Manda Scott first came across the phenomenon of the crystal skulls while studying shamanic dreaming in the early 1980s. Since then she has met with teachers and healers from tribal nations across the world. She has learned that the ancient Maya were astoundingly accurate astronomers, and believes that we should take their prediction that the world will end on 21 December 2012 very seriously indeed.

A veterinary surgeon by training, she has also written the bestselling Boudica quartet of novels which are available as Bantam paperbacks. *Rome: The Emperor's Spy*, the first book in her new series set in ancient Rome, will be published in early 2010.

For more details of readings, courses and events, please visit www.mandascott.co.uk. For information on the crystal skull itself please visit www.thecrystalskull.co.uk

2012
THE CRYSTAL
SKULL

Manda Scott

BANTAM BOOKS

LONDON • TORONTO • SYDNEY • AUCKLAND • JOHANNESBURG

TRANSWORLD PUBLISHERS
61–63 Uxbridge Road, London W5 5SA
A Random House Group Company
www.rbooks.co.uk

**2012: THE CRYSTAL SKULL
A BANTAM BOOK: 9780553824452**

First published in Great Britain
as *The Crystal Skull* in 2008 by Bantam Press
an imprint of Transworld Publishers
Bantam edition published 2008
Bantam edition reissued as *2012: The Crystal Skull*, 2009

Addresses for Random House Group Ltd companies outside the
UK can be found at: www.randomhouse.co.uk
The Random House Group Ltd Reg. No. 954009

The Random House Group Limited supports The Forest
Stewardship Council (FSC), the leading international forest
certification organisation. All our titles that are printed on
Greenpeace approved FSC certified paper carry the FSC logo.
Our paper procurement policy can be found at
www.rbooks.co.uk/environment

Typeset in Sabon by Falcon Oast Graphic Art Ltd.

Printed in the UK by CPI Cox & Wyman, Reading, RG1 8EX.

6 8 10 9 7 5

For my mother and father, with love

ACKNOWLEDGEMENTS

Four women were central to the writing of this book. In order of their appearance in the creation: Kate Miciak, Vice President and Executive Editor of Bantam Dell Publishing Group (US) sat over dinner and listened to the germ of an idea and said, 'Go for it,' and so made it happen. Jane Judd, my exceptionally patient agent, nursed us through the turbulent early stages before passing the baton to Selina Walker, editorial director of Transworld Publishers, without whom we would have no book. Last, but never least, my partner Faith Roper provided support throughout and then proof-read the final drafts against tight deadlines, with impeccable clarity and insight. My thanks to you all.

Along the way, my brother, Robin Scott, provided geological advice and Aggy offered to take me caving. Brian Gent of Blue Camas sent me his notes on crystal skulls and the Albion skull in particular and my teacher, Chris Luttichau, shared all that he knew of the Maya. My thanks to all of these; clearly any mistakes in comprehension or portrayal are entirely mine.

Finally, thanks to Nancy Webber and Deborah Adams and all those who work behind the scenes at Transworld for their sterling efforts.

That which you seek lies hidden in white water. Stone will be rendered unto stone, made safe in a place of hallowed beauty against the Enemy that seeks its destruction. Search north and then east, fifteen and twenty, behind the hanging thorns within the curve of the bow, in sound of the falling river.

Enter with courage. Go forward as far as the dark allows. Step through night's arch and come to the cathedral of the earth. Face the rising of the sun, and its setting, pierce the curtain to the well of living water and discover at last the pearl there entombed.

Find me and live, for I am your hope at the end of time. Hold me as you would hold your child. Listen to me as you would listen to your lover. Trust me as you would trust your god, whosoever that may be.

Follow the path that is herein shewn and be with me at the time and place appointed. Do then as the guardians of night foretell. Thereafter, follow your heart and mine, for these are one and the same. Do not fail me, for in doing so, you fail yourself, and all the worlds of waiting.

Item CO78.1.7 of the Cedric Owen archive –
the first of two ciphers discovered within the
text of the Owen ledgers by Drs O'Connor and
Cody in the spring and summer of 2007.

Text of both ciphers plus digital copies of the
original ledgers, with relevant markings high-
lighted, can be downloaded as pdf files from the
college website:
www.bedescambridge.ac.uk

PROLOGUE

To Dr Barnabas Tythe, visiting professor, Balliol College, Oxford, written this thirteenth day of July, in the year of our Lord fifteen hundred and fifty-six, greetings.

My dear friend – I write in haste and with regret that I must depart without a proper leave-taking. Cambridge is alive with accusations of heresy. Poor Thom Gillespie is already arraigned and faces death by burning for nothing more than questioning the use of a prayer book to mend a fractured wrist.

All those of us who practise medicine in accordance with the highest science, abjuring the superstitions of the Church, are in like peril. With a secret such as mine, I am doubly in jeopardy. Already there is a pamphlet circulating which states that I am in possession of 'a blue stone skull in the shape of an unfleshed man's head' and that I use it to gaze upon the stars. In our current climate, even so much would see me burn, but it cannot be long ere someone links the heart-stone with my healing of the sick which would, I greatly fear, lead to the stone's destruction as well as mine.

I leave, therefore, on the evening tide in the company of others who share my peril. They wait outside and we shall be away ere my ink is dry. But, before I go, I must tell you that I have been in close communion these past three weeks with Dr John Dee, who has lately been Astrologer to the Princess Elizabeth in her exile at Woodstock and has become the second of my teachers, behind only yourself.

As you know, it has long been my belief that if ever I have success in my physic, it is down to you alone. More than any other, you have taught me the rigours of anatomy and how observation of the patient is of paramount importance. But these last weeks Dr Dee has been most assiduous in showing me how the twin sciences of medicine and astrology may be brought together to hasten the restoration of the afflicted.

He has looked long and deep into the tissue of the blue heart-stone that has been my family's heritage and is of the opinion that it is of an age far greater than the oldest relics of Christendom. It is, he thinks, one of many that were birthed together in the temples of the heathen ancients, and sent forth to the world for the greater benefit of Mankind. He believes that there are those who fear the greater good that will be wrought by these stones in years to come and therefore seek their destruction. Thus I have Enemies of which I know naught, who will seek me out where ever I may go and will threaten the core of my life.

I am ashamed to confess that I have been in possession of the stone for a decade and yet am ignorant of its true nature, and this ignorance may be my death. It is pursuit of learning, therefore, as much as fear, that drives me from England to seek the help of any who might educate me as to the stone's purpose and my own.

In this regard, Dr Dee has observed my Part of Fortune, and the turning of my natal sun, and assures me that I will return to England at some future time when the climate is less dangerous.

I wish to believe him, and shall do so, knowing that only thus may I see you again. Until then, I must take my fortunes in France, carrying from Dr Dee his letter of recommendation to a friend whom he would trust with his own life and mine.

I have no knowledge of where this adventure will lead me, but am heartened by the scatter of the Constellations; on this day, Venus has come to rest on the fourth degree of Virgo, in near trine to Mars, as she did on the morning of my birth. Every felicitous part of my life has taken place under the good auspices of this star and her position now cannot but aid my cause.

With that to cheer us both, I take my leave. Know that I miss you greatly and will return to Bede's, and to you, when time and life allow.

For now, I am your most humble servant, honoured student and honest friend,

> Cedric Owen, Physician, Master of the Arts (Bede's College, Cantab 1543) and Doctor of Philosophy (1555).

1

*Beneath Ingleborough Fell, Yorkshire Dales,
May 2007*

BECAUSE IT WAS HER WEDDING GIFT, STELLA came first out of the tunnel. Filthy, wet and shivering hot-cold from the effort of the last fifty-metre uphill haul, she crawled on her belly, pulling herself face down into the empty blackness beyond.

She moved slowly, keeping taut the umbilical line that linked her to Kit, feeling first with her hands for the quality of the footing, then shuffling forward no further than the spilled light from her head-torch.

Like the tunnel, the cave was of chalk. Her gloved hands pressed on stone, washed smooth by century upon patient century of water. Her torch showed bright trickles of damp everywhere, washing over flat, undulating limestone. Beyond the splash of yellow light was unknown territory, unmapped, unexplored, as likely to be

17

a ledge and a bottomless fall as a flat cave floor.

With cold-stiff fingers, she established safety, set a bolt into the wall by the mouth of the tunnel, clipped in to it, and tugged the rope to let Kit know that she had stopped and not to pay out more rope. By the light of her head-lamp, she checked her compass and her watch and marked the incline and her estimate of its length and direction with wax pencil on the chart that she kept in her chest pocket, where it would not snag on tunnel walls.

Only after she had done all these things did Stella turn and look up and round, and send the thread of her torch into the vast, cathedral space Kit had found for her.

'My God . . . Kit, come and look.'

She spoke to herself; he was too far back to hear. She tugged twice on the rope, saying the same thing, and felt the single answering twitch and then the sudden slack as he began to move towards her.

Her hands coiled rope as a habit, without any conscious thought. Switching off her head-lamp, Stella stood in the roaring silence and let Kit's gift stand still in all its vast, black per-fection around her, so that she could remember it for the rest of her life.

Marriage is fine for the rest of the world, but I want to find you a present that will last us for ever, something to remember when the magic of now has grown to quiet domesticity. What is

it in the world that you want most, my lovely
woman, that will let you love me for eternity?

He had said it in Cambridge, in his river room that sat proud above the Cam, with the river running glassy green below, on the morning before they had gone to the registrar with their two witnesses and made themselves legal in the eyes of the world.

She had known him little more than a year; he the Bede's scholar to the depths of his bones, she the Yorkshire lass with a degree from a metropolitan university who knew nothing of the ivory towers. Between these two poles, they had found a meeting of minds that had carried them, in fourteen dizzying months, from discussions on string theory to marriage.

Then, lying at peace with herself and the world, there was nothing she wanted from him that he had not given, but it was a beautiful day and she was thinking of rock and how little of it there was in the flat fenlands of Cambridge.

'Find me a cave,' she had said, without thinking particularly, 'a cave no one else has ever seen. For that, I will love you for ever.'

He had come to kneel by the bed, to a place where his complex green-brown eyes could see and be seen. They were quiet then, more hazel than emerald, with hints of leafiness and summer. He had kissed her on the centre of her brow and smiled his driest, most knowing smile, and said, *What if I were to find you a cave with buried treasure that no one has entered for four hundred and nineteen years? Would that be almost as good?*

'Four hundred and nineteen . . . ?' She had sat up, too fast for the heat of the day.

Always, he surprised her; it was why she was going to marry him. 'You've found Cedric Owen's cave? The cathedral of the earth? Why didn't you tell me?'

Because I wanted to be sure.

'And are you now?'

As sure as I can be without going there to look. It's all in the cipher in the ledgers; the hanging thorns, the curve of the bow, the falling river. It had to be somewhere Owen knew like the back of his hand and the only place is Ingleborough Hill up in Yorkshire. He was born on the side of it. The thorns are gone by now but I found references to them in an old diary and there's a river that falls into Gaping Ghyll.

'Gaping Ghyll? Kit, that's the deepest pothole in England. The cave system running out from it goes for miles.'

It does indeed. And there are bits of it that haven't been explored yet, possibly a cathedral of the earth that no one has been in since Cedric Owen wrote his poem.

Would you like to go, as our present to each other? To find the cave and search out the white water and dive for the hidden pearl entombed therein?

20

Stella had known, then, that the gift was for him as much as for her. Cedric Owen's blue heart-stone was Kit's life's love, his project, his grail for ever quested for as long as she had known him; the great treasure of his college that had been sought by the high and mighty down the ages but never found.

They had not known where to look, the great and the good; they had not read between the lines for the hidden words and phrases as Kit had. It was his greatest accomplishment, and his greatest secret; by marrying him, she became a part of it.

Even so ... she wrinkled her brow and looked out of the window at the sandstone library and great lawned courts of Bede's College, with their five hundred years of tending and all the legends that went with them. She had learned those, too. 'I thought the skull killed all those who ever held it?'

He had laughed and slid his part-dressed body over the top of hers and said, *Only if they fell into the sins of lust and avarice. We won't do that.*

They were close then, eye to eye, nose to nose, heartbeat to heartbeat sharing each breath. She had held the weight of him balanced on the palms of her hands and looked up into the measure of his face and, quite truthfully, said, 'I could fall into lust for the first descent of an undiscovered cave. You can't begin to imagine what kind of gift that would be.'

But I can. You're a caver: it means to you what finding Owen's heart-stone would mean to me. It's why we can do it, you and me, bravely and together. Then we can tell the world what we have found.

She was the caver; hers the responsibility to bring the dream to reality. Which was why she had persisted after she found the rock fall that blocked the route, and why, when she had discovered an opening that might lead to where they wanted to go, she had gone first along the long, claustrophobic tunnel, where she had to become a snake and then an eel and then a worm in order to bend round the corners and slide under the overhangs and creep, inch by pulling inch, up fifty metres of a one in ten incline that brought her at last to the exit and the cavern beyond.

The rope went tight in her hands and then slack again as Kit rounded the final bend. She switched on her head-torch, to give him something to aim for.

Like a flickering cinema, her beam picked out random lengths of stalactites and stalagmites, closing like shark's teeth from floor to roof and back again. She eased the camera from the lid of her pack and turned a full half-circle, taking serial shots from floor to roof and roof to floor.

The flash reached out and splashed colour across the rising, falling calcite, drew rainbows from the constant sheen of water, sprinkled brilliant, living diamonds across the roof at each crack and angle of the rock.

She took pictures for the sheer joy of it, revelling in the beauty. Only as Kit was easing out of the tunnel to stand beside her did she follow at last the thunderous noise and turn west, to shed light on the cascading torrent of the waterfall.

'My God . . .'

'The cathedral of the earth. You clever, clever girl. I thought the rock fall had finished us.'

She was no longer alone. Kit's voice warmed her ear. Kit's arm wrapped her waist, immersing her in bittersweet joy; it was always hard to relinquish the purity of solitude, and yet, out of all the world, this one man understood her need for black aloneness and did not fear it.

She leaned in to him, dry-suit to dry-suit, and turned her light up to his face. Encircled by black neoprene, he was filthy and euphoric at once; a man on the brink of a promise.

She said, 'I can't think Cedric Owen knew about this route; you'd never get a Tudor physician in doublet and tights along that tunnel.'

'Nor any sane man, without his lady love to guide him.' He twirled a knightly bow and blew her a kiss. 'Mrs O'Connor, I adore you and everything there is of you, but I can't kiss you with a head-torch on.'

Laughing, she snatched the flying blessing from the air with her teeth. 'That's Dr Cody, until it becomes Professor Cody, and don't you ever forget it.' They had been wed for a little over forty-eight hours. Already the argument was old and private between them; in public there was never a chance he would steal her name.

She said, 'Have you a flare? It'd be good to see it all properly.'

'I have.' He was already rummaging in his pack. 'And then we have to find out where Owen came in when he walked the easy route. I'm rather hoping there's an obvious way out. I really don't want to have to do that second hairpin in reverse. Going down and then up and trying to turn at the same time wouldn't be any fun at all.'

'But not impossible. It matters to remember that.' She had been caught once in a cave where the way in was not a possible way out. She dreamed of it still, on the bad nights, when life pressed too close. 'Light the flare and let's see all that we haven't seen yet.'

'Ask and it shall be given.' Kit locked the flare in a cleft high up where he could reach and she could not; six inches' extra height was good for some things and bad for others. 'Stand back.'

He lit it with his hand covering his face, as she had taught him, and stepped back before the magnesium fully lit.

White!

Blistering incandescence spilled from the cavern wall. Under its light, the stalagmites were virgin snow, the waterfall was a cascade of living ice, and beyond all the jagged shark's teeth the cave's roof was finally visible, a greying white limestone arch halfway to the heavens.

'How high is it, do you think?' Kit asked. His voice was lost in the rush and thunder of the waterfall.

'A hundred metres? Maybe a bit more. We could climb one of the walls and find out if you're feeling keen.'

'Am I ever keen to lift my feet off the ground if I don't have to?' He grinned, weakly. 'I'd rather find the skull.'

He leaned back on the wall, bit his glove off one hand, delved into the hidden pockets of his backpack, and came out with the precious folded paper, the print of Cedric Owen's cipher, the pinnacle of three years' work.

'*That which you seek lies hidden in white water.* The waterfall is white.'

'And the water is full of limescale, which is another form of white. Read me again the bit that comes after having the courage to go forward?'

He was a poet at heart, for all that he buried his head in hexadecimal code and computer languages. He turned so that the flare cast his shadow behind him and read aloud:

*'Enter with courage. Go forward as far as
the dark allows. Step through night's arch
and come to the cathedral of the earth. Face
the rising of the sun, and its setting, pierce
the curtain to the well of living water and
discover at last the pearl there entombed.'*

He lowered the paper. Softly, he said, 'We
have come to the cathedral of the earth.'

'We have. So next we have to face the rising
and setting sun. But we didn't step through
night's arch to get here, we crawled through a
tunnel that wasn't there before half a ton of
rock fell into the route Cedric Owen took. We
need to find out where he came in before we can
work out where he went next.'

Stella stood at the margins of the magnesium
white and turned in a slow circle. Her head-
lamp cut a horizontal line along the wall,
cutting through stalactites, snagging on out-
crops, falling into a tall slice of darkness.

'There.'

She ran to it, soft-footed on wet rock. The
arch was more of a cleft, jaggedly asymmetric,
higher than her upstretched hands, broader
than her arm-span. She followed the dark space
cautiously, rounding a bend, moving into a
narrower passageway.

'Stell?' Kit was at the entrance, peering in.

26

She shouted back to him, cupping her hands against the echo. 'This is it. The rock fall's up ahead. It must be at least twenty metres thick. Our crawl-tunnel looped out and round to come out further along the cavern's wall.' She reversed back towards him, playing her torch over the passage walls. Here and there were smudges of colour that barely held her torchlight.

'I think there are cave paintings on the wall.' She could hear the awe in her own voice. 'We're going to have to tell people about this.'

She backed out, into the cavern, to the place where there was light enough to see, to look around, to search the high walls for other signs of ancient life.

'God, Kit . . . I take it all back. There *are* better things than finding a cave no one has ever been in.' She grinned at him, stupidly, her blood fizzing in her veins.

'Stell?'

The flare was fading fast. Gobbets of molten magnesium fell hissing to the ground. In the yellowing light, she saw him pull off his head-torch and strip back the black neoprene hood. His hair glowed like gold in the poor light. There was a line of clean skin where the cap had been. He had half a day's stubble, which had caught the mud. She saw what he was going to do and yanked off her own gloves, and touched her face and was glad that it was not clean.

27

He leaned forward, and lifted her torch clear of her head and stripped her cap back as he had his own. Coppery lights bounced off her hair and lit the water. He was near and warm and he smelled of sweat and fear and excitement and she loved him.

They closed the kiss in darkness, with no head-torches and no flare, and Stella was afraid, suddenly, for both of them, that from these heights there was only a long slope down.

He caught the swoop of her feeling. Hoarsely, he said, 'Are you ready to face the rising of the sun and its setting?'

She checked the compass on her wrist. 'I think that means we need to go east of the entrance and then west. There's a river over by the north side of the cavern. Can you set the second flare somewhere up there, so that it shines on the wall and the water together?'

They had three flares. She very rarely used more than one on any caving trip. He wedged their second between two stalagmites at the side of the water-cut channel in the chalk, where she showed him. The magnesium spat and flared and the black ribbon of the river became a thread of silver in snow.

Stella said, 'We don't know how deep it is and it's too wide to jump. We're looking for a bridge, or a stepping stone, or a pinch point where we can cross.'

Kit was ahead of her, searching. He was back

in neoprene with his lamp set at his brow. The smears on his cheeks made him more gaunt than he should have been. He said, 'Why are we trying to cross the river?'

'Because it's the only good reason to go east before we go west. There must be a crossing point to the east so we can walk back west along the north wall. The waterfall is a curtain and there's a pool at its foot that's as close to a well of living water as we're likely to get. It's also as far from night's arch as you can go in this cave. Owen was hiding his heart-stone to keep it safe for posterity. He didn't want it to be easy to find, but equally not impossible. Therefore, across the river, which you wouldn't do by chance, or even by choice, unless you had to.'

'Then we'll cross here, will we?' said Kit uncertainly. 'On the stepping stones that look like marbles?'

The stepping stones also rolled like marbles underfoot, so that, after a trial step on the first one, Stella made Kit wait while she set another bolt and strung out two lines at right angles to give maximum security before she tried again. She was glad of them when the third stone rolled under her feet and she felt the strength of the black current.

'You're cold,' Kit said, when he joined her.

She might have tried to deny it, but his hand

was on her arm, bouncing in time with her shuddering. She shrugged and made her teeth keep still from chattering. 'Caves are always cold. I'll be fine when we get moving again. And it's not a bad thing to be wet if we're going to have to dive for the skull.'

'You don't have the gear to dive.' He sounded anxious, which was not at all like him; the water had unnerved him more than either of them had expected.

'I have you. What more Kit do I need?' It was cheap, but she was in need of easy warmth. 'And we're not coming back, are we? It's too far and no cave in the world is as much fun a second time. I've got a mask and an underwater light. They'll do.'

'We might need the third flare.'

'No. We don't know what's ahead. We might need it to get out. Come on, let's have a look at the waterfall.' Already she was regretting the profligate waste of the earlier light.

'Face the rising of the sun and its setting. Pierce the curtain to the well of living water and discover at last . . . et cetera, et cetera.'

Her world was limited to the circle of her head-torch, and Kit's beside her. In all the looming blackness, the noise told her more than she had seen of the waterfall, of its size, and its volume and the plunging depth of the pool at its feet.

She tilted her head back to look up at the cataract, to guess its height. Her beam did not reach a point where there was no water, although right at the limit of its reach was turbulence, and a spray that reached far out into the cavern and danced like fairy lights so that she could believe the river's head might be there.

When she looked down, she followed boiling ice-cold water that plunged deep into blackness for an immeasurable depth. For the hell of it, she found a stone the size of her fist and threw it in. It spun like a leaf in the violent water and vanished.

'*Pierce the curtain*,' Kit said. 'Christ. How?'

'I don't know, but Cedric Owen did it four hundred and nineteen years ago without magnesium flares or a neoprene dry-suit and he came out alive, so we have to assume that it's not as terrifying as it looks. I think if we—'

'Stell?'

'Take a look at the northern end of the rock face where the waterfall ends, then we—'

'Stella . . .'

'—might find that there's a hollow in the space behind the water that will let us— What?'

'I don't think he did.' Kit's voice was flat, leached of all inflection.

'You don't think who did what?'

'I don't think Cedric Owen made it out alive. There's a skeleton here, with not a bit of flesh on it, and a huge amount of limescale deposit, which suggests to my untrained eyes that it's been here for a very long time.'

31

2

Beneath Ingleborough Fell, Yorkshire Dales,
May 2007

THE SKELETON WAS STARKLY WHITE, THE BONES
made thick and uneven by layers of chalky
deposit that welded it to the floor so that only
the top half was truly visible.

Stella knelt by the curved sweeps of the pelvis
and sent her light over all of it, tracing the lineage from toe to skull. A small, manic part of her
mind sang songs to keep the dark at bay. *The
toe bone's connected to the foot bone. The foot
bone's connected to the—*

She shook her head. 'It's hard to see through
all the calcium deposit, but there's nothing
obviously broken; no fractured spine or legs
bent at bad angles.'

Kit stood a little back at the other side. His
torch lit only the skull; a real skull, not the one
of coloured stone that they had come to find.

He said, 'It's so peaceful. It's laid out like a

knight on a tomb, everything in straight lines and its hands folded over its chest. All he needs is a sword and—'

'I think he's got one. Look.' Stella had a multi-function climbing tool on her rack, eight inches of light aluminium, strong enough to prod stubborn climbing gear from its wedged place in rock. She used the end of it to scrape the crumbling chalk from the thing that might have been a sword, but was too calcified to be clear. She said, 'Maybe he was dead before he came here. Or he walked in alive, but came here to die.'

'It's not like you to make gender assumptions. Are you sure it's a he?'

'I'm not sure of anything. I don't watch enough sexy pathologists on TV. Whoever he was, he was carrying something round his neck.'

Beneath the maybe-sword was something soft, which had not rotted away, but grown a shell of chalk. She wriggled it out and rolled it between her hands to break the stone.

'It's a leather bag, lined with something that's kept the water out.' With an effort, she teased apart the neck and tipped the contents into her hand. 'It's a pendant. Bronze, maybe, or copper.' She rubbed the silt from the face. 'Must be for you.' She held it up. 'It's got Libra scratched on the back.'

At another time, in another place, they would

have made a joke of it; one of the glues that bound them was a shared scorn of the gullible. In the presence of the dead man, it had value.

'Show me?' Kit's torch angled down her shoulder.

'It's been scratched on with a nail, or the point of a knife – see? Libra with the sun and the moon at either end. If we turn it over—' She did just that, rubbing it with her thumb. 'There's a crest. One of your ancient medieval cryptic sigils. Have a look.'

He cupped it in his ungloved hand and lifted it into the light of his head-torch. Because he was bending close to look, she saw the colour bleed from his face before he spoke.

'What?' she asked.

'It's a dragon under the risen half-moon.' He was as Irish as she had ever heard him, as if Englishness bled from him in the presence of death. 'That's the Bede's College crest. It's on the stained glass window outside my bedroom; it's above the gate to the Great Court and the archway to the Lancastrian Court and the door to the Master's suite. As a medallion like this, it's only ever worn by the Masters of Bede's or their emissaries, in the days when they had emissaries.'

He dangled it over his forefinger like a rosary. Its shadow swept in arcs along the length of the skeleton. 'This can't be Cedric Owen. He was never anyone's emissary.' He spun a circle on his heel, sending his torch's light bobbing out into the darkness. 'In any case, he died at the gates to the college on Christmas Day in 1588, everyone knows that. I wonder if someone else has tried to come here to find the skull-stone?'

'How? No one broke the code before us.'

'No one that we know of.' He handed her back the pendant, folding her fingers over it. 'Will you keep this? We can try to find out whose it is when we're back.'

She felt it cold through her gloves. 'If it's not Cedric Owen, then someone else died within reach of the heart-stone, exactly as the legends promise. "Everyone who has ever held this stone has died for it." You told me that, and Tony Bookless said it again at the wedding. I don't remember much else, but I remember that.'

'Do you still want to try to find it?'

'Definitely.' She swept her light up the length of the cataract and down again. 'Just let's try not to add to the statistics.'

Stella had to dive in the end, and was glad of it.

After the edgy blackness of the cavern, the water was so rigidly cold that she had to clamp her teeth not to gasp against it and drown. Her diving head-light cast a beam three inches wide into the churning water. Kit held the rope and paid it out too slowly. She came up for air and silently took some more slack and breathed out all her carbon dioxide, breathed in half a lung-ful of air, and dipped under again.

On a good day, in a river, with sun above, she could hold her breath for a little over three minutes. Underground in temperatures this bad, she hoped for maybe half that. She had an idea, and barely enough breath to test it. She sent the line of her light due west, past the churning edge of the water to where the swirling currents cut alcoves and potholes in the rock. She could see nothing but white; white water, white rock, white light, so that only textures made them separate and only her hands could truly be trusted.

Still, the idea burned, and, more than that, growing as she came closer, was the sense of something waiting, welcoming, that whispered her onward, that asked her to have courage, and sent fire into her marrow against the terrifying cold.

Three times she came up for air. Three times, the swooping eddies pushed her back before she could reach the place where an anomaly of the current held the water still and the white rock lay wide and round as a cauldron.

She had a rule: always try three times and then stop. It had kept her alive in caves where 'one more try' would otherwise have become ten more tries and the exhaustion of failure would have left her too tired to turn round and climb out.

She was ready to stop now, but for the whispered encouragement, the promises and the urgent insistence that made her take more rope from Kit and duck down again and kick forward hard through the wall of white turbulence to the black space beyond.

There, in the dizzy light of her head-lamp, was the lip of cavitied rock. She grabbed it with both hands and tilted her head to spill light down inside, to see what Cedric Owen had hidden there four centuries earlier.

They had come looking for a blue stone in the shape of an unfleshed man's head. What lay in the black water before her was a blob of chalk, a lumpen, misshapen pearl with barely a shadow of eyes and nose and mouth to suggest the skull within. Even so, to her eyes, it was beautiful. She balanced on her waist and leaned down to reach it.

Blue!

A blinding intensity of blue, that made her gasp even as her heart leaped like a salmon in her chest. She lost a mouthful of air and choked and spat water and came to the surface in a flurry of panicked coughing.

'Stell, you've been in too long. Come on out. No piece of stone is worth dying for. We can leave it.'

Kit was at the water's edge, leaning in against the pull of his three-line belay.

'No!' She waved an arm high over her head. 'It's there! I can get it. One last time . . .'

Once more, she ducked down into the black

water, kicked back to the cauldron's edge and sent light into it. Stiff with cold, her hands reached down into the churning dark, to the pearl beyond price that was Cedric Owen's skull-stone.

The blue was less intense a second time, and she was waiting for it. The skull-stone came to her hands, singing its welcome.

'Stell, you're freezing. We have to get moving, get you out, get back into sunlight.'

'Give me chocolate and hold me and I'll be fine.'

She was stupidly, insanely cold. Her marrow was a solid lump of ice. Her hands had lost all feeling. Experience told her she would have a sore throat in two days and be coughing in five. She sat in torch-eating darkness, ten feet from a skeleton of unknown gender, age, race and name, clutching an ugly, uninspiring lump of limestone that was barely identifiable as a skull – and she was as happy as she could ever remember.

She let Kit hold her, let him fold his arms and his legs and his whole body around her, let his warmth feed her and keep her safe.

'Kit?'

'Yes?' He was miserable, and not truly cold, which was sometimes worse than freezing. He had not asked to see the skull-stone yet, which surprised her.

She said, 'This is the best wedding present in the world. Thank you.'

'We're not out yet.'

'No, but it won't be long. The draught is all from east to west. If we go left of the waterfall, where we haven't looked yet, I'll bet there's a walk-out that joins up with the White Scar complex and takes us out near the car.'

'If it's an easy walk, people would have been in here by the hundreds.'

He held her less tightly. They shivered equally now, which was an improvement. Stella wriggled from his grasp and wrestled with her pack, setting the skull-stone safe inside, close to the bronze pendant on which a dragon unfurled its wings beneath a high half-moon. She held out her hand for Kit to pull her up to standing and grinned into the tentative light of his torch.

'OK, so there might be a bit of a climb. And maybe a tiny bit of a crawl through an entrance so small nobody's been dumb enough to try it yet. But the poem said *Find me and live*, so we have to do exactly that.'

'Bravely and together?'

She thought he had forgotten saying that. She pressed a kiss to his hand. 'Absolutely. Come on, we'll make a caver of you yet.'

They had climbed and crawled and were on the second pitch of a downward climb when Stella heard a stone fall in the darkness. She was standing at the belay point, winding in rope.

She looked up, letting her torch beam catch Kit's feet. 'Did you hear something?'

'Other than the blood rushing in my ears, the chattering of my teeth and the premonition of my screaming body falling ten thousand feet into the centre of the earth down this devil's climb you've magicked out of nowhere? No. What I would like to hear is the sound of traffic and real, live people. We've been in here for eternity.'

'Two hours. That is, two hours since we left the cavern. Four hours since we last saw daylight. And it's nowhere near a ten-thousand-foot drop. Nothing in Yorkshire's more than four hundred, tops.'

'That's enough to kill us when we fall off and hit the bottom.'

'We're not going to fall off.'

It was not even a four hundred foot drop, but it was not trivial either and they were climbing down, which is always harder than up. For an avowed non-climber, Kit was coping astonishingly well. And he was cheerful again, which was little short of a miracle.

Stella stood to one side of the ledge keeping the belay safely taut, but not so tight it pulled him off the rock.

His feet reached her first, and then his hands and he was down beside her.

'Where now?'

She tipped her torch on to her plastic map pocket. 'If the charts are right, this ledge is part of the White Scar complex, but quite far in. We're on a route that was only opened up nine months ago. It's not surprising nobody found the way into the chamber. It's hard enough getting along this ledge; anything else would need specialist equipment and a team who knew exactly what they were doing. We'll be fine as long as we don't stray into Gaping Ghyll.'

'The pothole with the river falling into it?'

'The pothole with the longest waterfall in England falling into it, with the biggest cavern below it and a sump below that. If we needed to climb out, it's eight pitches of extreme rock with water tumbling past our ears and neither of us is up for that.'

The Ghyll was her home territory, the place that had brought her to caving and left her wanting more, but not so badly that she wanted to be lost in it.

She traced a line with her index finger. 'As far as I can tell, this ledge carries on for about half a mile to a fork where we take a left. After that, the ledge gets narrower and the drop deeper. If we're lucky, there'll be bolts and a rope to hold on to but even if not, as long as we don't go near the edge, it's a cake walk.'

'A cake walk . . .' Kit let his light play over the side wall, and the ledge and the black nothingness below. Experimentally, he kicked a stone from their ledge. It rattled briefly against the side and then fell in absolute silence to a floor that was too far away to hear.

'And you do this for pleasure. Stella Cody, you *are* certifiably insane and I'm as bad for having married you. Remind me to divorce you as soon as we see daylight. Mental cruelty. No contest.'

He reached for her shoulder and squeezed it, softly. His accent was barely Irish. He was no longer shaking from either cold or fear. She tried to remember her first cave, and how long it had taken her to learn to love the fear as much as the dark.

He dug out his water bottle and drank, then passed it to her. The slosh of water very nearly covered the clatter of a distant stone.

She said, 'There!'

'What?'

'A rock fell.' She said nothing more. How to tell him that the skull-stone was coming alive, that she could feel its presence on the edges of her mind, and that it sensed danger nearby? 'There was one earlier,' she said. 'Before you came down.'

'In the middle of a mountain, made of rocks piled on rocks, you heard a rock fall on to another rock?' He flashed his head-lamp at her face, dousing her with light. 'Is that unusual?'

His buoyancy was infectious. She wanted to float on it all the way home. The skull-stone twanged at her nerves. She smiled, to bring him down gently. 'It is, actually. You only ever hear rocks fall in caves when there's somebody sending them down, like you just did. I think we have company.'

'Do we mind company?'

'Possibly not, but we're in an unknown part of an unmapped cave and we've just picked up an artefact that people have been hunting for the past four hundred years. Before that, it has a long history of associated violence. If someone else wants the stone badly enough, he could add two skeletons to this cave and who would ever know? I think we should keep moving, and try not to make too much noise.'

'Stell, that was definitely a rock bouncing on another rock.'

'I heard it. And the one before. They're coming at thirty-second intervals.'

The ledge on which they walked had narrowed to less than eighteen inches across. Stella kept her torch beam angled so that the light overlapped her feet and she never stepped further than she could see. There were no bolts and no rope to hold on to. Empty blackness yawned to her right, with that sucking magnetism that drew in living bodies and made them dead. Gravity sucks. Every caver knows that underground it sucks more strongly. Stella had never mentioned that to Kit. She said,

43

'Whoever's following doesn't mind us knowing he's there. Actually, he wants us to know.'

'What do we do?'

'If I said that the skull-stone thinks we should run like fuck, would you divorce me again?'

She was the one sounding Irish now. He always said she had a chameleon accent and it came out under stress, striding west from Yorkshire to Dublin with each rising notch of adrenalin.

'Pass. I need to have notice of that question. Does it say why?'

Kit was making such an effort to sound calm. She loved him, just for that. She said, 'It doesn't want to meet whoever is behind us.'

'A stone-hunter?'

'Of the nastiest sort.'

'The type that leaves skeletons behind?'

'Definitely.'

'Let's run then. Last one to daylight's a chicken. Can we switch off our head-lights and hope to stay alive?'

'Definitely not. And we can't run. We can just walk a bit faster.'

'*Kit!*'

It came out muffled, into neoprene. His hand was over her mouth, the other fumbled with her light and switched it off. His own light had already gone. His whole body held her against the rock. They stood in absolute dark, with a drop of unknown depth eighteen inches away. Somewhere, not so far back round a left-hand bend of sixty degrees, a rock tumbled quietly to nowhere.

'*Whisper.*' Kit's voice in her ear. 'We're being herded, not hunted. Whoever it is wants us to go faster. Is there something bad we're going to blunder into up ahead? Or does this ledge simply run out and leave us nowhere to go?'

The chart, such as it was, was burned into her mind. 'There's a pinch point two hundred metres from here. The chart doesn't define it in any more detail except that it's hard. There should be bolts and a rope by then.'

'But if we're pushed too fast, we'll miss them, and then we'll go over.' Kit's lips were on her forehead, beneath her lamp. There was no fear in him now, only a bright, sharp anger that could move mountains. 'So here's what we'll do. I'll take your spare light so it looks like there's two of us and go ahead fast and messy. You wait until the bastard has passed you and come up behind. If he's trying to push us off, he won't get both of us, and if we're lucky you'll get a good look at who it is. Just don't do anything about it down here; wait till we're safely back in daylight.'

'Kit, that's madness. Which one of us is the caver? If we're going to split, let me go ahead.'

He shook his head; the shiver of it ran through his shoulder to hers. 'I'll have both lights. You're the one left behind in the dark.' He bent down so their heads were level. She could feel the shine of his eyes. 'Stell, don't you trust me?'

A stone clattered, closer than before. Urgently, Stella whispered, 'It's not about that.'

'OK, but you're the one with the skull and it needs to be protected. *Find me and live* – remember? You can climb up the wall and get out of sight and out of the way. I couldn't do that if my life depended on it.'

She had no answer to that. He gripped her arm, taking silence for agreement. 'How much more after the pinch point before we see daylight?'

'About half a mile of easy going and then you're in the main Battlefield chamber. It's one of the biggest showcase caves in England; all fluorescent stalactites and prehistoric mudpools. A hundred tourists a day do it with their eyes shut. It *is* a walk-out from there.'

'Sorted.' His hands clasped her face and hugged her close. They clashed, head-lamp to head-lamp, and sketched the barest kiss. 'I love you. Now give me your underwater light and I'll see you back at the car.'

She loved him. She gave him her second light and listened to him make noise enough for two, if those two were trying to be quiet. He was right; he could move faster alone than when

46

he was following her; he was less cautious.

The dropping of stones halted for a moment and then came along faster. *You can climb up the wall and get out of sight and out of the way.*

It was madness. It was necessary. Blindly, she felt for handholds in the rock wall at her side, making herself a gecko, a squirrel, a tree-frog, able to adhere to wet limestone and never fall back into the swooping, sucking dark.

Footholds came to her hand, and then her feet; small nubs of rock that accepted her offer of neoprene and held it. She turned her face sideways to the rock, and glued her cheek to it, breathing in the wet, hard stone, as if breath alone might hold her.

Space loomed out and down and round and all that kept her alive was four points of damp rock. She tasted gritty, earthy mud, full of salt and silt, and did not spit it out, but opened her mouth and welcomed it as another way to glue her to the rock. She did not allow herself to think how she would get down.

He came soon, whoever he was; a passing solidity of flesh and breath and the smell of male sweat and neoprene and mud, that moved fast, and sure-footed, with only a pinprick of light.

He did not look up to where she was, even when the skull-stone screamed a furious warning and flashed a spark of pure blue lightning that existed, as far as she could tell, only in her mind.

She waited a long time, holding to wet rock with fingers that were locked with fear as much as cold. The sound of padding feet died to nothing. Kit was long gone.

'Kit, please God, Kit, be safe.'

Silence answered her, with no falling stones.

When she had counted a thousand, and again, she risked her light. The ledge was far narrower than she had thought, the handholds smaller. There was nothing but blackness beyond it, and the sucking void of vertigo.

She flexed her fingers and jammed them in a crack and lowered herself down, on to toeholds that sloped down and out, to a ledge that was exactly the width of her two feet set toe to heel. Beyond it, her light probed the darkness and saw nothing. She risked a lean forward and sent the light straight down the cliff's edge. The beam reached two hundred and fifty feet and did not touch the rock bottom. She turned her lamp forward, and began the long walk out.

The chart did not lie: the pinch point was difficult. What it did not say was that the ledge narrowed to eight inches and began to slope outwards, tipping her gently, softly, subtly towards the dark. Its treachery was supported by the wall on her left shoulder which had, until now, been her friend, her support, her safety in the world of sucking gravity. Now it, too, began to lean against her, pushing her ever outwards, easing her centre of gravity over the lip of the ledge.

Walking was an act of will. When it became impossible to walk, she dropped on to her hands and knees and crawled, feeling her way along a ledge barely big enough for her two knees. Her right hand gripped the angled edge. Twice, it slipped away, tipping her sideways, outwards. Gravity sucked. She spat back. The skull-stone sent its weight left, to keep her on the rock. *Kit . . . please tell me you didn't try to walk this.*

When it became impossible to crawl, she dropped on to her belly and stretched her arms out in front of her and used her left hand only to pull herself forward and inward, against the quiet whispering darkness that said how easy it would be to let go and roll gently off to a place of no resistance.

Find me and live. She took that now as a promise, to both of them.

She reached a place of safety and knelt upright, sobbing with fear, talking to herself in savage bursts through teeth that clattered too much for coherent speech.

She drank water and made herself steady. With some effort, she built a picture of Kit, alive and whole, waiting for her at the cave's mouth.

Unaccountably, the thought of him made her weep.

'Kit . . . Please be safe.'

The touch of his voice echoed in her head. *I'll see you back at the car.*

She looked at her watch. It was barely two thirty in the afternoon; five hours exactly since she had last seen daylight. Aloud, she said, 'I'll be at the car by three o'clock. We'll have a late lunch at the hotel. Or, better than that, we'll order room service and stay in and celebrate our wedding present.'

She stood in a wide tunnel, with no threat on any side. The rock was dry and smooth and sloped upward at four or five degrees. Somewhere, in the far distance, was the first taste of greyness in all the black. Stella Cody checked her compass, her chart and her watch, hitched her backpack higher on to her shoulders and began to run towards the light.

Very quietly, so that she had to strain to hear it, the skull-stone sang a single note of warning.

3

Paris, August 1556

PARIS LAY ASWEAT UNDER THE PALL OF SUMMER.
Smoke from the cook-fires hung as a
blanket over tiled rooftops and the stench of
sewage clogged the streets. Life slowed almost
to a halt. In the streets and alleyways winding
on either bank of the Seine, there was nothing
to be done but wait for rain or wind or, if God
were good, both, to clear the air and flush the
gutters.

Some things took no notice of the heat: birth
and death amongst them. Thus did Cedric
Owen, known to those around him as M. David
Montgomery – ostensibly a Scot with loyalties
entirely given to France's most serene majesty
and his ally the Pope – find himself up to his
arms in the slime and gore of a difficult
childbirth.

It was his fourth since coming to France. The
first had gone well and so earned him a

reputation amongst the street folk to whom he ministered. The second was for the wife of a tailor who had once sewn the points on to the hose of M. de Montpelier, who was something small at court.

The third came at night and he was called from his bed by a man who rode a horse and carried his own sword. The woman brought to bed was his mistress and her white linen sheets were ripped up to make staunching pads when she bled. That she survived was considered a minor miracle, the majority of which was attributed to Owen's refusal to countenance the use of leeches. The woman's lover, it transpired, was a cousin of M. de Montpelier and something rather more substantial at court.

And so, without any wish or effort on his part other than to follow his chosen profession, on the afternoon of the seventeenth of August, less than three weeks after his arrival in France, with Venus now at the mid-point of Libra and Jupiter in kind trine to Mars, Cedric Owen came to attend a chambermaid to the Queen, gone into labour nearly a month before her time and like to give birth, so wailed the women attending her, to a hare or worse.

She was not giving birth to a hare, but perhaps not much better. Naked to the waist, Owen lay on floorboards at the foot of her birthing-bed with his eyes shut, the better to see with his fingers, which were at full length inside, at the place where the babes lay. He felt bad news.

His French was passable and they thought his accent Scottish and charming. Speaking thus, he said, 'My lady, I feel two heads. You are about to be delivered of twins. Whether they yet live or not, I cannot say, but the Part of Fortune, if calculated by the modern method, lies at this time of the day in the constellation of Gemini which can only be to the good.'

Her face was a long way beyond the beached mound of her belly. Her eyes sought his and he gave her what compassion he could, knowing the intimacy of the moment, greater even than the moment of conception, and wishing not to taint it.

More gently, he said, 'The two babes are evenly placed in your womb. I must send one back to allow the other to advance. Have I your permission, and that of your husband, to choose which of your children is to be born first?'

It was not a trivial question; lives had been made or broken on the order of birth. He expected some hesitancy, or a wish to be part of the decision. Already he was feeling each head, testing for an excess or deficiency in any of the three elements that made up their nature, seeking anything he might pass on, that could be held later to have been a sign that one was inherently the stronger.

He thought perhaps one had a swelling on the crown that could indicate a strengthening of the mercurial aspect, which was enough to go by. Feeling the other to ensure there was no mistake, he became aware of a thickening in the silence about him that did not grow from indecision.

Opening his eyes once more, he looked about and saw the sign of the cross being made over and over on the breasts of those who stood in attendance; most particularly on the breast of Charles, the youth come early to manhood who had introduced himself as the father. Ashen-faced, the boy leaned back on the lime wash of the wall and crossed himself, again and again.

Owen had never been greatly impressed with the combination of youth and money that infected all courts. He allowed an edge in his voice that he would not normally have brought to the birthing chamber. 'Sir? God may guide my hand, but I need your permission before I act.'

He might have spoken Portuguese, or English, so little notice did they take. Dully, the young courtier said, 'The Queen had twins in June, both girls. One died at birth. The other, Victoire, lies in the care of the best physicians in the land. Some say she will live. Most do not believe it. We cannot have twins as did the Queen. The King will see it as ill luck.'

Owen eased his hand out of the tight confines of the birth canal and looked up along the swollen belly-line to the woman in labour. The fear in her eyes was more for her children and the racking pains of her body than for any superstitions of the court.

He laid his hands where they might not be seen in all their blood, but might give her comfort, and addressed her directly.

'Madame? Maybe there are three children within you. It is not unknown. Even if not, there is nothing to be done but let them see the light of day. King Henri is not known for his illogic. I doubt if he will truly see you as an ill omen for his child.'

He saw her mouth move and could not make out the words. She wet her lips with a dry tongue and tried again. 'Do what you must. Choose well by your own lights.'

The raw courage in her gaze was what had first brought Cedric Owen to his calling and what kept him there in the face of idiocy, superstition and plague. With a strange, familiar ache swelling his breast, he sent the most coherent of the serving women out for more hot water and clean linen and then sought out in his mind the sense of the blue stone that had shaped the path of his life and aided his vocation at every turn. It lay concealed beneath a floorboard in his lodgings, wrapped in brown hessian and well hidden, but its touch reached him, as it had done since his first foray into medicine, so that for a moment he floated in a clear blue sky and saw the world from above, with all the tumult of humanity as so many ants below. Among the ants, precious as gold dust at harvest, were his patients, and he cared for them.

Coming back into himself, holding the distance and the closeness equally, Cedric Owen turned every part of his newly honed attention on the woman and the two new lives he had felt under his fingers.

'M. Montgomery?'

He heard the voice from a long way off. He sat on the scrubbed wooden floor, still damp from the wash-mops of the serving girls, and listened to the one living child suckle its mother. The Part of Fortune had remained in Gemini long enough for this one to be born under its blessing, but had moved on before the second child could be brought to life, and the claws of the crab had crushed its breath. That one was already wrapped in linen and laid to the side. A priest had been called and had spoken Latin and then an archaic French that the young mother had understood, and had left again, crossing himself.

Owen was lost in the world beyond exertion where the cramping pain in his arm had become something sweet to be treasured and the closeness to new life was a gift that transported him beyond the fears and hopes and trivia of those around him.

It also temporarily caused him to forget the pseudonym he had taken.

'M. Montgomery? The Queen requires your presence.'

'The Queen?' He remembered very suddenly who he was and where. Catherine de' Medici was not known for her patience. 'Why?'

Charles, father to one dead girl and one living, was now a sick shade of grey. He bared his teeth in a grimace that made pretence of a smile. 'Word has reached her majesty of our . . . felicity. She wishes to see the young Scottish doctor who has brought a healthy girl-child into the world.'

They had both been girls. The living one, perforce, had been named Victoire after the daughter who had come to grace the lives of Queen Catherine of France and Henri II, her husband.

Therein lay the problem. Not only had the King's sister married James V of Scotland, France's strongest ally in the complex wars of politics and person that assailed Europe, but James's daughter, the young Mary, Queen of Scots, was betrothed to Henri's eldest son. The French court was home to as many Scots as Frenchmen – any one of whom would discover in the first minutes of conversation that the carroty-haired young Scotsman with the eyes that looked brown in some lights and green in others and so appealed to the ladies had precious few memories of Scotland, its people or its politics.

If they discovered he was English, they might send him home to be tried for heresy. Or they might simply invite one of the many representatives of his holiness Pope Paul IV to do it on the spot; the Inquisition was as active in Paris as any other place in Europe. Either way, he would die at the stake if he were lucky, and under torture before that if he were not.

Cedric Owen pushed himself to his feet and reached for the shirt he had left folded on a clothes press on one side of the room. Even more than the English, the French court was notorious for its licence, and the Queen was foremost in the setting of fashion. Owen looked down at himself. He had always eschewed the London fashions that filtered down to the court-in-miniature that was Cambridge. His breeches were clean, which was the best that could be said for them; the weave was as good as anything to be got in Cambridge, but it was homespun and not likely to appeal to the most riotous nobles in Europe. His cloak was of good velvet, but, like his suit, it was brown. He recalled – and now regretted – believing the draper's daughter who had said the colour matched well with his eyes. In any case, he had left the thing at his lodgings, together with his cap.

He looked up and found Charles staring at him. 'The Queen will make allowance for your dress. It is your skill she seeks, not the references of your tailor.'

Owen bowed low, because it was easier than speaking, and gestured to the door. They passed the small casket containing the dead child on the way out.

In all his life, Cedric Owen had never been to any court. He passed through corridors that dwarfed those of his old college at Cambridge, and he had thought those beyond all grandeur. He climbed stairs that went on for ever and was ushered into an antechamber to the ailing infant's bedroom, an oak-panelled place that smelled of sulphur and rosemary oil and more faintly of rosewater and sickness. The narrow windows were shuttered on one side against the glare of the evening sun, but open on the other, so that there seemed the faintest breath of a breeze in the room, which was as close as Cedric Owen had come to witnessing a miracle.

At one side of the room stood a clutter of middle-aged men who shared in common the belief that long beards and black gowns gave them an air of studious learning. Owen noted them peripherally and accounted them little danger.

It was the Queen who held the better part of his attention; the vision of ivory silk with primrose yellow bows about the waist and hem and diamonds worth an emperor's ransom set about her throat and hair. His one glance told him that she had been weeping, although the women who attended to her appearance had done an excellent job of covering it.

The part of him that was always professional admired her fortitude. Catherine de' Medici was two months past her own confinement and it could as easily have been two years for all that it showed on her body or her face. The entirety of her court knew that her husband, the King of France, was in love with his mistress, Diane de Poitiers, and slept with his wife only as was required by his duty to create heirs to the crown. That the woman could look as regal as she did in such circumstances was a testament to her Medici breeding. Power begets power and the Medici were never starved of the stuff of rulership. It radiated from her now, making smaller the men in the room.

Left alone, Owen bowed as low as he knew how and then stood awkwardly with folded hands and his eyes downcast, not knowing how he should deport himself in the company of a queen.

'You may view us.' She spoke her French richly, and with only the trace of an Italian accent. 'And then you may view more closely our daughter. For how else may you heal her?'

'My lady . . . your highness . . .' Owen's French came out in poor order. 'I am a bringer to birth and a giver of such medicines as I might find useful. I can scry the heavens for their wisdom and test the elements of a man or woman and bring them back into balance. I regret that I have no skills in the treatment of children. Your majesty has in this room physicians far more skilled than I.'

There was a rustle amongst the black crow-men who were pretending not to listen. He was not winning friends amongst them.

The Queen said, 'We have men who have so far neither freed our child of her fever, nor permitted her to thrive. We would have a fresh eye and a clear mind assess the case. They say you do not consider the four humours to be chief in aiding your diagnosis.'

This was controversial and had nearly cost Owen his studies in Cambridge. The pressure in the room became delicately brittle, like new ice at the corners of a horse trough.

Somewhere in the depths of his own ears, beyond the hearing of others, Owen heard a high, bright whine, which was the warning sound of the blue heart-stone.

Always, when he heard it, his life took a new turn.

He took a breath and smoothed his sweating palms on his shirt tails and said, 'Your highness,

I believe that Paracelsus was correct and that life is better measured by the balance of the three elements: salt, sulphur and mercury. I still wholly believe in the testing of the six pulses at either wrist, but would rather read their speech in a newer tongue. The estimation of humours has its place, but it is not the full explanation of life.'

They hated him for that, the crow-garbed men, and they were not stupid; they could sense falsehood as easily as they could smell putrefaction. By the law of averages, at least one of them was likely to be a Scot, and so able to unearth his deception.

Owen was turning his back on them when one, the youngest by a good ten years, looked across the room at him and offered a subtle, but perfectly clear, inclination of his head. The Queen saw it. 'Michel, *mon ami*, you have an ally.'

'And gladly so.' The man bowed so deeply that the finger-grease on the crown of his skull-cap showed. His voice was surprisingly delicate. 'In which case, perhaps between us we may begin to—'

A wail began in the bedroom beyond them and rose to a shriek. Another joined it. The Queen spun, and staggered. She wore heels to her shoes to augment her height and they were not made for fast movement.

Within her daughter's chamber, a bass voice

stilled the shrieks, but only for a moment. Then the Queen reached the door and flung it open and the grief spilled out, enveloping them all.

There was a great deal of noise and consternation and very little sense to be made from it, except that the young princess, clearly, had died.

The small man with the delicate voice slipped unnoticed through the chaos and came to stand with his shoulder pressed tight against Owen's, moving them both back, closer to the far wall. 'When we can leave, we should do so. You have lodgings nearby?'

'On the south bank. Maison d'Anjou.'

'A plain place, but clean, as I remember it. You choose well for one newly come to a foreign city. We should go there forthwith, with but a small detour to my own lodgings en route. I have in my effects a letter addressed to me by a young man which contains within it a letter of recommendation from Dr John Dee, a gentleman of great renown. Would you know anything of it?'

In the heat of the day, a ball of ice formed in Cedric Owen's guts. 'I have sent a letter to a physician of even greater renown in Salon,' he said. 'None to Paris.' His voice, he was glad to hear, remained level.

He looked up into eyes that laughed and warned together. 'I was summoned here three days ago from my home in Salon. Your letter followed me, and a second one from my friend, Dr Dee, giving the description of a young man of great talent who was in possession of a particular stone,' said Michel de Nostradame, physician, astrologer and prophet. 'We should perhaps—'

Once again, the urgencies of the royal family interrupted him. The Queen stepped back into the antechamber, spitting orders, catlike, at anyone and everyone in her path.

Things happened fast.

A herald in blue and gold livery materialized at the door, took his instructions and left.

A priest passed through the crowd like a breath of old wind and joined the two already in the princess's chamber. This one wore cloth of gold and a crucifix of value to rival the Queen's diamonds.

A woman came bearing a black dress and black jewels and a hair ornament of jet and black lace for the Queen. They were approved and taken into an adjacent chamber.

Through it all, the failed physicians stood bunched in a corner like crow-caped cattle. The smell of fear came off them in waves.

Catherine de' Medici raked her gaze across them all. 'You will attend us,' she said, icily. 'Now.' It did not sound like a kind offer.

Cedric Owen did not need the high, urgent whistle in his ear to understand the closeness of death. By fate and the fortuitous sideways step made by Michel de Nostradame, neither he nor the physician-astrologer was anywhere close to the black-robed men. The Queen, it seemed likely, had forgotten their existence.

Owen felt a hand tug at his sleeve. A delicate voice said, 'We should go now. I, too, had not yet examined the infant; her blood is not on my hands. I would be honoured if you would join me for wine, perhaps, and some dinner at your lodgings? There is much to talk of that is best not spoken in public. In particular, I would see the stone you have, which has been the inheritance of your family.'

'Does it require your death, this stone?'

Michel de Nostradame asked his question casually, towards the end of the meal. The blue heart-stone lay on the table, a third interlocutor in a curious conversation that was both comforting and unsettling at once.

The wine was red and not overly sour. Mme de Rouen, proprietor of the Maison d'Anjou, may have kept a plain house, but she was discreet in all things, and a consummate cook. Her dish of pigeons roasted with almonds and port was the equal of anything offered in the palace. She had served it herself in Cedric Owen's chamber on the first floor, with a linen tablecloth spread across the trestle and the wine served in cups of good boiled leather.

The wine was cloudy now that they were

near the bottom of the bottle. Cedric Owen watched the swirl of it in his mug and considered the question. He was not sure, as yet, how to take Nostradamus; the man was not intrusive, indeed had been the soul of courtesy. He was not commandeering in the way that John Dee had sometimes been. Crucially, he neither was afraid of the stone, nor sought to possess it.

Owen had dared show his treasure only to those few men whom he trusted with his life. Most, on seeing the likeness of their own unfleshed heads, had found it at first disquieting. Some had continued to fear it, stepping away from him and avoiding conversation ever after, but others – and these were the more dangerous in his view – had begun to view it with a passion bordering on lust, so that he must needs take steps to avoid them.

Not the Queen's physician; Nostradamus had laid his napkin flat that Owen might set the stone down cleanly, had got up to check that the lock on the door was secure, and then opened wide the westerly shutters, the better to let in the long, cool slant of the evening sun.

The light had stirred the fires in the depths of the blue stone, so that the empty eye sockets filled with it, and the perfect arch of the cheekbones sharpened. In this company, it was accorded the wisdom and experience of any man, and came alive, knowing it.

Nostradamus had said, 'May I touch it?' and, on a nod, had done so, laying his hand at the nape of the neck, and been silent a long while. It was then, moving his hand away and raising his wine, that he had asked his curious question. 'Does it require your death, this stone?'

Owen took his time in finding an answer. There was no danger that he could feel. The urgent whine of the Queen's chamber was long gone; whatever fates had hung in the balance, they had been settled and a new path set.

Presently, he said, 'I have the stone from my grandmother. My first memory in this life is of the blue at its heart, calling to me, and me to it; such has always been the way of choosing. It should have come to me on my twenty-first birthday, but my grandmother was slain on the orders of King Henry's counsellors, he who is father to our present queen.'

'For heresy?' A soft question, asked with due care.

'What else? She was to be hanged, but fought the men who came for her and was slain at sword-point. I was thirteen and saw it happen from a hidden place in the hallway. My great-uncle, who was keeper before her, died in like manner and his mother before him was killed by a thrown knife from a thief who desired to possess the stone. It has come to be known in our family that the keeper of the blue heart-stone will die for their care of it, but also that the life lived before is both rich and long – none of these died at less than the age of sixty. This, therefore, is both the gift and the curse: that the stone gives a long life of great joy but the end must come in violence.'

Nostradamus made a steeple of his fingers and viewed him over the top of it. He blinked, owlishly. With the same soft care, he said, 'Even so, you care for your stone, do you not?'

Owen had not expected the question, and so had not prepared an answer. His heart spoke for him, without censure.

Rawly, he said, 'It is the core and light of my life, my greatest love.'

Even to himself, he had never made it so plain. Laid open as if naked, he wrapped his own hands on either side of this stone that he loved.

It was the size and exact shape of the human skulls he had handled so often during his training, with high, broad cheekbones and deep eye sockets that seemed to follow him as he moved around it. The lower jaw moved freely but was hinged somehow in place so that it could not be disarticulated and removed as could a true human relic – in this respect alone it was unlike that on which it was modelled.

The surface was polished to smooth perfection and seemed impervious to dust or dirt or finger marks. Today, in the upstairs room of the Maison d'Anjou, the crystal from which it was made was warm to his touch, as it had been once or twice in the years since it had become his. It vibrated under his fingers as its song rang through his ears.

The blue that suffused it was breathtaking; the pale, sharp, cool clarity of a sky seen at noon over an open sea. Looking into it was to gaze into infinity, a place with no walls or ceiling, but only an ever-stretching peace.

With only a little effort, Owen opened his mind fully to its presence. It was like entering a great hall, or the reading room of a library, in which an old friend waited for him. Always, it had been his private preserve. This time, he walked in cautiously, afraid that he might find Nostradamus ahead of him. The relief when he did not left him unmanned and wet-eyed. He reached for the wine beaker and found it pushed into his hand.

Michel de Nostradame said, 'It is no shame to love this thing; it is at least as marvellous as the pyramids of Egypt, as old and as wise. And yet it is more vulnerable than any of these; for there exist in our world those who would destroy it, to rid the earth of the promise it carries. You have done well to have come this far unscathed.'

Never before had the stone been so clearly seen. Even John Dee, for all his perspicacity, had not asked his questions with such tact, nor so readily understood all that could not be spoken.

Feeling a freedom he had not known in Cambridge, Owen said, 'Dr Dee was of the belief that this stone is not alone, that there are others, and they will be called together at some time long hence, to keep man's greatest evil from afflicting the world. Would you concur?'

Unconsciously the two men had migrated to classical Greek, the language of physicians, which few others understood. It added an extra dimension to their conversation and their appraisal of each other.

In that language, thoughtfully, with his gaze resting somewhere in the infinite blue of the heart-stone, Nostradamus said, 'I have here another bottle of wine, bought from the inestimable Mme de Rouen. If you were to pour for us both, we might perhaps begin to speak the unspeakable.'

They rinsed the old wine into the hearth and poured new, of a better vintage than before. Its fruited scent filled the air, catching the blue shine of the stone.

Inhaling his appreciation, Nostradamus said, 'I concur with all that Dr Dee has told you and can add to it what I have learned from the teachings of Egypt. Your stone is one of thirteen that were created together after the flood that drowned the great cities of Atlantis. Those who survived wished to preserve their wisdom against the tide of ignorance sweeping the earth. To this end, they brought together stones of different hues from the different lands that circle the earth, and carved them with the skill and beauty you see here. Nine are coloured and are shaped for the races of men. Four are clear as glass and are made for the beasts that walk, crawl, slide and fly. Remember this. You will need knowledge of it later.'

He spoke the truth. The very stillness of the stone told Owen so. He listened with his whole body, so that his skin became an ear, and his heart, and his innards, all reverberating to this Frenchman, speaking verities softly in Greek.

'The magic by which the stones were carved, and the knowledge instilled, is beyond us, but it was done. After many generations, when the task was complete, the skull-stones were separated, as beads from a thread, and each returned to the place of its birth to be held in trust until such time as all are needed to avert the catastrophe that man will wreak on God's earth. In each land was set a lineage of keepers who guard the knowledge of what must be done with the stones in that end time.'

In the cool of the evening, Owen broke into a sweat. 'Then I have failed at the start,' he said. 'My grandmother died before she could pass to me all that she knew, and that was little enough. Too many of our family have died in the stone's name. If that knowledge was ever ours, it has not reached me, and thus I cannot pass it on.'

'Not true!' Nostradamus' hand slammed flat on the table. 'What has been lost can be found again! This is your life's work. Three tasks have been set you, Cedric Owen: to find the wisdom of the heart-stone, to record it in such a way that it can never be lost again – nor found by those who would misuse it – and last, to hide the stone so that none might come across it by chance or ill design until the end times are near.'

Cedric Owen had thought Michel de Nostradame strange, and light-voiced. He was not so now. Leaning forward in the dying light, his face was a feral mask of lines and shadows, his voice hoarse. He reached his two hot hands across the table, grasping Owen's chilled ones. 'You must do this. If any one of the thirteen skull-stones is lost before the end times, then the whole cannot be made from the sum of its parts and the world will descend into such darkness and infamy as to make our current sorry state seem like heaven by comparison.'

Letting go of Owen's hands, Nostradamus spread his palms around the stone, not touching it, but close, as if he could send his words into it, or receive them from it by some alchemy Owen could not feel. There was a long moment's waiting before he spoke again.

'Make no mistake,' he said. 'The attacks on your family were not accidental. There a force at work that does not wish our world made better; it feeds on death and destruction, fear and pain, and wishes these things to continue into the nadir of Armageddon. It bends men to its will; intelligent, thoughtful men who believe that they can take the power they are offered and wield it only for good. But the nature of power is otherwise; it breaks them, always, and its greatest desire is that the thirteen stones might never again conjoin to deliver our world from misery.'

'You speak of the Church?' Owen asked, whispering.

'Ha!' The Queen's prophet spat a flurry of wine into the hearth. 'The Church is ruled by infants, with the mean minds of harlot women and the jealousies of a cuckolded queen. They know that there are places they cannot – or dare not – travel and they would see us die at the stake rather than admit their incapacity, or permit those of us who walk between the worlds to tell others of what we find that does not accord with their infantile view of the universe.'

As if moved by the power of his blasphemy, his hair flew out around his head. He turned a wild and savage gaze on Owen. 'Yes, I speak of the Church, but it has not always been so in the past, and will not always be so in the future. The Church is but a vehicle for those who crave power. In centuries to come, the state will become as powerful, eclipsing the mewling priests. Men will arise then with power we can only dream of and your stone will be in even greater danger than it is now. This is why the lineage of skull-keepers must be broken and your heart-stone hidden from the avarice of such men.'

'I don't understand.'

'Wait.' The prophet held up his hand. 'We must draw the blinds before we speak of such matters, but first there is a thing you must see while we yet have the benefit of the sun. You must understand what it is that you hold. Dr Dee will have shown you how the light of the sun might be split by a crystal?'

'He did indeed.' It was the last of Dee's teachings, a gift to stretch intellect and spirit together. Owen was still bright with the understanding of it.

'Excellent. Then we shall perform that feat now.'

Nostradamus was a conjuror at heart. He pulled from his inner pockets a small shard of clearest crystal, and, with a flourish, set it on the table at a place where the sun sent its last rays. He tutted a moment, and moved it, and shifted the white napkin that the light spilling out of his fragment might fall on to brightness, not on to the undistinguished oak of the table.

He paused a moment, then moved his hand away. There across the table was shed a bright, brilliant rainbow, no wider than the palm of his hand.

Owen gave a soft exclamation; he had seen it once before, but it was not a thing of which a man might tire.

Gratified, Nostradamus said, 'Thus is the sun's light revealed to be made of seven colours. By this means also is a rainbow fashioned when light meets falling rain and is cast in an arc upon the ground.'

Owen said, 'And the fifth colour is the blue of the noonday sky which is also the blue of the heart-stone. In my earliest childhood, my grandmother showed me this; my family carries a part of a rainbow.'

The evidence was there again in front of him. The fifth colour in the array, wedged between grass green and midnight blue, was precisely the noon-sky blue of the skull.

'And did your grandmother tell you, then, why your stone is named for the heart of the world?'

Owen shook his head. Nostradamus smiled, pleased to be privy to more knowledge than a white-haired old woman. 'Then I shall show you.'

Quick-fingered, he brought a piece of jet and a white pebble from his pocket, and set them at the end of the rainbow strip, black before white.

'The colours of the world are nine in total;

the seven of the rainbow, plus the black of no-light and the white of all-light. Blue is fifth of the nine, the central colour, the fulcrum about which all turns, the keystone of the world's arc. The ancients knew this, which we have forgotten. To the blue was given the heart of the beast, and the power to call together the remaining twelve parts of its spirit and flesh so that the whole may be joined again.'

Owen frowned. 'What beast?'

'The Ouroboros, spoken of by Plato, the ultimate beast of all power, that embodies the spirit of the earth and will arise at her time of greatest need. What else could free the world from the wrath of Armageddon?'

Seeing the incomprehension on Owen's face, the little man stood, his added height giving weight to his words.

'The flesh of the great serpent is made from the four beast-stones. I know not the nature of the beasts, nor how they may be brought together – you must find this. What I can tell you is that the life-spirit of the beast comes from the nine rainbow stones that encircled the earth.

'The ancients knew of the lines of force that flow around us, unseen and unfelt. They mapped them and built on them great artefacts: pyramids and stone circles; tombs where the dead guard the points of deepest power. At nine of these points, they fashioned sockets to receive the stones and hold them on the earth. At the appointed time, when the stars are in propitious alignment, if all nine are set in place, then can the coloured stones of the rainbow arc join with the four beast-stones to become the Ouroboros.'

Owen stared at him, trying to imagine such a thing. The prophet leaned forward, his hands flat on the table, his eyes narrowed. '*The thirteen stones make the beast*. Do you understand?'

'But why?' Owen asked. 'To what end? What can such a beast do?'

Deflated, Nostradamus sat. 'That we do not and cannot know, for the circumstances are not yet upon us that would require it. If man is, indeed, the instigator of all evil, then it may be that the only answer is to cleanse the earth of our sorry presence. I would hope that this is not so, that it is possible for so great a thing as the earth-serpent to find hope in the race of men and thereby turn the tide of devastation, but we cannot say for certain.'

The sun was all but gone. The rainbow faded to nothing. The heart-stone drew in the light of the fire and shed it softly blue across the table. Heartsick, Owen said, 'Then it may be that I hold the end of mankind in my hands. I would not wish to harbour such a thing.'

'But you may hold its saving. Do not deign to judge, for that is not your place.'

The Queen's physician swept his hand across the table, gathering his stones, then turned to close over the shutters and used his flint and tinder with some élan to light the two tallow stubs left on the table. New light and new shadows furled about the skull-stone, dancing with the fire at its heart.

In the changed atmosphere, Nostradamus poured more wine. 'Let us review your tasks in reverse,' he said. 'When the time comes, you must hide the stone so that it cannot be found by any until the end times. Before then, your task is to recover the wisdom that your ancestors knew, and to preserve it for those who come after.'

Frustrated, Owen threw himself back in his chair. 'How? Who is left who will teach me this when all of Europe is under the thrall of the Inquisition?'

'You will not remain in Europe.'

Nostradamus pulled his seat round to sit with his shoulder pressing Owen's. He moved the candles so that the two flames shone through the unblemished blue of the skull, alight in the places eyes would have been.

Heavily, he said, 'Now is the time of revealing, limited though it is. You, Cedric Owen, ninth of that name, are the one chosen to make the bridge between past, present and future. You have no choice in this, as I have no choice but to tell you. This stone does require your death, but it offers, as

78

you know, a life lived full and long, with great joy to balance the pain of loss that must come at its end.'

The prophet's eyes were quite black. His hands were still as death and whiter than bone. His voice came from somewhere else in the room and was entirely powerful, while yet no louder than a whisper. Afterwards, Owen was not even sure what language had been spoken. He thought it might have been Latin.

'You will go to the place south of here where the Mussulman once ruled, where the river runs into the ocean. From there, you can take ship to the New World, therein to find the oldest part of the Old World and there to meet those who understand the nature of the battle that will be fought at the end of time, and the ways in which we might survive it. It is they who know the heart and soul of your blue stone. They will tell you how best you may unlock its secrets and preserve them for all eternity. I who am an amateur in these things, and serve merely to purvey the prophecies of others, can tell you only that you must return at last to England, and find the place of white water and stone. Hide your secret there and afterwards ensure that those who follow may understand what they have and what they must do.'

Owen waited a long time for the life to return to the other man's eyes. Long enough to think how he might go south to the place where the river ran into the ocean. He heard the noises of gulls and of fisherfolk and did not question the truth of his ears. He felt the floor move beneath him as a deck and smelled the bitter, brackish sea.

As from an equal distance, he saw Michel de Nostradame come back into himself and pause and view him and nod and smile his small, succinct smile.

'Good. It is done. I have fulfilled my part of our bargain. Now, I have a question which will seem to you strange. Are you a physician or a surgeon?'

'A physician, always. I have no common cause with the barbers and wielders of knives.'

'Nevertheless, you will need to gain some knowledge. I have in my lodgings a monograph by Dr Giovanni da Vigo, who was surgeon to the Pope himself, and several from the Moor, El Zahrawi, whom you may better know as Albucasis, who is in my belief the best man to bring the sciences of medicine, surgery and astronomy together. Do you speak Spanish?'

'Yes. As part of my studies, I spent half a year in Cadiz, learning the ways of the Moorish physicians there.'

'Then you will already have a foundation for what I shall teach you. Excellent.' Nostradamus gave his bow again, that showed the crown of his skull-cap.

'It is too hot for you to travel and all Paris

must enter mourning for the young princess. You will be unable to leave for at least a tenday. If you will come to my lodgings at six of the clock tomorrow morning, I will give you these two books and you may read them in my company. You may ask of me what you will, and at the end you will know enough to perform such surgery as might be needed. Amputations, particularly, should be your field of study.'

At the door, he turned, his gaze still black. 'Until tomorrow, I will leave you with your heart-stone. You have my best wishes for the success of your venture. On you rests the fate of worlds and of men.'

4

Ingleborough Hill, Yorkshire Dales,
May 2007

STELLA WANTED TO GO INTO THE CAVE AGAIN,
and the rescue would not let her.

She had reached the car at eighteen minutes
after three. By half past, when she had stripped
out of her dry-suit and changed into shorts and a
clean T-shirt, wet-wiped her hands and face,
drunk half a bottle of water and tipped the rest
over her head, found somewhere to pee that was
hidden from the road and eaten the cheese and
tomato sandwiches, gone limply acid after a day
in the sun, and there was still no sign, she had
called Kit's mobile.

By quarter to four, when there was no
answer, she had called the hotel, and Bede's
College in Cambridge and the two friends of his
she knew in North Yorkshire who could be
relied upon not to panic. She had told all of
them she could not find Kit. She had not

told any about the skull, or the pearl-hunter.

At four thirty, with the summer sun still warm on her back and her hands so cold she could barely hold the phone, she had called the police, who had called Cave Rescue who had come out in force; a dozen men and women who lived for the chance to go underground.

They were efficient and well equipped, with their short-wave radios and clinometers and ascenders and descenders and pulleys and cow's tails and compasses and charts that mapped the entire White Scar complex, beside which her hand-drawn effort looked infantile.

Still, they were cavers, and they knew her as one of their own, and did what they could to be kind about it. 'That's good . . . it's really good. We did this one in November and it was hell on wheels. Easy to see how he'd fall at the pinch point . . .'

'That crawl along the ledge . . . nightmares-ville . . . We should have bolted it when we first went in. He went off there, did he?'

'The drop over's at least four hundred feet. Is that where he went off, aye? At the pinch point?'

'. . . water at the bottom. Might still be alive . . .'

'You think there's an opening up in the wall? Really? And cave paintings in the cavern? We could try for it tomorrow, maybe. You'd get first claim on the route, of course, but we could map it out properly. Andy? Where's Andy? Has anyone seen . . . ?'

'Good thing you weren't roped together. That was good planning. It was here, at the pinch point, yes?'

'*I! Don't! Know!*'

The echo of her shout rolled round the mountain. A thick silence rolled after it. Stella could feel the glances exchanged over her head and the half-rolled eyes and the sudden switch to brisk efficiency which saw them all pack up their gear and make ready, communicating by hand signals and eye contact.

They left her in the charge of the young woman police sergeant who was working the radio and had been asking all the right kinds of questions. All the time, the skull-stone lay in her backpack, radiant as lightning, whispering its constant warning.

For the skull-stone, for its urgent insistence, she told half-lies with no telling the consequences at the end of it. For the skull-stone and for Kit, because he had risked his life for it, and the danger had been real and she did not know yet if he was safe.

For both of these, she did not say why they had been in the cave or what they had found in the cavern or that she had no idea where he had fallen or even if he had fallen at all because she was too far behind; she simply said where

84

she thought it most likely to be and prayed that she was wrong.

'We'll be an hour in. Maybe a bit longer. You should eat something, aye?' A neoprene hand patted her shoulder. Half a dozen faces grinned at her and offered themselves in to the dark on her behalf, for an untruth, poorly told. She smiled for them and tried not to look hysterical and went down to stand by the car.

'Mrs O'Connor?'

A new police officer came for her; a tall man in a flat hat with more polish to his uniform than the young WPC she had left at the cave's mouth. He strode long-legged down the hillside, alive with urgency.

'Mrs O'Connor . . .'

Sheep grazed, half hidden in the bracken; ewes and their long-tailed lambs, which still thought more of playing than feeding. A buzzard wheeled in the high blue. The skull-stone reached a single-pitched note of warning, just as it had in the cave.

Stella wondered if perhaps she were going mad, and stooped to look in the car's wing mirror, to make sure she was still the same woman who had risen that morning, with joy firing her heart. Her own face looked back, angular, sharp-boned, with too many freckles ever to be elegant, and now too much mud where the wet-wipes had missed and unattractive lines of red and then weary blue beneath her eyes. Kit's ghost kissed her hair. *Beautiful woman. I love you however much mud you choose to paddle in.*

'Kit . . .'

'Mrs O'Connor—'

Breathless, the officer reached her. He bent and placed his palms on his braced knees and fought to make his straining lungs work.

'Mrs O'Connor . . . we need you to . . . come up the hill. The caving team are . . . on the radio. They think they've found—'

A car door slammed, solidly. 'Her name's Cody. Dr Stella Cody. You're not doing anyone a service by diminishing her achievements.'

'*Tony!*'

She swayed. Her knees unlocked. Tony Bookless was a tall man, with an impeccably tailored suit and short silvery hair. He caught her arm and held it. She found her voice and made it work for him.

'You didn't have to come . . . I didn't call to ask you to come . . . it's such a long way.'

He hugged her close. His voice hummed through her chest, deeply. 'I didn't come from Cambridge. I was in Harrogate, at the conference; it's no distance at all. The office phoned me just after you'd called them and I left as soon as I could. Tell me what you need me to do?'

Tony Bookless, forty-third Master of Bede's

College, Cambridge, was old enough to be her father, solid, certain, sure, with the bearing of long-ago military heritage and a mind honed by years in the ivory tower. He had been one of the two witnesses at her wedding. Stella gripped the hand he offered and felt human again for the first time in hours.

'Make Kit be alive?' Her voice sounded harsh in the sudden silence.

'Oh, Stella . . .'

He drew her in to his chest, where the world was safe. Over her shoulder, he held out his hand and introduced himself to the officer behind her. 'Professor Sir Anthony Bookless, Master of Bede's College, Cambridge. I was – am – Dr O'Connor's employer. I will shortly be Dr Cody's employer. If I can be of assistance, please tell me. You are . . . ?'

'Detective Inspector Fleming, sir, North Yorkshire Police Authority. Our caving team has followed Mrs O'Con— that is, Dr Cody's excellent directions and they have found . . . the place she described. They're at the bottom of a four-hundred-foot wall and they believe they have found . . . what they were looking for.'

Four hundred feet. Gravity sucked at her again, the yawning blackness, the sliding slope of the ledge to an unknown drop.

That's enough to kill us when we fall off and hit the bottom.

We're not going to fall off.

Four hundred feet.

She looked up. Two men were looking back at her, waiting.

Numbly, she said, 'What do you need me for?'

Fleming stared at his feet. He was sharp and polished and had none of the people skills of his colleague. 'At some point, we'll need an . . . identification, but not until they come out, which won't be for a bit yet. In the meantime, it would seem we may have a . . . murder investigation. Sergeant Jones tells me that there was someone following you in the cave – that Dr O'Connor may have been pushed off the ledge. You have given a statement to that effect?'

He was speaking around her in wide ellipses of meaning through which only one fact stood out. She said, 'You've found Kit? Is he all right?'

'My dear, we are rarely asked to identify the living.'

Tony Bookless had never treated her as less than an equal. While Fleming pursed his lips and tried to think of new ways to obfuscate, the Master of Bede's, Kit's mentor, employer and friend, took Stella's shoulder and turned her away, bringing himself down so that his eyes and hers were level. In the simple, steady compassion of that act was the truth she could not face.

For the first time in her life, Stella felt reality break apart around her. Part of her stood on a hillside, facing an inspector of the police who wanted to start a murder investigation. The greater part was in darkness, standing on a finger's width of rock, with a light bobbing past below. In that part alone, Kit was still alive.

She saw Tony Bookless's mouth open and close, like a fish under water. From a great distance, she heard him ask a question. 'Inspector Fleming is asking if there was some-one else in the cave, someone who may have wished you harm. Can you remember?'

A part of her that could still function said, 'I was looking down on him. Perspective does strange things, but he looked big, the same as both of you.'

'It was a man, then, you're sure of that? You saw him?' Fleming flashed his notebook out.

She had had her fill of Inspector Fleming and his clinical enthusiasm. Anger made her lucid. 'No, I didn't see him. Yes, I think it was a man but I couldn't be certain. I was on the wall above the ledge. Kit took my spare light and went on ahead – he's a runner, he thought he could get out faster alone than with me. I climbed up the wall above the ledge to get out of the way. Whoever it was passed beneath me. I didn't see more than his head-torch.'

'You climbed a cave wall in the dark, with no lights?' Tony Bookless looked at her with a new kind of awe. 'Stella, that's . . . immensely dangerous.'

It was a compliment, of sorts. She felt herself flush. 'I was desperate.'

Fleming was not so easily impressed. He came to stand over her, with his hand on the car roof. 'There must be something you can give me. We're four hours past the time of the event. Every passing hour loses us evidence. You do understand that?'

She stepped out from under his gaze. 'I had no light. I was holding on to rock with a ten-degree overhang. I was trying not to fall off and die.'

'We'll see if we can send in anybody to find any prints, then, aye?' Fleming had a radio in his pocket. He turned away and spoke into it, urgently.

Tony Bookless sighed. For her ears only, he said, 'There stands a man who believes what he sees on television. He'll have a team up here in the night, running reconstructions, just see if I'm right.' His eyes were on her face. 'At least that made you smile. I'm glad. But I still don't understand why someone would be chasing you in a cave. You and Kit are the last people on earth to have upset anyone that badly.'

'He wasn't after us. We found—'

She was shrugging off her pack to show him the stone. The words were shaping on her tongue, of discovery, of explanation, of triumph that only a man like Tony Bookless would fully understand.

They never took form. In the blue place of her mind, the heart-stone stole her words and slid in others of its own.

Glibly, she said, 'Kit had the crystal skull. Cedric Owen's blue heart-stone. It was in his pack. Whoever it was wanted the stone, I'm certain of that.'

'Cedric Owen's heart-stone?' Tony Bookless's eyes were sudden windows to his soul and it ached. 'It went over the edge with him? It's lost?'

To hide her own face, she gave him another hug. 'I'm sorry. It won't have survived a four-hundred-foot fall on to rock. The best we can hope for is that they find his pack. At least we could have the shattered pieces of it to show why we went in.'

As all lies do, this one grew roots and became real.

With Tony Bookless and DI Fleming tracking behind, she retraced the path to the cave's exit, where Sergeant Ceri Jones doubled as the radio operator for the Rescue. She sat close to her set, listening to the crackle and wheeze of short wave transmitted in relays to the surface, because however new the technology there will always be limits to the human ability to communicate underground.

She fed out the news in bursts of static, a slow drip-feed of hope and unhope. 'They found

91

water at the base of the wall. No one's been down there before. They didn't know.' She was wiry and blunt-nosed and kind. She spoke directly to Stella, not through the two men; caver to caver, Yorkshire lass to Yorkshire lass, in the accents of home that had always held hope.

'Water?' Stella said. 'Not rock?'

'Water.'

And so hope.

A breeze curved round the edge of the slope, lifting strands of hair, taking the edge off the wild sun. Stella clutched her hands across her body and stared at the cave's mouth and saw nothing.

The radio crackled again. Ceri bent to it, playing with the reception. 'They're pulling him up on a stretcher. The medics think . . .' Kind eyes met hers. 'Don't hope too much.'

'Do they have his pack?' Tony Bookless asked. His hands were on Stella's shoulders. 'I'm sorry, but it *is* Cedric Owen's stone.'

Ceri Jones stared at him, flatly. 'They didn't say. Probably not high on their list of priorities. They'll be here in ninety minutes, give or take. You can be patient till then.'

Jones was a caver before anything else; she rated her world by the ability to crawl a sloping ledge and climb a wall at the end of it. Professor Sir Anthony Bookless did not feature in her scale of reckoning and it showed.

Stella saw him discomfited for the first time

in her life. He stepped away from her and sat on a rock, twisting his hands over each other. 'I wish I'd known you were going for the stone. I could have helped; made sandwiches, held a radio outside . . . something.'

'It was Kit's present to me, that we should do it together, alone. After Friday . . .' On Friday they had married, with Tony Bookless casting rice in handfuls over their heads.

'Ah.' His smile was brief and sad. 'Private.'

Stella said, 'Kit thought you knew at the register office when you warned us of the deaths that attended the stone. He thought he'd said something incautious and blown it.'

'Did he? I'm sorry, perhaps I wasn't paying enough attention. I knew the two of you were looking for clues to the heart-stone's location, but it didn't occur to me that you might already have found it. I suppose I was arrogant enough to think Kit would have told me.'

Professor Sir Anthony Bookless had made his name co-writing the definitive biography of Cedric Owen. More than anyone else, more than Kit, far more than Stella, he was linked to the blue stone and all it represented. The hurt in his eyes was a tangible thing.

Gently, Stella said, 'Kit wanted to bring the stone back to show you as a surprise. You were so clear in your reading of the legends, about the dangers that went with the stone, but he thought you'd change your mind if—'

'Stella . . .' Bookless edged off his rock and came to sit on the heather at her feet. He held her two hands between his own and looked up at her earnestly.

He was so polite, so very English.

She said, 'What?'

He looked down at his hands. His signet ring bore Bede's fiery dragon faced by an un-armoured knight, wielding a delicate sword. He said, 'It's not about changing my mind, it's about the integrity of scholarship. Cedric Owen is the closest Bede's College has to a saint. He took his degree with us, he shed his life-blood at our gates, that he might bequeath to us his very considerable fortune. He left us gold and diamonds enough to lift us from being a second rate Plantagenet project to punching so far above our weight that we're on a par with Trinity and King's and the Ivy League in the States. On top of all that, he left us thirty-two years of quite astoundingly meticulous accountancy ledgers, which have set us on the map of academic excellence in a way nothing else could have done.'

'Tony, I've been at Bede's nearly a year. I do know the history—'

He caught her arm and dropped it again. 'I know you do, but listen to me. Owen's skull-stone has not been seen since his death. Sir Francis Walsingham, spymaster to Elizabeth I, the man with the most extensive network of informants the medieval world had ever seen, searched the length and breadth of England looking for it after Owen's death. He failed to find it. As have at least three dozen others in the time since. Could you tell me, then, what Kit found that four hundred years of dedicated scholarship failed to uncover?'

The truth was harder to tell than the lie. Stella reached for her water bottle and drank, and felt in the recesses of her mind for where the skull-stone crouched, catlike, cornered, or waiting; she could not tell which.

Her fingernails were still dirty. She picked at one forefinger with the other and then clenched her hands and pushed them under her knees.

In his perfect, assured, Cambridge voice, Bookless said gently, 'Stella, you can tell me. Whatever it is, it can't be worse than Kit's death. Believe me, if he could be made alive, I would give my own blood to do it.'

They were on a hillside, in late afternoon, and there were at least two others listening. Even so, her world had shrunk to this one man and the ease with which she could rock his foundations.

Quietly, distinctly, over the crack and hiss of Ceri Jones's radio, Stella said, 'We broke the cipher in the Owen ledgers. It wasn't written by Cedric Owen. Kit thinks it was written by Francis Walker after Owen's death.'

Tony Bookless frowned. 'I'm sorry?'

'The ledgers are fakes, Tony. At least the last half-dozen are, and if they are, the rest might as well be.'

There was no way to say it kindly and Stella did not try. Bookless stared at her. His eyes were a pale brown, made richer by the descending sun. They searched her face now, as if an answer might be hidden in the streaks of grime from the cave.

It was easier to speak than not. Patiently, she said, 'When Kit finally got his software to work, he wanted to test it on the Owen ledgers: thirty-two volumes, written by the same man over thirty-two consecutive years, with almost a fifty-fifty mix of text and numbers. He thought that if the algorithms could make sense of a medieval accountancy manuscript, they'd chew through our modern attempts at scribbling signatures in seconds.'

'I know this. He came to me to ask permission to enter the archives.'

Before he was a teacher, Tony Bookless was the Master of Bede's; it mattered to him that the world know its history. He looked up to Ceri Jones and Fleming. 'Bede's has some of the most advanced archiving facilities in Europe. The Owen manuscripts are a set of accountancy ledgers dating back to Owen's time in the New World. They're our most precious academic resource and we keep them locked in a sealed archive with temperature, humidity and atmospheric controls. The copying process was long and very slow. Kit was commissioned to write a program that would analyse and compare any handwriting by any individual at any point in their life and verify it as authentic. He only started the analysis in January of this year. He's been very quiet since. I thought – forgive me, Stella – I thought he was preoccupied with other things.'

Other things. You.

She tried to imagine Kit distracted from his life's joy, and failed.

To Tony Bookless, she said, 'No. He was preoccupied with how to tell you that Bede's entire academic basis is a sham. The ledgers were written in five years, not thirty, and by two different people. Cedric Owen wrote the first two dozen or so volumes; someone else wrote the remaining six. They tried to copy his handwriting and to the untrained eye it looks the same, but when Kit scanned it in, it blew his program out of the water. Cedric Owen may have written the first lot, but he didn't write the last half-dozen; the handwriting for those matches a letter sent to Barnabas Tythe after Owen's death signed by someone calling himself Francis Walker.'

'Why?' Bookless was standing now, pacing a swathe through the bracken. 'The ledgers are the rock on which Bede's stands. Owen knew they would be, it's why he hid them before his death, so that Walsingham's pursuivants couldn't destroy them. Why, *why*, would he do this to the college he loved?'

They had asked themselves that, Kit and Stella, in the solitude of the river room, floating between air and water. *Why?* And out of the asking, had come an answer.

'To hide the skull where only someone like Kit would find it,' Stella said simply. 'There's a code in the ledgers. On the last twenty pages of the last volume, there's shorthand of the kind used by John Dee, the Elizabethan astrologer. It told us where to look for the skull-stone, in the cathedral of the earth, in the white water. We went to look for it, and we found it, and Kit had it, and if they don't bring it up with him, then it really has gone.'

Find me and live, for I am your hope at the end of time.

There was nothing else to say. They said nothing. In the quiet afternoon, the radio hissed and popped. Ceri bent to her headphones and came away, smiling uncertainly.

'They're ten minutes from the entrance. They've asked for a helicopter. They think they have a pulse.'

5

*Ingleborough Hill, Yorkshire Dales,
May 2007*

THEY BROUGHT HIM OUT TO HER IN THE evening sunshine, strapped by arm and leg and head to an aluminium stretcher.

His hands were folded over his chest in peaceful repose. His legs were bound straight, hiding the break that Ceri had already told her was there. The sun lit his face, giving colour where the water had leached it all away. His eyes were shut. A graze-bruise down one side of his face leaked up to a bloody mess in his hair above his left ear.

Wanting to touch him, not able to make herself, Stella touched the clot instead. Hours of cold had made it hard, like plastic, so that her fingers skittered over the surface. To no one in particular, she said, 'How . . . ?'

One amongst the team was a medic; a short man, closer to middle age than the rest. As he spoke, he cut Kit's dry-suit and stuck on patches for an ECG. 'We think he hit his head on the side of the wall before he fell over. He was probably unconscious when he hit the water. His pack saved him; he had a plastic lunch box in there that held air and kept him up.'

'No stone?' Tony Bookless asked from just behind her.

The medic stared through him and said nothing. He fixed the wires to the patches and set the screen on the end of the stretcher. The green line blipped . . . and blipped . . . and blipped.

Stella stared at it, and choked and stuffed her knuckles in her mouth.

'Thought so.' The medic reached for her arm and patted it, smiling tightly. 'Your man's alive. Whether he'll regain consciousness, or when, is entirely another question. We need to get him warmed up and on oxygen and get a scan of his brain. If there's scrambled eggs in there, you might wish he'd died in the water.'

'No, I won't, I promise you. I'll never wish that.' Behind, on the hillside, the blast of a rotor scattered the ewes and flattened the bracken. 'Can I come with you to the hospital?'

'Sure.' The medic glanced past her. 'And your father, if he wants to.'

Stella's lie unravelled in the hospital later that night, with only Tony Bookless to hear it.

Kit lay in a white room under white sheets with a white curtain drawn about. Wires and drips rose from him like cobwebs. Green lines drew the rhythm of his life and numbers charted his oxygen tensions, pulse pressure and heart rate. His face was white, except at the left temple, where a great black bruise spread down towards his jaw. He had not yet opened his eyes, or spoken. The medics did not know if he ever would.

Miraculously, the right half of his face was almost untouched. If she looked at that alone, Stella could believe him simply sleeping. When Tony Bookless left her to make a phone call, she sat alone, holding Kit's hand, and focused on the right half of his face and recounted for herself the full litany of shared memories, from first meeting to last parting in the cave.

First meeting was best and sharpest and she came back to it when all the others had passed. He had been sleeping then, too, or she had thought so; one of the half-dozen post-grads lying in the sun on Jesus Green on a Wednesday afternoon halfway through the Lent term, with games of rounders going on all about and the first tourists punting badly up the Cam.

Stella had been new to Cambridge, still learning the geography of the landscape and the politics, still mapping the internal minefields of protocol and preference, too busy to lie on the grass on a warm spring afternoon, too preoccupied with the next day's paper presentation to notice the long, lean arm that snaked out and caught her ankle.

In Manchester, she would have screamed and tried to run. In Cambridge, she stood very still and looked down. At eleven o'clock in the morning, the man at her feet was unshaven, his hair was a mess, his T-shirt had grass stains across it.

In lilting Irish, he said, 'I came to your talk at the Caving Club last night. Gordon said you were the best he'd ever met. If I were to offer to take you to dinner with Martin Rees at Trinity tonight, would you teach me the wonders of caving at the weekend?'

It was his voice that caught her, and then the sharpness of his eyes, and only last what he had said.

'Martin Rees? *The* Martin Rees?' She sounded foreign, as he did, so far into Yorkshire that it could have been another country.

'The Martin Rees. Astronomer Royal, Professor of Cosmology and Astrophysics and President of the Royal Society and Master of Trinity College. The very one. There's a formal Hall at Trinity and I can get us invited. At least, I can get myself invited, plus whoever is currently my partner.'

'Your partner?' The idea made her head spin. Three years as an undergraduate in Manchester had been an academic miracle nearly lost in a series of relationship disasters. For Cambridge, she had promised herself three years of hard work with no distractions of the heart. She was barely into her second term.

Kit had shrugged. Even then, she had read volumes into it. 'The arrangement can be as transient as you like. We can discuss the caving afterwards. I'm afraid of the dark, really. But Gordon did say you were the best he had ever met.'

Gordon was the best in the country; both of them knew that. If Martin Rees was the reason Stella had come to Cambridge, Gordon Fraser, chance met in a Cheshire cave, was the man who had drawn her to Bede's. It was on his recommendation, in a roundabout way, therefore, that she had gone to formal Hall and sat three tables down from Martin Rees and barely noticed the great man was there.

She had taken Kit down one small cave that weekend, just for the completeness of it, and then never again in the fourteen turbulent, productive, much-distracted months of their togetherness; until now. For the first time in her life, she had found that her world could encompass work and love and that both were better for it. To lose love – to lose Kit – was unimaginable.

What if I were to find you a cave with buried treasure that no one has entered for four hundred and nineteen years?

In the harsh whiteness of the hospital, she pressed his hand to her face and felt the coolness of his skin and never heard the footsteps as Tony Bookless came back from his phone call.

His hand came to rest lightly on her shoulder. 'You're thinking too much. Would it help to talk?'

'I was thinking that I'm the caver. I should never have let Kit go on ahead.'

'But you thought you were being chased, and he was the better runner.' Bookless found a chair and pulled it up. 'As long as you're sure there was someone there? The ardent DI Fleming, I feel, is downgrading this all the time. If you're lucky, he'll hold it over as a suspected murder. If not, he'll write it off as an unfortunate accident with you as the paranoid hysteric.'

'There was somebody there, Tony. He was hunting Cedric Owen's skull-stone.'

She felt stupid saying it, here, with everything so starkly white and perfect. She stared a long time at the cardiogram. When she looked up, she found Tony Bookless waiting for her. 'What did he do, this . . . hunter?'

They were edging closer to the truth. Amidst all the technology, the stone still occupied a part of her mind, keeping her watchful and wary. Stella drank plastic vending-machine coffee to dull it.

'He threw stones, so that we could hear them;

a steady rhythm, one every thirty seconds, so that there was no chance it was random. Kit said we were being herded and that if we separated, he could draw off the danger. He took my underwater lamp and went ahead. He thought he could run to safety.'

'On that ledge?'

'We didn't know how bad it was.'

'And so he fell, and took the skull-stone with him. One final death added to its toll of dozens.'

Tony Bookless sat back, deflated. He had not been the same since she had told him the Owen ledgers were a fake. She wanted to give him something worthwhile. She drained the last of her coffee to drown the warnings of the skull-stone and offered her only gift.

'No. He fell and left the stone with me. That was the point. He was only ever the decoy.'

It took all her will to say it. The stone screamed until all she could hear was its screaming, a nail driving into the soft parts of her brain.

She put her head in her hands.

'What is it?'

'The skull. It's become part of me. It's driving me crazy. Earlier, I thought it was trying to help Kit – to reach to him when he was in the MRI machine, but now it's just making so much *noise* . . .'

She pressed the heels of her hands to her eyes

and her fingers in her ears and it made no difference. 'Tony, we should never have touched it. It's driving me mad and there's some lunatic out there who wants this thing badly enough to kill for it.'

She reached for her bag. Tony Bookless's hand caught her arm. He said, 'Please don't. I don't want to see it. It carries too much blood, most of it from people I hold in highest respect, of whom Kit was only the latest. I don't want yours added to it – or anyone else who might be hurt by its having been found.'

Stella slumped in her chair. 'What do I do?'

'Do you want my very sincere, absolutely honest advice?'

Tony Bookless was tired. Lines etched patterns on his face that she had never seen before. He smiled wanly. 'This is probably the greatest artefact our college could have. It would make the truth of the ledgers a victory, not an abject failure. But all that we know, all of its history, says that everyone who has ever held it has died, up to and including Cedric Owen. No stone is worth dying for and this one carries the blood of too many people already. Get rid of it, Stella.'

'How?'

'Take it back into the cave to the place where Kit fell, and throw it into the water where it should have gone this afternoon. When you've done that, and the world is safe, come back to me and I'll throw my weight around until people listen. We'll organize for Kit to come to Addenbrooke's, where they have some of the best minds in coma medicine in the world, and you'll let me drive you back to Cambridge to be close to him. I'll talk to the people at Max Planck and push through the fellowship you were going to get anyway, and you'll make of your life the very best that it can be until Kit is well enough to join you, whenever that may be.' His voice said it may be never, where his words skated over the truth.

'I can't . . .'

He gripped her hand. 'Stella, you're a caver. You can do anything you want to. And Kit will be here when you get back. I'll watch him if you want, or come with you if you'd rather.'

'It's not that. I can't go back to that cave tonight. I haven't got the bottle, Tony. I'm not sure I'll ever try a cave again.'

He had the good grace not to argue. 'Is there somewhere else, less . . . intimidating?'

'Gaping Ghyll maybe. It's the first wet cave I ever went down and this is the only year for the past ten that I haven't been back. It's the deepest pothole in England and the entrance isn't far from here, but I don't want to go in the dark.'

'I'll take you there tomorrow morning, then. And afterwards we'll head back to Cambridge.'

'Don't you have a conference to go to?'

'I have a conference to chair, but they'll live without me. Some things are more important than listening to a hundred earnest professionals discuss how the government is steadily eroding our civil liberties. If you're going to stay here all night, we should organize a bed. Or would you rather go to the hotel?'

'I don't think I should leave . . .'

Bookless read the conflicts in her eyes and forced a smile. A hand under her elbow helped her to rise.

Gently, he said, ' "Should" is a word to erase from your vocabulary. Kit's not going to wake any time in the next twelve hours. The consultant was quite clear on that. You're not doing him any disservice by leaving, and you'll be better able to make decisions in the morning if you've had a good night's sleep. Will you let me take you to the hotel?'

It was not a time to argue. She leaned in and kissed Kit's cold, plastic cheek and let Tony Bookless drive her back to her hotel and see her to her room; a different room, because he had talked to the hotel manager and they had already moved everything out of the suite she had shared with Kit into a corner room on the floor below which was smaller, but had a better view of the Dales, could she bring herself ever again to look at the landscape and feel it home.

'I'll see you tomorrow. Don't forget what I said.'

He pressed her arm, quietly, sanely comforting. For the first time in months, she opened the door to an empty bedroom. From its place in the depths of her backpack, the skull-stone sang to her sadly, in waves of quiet blue.

6

Seville, late August 1556

'SEÑOR OWEN, MY SHIP IS FITTED OUT AND ready to sail with the dawn tide. She will take me to New Spain, where I will make my fortune. For the duration of the trip there, she will be part of a small convoy which includes two warships that will keep us safe from privateers, and we will therefore have no use of further swordsmen. You want me to take you with me, but then so does half of Seville. I have refused to take any man, however well bred, unless he can prove himself of use to me. None has so far done so. If no noble son of Spain can assist me, can you give me one good reason why you might do so in their stead?'

'I can give you three,' said Cedric Owen flatly, 'and you can choose for yourself which one finds the highest favour.'

It was hot and two fat, green flies swam on the surface of his wine and he had already decided that Fernandez Alberto Garcia de Aguilar was a primped Spanish popinjay with an expensive taste in doublets that matched his elevated estimation of his own esteem and a quite catastrophic affectation to do with gold jewellery that dangled from the lobe of his left ear.

Wind and tide and the gentle nudgings of the blue heart-stone had brought Owen here, to this table with this man, and he had expected, for no better reason than that, to be welcomed. He was tired of the word-joust before it had truly begun. Only his English manners held him in his seat.

Above him, an awning of striped silk kept the afternoon sun from his eyes. To his right, that same sun glanced in brightest silver from the ribbon of the river as it made its long reach to the sea.

Behind, the high white walls of the Moorish fortress made scimitar curves against the too-blue sky. Someone had recently scratched a crucifix into the stone so that the lines were still sharp; Seville was only three centuries from her release back into Christendom and she was still proud of her battles.

Fernandez de Aguilar certainly was proud of his city's history, and of its battles, past, present and future. He was proud also of himself, his family and his ship, possibly in equal measure, although it seemed to Owen that he was proud chiefly of himself.

The Spaniard tapped his finger to the perfect bow of his lips and said, 'Your three reasons, señor?'

'For the first—' Owen dipped his finger in his wine and made a mark with it on the weathered oak of the table. 'I am a physician of some worth, for the proof of which I travel with a letter of affirmation from Michel de Nostradame, physician to the Queen of France. I am prepared to minister to the sick and injured on your ship for no charge for the duration of our voyage.'

'*Our* voyage?' The Spaniard had the flawless, sun-olive skin of his race, with the blackest of black hair that fell in coiled, oiled ropes to his shoulders. Only his eyes set him apart from his countrymen: they were wide and grey-blue so that it was hard not to look at him oddly, and to wonder at his parentage. Just now, they were brimful of affronted dignity.

'You are presumptuous,' declared Fernandez de Aguilar. 'And arrogant. The Queen of France, they say, lost both of her daughters within months of their birth, and while the subjects of his most Christian majesty of Spain can only be glad that the French goat Henri has not sired more living goatlets, their loss does not say much for his wife's physicians. I value my crew highly. I would not want such a man as you to tend them if they were sick, and in any case, a ship has more need of a surgeon than a physician and you have already told me that you are not qualified to wield a knife in case of emergency except in the dubious area of amputation in which you consider yourself still an apprentice. I am not filled with admiration. Your second point?'

'For the second, my mother's father sailed with Admiral Sir Edward Howard, who served King Henry of England, our queen's late father. My grandfather was with Howard when he captured the Scottish pirate, Andrew Barton. He came to live close to us in his elder years and spoke of it often. I have from him a deep and abiding understanding of the sea.'

'So perhaps you will also try to captain my ship? I will tell you that my father's uncle, Geronimo de Aguilar, sailed with Juan de Valdivia, the bearer of his majesty's most sacred purse. Their ship sank off the coast of New Spain and my great-uncle was one of only nineteen who survived to join the lifeboat. They languished under the sun, at the mercy of the winds, for two weeks until they made landfall and were taken captive by the savages. Five were eaten immediately – yes, that shocked you, did it not, Englishman? They eat men where we are going.' His smile was widely mocking, a flare of white teeth in brown skin.

'My great-uncle and one other man escaped death and were held as slaves until, eight years later, my relative escaped and returned to the fold of Christendom, becoming translator to the great Hernan Cortés as he conquered the Aztecs and made his fortune. He wrote back to us, his family, of how barren was the landscape and how poor the people, and yet he stayed to live and die there, when he could have come home and been a hero. Do you not think that strange, Englishman? I do. So I am taking a ship to see why he chose to stay there, and to make the fortune he did not see in the green gold around him. I have as yet heard no reason why I should take you with me when I have turned down so many among the great and the good of my town.'

The Spaniard reached a long, lazy arm and poured himself some more wine without offering any to Owen. In England, men had died for insults less starkly made than that, although none of them at Owen's hand: he had been the bane of his swordmaster's existence, sent packing with the advice never to risk the ignominy of a duel.

De Aguilar grinned savagely and said, 'I am not greatly taken by your first two reasons. For your third, you are not, I hope, going to suggest that I should take you on because my king has these past two years been married to the unloveliness that is your queen? His marriage is a sham and all true Spanish men pity him the chains of necessity that he must endure for the betterment of us, his people.'

Cedric Owen rose to his feet. He had been going to say exactly that, if in different words, which was humiliating if only because it was an idea he had made in jest as he travelled and had thought would be put in good-humoured company where the irony would be understood between men of the world who were acquainted with the vagaries of royalty. De Aguilar, clearly, had no sense of irony and his good humour was reserved for his own countrymen, who were welcome to it.

Owen had removed his hat at the start. He replaced it now, a shabby cap by comparison to the silked, befeathered effigy that sat at de Aguilar's side. He bowed stiffly, from the neck only. 'Señor, I am wasting your time and mine. I will find another way to travel to the barren landscape you describe, which I have heard is a fertile forested land of great wonder and civilized peoples. I apologize for interrupting your day and offending your hospitality. If you will allow me to pay for the wine . . . ?'

He had not expected that offer to be accepted. The fact that it was, and that the tavern owner charged at least ten times what the wine was worth, left him with a much reduced purse and a foul temper.

Some hours later, in the cool of the evening, Cedric Owen found a tavern where his imperfect Spanish was greeted with the warmth he had once so fondly expected, and the fish soup was rich and plentiful and did not lighten his pockets too much further.

He fell to talking with an actuary who had once been an employee of the Medici bankers and the conversation meandered from the New World to the Old and back again, with detours into the many ways a man might make himself rich and then save what money he had earned without losing it to the ravages of taxation and monarchs who thought of the banks as their own private lending service.

None of it touched on the 'green gold' of de Aguilar's dreams, but it was interesting and stimulating none the less and became more so as the evening progressed.

Owen took more wine than perhaps he should have done, but it was the first time he had relaxed in amenable company since leaving France and it was a cheerful man who left the tavern to return to his lodgings up near the Moorish walls when the landlord ushered him out.

He liked Seville better by night than by day. The air was warm but not too hot and the flies were gone. The sky was a shimmer of stars that looked sharper and closer than those he was used to viewing from the flat fenlands of Cambridge. Owen stopped halfway up the hill and stood with his back arched over and his neck craned so that he could stare straight up at the sky the better to appreciate the arc of the heavens and all that was in it. It revolved slowly, and unsteadily, which was unsettling, but not unduly surprising.

'Help! Murderers! *Help!*'

The cry was in Spanish and came from his left. Without thinking, Cedric Owen ran towards it, skidding round a corner to enter a narrow, angular alleyway that was barely wide enough for his shoulders, more of an open drain between two neighbouring rows of white-limed villas. No candles or torches were lit there. The milky shimmer of the starlight was cut out entirely by the overhanging roof tiles.

The dark ate his shadow and turned the ground into a lightless void where he could not tell if he ran over solid ground or a pothole – or decomposing fish guts, which sent him hurtling into a stack of boxes he had not known were there and from them into a barrel of old fish, which upended, sending him at last to the ground, which was firm and hard and drove the last of the wind from his lungs.

'*Aaaayeeeeh—!*'

The scream started low, rose fast to a screech, and then stopped, abruptly, to be followed by a dull silence, and the discordant rhythm of wood beaten on flesh.

Owen thrust himself to his feet. Bracing both hands against the side walls of the alley for support and direction, he hurried as fast as he

117

could round the elbowed bend towards the sounds.

A spill of light from a part-open door revealed a huddled shape on the ground and two others bent over it. The grunts of pain that came from the figure on the ground were animal in their nature, so that Owen could not tell if it were a man or a woman, or of what race. The sounds of beating ended. A long iron blade flashed dully in the poor light.

'Stop! Stop now!'

Outnumbered, unarmed, unsober, and against all the urgings of his fencing master, Cedric Owen flung himself on the figure holding the knife.

The fight was brief and painful and the first surprising thing about it was that Cedric Owen did not die immediately.

The second surprising thing was that, lying in the gutter with his head cracked open and blood streaming down his face and that same knife poised high above him, he felt no fear at the certain prospect of dying, only an opening of the doorway in his mind that led to the blue heart-stone, so that the future blazed through, and was open and beautiful and he could walk towards it in peace, forgetting the burden that Nostradamus had laid on him.

The final surprising thing was that the raised blade never struck home. As Owen stared out into the blue and set his thoughts in order, he felt a hand grasp his shoulder and lift him to sitting.

'Well, that was an intriguing thing, was it not, Señor Owen? I am attacked by cutthroats in my home city and the only person who comes to my cry in the whole of Seville is a drunken, fish-stinking, English doctor.'

The bruised and bloodied face of Fernandez Alberto Garcia de Aguilar grinned at Owen. With one hand, the Spaniard helped him to his feet. The man's other arm hung limp at his side, with the hand turned out at an unnatural angle. Blood flowed in a slowly clotting stream down his wrist and on to the ground.

Owen spat a lump of his own blood on to the stones beneath his feet. Through swollen lips, he said, 'Your arm needs urgently to be set.'

'It does indeed. Is that within the purview of a physician?'

'I can do it, yes.' Silently, he thanked Nostradamus for that.

The Spaniard was in wild, high spirits, such as men are who have fought against heavy odds and won, but his eyes were steady and the soul behind them was not the primped, self-opinionated popinjay that Cedric Owen had met in the afternoon.

'If you would care to assist with its setting, then perhaps afterwards we could review our conversation of this afternoon? Perhaps your queen is not the unregarded spawn of a rutting boar that I believed her to be and it may be that there is room upon the *Aurora* for a physician who can set bone and can tell me when the moon might not be in opposition to the warrior-star. We sail in two weeks' time. It is my turn, I believe, to buy the wine?'

7

Aboard the Aurora, third ship of his Spanish majesty's convoy sailing under Fernandez de Aguilar, Atlantic Ocean: westerly course, September 1556

ITS POSITION FIGURED BY THE NIGHT METHOD, instead of the day, the Part of Fortune crossed from the Goat to the Water Carrier and lay in wide squares to both Venus and Saturn, which lay in mutual ill-omened opposition.

Accordingly, a steady rain smeared the sky into the sea and the fish were not biting. Cedric Owen was sitting with his feet over the ship's stern, holding a useless fishing line in his hand, feeling seasick and sorry for himself when Fernandez de Aguilar came to find him.

The rain was not hard enough to drive him inside, more of a soft, insistent patter that soaked through the brown worsted of his suit until it chafed at every crease of his skin.

He was not, either, feeling sick enough to

keep to his cabin as he had for the first ten days of the voyage. During his early training in medicine, he had sailed several times to France and Spain and had thought himself a seasoned traveller, but the sudden change to the open ocean, as they sailed south and west from Seville, had left him semi-conscious and vomiting, so that Fernandez de Aguilar had threatened to break apart their six-ship convoy and turn the *Aurora* back to put him off at the nearest port rather than have him puke up the root and fire of his guts and die on board.

Owen had begged leave to remain, in part because his pride would not let him turn back, but chiefly because his blue heart-stone was as happy as he had ever known it. It remained a calm and steady presence at the back of his mind, radiating contentment like a lover given the ultimate gift, and he would not have taken that happiness away from it for something as trivial as his own discomfort.

He had stayed, therefore, and managed to drink enough clear water to prevent the salt of his body from overwhelming the mercury and sulphur and on this, the tenth morning of the voyage, had emerged tentatively to sit on the aft deck of the *Aurora* with his booted feet dangling over the stern and a long line in his hand, waiting for the lean, oily fish that swam far below the surface to take his bait of salted beef, a thing they showed no inclination to do.

De Aguilar, as ship's captain, had shown no sign of illness at any point, nor did he now. Perfectly at ease, he leaned both elbows on the stern rail and looked out along the long, silvered tail of the ship's wake, showing off his perfect profile.

He was, Owen decided, more Latin than Spanish, a youthful, vigorous Trajan, lacking only the beard to cement his authority. His hair was long and thick and coiled into wet ropes that spread out around his shoulders as it dried. His caustic grey eyes were thickly lashed, like a girl's. Even soaked to the skin, he managed to look regal. To the right kind of man, he would have been beautiful.

Owen had met such things only peripherally at Cambridge, and taken pains to avoid them. Struck by a new awareness, he wondered which of the crew would look thus on their captain, and whether any of them would dare act on it, or be welcomed if they tried.

De Aguilar said, 'Now that you're well enough, you should go barefoot. It makes moving on deck far easier.'

The comment was so unexpected that it took a moment before Owen realized it had been addressed to him. Stiffly, he said, 'You do not.'

'Hose and boots are the penance of the captain and his mate. They are not necessary for those unbound by the restrictions of rank. You are not so bound. If you abandon your shoes and your jacket, what remains of your brown suit will fit exactly with all that you need: warm in the cold, cool in the heat, and it will dry out when wet. You only need change your shirt once in a while and the men will still think you dress a world above them. Thus you will not lose your dignity.'

'I see.'

They fell back into an awkward silence.

De Aguilar stared thoughtfully at the sea and the three boats of the convoy that sailed just far enough back to be visible. 'You have never been on a long sea voyage before?'

'No.'

Owen was about to tie fast the fishing line and untie the cord that held his waist when something big grabbed at his bait and caught fast.

He would have let the line go but that it was borrowed and he did not wish Dominic, the ship's boy, such ill will as to lose it. He could have sat there watching it cheese-wire through the waves but there were levels of foolishness to which he was not prepared to stoop. He began, cursing, to haul it in, hand over hand, dreading the inelegant final struggle to bring its catch aboard.

'You're not enjoying it?' de Aguilar asked presently.

'The fishing or the voyage?'

'Both. Either.' The captain did not offer to help.

'I did not come for the pleasure, only for the destination.'

Owen's fish broached the surface, thrashing. It was big and fit and did not want to leave the sea. He braced both feet against the stern rails and hauled it up, becoming ever more aware that he stank of sick and sea-salt and sweat, and that de Aguilar, by a process of unexplained alchemy, did not.

The fish came out of the water, fighting. It was as long as his arm, slick and silver as the moon, and bucked over the rail. The hook had caught it across the cheek, under its eye. Owen felt a stab of guilt at his dragging of an innocent thing from safe security into a medium of which it knew nothing and then threatening it with untimely death.

He could have jammed his fingers in its gills, ripped free the hook and priested it with the small ironwood handle that the ship's boy had left to hand for just that purpose.

Instead, he managed a more dextrous thing: he tugged loose the hook and fumbled his hands so that even while it looked as if he was trying to bring it aboard, the fish slipped free. It hit the white water and twisted and was gone. He thought it was still alive.

There was silence, and the quieter splash of the sea against the ship, and then de Aguilar said, thoughtfully, 'Well done,' which was quite the least thing Owen had expected.

The rain was almost gone and the cloud was lifting. The sun leaked through patchily, sending intermittent shadows aft along the ship's length. Something about the quality of the light lifted Owen's gloom. He tied off his fishing line and began to untie the sodden cord at his waist.

His action broke whatever spell had held them. The captain turned, leaning his back on the stern rail in a way that looked entirely unsafe. Concerned, Owen said, 'If the rail should break . . .'

'Then I have not built my ship to last and I will fall overboard and follow your fish to the ocean's floor, carried under by the weight of my own gold. I know. We both have to hope, therefore, that I have built the ship with this in mind and that my wearing of gold is proof of my belief in her, not my undoing.'

It had never occurred to Owen that the Spaniard's excess of gold was anything more than vanity. It seemed to him still that it was not. The idea that the crew might view it differently brought him round again to the captain's status as demi-god with his men.

Watching him closely, de Aguilar said, 'When we spoke of your coming on the voyage, we never considered your family and how it might affect them. Have you a wife who is mourning your absence?'

'I have no wife.'

'For one so talented? I find that hard to believe. A lover then, of a stronger wine?'

That was very much too close to the bone. Owen flushed rarely, but when he did it was spectacular, such as now, when hot blood breached the wall of his neck and flooded his face.

Stiffly, he said, 'I have no lover, nor any desire for one. At some point, I may hope to have a wife, but that time has not yet come. In the meantime, I remain continent. It may not be fashionable in Spain, and certainly was not in England under the late King Henry, but I have no wish to make the demands of intimacy upon any woman without the benefit to her of marriage. If you find that risible, I would ask you to keep your humour private while aboard ship. A physician needs a certain amount of respect from his patients, or his skills are rendered worthless. You, of course, are exempt. I expect no respect from you, nor wish any to be expected of me.'

Whatever you do, never force a duel unless it be of the mind. Keep your insults more subtle than those of any man you choose to upset. It is the only way you will survive. So his fencing master had said. Owen apologized to him in his mind.

He needed to leave. Anger at last made his fingers nimble, so that the cord holding him seated was not impossible to untie. He struggled with the last two turns of the knot.

Peaceably, de Aguilar said, 'I apologize for offending you. You are that rare thing, a nobleman in the true sense of the word. I had thought it, but was not certain. I will not, therefore, send Dominic to your cabin tonight. I'm sure he will be most relieved.'

'As will whoever he might have stayed with instead, I have no doubt. You, perhaps? Or is that place reserved for the first mate whose shoulder I set yesterday? You should know that, as his physician, I recommended that Juan-Cruz refrain from rigorous exercise for a half-month. I apologize if this causes you inconvenience.'

Barring a minor accident with the rigging, which had dislocated his shoulder, Juan-Cruz was a supremely competent seaman. He was also the ugliest man on board and to link him thus to the captain was an infantile insult. Owen regretted it on every level. He stood, shaking, facing de Aguilar, certain that he would die, and equally certain that nothing would make him retract what he had said.

Rage made him slow to look up and slow, therefore, to realize that he was standing in silence because Fernandez de Aguilar was laughing too hard to answer.

'I have said something amusing?'

'No . . . Yes. Obviously . . . Yes.' With the back of his hand, the captain wiped his beautiful shark-grey eyes. He produced a linen kerchief from his sleeve and blew his so-elegant nose.

Shaking his head, he said, 'Rigorous exercise? My God, remind me never to offend you again. Juan-Cruz, I am sure, will refrain from "rigorous exercise" if you have told him that it is necessary, and if he does not, it will be none of my doing. Nor will he or I or anyone else offend young Dominic, unless it is that the boy's stutter catches the men on a bad day and they hurl him overboard in an effort to effect a cure. If you inform them it will not work, I'm sure they will listen. You are counted among the angels by those who believe in such things and among the gods by the rest, who do not.'

'I would prefer that they view me only as a man who is doing his best, imperfectly, to learn the art and science of medicine.'

He sounded frigid and could not help it. The captain shrugged.

'You are far too late for that. Better to know your state and enjoy it. Better, also, to know that you are safe from unwanted attentions. On this ship, such things are not done. I was pandering to your more evident fears and I apologize, but I do believe it helps to have these things spoken aloud. If Dominic ends this voyage deprived of his virginity, it will be of his own volition. I thought you should know it.'

So saying, de Aguilar nodded amiably, unhitched himself from the stern rail, and left.

Owen sat down again. He stayed a long time, watching the quiet sun fall to kiss the sea before he stood up and retired to his cabin.

He ate alone that night, on boiled beef, and slept badly. The next day, he abandoned his hose and stout shoes and went barefoot. Nobody commented, but he found by noon that he could walk more easily, and by dusk that he could stroll as he might have done along the banks of the Cam.

Cedric Owen split his lip open on the heaving deck and tasted hot salt in all the cold salt of the sea.

The slop bucket broke free of its moorings and the stench of a night's shit and piss slewed around the cabin before the storm smashed over the bulkheads and everything was wet and cold and smelled of seaweed and harsh, unforgiving air.

He woke, gasping, and brought his hand to his mouth. There was no blood and no pain. The *Aurora* swayed as gently as she had when he had first fallen asleep. The night smelled sweetly of a benign ocean, not at all as he had imagined. The blue heart-stone that shared his bunk rolled a little with the tilt of the waves and came to rest against his ribs, a warm thing in a warm night. He felt its presence as a sleeping lover, but that it was not asleep, and it had a message for him that broke the night apart with its urgency.

Does it require your death, this stone?

Nostradamus' voice echoed in the small of Owen's ear, even as he was already upright, dressing. His fingers fumbled for buttons in the dark, tucking in shirt tails so that he might present himself as a gentleman. He had long ago given up on his jacket, but he retained his shirt, even though the linen was harsh with salt and chafed against raw skin at his armpits and wrists.

He yawned and grimaced and stepped out into a wide, black night, lit by stars he could not name and a dish-faced moon that flooded light across the flat sea.

Behind them sailed three other merchant ships of a similar size to the *Aurora*, and far out on the port bow was a naval warship laden with cannon, set there to ward off privateers by her presence alone. Somewhere behind was another the same, although it was well known that the privateers set their targets on the rich ships returning from New Spain to the old country, not those going out.

From the start, Owen had seen the warships as an insurance, not a necessity. With the per-spective of the blue stone, he saw them newly as a burden to be shed, and quickly, only that he was not certain why or how.

'Sir?'

Owen scratched at the captain's door. The sound was lost in the ruffle of waves and the

131

slow thrum of the rigging. He knocked a little harder. 'Don Fernandez, are you there?'

'Señor Owen? Wait – I will come out.'

The astonishing thing – one of the several astonishing things – about Fernandez de Aguilar was the speed with which he could don his outrageous doublets. He slept, obviously, with his fortune in gold in his ear, but he could not have slept in his doublet and emerged looking as fresh as he did now.

Weeks ago, at the start of their voyage, Owen had made a small promise to himself that he would watch the man dress one day and see how it was done; but not this night, at this hour. Even as he thought it, the captain emerged decently sober in midnight blue with only a small prince's ransom in his ear.

'A beautiful night.' De Aguilar braced a hand on the starboard rail and studied the Englishman. 'May I ask what it is that has brought you out in it so late, and me with you?'

'There's going to be a storm.' It sounded lame, there, under the flawless stars. 'Bigger than anything we've seen already. It will break the convoy apart, possibly sink us. We need to . . .'

Owen struggled for words. His Spanish had been serviceable at the start and, after six weeks at sea, was much improved, but he would have hesitated now in any language.

'There are things that need to be done but I

don't know what they are. Only that you must do them so that we come through alive and so that, at the end of it, we are no longer part of the convoy.'

'Not part of . . . ? I don't understand.'

At least de Aguilar was listening to him, not sending him to his cabin with a draught of laudanum to keep the night-fears at bay.

Owen said, 'We must not cling to the other boats; that way danger lies. If we can steer clear of the others we have a chance; there are no privateers, but we *must* make our way to New Spain alone, without those who might hamper us, or alter our judgement.'

'So? I said once you might try to captain my ship. I did not believe you would do it in truth.' De Aguilar spoke thoughtfully, without the sharp pride of which he was capable. 'Will you tell me how you know this?'

It was Owen's turn to stare at the sea. Nostradamus had pointed out that the blue heart-stone was a death sentence in the wrong company, but the concept was not news; those who held it had known the full weight of what they carried all down the centuries, and had grown used to the necessary subterfuges.

Still, the lie came less easily than he would have liked and left a bad taste on his tongue.

'As I told you once, my grandfather sailed with Sir Edward Howard. He spoke to me as a child of the peculiar smell the sea makes when a storm is coming; like iron that is made white hot then plunged into water. I smelled that now, coming from the port bow. The storm will come from that direction. As to the rest, I thought to compare your natal chart with that of the present moment, setting our location here on the ocean, as best we know it. I should have seen this far sooner, and deeply regret that I did not.'

This part, at least, was true. More confidently, Owen said, 'The Part of Fortune for this night lies conjunct now to Saturn and is in quintile aspect to your Part of Fortune, which lies in wide conjunction to your moon. If these two sat in opposition I believe we would see such a catastrophe as to die. Because they lie quintile one to the other, we may prevail through your courage and the use of your instinct.'

De Aguilar stared out over the starboard bow. The sea rocked them a long time before he spoke again.

'Perhaps one day you will honour me by sharing the truth. For now, we will believe there is a storm coming and wake Juan-Cruz and his men and tie down the rigging and alert the other boats so that they may do the same. Afterwards, if it proves not to be true, I will call the crews of all six ships together so you can tell them the story of your grandfather who so staunchly served the reiving King Henry, and I will let them cast you overboard if they do not like your tale.'

He grinned as he spoke. There was room to believe that he might have been in jest.

The ship came awake startlingly fast. Juan-Cruz was already half dressed, his preternatural link to de Aguilar and the ship having given him some warning. His face showed no emotion as he listened to Owen's fabricated story; he only swivelled his healing arm around his head and set to work on making the *Aurora* bend to the captain's bidding.

Within moments, whistles twittered in the rigging and flags were run up the stays, clearly visible in the moon-washed night. Sleeping sailors were shaken awake. Spanish sang from the yardarms of half a dozen ships, cursing the night and the crazy Englishman, and very carefully not cursing the captain.

With nothing at all he could do, Cedric Owen retired to his cabin and sat on his bunk. The blue heart-stone lay under the blankets at his side. He felt a fresh alertness in its waiting, such as he might have felt from a hound at the start of a night's coney-catching, knowing that it sensed beasts he would never see until they were retrieved to his hand, soft and warm and quite dead.

He said, 'You have never asked anything of me that I have not willingly given, but more

135

men's lives are at stake now than mine. Will you bring us safe to land as I have said?'

The stone gave no answer; it had never done, but in the blue that inhabited his mind was a renewed peace, and a sense of almost-there, as of homecoming from a long and arduous journey. He turned on his side and lay on his bunk, staring at the moonlight that came through the cracks in the doorway.

Quite soon after that, the wind began to thrum faster on the rigging.

8

Ingleborough Fell, Yorkshire Dales,
May 2007

STELLA WAS ALONE WITH THE SHEEP AND THE skullstone on the slopes of Ingleborough Fell.

The night was cool, but not cold. Threads of cloud drew fine lines between the stars. High up, Fell Beck poured its black water into the blacker hole that was Gaping Ghyll. The stone was light in her backpack. She was beginning to understand the different feel of it. Here, now, neither she nor it were in danger.

The low path by the stream gave way to a left-handed climb. She trod lightly through the bracken and it buoyed her along as it had done since she had woken in the hotel room, with Tony Bookless's words sounding over and again in her ear.

No stone is worth dying for . . . Get rid of it, Stella.

She had gone to sleep hearing him and woken to his voice in the black heart of the night. The skull had made no protest; there had been neither blue lightning nor a screaming pain in her mind as she rose and dressed and drove out along the unlit lanes to the car park in the village at the foot of the trail.

She walked up now, empty-headed, feeling the night air tight on her skin, and the drawn ache of muscles pushed hard the day before and not yet eased back to peace. Here, in the high place above the village, the air smelled of night-dew and bracken and sheep-oil. The sound of cascading water drew closer. She walked more cautiously, testing her footfalls, feeling the gradient before she set her weight on each foot.

I don't want to go in the dark . . . Yorkshire was her home. She had been to the Ghyll more times than she could count, but only in daylight, when the route was clear and the thundering spume of the falls clearly visible. She had no intention of wandering into the mouth and adding one last body to the count of the skull.

Sheep stepped sleepily out of her path as she took the last steep rise and then over the elbow to the flatter landscape beyond. The slide and hiss of the waterfall called her on. At the half-remembered sheep fence, she stopped, and took a step back. Before her feet, the moor fell abruptly away. Fell Beck crashed down into the vast space of the cave beneath.

In a world of greys and deep, sucking blacks, she sat on a slope of grassy earth, well back from the lip of the pothole. Ahead, the waterfall threw spray up into the starlight, the only touch of silver.

She took the skull-stone from her pack and held it in her hands for the first time since she had sat shivering in the cathedral of the earth with its first blue flash still searing her brain.

It was quieter now. The lime-chalk coating had roughened a little in the rub of her bag, so that it shed flakes into her palms and was smoother. Starlight gave it faint shadows; with her forefinger, she traced the outline of eyes and mouth and the vague triangle of the nose.

In this light, shadowed and white, it looked enough like Kit's bruised, broken face for her truly to hate it and the destruction it had wrought. Tony Bookless's voice whispered in the rush of the water. *It carries too much blood. Get rid of it . . .*

And yet . . .

It was hard to surrender the passion with which she had first held the stone. Even under-water, cold and close to drowning, the sense of homecoming, of welcome, of a pact long made that she had forgotten and was only now remembering, had been overwhelming. Traces of it were left in the sharpness of her senses.

A night breeze lifted spray from the beck and

spattered it across the backs of her hands and her face. She picked a stalk of grass and chewed it. The broken stalk tickled her tongue. Sharp, sweet sap made her salivate.

Closing her eyes, Stella searched for the touch of the heart-stone's presence, for any sense of what it might give to mitigate the deaths that surrounded it. It had been with her all the way up the side of the beck. Unaccountably, now it was gone, or so quiet she could not feel it.

She opened her eyes again. By a trick of the light, Kit's face stared back at her from the white limestone, broken and vacant, plastic like a doll. Tony Bookless's voice thundered from the falling beck and this time a passing shadow brought back the memory of a man passing beneath her feet in the cave, intent on Kit's death. Her mind flinched from it, as her body had not dared to.

Get rid of it!

Gaping Ghyll gaped at her feet. Fell Beck fell the longest distance of any waterfall in Britain, into the cave below, and from that into an underground sump that made even cave divers blanch.

She balanced the weight of the skull-stone in her hands and raised them for the throw.

The shard of blue lightning in her mind was so far away, so tired, so old and worn, so nearly spent of all its reserves of calling. Or young, perhaps, like a lamb dropped from the ewe into

140

the cold of a winter's night that has cried all it can and not been fed, and grows weak from the bleating.

Stella lowered her arms. With unexpected care, she cradled the stone to her sternum, feeling its rough chalk through the thinness of her T-shirt. Her heart beat for it, as it had only ever beaten for Kit, but differently; she had never wanted to protect Kit in the way she yearned to protect his lump of mucky limestone. Aloud, she said, 'We should clean you up, make you whole again.'

The blue spark flickered and held more strongly in the way of a candle taken from the draught that had threatened to extinguish it. Holding it close, Stella stood up and looked around.

Dawn was near. The sheep were waking. The sky was lighter than it had been. Gaping Ghyll yawned more blackly and the beck dropped as fast. They waited, these two, with the same ancient intelligence as the stone she held. Instinct said they must be fed.

She set the stone in her backpack, swaddled in a towel, and set to looking for a stone the same size and shape in the sheep-shorn turf.

Her search took her in a wide circle, through the wire fence and out on to the moor until she found what she needed and brought it back.

There was colour in the green moor when she returned, and a multitude of silvers in the falling beck. Only the pothole was the same vertiginous black. With the rising sun behind her casting a shadow across the water, Stella bowled the new-found stone underarm into the centre of the gap.

It vanished terrifyingly fast. Some time later, she heard the shatter of breaking rock.

'Well done,' said Tony Bookless from behind her. 'I wasn't sure you'd be able to do it.'

She stood still. He completed his ascent of the fell. His shadow welded to her shadow, extending it, so that their twinned heads fell over the pothole.

She said, 'I dreamed of Kit. It seemed as if the stone . . . that it needed to come here.' In a corner of her mind, the thing that had become a part of her held its breath, waiting.

He said, 'I heard you get up. When you didn't come back, I thought you might need help.'

'Thank you.' She was back in the lie again, and this time the stone had not made her do it. She had no regrets.

Bookless lifted his phone. 'I just had a call from the hospital. Kit has regained consciousness. He's asking for you. Will you come with me to see him?'

9

THE SEA LAY CALM ON ALL SIDES. FOR THE FIRST time in the week since the storm, the *Aurora* dared full rigging and ran lightly ahead of the wind. The air was alive with the rush and hiss of the waves on the bow and the flagging of sails on the three masts and the judder of the ropes and stays, and somewhere in the distance the long, forlorn cry of a sea-bird.

Cedric Owen rose before dawn and came to stand with his back to the foremast at a place where the breeze of their passage pushed his hair back away from his face. Beneath his feet, the bow dipped and rose in a peaceful sea, sending waves creaming towards the stern.

The night was much as it had been on the first day of the storm, but that they sailed alone now, with no boats before or behind. As the blue heart-stone had warned, the *Aurora* had become separated from the rest of the convoy in the chaos of wind and rain that had ripped at least one of the other boats apart.

The *Aurora*'s crew had seen only one ship sink; the rest had been lost in the teeming rain and the savage, spiralling wind. Against all sanity, de Aguilar had spent two days sailing in circles in an unsafe sea searching for a sign of flag or sail or, more frantically, for living men among the wreckage that danced on the waves in ever smaller fragments.

Finding nothing and no one, and under assault from winds that threatened to uproot the masts, they had finally, reluctantly, set a westerly course again, not knowing if the other ships were searching for them in like manner or had fallen to the wrath of the storm. Every man on board had felt the cut of separation far more sharply then than when they had first sailed from the harbour in Seville six weeks before.

Sailing alone was a different thing, like walking along a cliff's edge in a gale with no guard rail for safety. In the beginning, Owen had found the sense of isolation unnerving, but a week's peace and the quiet assurance of de Aguilar's captaincy had changed that until he felt the exhilaration and freedom of their aloneness, and never wanted it to end.

Only the blue heart-stone wanted more. Its urgings had woken him before dawn, bringing him out to this place at the masthead where he could look out across the black void of sea and sky, to the place on the undefined horizon where they merged.

Never before had he been in night so complete. The dark-light boundary of the horizon was gone, welding sea and sky into one. Endless constellations reflected in the ocean and back up to the sky, so that Owen was surrounded by pinpricks of light in a darkness that had no ending.

Only at one place was there a difference: ahead and a little off the port bow was a light that looked more orange than the stars, and flickered occasionally in a way that mimicked fire.

He was watching that, and wondering as to its nature, when the blackness broke apart, letting the first knife-edge of sun streak out across the water. Displayed for his admiration alone was the priceless moment when the sea abandoned the inky mystery of the night and opened to the blinding blue and gold of the dawn.

It was heart-stopping in its beauty. Lacking any sense of a god to be worshipped for its benevolence, Cedric Owen followed a lifetime's habit and opened his heart to give thanks for it to the blue stone that had brought him here in the face of all improbability.

'It is worth it all, just for this, is it not?' The

soft Spanish came from his left side, where the dawn was not. Fernandez de Aguilar could always traverse his own ship quietly.

Owen startled and settled and found he was not entirely unhappy to have shared the moment. He said, 'If I were to die now, having seen this, I would not feel my life ended too soon.'

De Aguilar clucked his teeth lightly in reprimand. 'You should be careful what you say. An invitation to death is not a thing to give lightly. We will make land by nightfall, did you know?'

'I thought as much. Do you know where we are headed, now that the storm has sent us so far from our original course?'

'I would be a poor captain if I did not know where I had brought my ship.'

The Spaniard slid his back down the mast to sit with his heels drawn in and his knees clasped against his chest. He was the most casually dressed Owen had ever seen him; his white shirt tails hung loose about his hose, with the cuffs open and dangling and the collar wide. He still favoured his broken arm, but the bandages were thinner than they had been, and Owen believed they could be dispensed with by the end of the month.

'We were due to berth in Campeche,' de Aguilar said. 'It lies north of here and along the western side of the peninsula. We have not food

146

and water left to reach there, so we are headed instead for the city named Tulum by my grand-uncle, for the vast wall that stretches around it. The natives call it rather Zama, which means dawn, and I suspect we have just seen the reason why. At night, those who live there keep the coasts safe by warning ships of the rocks. If you look across the port bow, away from the sun, you can still see the fire they keep burning in the tower that looks over the sea.'

'It is a fire, then? I had wondered. I had not imagined the savages to understand the concept of a lighthouse.'

'They understand a lot you might not imagine from what we are told of them. It is to the King's advantage to make them seem as primitives, whom we may freely scorn. My grand-uncle began his time here thinking them ignorant brutes, fit only to be slaves to the grandeur of Christendom. His comrade, Gonzalo de Guerrero, realized soonest how wrong that was and fought for thirty years alongside the natives against Spain.'

'Even so, you come amongst them to conquer?'

De Aguilar shook his head. 'Never that. I come to make us and them rich in the new world which will destroy the old. The ones you name as savages are not stupid. They have painted their entire city blood red, as a warning to their neighbours not to attack, and yet they keep the coasts safe by an effort of engineering that would leave our architects weeping with envy. The lighthouse whose fires you see is not a rude column such as mars the coastlines of England and Spain, but a square-sided pyramid, of a size and grace that would match any of our cathedrals. The carvings and murals are of a complexity to outdo Egypt, and their writing is as opaque to our understanding as the paintings on the walls of the pyramids. The beauty of it is that these people are alive and may teach us what their carvings mean, when all of Egypt's antiquity is beyond our ken.'

'And will they teach us? Or do they offer war, as they did to Hernan Cortés?'

De Aguilar picked a sliver of grit from beneath one fingernail. Looking up, he said, 'I hope they will not offer war, but have no certainty. Zama perches on the edge of the ocean and faces east so that its citizens have seen every morning that with which we have only now been blessed. I would like to believe that being bathed in the light of a sunrise such as this on every day of one's life predisposes a man to reflection and farming, rather than war, but I may be wrong.'

'Then, in case you are, we had better make the most of what we have.'

Owen too slid down the mast to sit with his face to the sun. He tilted his head back and closed his eyes against the familiar blue of the sky. The wider, vaster, internal blue of the heart-stone stretched out and became tinged with red at the edges, only a little, but enough to be a warning.

With his eyes still closed, Owen said, 'However they paint their walls, I think the natives are not our only danger.'

'No. If my information is correct, there is a priest in Zama who is second only to the bishop of Yucatán in his desire to bring the Inquisition to New Spain. He is a Jesuit who fears the deterioration of the mother church in Europe, where the Germans, Dutch and English are sacking the monasteries and stealing their gold. He seeks to replenish her coffers with treasure from the New World. He does not say so openly, of course; in his letters home, he writes that he seeks to bring heathen souls to God and so save them from an eternity of burning. To do that, he will inflict on as many of them as is necessary the more temporal burning of death at the stake.'

There was a pause. Owen heard a rustle of cloth as de Aguilar turned a little to face him. Then came the quiet, eloquent voice: 'You should be careful, my friend. Many of those who have died have not had such a thing as a skull of pure crystal to carry with them into the executioner's fires.'

There had been no warning. Owen opened his eyes and stared up at the impossible blue of the sky.

After a while, he asked, 'How long have you known?'

'Nearly a week. If you remember, there was a night of calm before the second, worse part of the typhoon. I excused myself then from dinner. I do not expect your forgiveness, but you must know that I could not risk taking my ship and its men on an unplanned, poorly charted leg of the voyage without knowing for whom, or for what, I was doing it.'

'And so you went to my cabin and sought out the stone?'

'It was lying in the open, waiting to be found. I did not touch it; such a thing would be sacrilege, but I felt from it a welcome such as I have only before received from Deaf Pedro, who taught me all I know of the sea and still welcomes me into his home like a beloved grandson when I return to visit him.'

Owen turned his head a little, to bring the other into view. 'Every man I have met, with the exception of Nostradamus, has either feared that stone or desired to possess it. Are you, then, another exception, or has the skull lost its power to command the minds of men?'

There was silence, and the slapping of waves on the hull. Presently, de Aguilar said, 'If I had a wife of exceptional beauty and wisdom, such that you saw in her everything you had ever desired in a woman, would you wish to take her from me?'

'I would take nothing from you, but especially not a free heart, freely given.'

'So, then, why would I not do likewise? The stone is clearly yours in all ways. It is not that I do not see it as desirable, but that I choose not to desire it.'

Owen said, 'Your integrity shames me. You are captain of this ship and I owe you my life. More than that, I have seen how you treat your men and respect every aspect of what you do. I would not have kept the knowledge from you, but—'

'But it is hard to know whom to trust, I know. And perhaps you would not wish so to burden a friend?'

Owen had not thought of Fernandez de Aguilar as a friend, nor imagined he might be considered so in return. Spoken aloud now, after all that had just passed, he saw the truth of their friendship and could trace its growth in the series of meaningless conversations that yet held meaning and honesty; in the slow, cultivated growth of his respect.

As he had once feared, he had been wooed, and had succumbed, and did not regret it. He said, 'Why did you do this?' and was grateful that de Aguilar did not pretend misunderstanding.

'You saved my life; is that not reason enough?' The Spaniard shrugged. 'And you present a naivety that is easy to believe, but there is a strength beneath it that is the worth of a dozen vanities.'

'I would never love you as a man loves a woman.'

'I know that. I would not ask it of you. Nor, actually, would I want it; I, too, will find a wife one day. But there is such a thing as a meeting of minds between men of equal valour that holds easily as much value as the immersions of flesh, and may outlast the heady days of carnal love. I had hoped we might share such comradeship, and that, in doing so, you might find that you could tell me a little of your blue stone's history, as much as is safe.'

'I might . . . indeed I might.' Owen swept his hands across his face and had no idea how young that made him look, or how uncertain. 'I have lived with the weight of the stone's existence all my life. I love it and all that it brings, but I would not inflict that burden lightly on another, particularly not on a man I admire. And yet . . . That night, when I came to dinner, I did not leave it in the open – it was as well hidden as it has always been.'

'The stone let me see it?'

'It would seem so.'

There was silence a while, and the slice of the boat through water and the lift and rock of the sea. The cries of the sea birds returned, more insistent than before, the birds themselves faded scribbles on the horizon.

De Aguilar reached into his shirt and brought from an inside, hidden pocket something of gold.

'The priest at Zama is a Father Gonzalez Calderón. By all accounts the man is a fanatic who revels in the pain of others and I believe we should tread very carefully in his presence. At the least, we should appear to be men of God. If it does not offend you greatly, perhaps you could accept this?' A small gold crucifix of quite exceptional workmanship dangled from his fingers. 'It was my mother's,' said Fernandez de Aguilar simply. 'But a man may wear it.'

The sun caught the cross as it turned slowly in the freshening breeze and made of it a small penumbra of light, far beyond the metal of its making. Cedric Owen reached for it and the blue stone, which had recoiled from every other artefact of religion, did not flinch from this one.

'Thank you,' Owen said. 'I would be most honoured.'

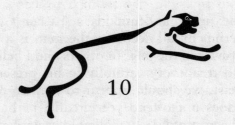

10

Zama, New Spain, October 1556

ON CALM WATER THAT SPARKLED UNDER A
noon sun, the *Aurora* slid slowly into the
small natural harbour below the city named
Zama for its view of the dawn.

High white limestone bluffs stood as sentinels
of purity, drawing them in to a city of startling
blood-red stone, walled on three sides and faced
on the fourth by the vast, red, pyramidal tower
that was its lighthouse.

On board, men lined the port and starboard
sides from bow to stern, taking soundings with
leads dipped in soft wax, that they might find
both the depth and nature of the sea's floor
beneath them.

A relay of quiet voices sent reports back to de
Aguilar, who stood with Juan-Cruz at the
wheel: 'Port stern, third man, five fathoms,
sand'; 'Port bow, fourth man, four and a half
fathoms, lost the sand, probably rock';

'Starboard bow, first man, three fathoms, weed and mud.'

From this uncertainty, inch by careful inch, did the captain bring his ship in to a place where he could safely anchor and set down the small-boat for himself and his favoured companions to make first landfall.

Their arrival was not unannounced. For the last hours, since they had been able to see the harbour, they had seen also the growing crowd of natives awaiting them, dressed in colours bright as birds and with a quantity of green feathers set about the crowns of their straw hats, so that Cedric Owen, who had been at sea far too long, fondly imagined them to be women, and the things that they carried to be for trade.

He had no such fond imaginings now. This close, it was clear that every one of those waiting was a man and that the things they carried were the arms of war. At least a dozen in the foremost rows held guns as if they knew how to use them. The rest, for the most part, bore spears or long wooden clubs made black at the edges.

'They call them *maquahuitls*,' said de Aguilar quietly. He stood at Owen's side in the bow of the small-boat with a coiled rope in his hand, ready to leap ashore. Behind him, six men rowed in trained synchrony. 'My great-uncle described them as the greatest hand-held weapon he had ever seen in action. They're made of hardwood with blades of obsidian set along the edges. The warriors of the Maya are not large men, so they wield them two-handed, which gives a greater arc and more force to the strike. Pedro de Moron, who fought with Cortés, had his horse decapitated by a single blow from one of these. Cortés had offered iron swords to those of the natives who swore him fealty, but they believed their obsidian to be sharper and stronger. It took a dead horse to prove to him that they spoke the truth.'

'And now they wait to prove the same to us,' Cedric said. 'They're hard to count all crowded together like that, but I'd guess we're out-numbered at least three to one and they do not look to me welcoming, however bright their clothing or their feathers.'

De Aguilar nodded peacefully. 'Then we will die swiftly, having seen that blazing dawn. I would prefer it to the alternative. The man walking through them now, dressed all in black with a fortune in silver at his neck, is Father Gonzalez Calderón. In his presence, we have to hope that if they hate us, we are given a native death of swift black stone, not a European one of torture and fire. What does your blue stone say?'

'That it is nearing home, and cannot reach land soon enough,' said Owen, who was having trouble thinking through the wild singing in his

156

head. 'It says nothing of how welcome we may be when we take it there. Are you going to throw the rope to the priest?'

'Who else?' asked de Aguilar, grinning. 'Watch closely, and learn what it is to speak softly to the natives.'

The wooden jetty was so new that the barnacles had not yet set up residence on it. The black-robed priest stood at the farthest end from land, and caught deftly enough the rope that was thrown him. Two native men stood a pace or two behind. Alone among their brethren, their trousers and smocks were of plain, uncoloured cloth and they bore no weapons.

The priest leaned back on the rope and made it taut. There was a moment's drifting impact and then Fernandez de Aguilar jumped lightly to the wooden planks and stood there, rocking gently for a moment, as if the sea still moved him. Then, before them all, he swept the lowest, most elaborate court bow Cedric Owen had ever seen performed by any man.

'I present myself, sir, Fernandez de Aguilar, a ship's captain of little worth, but I bring with me Señor Cedric Owen, our ship's physician and most astute astrologer. He comes with a recommendation from Catherine de' Medici, the Queen of France herself. I commend him to you and your friends in that vein. You, of course, are Father Gonzalez Calderón, priest of the mother church in Zama, New Spain. We were speaking of you only this morning and of how pleased you would be to meet our esteemed passenger. Wait, we will set down a plank so that the good doctor can come to land.'

'No.'

There fell a silence even the gulls dared not break.

The priest was an ox of a man, broad of back and girth and all of it sinew and muscle. His neck was thickly corded with a layering of chins. Across the broad, black sweep of his chest lay a crucifix in raw silver that was the largest and heaviest Cedric Owen had ever seen.

His single word held all the harbour still. Watched now by every man on boat, ship and land, he coiled the rope in his hand and threw it neatly back to Cedric Owen's feet.

Raising his voice to be heard, he said, 'You should know that we have had smallpox here. It has passed now, but before it did so, God took to Himself over half the men, women and children of our city. We are wary, therefore, of incomers who might bring the same again, or worse. Can your so-esteemed physician swear to me in the name of God that you carry no disease?'

The priest addressed de Aguilar, but his gaze, resting on Owen, was hot and angry, as if the pox held his mind in thrall.

The sudden scream in his mind's ear was of a different pitch from any Owen had ever heard. In an effort to escape it, he lifted his gaze beyond the black-garbed priest and on to the two native men who stood immediately behind—

—and stopped, because thought had become impossible.

The two men behind the priest were dressed plainly in trousers and smocks of unbleached cotton; both were clean-shaven with wide faces and wider eyes and dense black hair that hung plumb-straight to their shoulders. The one on the left fingered a small wooden cross at his chest and stared without interest at the *Aurora* and her crew.

The one on the right was staring directly at Cedric Owen – and straight through him into the blue of the heart-stone.

Never before had Owen been so immediately, so cuttingly exposed. A bitter wind sliced at his flesh, as if his own clothing had been stripped from him, taking half the skin with it.

In the long paralysis of the moment, it came to him that, unlike his fellow, the native had the stance and countenance of a warrior. A broad zigzag scar that looked deliberately made coursed down his left cheek. With his gaze locked on Owen's, the man laid the first two fingers of his hand flat across it and then turned his head away.

With the searching gaze gone, the scream in Owen's ear fell back almost to nothing. He was able to hear things in the outer world again, chief amongst which was the priest saying, 'Señor Owen? You are a physician as well as a caster of charts. Can you swear before God that your ship brings us no disease?'

The priest threw a shadow like a mountain. It was easiest to look at him and the vastness of his bulk and consider the threat he might pose, and thereby to forget that one had been stripped naked and then reclothed again by a single look from a scar-faced savage.

They were waiting for his answer.

'No,' Cedric Owen said. 'I can promise nothing and would certainly not swear so in the name of God. I can say that I have been at sea with these men for two months and that there has been nothing beyond the usual intestinal instability and a single case of a torn shoulder when a man held too long to a lanyard. I can say that we stopped in Panama to take on board more food and water and that we took on then a native youth who wished to make his way at sea. It is my belief that if there were any disease on board, he would have succumbed to its effects, and similarly that if he brought ill humours, we would have fallen ill by now. In view of that, I will swear in any way you like that I have seen nothing to indicate illness, but no more than that. If you wish us to put back to sea, with our hold full of guns and powder, lead and steel, then you may do so. I am sure that the followers of King Philip at Campeche will welcome us.'

He had planned none of that. The words fell out of his mouth and he heard them at the same time as the others, and with as much surprise.

Fernandez de Aguilar shot him a look of pure astonishment, which turned to something more thoughtful as the priest inclined his head as if in prayer, then said, 'Well argued, Englishman. If you had sworn by God that your men were clean, I would have had you shot and your ship burned in the open sea. The jetty would have been destroyed with it, as was the last one that brought us infection.'

'And all in vain,' Owen said. 'You have been close enough to Don Fernandez to be a source of infection if he did, indeed, harbour disease. You would have walked back among your people and spread plague wherever you walked.'

'Except that I would not have walked among them at all. My clerk here, Diego' – the wave of his hand indicated the scar-faced native – 'has orders to cut my throat and then his own. Domingo' – a lifted finger indicated the quieter of the two clerks – 'would have walked into the sea, this being his choice of death. With us gone, the second rank of warriors would set the fire arrows to your ship. No child willingly

161

shoots his father, but they would kill me on my command; this much I believe in them.'

Owen saw Fernandez de Aguilar sharpen. 'These people see you as their father?' he asked.

Gonzalez Calderón's face was unreadable. 'I see myself as their father under God,' he said. 'I believe that if I tell them that you do not carry pox and come instead to bring gifts and knowledge to help us to recover our losses, they will allow you to land your ship. What happens thereafter is in God's hands. I cannot guarantee your safety any more than your physician can guarantee the clean health of your men.'

11

Bede's College, Cambridge, June 2007

A SINGLE STEM OF WHITE LILIES LEFT OVER
from the wedding decorated the low ash-
wood table in Kit's river room.

By a feat of Tudor engineering, over half of
the room's length projected out over the Cam.
Windows on three sides let in the strong
summer sun. The river ran greenly beneath. An
open window lifted the smell of nearly still
water to mix with that of the more colourful,
shorter-lived sprays dotted about the room, sent
by friends to welcome Kit home from the
hospital.

Because they were his friends, they had the
sense not to be there when he came home, but
let Stella help him out of the ambulance on his
two sticks, and manoeuvre him up the stairs
into the wide, light space that was his home.

He stood swaying by the table with the
flowers, but it was the river running beneath

the window that caught him; the slow slide of green-grey water, and the shimmer of air above it and the odd tricks of light and glass that made it seem as if the part of the room projecting out over the river was the greater, that it floated alone, 'suspended 'twixt sky and water' as its Tudor designers had intended.

He turned a full circle, taking in the sky and the thin strips of cloud, and the parched, busy grass of Midsummer Common; the crowded river, full of tourists on punts and late students celebrating exams; the perfect lawn of the Lancastrian Court, with its cloistered surround and the bronze statue of Edward III, the Plantagenet monarch whose son had established Bede's as an act of filial piety in commemoration of his father's victory over the French at Crécy in 1346.

Stella watched Kit come back to the room, and to himself; to the memory of what he had been, and what he had become. His sticks faltered and stopped. His eyes met hers, green-brown and turbulent, full of new passions she could not read. 'I remember the lilies,' he said.

'Kit . . .'

She could not move. A patch of sweat grew cold on the back of her neck. From the moment she had met him in the ward, he had been cold and withdrawn and quite different from the man she thought she knew.

Now, she saw him gather himself to deliver

something prepared that she did not want to hear.

His face was a harlequin's: greenly bruised on the one, still side, alive and mobile and white on the other. With that half alone, he made himself smile. 'You should leave me. Now, while the memories are all good ones.'

His beautiful rolling voice was broken, and spilled over at the edges. He heard it and winced. His eyes never left hers.

'Don't . . .' She was weeping, which she had promised herself not to do. 'I won't leave. You can't make me.'

'I can ask you. For both our sakes.'

'You don't mean it. You married me less than a month ago. I married you. It's not time to give up.'

He frowned and shook his head. His hands were unsteady on the walking sticks. She wanted to step forward and catch him, to find him a chair, to reach for the electric wheelchair and make it ready for him, to sit and sleep and be home again and not to worry. She could do none of these things until they had settled a future they could both believe in.

His body did not answer him as he wanted. He lifted his one good shoulder in a shrug. 'I don't want to be with you as less than I was.'

'God, Kit . . .' She wiped her face with the heel of her hand and struggled in the pocket of her shorts for a tissue.

He was not what he had been, that much was indisputable. Even so, he was not as bad as the medics had promised at first examination. That he was able to walk at all was a miracle of modern science and testament to the therapeutic value of intravenous dexamethasone given in doses sufficient to drown an elephant, or so she had been informed by the consultant at the hospital in Yorkshire and again, in more measured terms, by the neurology team at Addenbrooke's in Cambridge, who had run their own MRI and CT scans and concluded that either they had been sent the wrong set of films, or the gods of caving had been exceptionally benevolent in awakening Dr Christian O'Connor so early and so relatively intact from his coma.

What they were not able to do was perform further miracles and give him back to her fully mended. They sent him home half done, a man prone to falling asleep without warning, who could only smile with half of his face, who could not move his left leg fully, who had only partial use of his left arm. They sent him with sticks and a wheelchair and a regime of exercises from the physiotherapist to keep him occupied and perhaps on the route towards healing. They thought, with time, he might be able to dispense with one of the sticks.

They could not say whether he would walk normally, or run, or if the full quirk of his smile would come back from the near-plastic blandness that afflicted the left half of his body.

They could not say, either, whether he would ever recover his memory of the cathedral of the earth, of the white limestone skull they had found there, of the run-crawl along the ledge with two lights and the fall that came after it, with sufficient clarity to be able to persuade Detective Inspector Fleming to reopen the case as attempted murder. At the moment, he could barely remember the details of his own wedding.

I remember the lilies.

Only his eyes were truly alive. She had never been able fully to read them, but always before there had been a clear, sharp humour that had drawn her in to his life. Now, they were shields that kept her out; she met his gaze and had no idea of what he thought or felt.

Quietly, he said, 'You know I'm right.'

'No.'

Desperate, she reached down for the backpack she had left beneath the table. Her plans for it had been quite different.

With one hand, she opened the fastenings, drew out the crumbling white stone that had been Kit's life's quest and set it on the table, a plain, ugly thing that shed flakes of chalky dandruff on to the bare wood floor.

She felt nothing from it; none of the blue lightning that had seared her mind, or the sense of newborn-ancient vulnerability that had so moved her on the moors by Gaping Ghyll. For three weeks, it had languished in her bag, unseen and unheard. She had not been able to bring herself to look at it. She felt no better now.

She said, 'I didn't throw it away.'

'Clearly.'

His face had become quite still; this once, it was symmetrical. 'Perhaps I should sit down?' He swayed on his sticks, and cursed and shuffled stiffly round to his wheelchair.

She wanted him to be glad of her help. He tolerated it with bad grace, letting her bring him to the chair and settle him as the hospital had taught her. Unresisting, he let her place the skull-stone in his lap. For too long, he stared into it and through it in cold silence.

When she thought the pressure might kill them both, he lifted his head and took himself in a whine and squeak of new wheels to the window where he could look down at the water.

The ash table lay between them; a wedding present from her to him and him to her, bought in another era when they were different people. She sat on its edge. 'If you hate it that much, we can throw it in the river now.'

'Would that keep us safe?'

'Is that what this is about? Our safety? It feels deeper than that.'

His face twisted. 'Someone tried to kill me for this, Stell. How much deeper do you need?'

'So throw it away.'

'You told me you'd already done that.'

They had never fought before. This sharp, edgy friction was new and unexpected and terrifying.

She found she was clasping her hands and made herself undo them. 'Tony Bookless told me to,' she said. 'I tried. I couldn't do it.'

'But you let him believe you had. And me.'

'So I'm a liar on top of everything else.' She spun away. 'I thought you'd be pleased. I was saving it as a surprise for when you came home. Are you going to leave me for it? Is that what this is about?'

She could not sit. She paced the length of the window, keeping her back to him, watching students play rounders in the sun on the common, wishing she could go back to a time before and make things different. She had completed three full lengths of twelve paces each before he spoke.

'You're not a very good liar. He didn't believe you'd thrown it away. He thinks you're in love with the stone. It does that to people, apparently. It's why they die.'

The sound of his voice stopped her more than what he said; a soft throatiness she had never heard before. She turned. His eyes were rimmed red. He made himself look up at her.

'Are you crying?'

'I'm trying not to.'

'Oh, Christ. Kit . . .'

She had to lift him out of the chair to hold him properly. In that long, wordless moment was more connection than they had managed in all the three weeks since the accident.

Under the haze of hospital-clean, he smelled the same as he had always done. She opened his shirt and pressed her nose to the soft skin under his collarbone and spoke to flesh and bone and the heart beneath. 'When did Tony tell you?'

'Last night. He came back again after you'd left for the night.' His hand teased out her hair, newly cut for his homecoming. It was shorter than before; less than a finger's length on top. He ruffled it and kissed her crown and she could feel the half of his mouth that worked properly. He said, 'I promised him I'd get you to destroy it.'

'Kit, I . . .'

'Which was stupid when I hadn't spoken to you first, I do know that. But I don't want you to die, Stell. I've lost so much chasing after a pipe dream of my own making. I don't want to lose you too. I couldn't bear that.'

She lifted her head away from his chest. 'Why should you lose me?'

'Because Cedric Owen didn't write his verse for its poetry alone, he wrote it as a guide and a warning.'

He closed his eyes and spoke from memory.

'*Find me and live, for I am your hope at the end of time. Hold me as you would hold your child. Listen to me as you would listen to your lover. Trust me as you would trust your god, whosoever that may be.*'

He opened his eyes. His gaze was green-brown and opaque. '*Hold me as you would hold your child. Listen to me as you would listen to your lover.* Are you doing that?'

She said nothing, there was no need; Kit could still read her even if she could no longer read him. He grasped her two hands and pulled her forward and held her, so that his eyes were all she could see, wide in their earnestness.

'Stell, everyone who has ever held that stone, and cared for it, has died. I would have done if there hadn't been water in the cave. You're in more danger. You're in love with it.'

Bringing her closer, he ran the tip of his finger over the arch of her ear, in a way that sparked down the length of her spine and into her core.

For three weeks, she would have given anything to feel that. Now, she caught his wrist and held it. 'Kit, listen to me. It's not the stone that kills people. It's people who kill to get hold of it, or to destroy it.'

'Which?' His hand lay unmoving in hers.

'I don't know. Probably both. In the cave, the pearl-hunter wanted to destroy it, not you. I really believe that.' Her focus was poor. She stared out of the window and saw only slews of different greens. 'Not that the police believe us. They think what happened to you was an accident. The Rescue have written us off as a pair of day trippers who got lost in a new cave.'

Kit laughed unevenly. 'So whoever did this is still out there. He knows exactly who we are and we haven't the first clue who he is. Christ, I didn't manage this well, did I?'

'You didn't—'

'I did. I made this happen. My pipe dream, my push, my idea for a wedding present. Please let's not argue about that as well. If you want to go on with it, you can take all the responsibility from here on in, but this far, it's mine. Deal?'

'Deal.'

'Thank you.' Clumsily, he turned Stella round, so they were both looking out of the window, and hugged her in to his chest.

Beneath, a student in a straw boater punted a group of tourists along the river. For show, he poled one-handed, holding a full champagne glass in the other hand. American voices floated up, commenting on the river room as they slid underneath.

There was a long moment's wait; time to feel the warmth of the one thing he said that she could hold on to. *I've lost so much. I don't want to lose you too. I couldn't bear that.*

The punt slid on past. The strangers' voices faded. In their echo, with ice gnawing her stomach, Stella said, 'If you stay here and I go away to find what the skull's about, it doesn't mean I don't love you. It doesn't mean you're losing me. You do know that, don't you?'

'I do. And you need to know that if I come with you, it doesn't mean I'm jealous of a stone.' A spark of laughter grated in his voice, and something else she had to strain to hear. He kissed the top of her head. 'You are a very brave woman. I do love you, did I mention?'

'Not since the cave.'

Her cheek was against his chest. His heartbeat pushed against her. She raised her head. His face was just above hers. Slowly, not quite accurately, he bent to kiss her.

The need for sleep caught him soon afterwards, for all that it was only a kiss. He lay back in his wheelchair, his face childlike in its peace. Stella sat cross-legged on the bare oak floor and looked out at the river and tried to keep her mind empty. The skull-stone lay on the low ash-wood table between them; an unexceptional, uninspiring lump of chalk that might have been the shape of an unfleshed man's head.

Or it might simply have been stone pulled

from a calciferous eddy pool in an underground cavern.

Her mind remained hers alone; the tenuous thought-feel of a presence that had left her at the mouth of the pothole in Yorkshire was a memory, and even that was fading so that it might have been imagination, pushed by the fear of the cave.

She pushed the skull-stone out into the strong summer sunlight, to the place where its shadow fell most crisply. A noon breeze lifted the smell of slow-running water from the river and brought with it the slow natter of the mallards, and the crisp certainties of a young tour guide leading a group of visiting scholars.

'. . . the river rooms, which appear suspended over the River Cam, a unique example of this kind of extreme Tudor architecture. They were home for a while to Dr Cedric Owen, the college's foremost benefactor and author of the Owen ledgers. The rooms were later occupied temporarily by the playwright and spy, Christopher Marlowe, and there is a rumour that King Charles I was hidden here for eight nights during the latter stages of the Civil War. From here, we can walk on round to the small stone at the outer gate to the Great Court which marks the spot where Owen died on Christmas Day in 1588. His body was buried in a pauper's grave somewhere near the plague pits, but before his death he . . .'

The voice faded into the background murmur of the afternoon. Stella propped her elbows on her knees and her chin on the hammock of her laced-up fingers and brought her eyes level with the skull's.

'Before his death, Cedric Owen hid you in a place where time and hard water could have kept you secret for ever. But someone wanted us to find you so badly that they usurped Owen's manuscripts to plant their own code. *That which you seek lies hidden in white water*. Why did they do that?'

Why?

Kit had asked it first, when he had analysed the ledgers and found them written by two different hands. It was the only time in a year of knowing that she had seen him un-calm, pacing the length of the big window, raking his fingers through his hair.

Why? Everything we know about Cedric Owen says he was a decent, honourable man. He planned everything else so carefully; he hid the money and the ledgers, and left a letter with a lawyer, to be opened a century after his death so there was no way the Crown could confiscate his estate. Once it was safe for them to be found and brought to the college, he left orders that the ledgers be kept available to the public at all times, 'preserved against all harme, and made free to alle as may wysh to view them for the purposes of personal or academic studie.' *He knew exactly how much they would enhance the college's academic status. If they're all fakes, there has to be a reason.*

It had been raining that day with a dense mist lying over the Cam. The river room balanced on the shelf of it, a place of grey-green light and the hypnotic drumming of water on water.

Without undue thought, Stella had said, 'There must be something else hidden in the text. You're the cryptographer. You've got the whole lot on disc – why not crunch the numbers and see what comes out?'

He had loped across the room and kissed her on the forehead; the dry warmth of his lips had stayed with her longer than the laughing Irish voice. *You're a genius, did I mention?*

Stella had known him a year by then, and loved him for half of that, but she was only just beginning to know the man beneath the voice, and the mind behind the eyes. She had offered to help with the search for a code as much for an excuse to study Kit as out of curiosity for his hidden text.

She was an astronomer. She knew nothing of history, but she had submitted her thesis and was waiting for the summons to her viva and time was weighing heavy on her hands. In the weeks that followed, she learned more of English history than during any amount of half-heard lessons at school, and found she enjoyed it. While Kit had crunched the numbers in the columns of the accounts, Stella had taken the printed copies of the original text and learned to read the difficult looping manuscript.

Weeks later, after the endless – and fruitless – round of numeric analyses of the integers, when she was beginning to dream of cramped, crabbed Elizabethan handwriting every time she closed her eyes, Stella had seen in the last pages of the last ledger the smears and errors on the page that were not, as had always been said, the result of writing on board ship, but the deliberate masking of a known shorthand.

It had taken her less than two hours to transcribe it and half of that was spent in the library finding notes that led her to the contemporary translations of John Dee's shorthand.

That which you seek lies hidden in white water . . .

Stella had found the text. Kit was the one who had understood that it directed them to Cedric Owen's lost heart-stone, Kit who had spent his days reading the biographies of Cedric Owen to find the places to which the cryptic lines might refer, who had unearthed maps and the earliest ordnance surveys, who had cruised Google Maps until his eyes were square; and Kit who had cared enough to plan the trip and make it happen and had shouldered the responsibility now, when death stalked them both.

But it was Stella who had dived into the white

water and picked up the ugly mass of white lime, Stella who had come to care for it and was left with unanswered questions that ate at her sleep and shadowed her day. She stared at it emptily.

'What am I missing?'

Kit's laptop lay under the low ash table; repository of the entire Owen archive, plus the hundreds of files of failed cryptography, and the single one that had succeeded. Pulling the file on to the screen, she skipped down to the stanza that Kit had remembered.

I am your hope at the end of time. Hold me as you would hold your child. Listen to me as you would listen to your lover. Trust me as you would trust your god, whosoever that may be.

Follow the path that is herein shewn and be with me at the time and place appointed. Do then as the guardians of the night foretell. Thereafter, follow your heart and mine, for these are one and the same. Do not fail me, for in doing so, you fail yourself and all the worlds of waiting.

She chewed on the end of a pen. 'I have held you as I would hold a child. I am listening in all the ways I know how. I am prepared to trust you, if you'll give me something to trust, and I didn't throw you into Gaping Ghyll, which must count for something between us. I would follow the path that is herein shewn if I had the slightest clue where you might shew me anything usef—'

It was not blue that lit her mind, then, only a sudden slamming thought. 'Stella Cody, you're an idiot. And a blind one at that.'

She pushed herself to her feet and ran for the desk in the far corner of the room, to where Kit kept all his files, with a neatness bordering on pathology that nevertheless meant she could find anything as long as she knew what it was that she needed.

She knew exactly what she needed now; she pulled out a box file full of printed copies of the first three ledgers, a pad and a new pen and took it all back to her space by the window, pausing to kiss the back of Kit's hand as she passed.

'If I ever again accuse you of being scarily, certifiably anal, please remind me of this.'

She said it quietly and did not see him wake then, nor apparently in any part of the afternoon, while she sat in a messy cascade of papers and scanned images and asked of herself the question she had not asked before, and found, perhaps, the beginning of an answer.

'Hello? Anyone at home?'

The sun was leaning far to the west, sending amber light to glance off the river. The breeze was cooler and less laden with water. The tour guide and the visiting scholars had gone. The ducks had all moved upriver, to be fed by tourists at the cafés on Magdalene Bridge. Stella sat cross-legged in the evening's quiet light chewing a pen and making notes on her A4 pad.

'Am I not welcome?' A stocky figure stepped in through the doorway, letting in a draught that lifted the paper's edge.

'Gordon! Of course you're welcome. Come on in . . .'

Professor Gordon Fraser BSc, MSc, CGeol, FRS and prime contender for the Master of Bede's in the unlikely event that Tony Bookless ever renounced the post, was a sedimentary geologist and caver of international renown; he was also one of Stella's closest friends in Cambridge.

A short, wide man, he bore a carroty beard that jutted ledge-like from the angle of his lower lip and gridiron sinews that stood out along his shoulders like lanyards. His hair ranged across his head in wild curls that would have been the envy of any woman and he wore a Cambridge Climbing and Caving Club T-shirt that proclaimed a list of first descents that would have been implausible except that Stella had been with him on the latest of them and knew the rest to be genuine.

He spoke his English from the north-west of Scotland and had been known to wear a kilt, although Stella had only seen evidence of that once, three weeks before, when Gordon the Dwarf had been the second witness at her wedding.

He stood awkwardly on the threshold now, holding a bunch of freesias, peering in round the edge of the door. The skull-stone was not in his line of sight. Stella slid her pack over it before she stood.

'I'm sorry, I was lost in the ledgers. Let me make you coffee and then we'll see if Kit wants to wake up. He'd be sorry to miss you.'

From his wheelchair by the window, Kit said, 'Kit's awake.'

He spoke in the lazy slur that made it impossible to know if he were still half asleep or had been awake for the past three hours. A whine of batteried wheels turned the chair. He shrugged his better shoulder.

'I'm sorry.' He answered the look on her face. 'I should have said something sooner. It was good to watch you work.'

His cluttered gaze met hers, saying more: that he, too, enjoyed his solitude; that he needed the freedom simply to sit; that there were parts of him that he needed to keep private, but was sorry for it.

Lightly, he said, 'I need to pee. If you make coffee, I might be done by the time it's ready and then you can show the two of us what you've made of Cedric Owen's ledgers.'

The kitchen was a galley in the corner of the room; a remnant of Tudor planning that had seen no reason to keep the heat of a cooking fire away from the bedroom or study.

While he was gone, Stella made coffee the slow way, setting Gordon to grind the beans while she boiled the milk in a thick-bottomed pan. They talked of caves they both knew, and not of the accident; all of that talking had been done at Kit's bedside in the three weeks before he came home.

In that time, other cavers had repeated their route in both directions and mapped it; pictures on the web showed the cathedral of the earth with its chandeliers of dripping stone. Anthropologists were already studying the cave paintings, naming them, classifying them, dissolving their mystery.

Kit's wheelchair whined back from the bedroom and lavatory beyond. He had changed his T-shirt and dashed water over his hair, leaving it rumpled, and more brown than gold. Stella noticed these things as she would have done a month ago, but with a different kind of care.

'And so?' He found his space by the three-sided window and moved the low table with his foot. 'You've spent three uninterrupted hours studying Cedric Owen's ledgers. What did you find?'

She was not ready. The part of her trained to science wanted to finish the search, to quantify the results, possibly even to decipher their message.

They waited, kindly; two of the three men she trusted most in the world. She said, 'I hate to say this, and I'm not sure I can bring myself to face him again, but Tony Bookless should be here.'

Knowing her a liar, he had none the less confirmed the funding for her fellowship within a week of coming home. Her conscience was a needle in the back of her mind that would not go away.

'He's stuck in a meeting at the Old Schools,' Gordon said. 'He'll not be finished till after formal dinner.' He wrapped his thick fingers round the mug Stella gave him and jutted his beard at her notes. 'I watched you in the window all the way across Jesus Green. You were way lost in something that didn't look as if it'll wait until then.' Then, when she did not answer, 'What have you found, lass?'

She swirled her coffee and looked at Kit and tried to forget Tony Bookless. 'I found the second cipher in the ledgers. The one "that is herein shewn".'

It should have been said with flashing lights and a fanfare of trumpets. She had a chorus of mallard drakes assaulting a duck, and the thin, high cry of a lost child on the river bank.

And Kit, smiling broadly with the half of his mouth that could manage it, said, 'Which is why there are thirty-two volumes, not just one. You clever, clever girl. I thought it was an awful lot of work for two men just to leave us a single page of poorly cadenced poetry. What does it tell us?'

'I don't know. It's a hieroglyph. I've spent half the afternoon on the web trying to find out what it is. Look—'

She made a stack of her notes and set them on the table.

'It's like the shorthand: each page has half a dozen marks that look like random slips of the pen, except these ones are better hidden and the end result is more convoluted. It's there in all of the books. See here near the bottom of the page . . .' She picked up a volume at random and ran her finger under a line.

21 August 1573, To Imagio, son of Diego, For: 2 brayce hunted fowl: 2d

'If you look closely under the figure 3 of the year, and again in the s of son and the y of brayce, there are curls and lines. If I copy these across the page . . .' She laid a sheet of thin tracing paper on top and copied them through to it. 'And then repeat again for the next line . . .'

22 August 1573, To Father Calderón, For: rent for 2 persons, viz, myselfe & don Fernandez

As she spoke, Stella picked out marks and copied them. 'That finishes this page. It's not very coherent yet.'

'It's gibberish.' Kit picked up the sheet and held it at arm's length, frowning. 'It hasn't got any of the hallmarks of a shorthand script.' His speech was less slurred after sleep.

'That's because it isn't a shorthand script.' Stella took the page back and picked up three others. 'It's a composite. If we fit the pages together in groups of four, and match these dots down in the bottom left-hand corners . . .' She caught her tongue between her teeth and fitted the pages together. 'We have the magic of human communication. See?'

Four pages of tracing paper came together to make an array of strange curling glyphs, of half-seen goggle-eyed men and animals, of gaping mouths and suns and trees and moons and coiled snakes and jaguars and none of it intelligible.

'Christ.'

Stella had not often known Gordon rendered speechless. It was good to see it now.

She said, 'There are marks and alignment dots on every page from the first volume to the last. I can't think why we didn't see them before.'

'We weren't looking,' Kit said, 'and now we are. You are, at any rate.' He was bending over dangerously far, fumbling with the pages on the low coffee table. 'Although I, clearly, am too befuddled to see the obvious; I can't understand a bit of it. Gordon, who is wise and sage and hasn't had his brains knocked to dust, will doubtless succeed where I am failing. Gordon?'

Quite dexterously, he flicked a set of four pages to the blunt Scot, who studied them, one after the other.

'Maybe. Maybe not.' Gordon passed the pages to Stella. 'Could you show me that again?'

She chose different pages, with different marks, all very clear to her eyes. Taking a thick fibre pen, she marked them rapidly on each page, traced them, matched them and drew out the final glyphs.

'They come in blocks of twelve by twelve,' she said. 'I scanned them into the laptop and ran some web matches and I think they're old Mayan glyphs. Maybe Olmec if we're splitting hairs, but Cedric Owen was in the Mayan lands for thirty-two years of his life, so I'd bet on that.'

'Can you read them?' Gordon asked.

'Are you kidding? Not a chance. I could learn to, perhaps, but it could take me years. We need someone who's already steeped in this stuff.'

'Of which I imagine there are very few, and fewer still in England whom we could trust not to shout this to the whole world before we're ready.' Kit was looking at her, in the way she remembered. 'But you've found the one who knows it all?'

She grinned. 'Maybe. I Googled "skull" and

"Mayan" and got half a million hits of flaky nonsense about the end of the world. Then I added "Cedric Owen" and got down to two pages, all of which eventually linked through to Professor Ursula Walker of the Institute of Mayan Studies, which is part of Oxford University. This woman's amazing; the Institute is based at her home, which is a Tudor farmhouse in the Oxfordshire countryside. Her family have owned land there since the Domesday Book and it happens to be the place where the Owen ledgers were found so you could say she has something of a family interest. She got a first in anthropology—'

'From Bede's?' Kit said.

'Of course, and then, if Google's telling the truth, she spent four post-graduate years writing the definitive biography of Cedric Owen – with Tony Bookless.'

Gordon smacked his hand on his head. 'I thought I'd heard the name before.'

'Exactly. But she didn't stick around so everyone has forgotten her. The pair of them got their PhDs together and then went their separate ways: he joined the army and became a military historian; she became a field anthropologist. From her output, I'd say she's spent a lot longer than we have looking for the skull-stone and trying to work out what it's for. The only problem is that it looks like she's gone native in the process.'

Kit rolled his eyes. 'What kind of native?'

'Every kind there is. You name a native, she's gone it. As far as I can tell, she spends at least half her life in the field. Have a look . . .'

Stella lifted the lid of the laptop and turned the screen so they could both see it. A brisk-eyed, wind-tanned woman in her mid-sixties glanced out at them. Behind her, the scenery was densely green.

Gordon twisted the screen round to get a better look. 'Looks more like jungle than field.'

'That's the last trip to the Yucatán in June 2005,' Stella said. 'Sadly I can't find a picture of winter 2006 which was spent in the frozen wastes of the Arctic tundra getting stoned on reindeer urine with the Sami Laplanders.'

'*Stella?*' For the first time since the cave, Stella saw Kit laugh. Her heart danced.

Straight-faced, she said, 'It's a well-known procedure in modern cultural anthropology, apparently. The reindeer eat hallucinogenic mushrooms and piss out high-octane urine. The reindeer herders eat the yellow snow and then their shamans do whatever it is they do to keep everyone happy.' She let go and felt a grin stretch her ears apart. 'What else do you do when there's thirty seconds of daylight every twenty-four hours and the ambient tempera-ture's cold enough to freeze the balls off a cat?'

'Maybe you stay at home where it's safe and warm like the rest of us?' Gordon said faintly.

Stella laughed and it came out reckless and foolish and she did not care. 'As the man who soloed the top pitch of Greasepaint Chimney, you can hardly talk about staying home and being safe, Gordon Fraser.'

'Fair point.' He chewed the edge of his thumb. 'So if she's off the happy juice, can she translate the new cipher?'

'I think so. I sent her an email. We have an invitation to go and visit her tomorrow. There's a conference at the Institute, but it'll be over by the afternoon.'

We. Stella was watching Kit as she spoke; for all the laughter, she could not read him yet. He saw her looking and smiled unevenly. With great care, he reached across to the table and snapped a single bloom off the stem of white lilies.

She sat very still as he manoeuvred his chair round and slid the flower in behind her ear. With his hand on her shoulder, he said, '*Follow the path that is herein shewn and be with me at the time and place appointed.* We've got this far. Do we want to be at the time and place appointed?'

She wanted to cheer out loud. She said, 'We have to find them first. That's why we're going to Ursula Walker's.'

'Knowing somebody else will be dogging our every step?'

'We have to be careful; we already know that.

189

And the stone will warn us if there's real danger. We have to believe that.'

She had not mentioned the stone in company before. Kit looked at her, surprised. 'So . . . can we show Gordon what we've got?'

'I don't see why not.' Experimentally, Stella said, 'Gordon, I think we have something to show you.'

There passed a short silence, in which Gordon had the good sense to remain silent, and Stella braced herself against the screaming protestations of the skull-stone – which did not come.

On the contrary, somewhere in the distant blue of a summer's evening was the first stirring of connection: an awareness, an awakening, and a weak, uncertain love.

'My . . . that's a bonny thing.'

Gordon sat on the floor opposite her, touching knee to knee, but not touching the skull-stone. She held it for him, as she might have held a newborn child, and turned it round so that he could see each part of it. She did not let him touch it; the new connection was too fragile for that. He did not try, but sat on his hands and looked with quiet awe.

'Can you clean it?' she asked. 'Can you do something to take off the limescale and make it back to what it was when Cedric Owen held it without hurting the heart-stone underneath?'

Gordon flicked a glance from under his caterpillar brows. 'We can give it a shot. It might be harder to hide then, mind you, but it would be a very lovely thing to see.'

He looked at his watch and the sun and at them both, then just at Stella. 'You and me could go over to the lab now, maybe, while everyone's out?'

12

Geology Department, Cambridge University,
June 2007

THE GEOLOGY DEPARTMENT LATE ON A SUMMER
afternoon was a quiet place. Stella followed
Gordon down three flights of stairs into air-
conditioned dryness that smelled, like
laboratories the world over, of unnamed acids
and alkalis and chromatography gel; the odours
of man, which had nothing at all to do with the
earth.

In this subterranean aridity, they came at last
to a white-tiled laboratory with steel benches on
the periphery and a space-age fume cupboard
on one wall with an electronic control panel fit
for a fighter jet at the front.

'This is Maisie. She's the real thing.' Gordon
stroked the cabinet's glass front fondly. His
accent, always un-English, broadened into
rolling, granular Scots. 'Before this beastie came
along, what we're planning would have taken

six months of slow tedium waiting for the lime to dissolve into an acid bath. Watching paint dry would be exciting by comparison. Now, thanks to the genius of a few of my colleagues, we can put your friend into our shiny new machine here and it'll all be done in the blink of an eye, more or less. Do you want to put him in?'

He slid open the glass and let Stella set the skull-stone on a plastic stand on the base of the cabinet. An array of fine tubes angled down from all directions. Flakes of lime peeled off the stone as she withdrew her hands but they were sucked into a vacuum system before they hit the floor. Under the white lights, the skull-stone looked more obviously of another age.

Gordon was a man in his element. He whistled through his teeth, more of a hiss than a recognizable tune.

'Well now, shall we see what a wee bit of ultrasound and high pressure acid at two hundred degrees can do to get rid of all the crumbling crap on the surface? This is experimental, you understand. We've not released it to the public, but I can't see it'll do any harm if what's inside is solid quartz.'

'Do we think it is?' Stella asked.

'If it's Cedric Owen's heart-stone, then there's nothing else it can be.'

The front of the cabinet closed with a pneumatic thud. Gordon began moving his

193

hands over pressure-sensitive controls at the front. Lights flickered. The array of pipes moved closer to the skull. A needling whine began to eat at their ears. Under it, Stella felt a faint, singing murmur; the stone was more fully awake now, so that the blue place in her mind was occupied again, watchful and alert. She felt the moment's panic that was not hers, as the acid began to spray. She promised calm and was heard.

She said, 'How long will it take?'

'Maybe a couple of hours.'

'So I could go back to Kit? If there's a way to get him down here, I'd like him to see the result when you're finished.'

'I'll call you. There's a lift you can use. I just don't like it much,' said the man who had led some of the hardest caves in Britain. 'Too claustrophobic.'

Kit was asleep again when she returned. She made a salad and cut the tops from some straw-berries and set them both to the side for when he woke.

She was sitting on the bare oak floor by the ash table, drinking green tea and watching the sun gild the trees on Midsummer Common, when Sergeant Ceri Jones, the young radio operator who had talked Kit's rescue party out of the cave, rang her mobile.

'I'm on Ingleborough Fell again.' At two

194

hundred miles' distance, her accent was broader than it had been in person. 'We finally got a police team together to look inside your killer cave. We just came out. I thought you'd like to know.'

'Thank you.'

'Is Kit OK?'

Stella turned to look at him. His colour was better than it had been and his face was symmetrical in sleep. 'They let him come home this morning. I think that's as OK as it gets.'

'I'm glad.' There was a pause and a breath of moorland wind and the sound of crows and cars in the background. Ceri said, 'I've got a web-cam. Are you on line?'

'I can be,' Stella said.

Kit's laptop had a lens in the lid that let her set up a video link. Ceri came up on the screen, windblown and wiry, with smears of mud on her face and curly dark hair wet-plastered to her head. She looked straight at the lens, sharply, a woman barely contained.

'What have you got?' Stella asked.

'Two things. The easy bit is the skeleton. You remember there was a body holding a sword lying in the cave with the ice-age art on the wall?'

'The cathedral of the earth. I've never seen anywhere as beautiful. I heard the anthropologists are all over the paintings?'

Ceri grinned. 'Like a rash. They're already

working out how to clear the rock fall to get in to see them without having to crawl. But we had a forensic pathologist on the team too, which means I can tell you that your skeleton was a man, five foot ten and in his sixties when he died. The important bit is, they think the body's at least four hundred years old, so he died around Cedric Owen's time. And the sword he was holding cleaned up enough to see some detail. Have a look . . .'

The screen blinked and Ceri was gone. In her place was a sword, photographed with a flash against whitish rock. The hilt was bronze, or brass, the blade rusted iron. A second picture sent a moment later showed a close-up of the crosspiece. Etched lines showed indistinctly.

'Are those initials on the hilt?'

Ceri came back on to the screen. 'It says RM, and then a number: XII.'

'Robert Maplethorpe was the twelfth Master of Bede's,' Stella said. 'But it can't be him, he was killed defending Cedric Owen at the gates of the college on Christmas Day 1588.'

'OK, so we'll leave it open until we come up with a better answer. I just thought you'd like to know.'

'Thanks. If that's the easy bit, what's the rest?'

Ceri frowned and looked over both shoulders before she spoke. Slowly, picking her words, she said, 'We've just been along the nightmare ledge

196

again. We set up bolts and a rope so it's safe now, but we went along it twice to get it set. There's a crawl and then something worse than that, but nowhere for someone to hit their head hard enough to smash their skull open like Kit did.'

She waited. When Stella said nothing, she said, 'It proves that you were right; there was someone else there with you.'

'He might have hit it as he fell.'

'No. The wall angles inwards below the ledge where he fell; there's no way he could have hit himself on the way down. Our forensic pathologist is sure that it wasn't an accident. In any case, while the others were all taking pictures, I went a little way up the fork to Gaping Ghyll to have a look. I found this . . .'

The image switched again. On the screen, briefly, where Ceri's head had been, her grubby hand held a plastic drinking bottle.

Ceri reappeared. 'It was bought at a motorway service station on the M6 and we have a date stamp on the side so we can narrow the time down a bit. If we had the money, we'd run a check to see whether there's any saliva and then if there's any DNA to run through the database, but we don't. At the moment, all it's good for is to prove that there was someone else in the cave around the same time as you. We're cracking our heads trying to work out a motive for an attempted murder. If we can find one, we might be able to persuade them to at least run a check on the CCTV at the service station to see who was buying water on the day Kit fell.'

It was half a question. Stella spread her hands wide. 'If either of us stumbles across a plausible reason why someone would want to kill Kit in a cave, DI Fleming will be the first to know. You can tell him that, from me.'

'I'll do that. Thank you. And I'll mail you with anything we get.'

They closed the connection. The sun was a red globe deep in the west. The bars and pubs up near Magdalene Bridge were coming to life, spilling multicoloured reflections on the river. The ducks slept, silently. Some time later, into the quiet evening, her phone rang again.

'Your wee stone's ready,' said Gordon Fraser unsteadily. 'I hope you are.'

Nothing could have made her ready.

An unusually subdued Gordon met her and Kit at the doors to the elevator and ushered them into the fluorescent hush of his laboratory.

Kit went ahead, sweeping his electric wheel-chair along the corridor and through the door with wild oversteer at each corner. Stella followed behind, losing him at the last turn.

'Dear God . . .'

He whispered it, hoarsely, in awe, or fear; Stella could not tell which. She stumbled into the back of his chair, cursing. Then she, too, stopped.

'Christ.'

Blue. All she could see was crystalline, perfect, unblemished-sky blue: such poverty of language for such heartbreaking beauty. She stepped forward to press her nose against the glass of the cabinet.

Gordon had not moved the stone from the small plastic plinth where she had left it. The white lights were as harsh as they had been, but were outmatched, now, by what they lit.

Colour flooded the space, a dense, dazzling, lucent blue that brought the morning sky underground and spread it into the far corners, dispelling dust and technology.

Stella crouched down, bringing her face level with its eyes. Freed from its limestone carcass, the skull was perfect, a thing of flawless crystal that drew the light inward in curves to make a soft, blurred flame at its heart.

On the outside, the smooth arc of the cranial vault gave way in front to two tunnelled eye sockets above sharply angled cheekbones. The nose was a clear triangle. The lower jaw looked separate, so that the mouth could open and shut if one chose to play such games with it.

Stella did not wish to play games of any sort. Softly, she said, 'Kit, have you got the bag?'

'Are you sure you want to do that?'

It was Gordon who spoke. He stood at the far side of the room, white and wide-eyed, and had not come near her.

In the same, shaken voice as he had used on the phone, he said, 'Myself, I'd want to be sure I could put that thing down before ever I picked it up.'

'What do you mean?'

'I'm not sure. Just that it's a thing to steal the soul and I'm not sure I want mine stolen. It's too beautiful. It's just asking to be picked up, and when you do, I don't think you'll ever put it down again. To be honest, I think you'd be safer putting it under a pile driver. We have one, if you need it.'

There was silence. Stella looked at Kit instead of the stone. 'What do you think?'

He shrugged his one good shoulder. 'Tony says it kills anyone who handles it. It all comes to the same thing in the end. Either you believe that it's lethal, and no stone is worth dying for, or you think it has something to teach us and is worth the risk. We've been round this circle before. If you've changed your mind, I'll gladly go with the pile driver.'

'Do you think it has stolen my soul?'

'Honestly?' He glanced up at her and for a moment she saw the brief battle his eyes could not hide, as he struggled to find the balanced view he had always held so easily before. He made himself smile. 'I think you're stronger than that. If you weren't, we wouldn't be having this conversation.'

'Are you not afraid of it?' Gordon asked.

Kit pursed his lips. 'Not that I'd noticed. It's
. . . striking, but I can't see what's to be afraid
of.'

'You're a stronger man than me, then. Maybe
I'm just a milksop at heart.' Gordon eased back
his shoulders, as Stella had seen him do in a
cave at the start of a hard pitch, and came forward to open the cabinet for her.

More normally, he said, 'If you want some
jargon to keep the bean counters happy, then
you should know that your bauble is made of a
single piece of blue quartz, better known as
sapphire.'

'*What?*'

His grin split his beard right across. 'What
you're looking at is probably the biggest gemstone ever dug out of the northern hemisphere.'

Kit said, 'What's it worth?'

'Pass. More than you or I will see on a
university salary in a long, long time, but if
you're looking for a motive for murder, I don't
think this is something you steal so you can cut
it up and sell it to the footballers' wives. It's got
the kind of tingle to it that would make a man
want to keep it whole for himself. There now,
it's all yours . . .'

He slid open the cabinet door. Stella lifted up
the stone. Blue light enveloped her. A sense of
welcome, of homecoming, of friendship re-
kindled soaked her soul.

Distantly, she heard Kit ask, 'Where exactly is

it from?' and Gordon answered, 'Scotland. I've seen one or two of that colour from the basalt layers at Loch Roag on Lewis, but never one that big without flaws in it. If it matters, we could run a scan and analyse the colour bands. That'd give us more of a clue where it came from, although there's no saying it was cut there; it could have been taken halfway round the world before anyone touched it. Either way, it's been cut against the grain of the crystal, which is hard to do without breaking it into a thousand tiny pieces. Certainly it's not a German fake; they don't know how to do it without shattering the stone.'

Stella was only half listening; all of her attention was on the skull-stone. She cradled it in the crook of her elbow.

I am your hope at the end of time. Hold me as you would hold your child. Listen to me as you would listen to your lover. Trust me as you would trust your god, whosoever that may be.

Gordon was right, the stone had hold of her soul; and he was wrong, it was not an unsafe thing to permit. She trusted it and it her. The relationship was more even now, as if the stripping of the chalk shell had opened a channel that let the stone return an equal care.

In the new parts of her mind was the space of

the open sky, offering a peace she had not known possible. Stella stepped into it, as she would have stepped into a cave, with the same need to explore and the same unknowing of what she might find.

Kit must have asked another question, because Gordon was answering it.

'The Germans are the masters when it comes to cutting quartz.' He closed his cabinet and switched off the lights. The deep blue flame burned on in the skull's heart. 'There's a village somewhere in the blackest part of the Black Forest where they make crystal skulls and sell them to gullible Yanks. This is not one of those. I'd put my career on that.'

He pointed a blunt finger at the stone lying on Stella's arm. 'See how the zygomatic arches pull in the light? And the eye sockets are lenses, to focus it into the cranium? You don't get that kind of workmanship from the twenty-first century. There's nobody left knows how to do it.'

He took a step across the room and stood at his computer rattling his big fingers across the keys. 'The provenance makes or breaks this thing, clearly, so I took the liberty of firing off a few photographs before I started. If you look on the big screen at the back there' – his hands waved to the far wall of the laboratory, where was a wide screen of cinematic proportions – 'you'll see the picture of the fissure in the rock.'

A cleft of dense white chalk showed blue at its base. The quality of the image was breathtaking. Close up, in high definition, even limestone looked inspiring. Gordon waved a laser pointer at it. A red dot spiralled over crinkled laminations.

'These are sequential deposits. The density and depth varies with seasonal cycles. We're not what you'd call precise at this resolution but if you'll excuse a grubby approximation, we can safely say that your rock there has been sitting in water of high calcium carbonate content for four hundred and twenty years, give or take five per cent.'

Kit said, 'So it is Owen's.'

'It's in the right time frame. That's as much as geology can do for you. The rest is up to you, but I don't think there's much doubt.'

'So we're no further forward, really, are we? We're still trying to stay alive long enough to find the time and place appointed, if we had the first clue what they were,' Kit said. 'Trivial.'

'We need to know who it is first,' Stella said, from the floor.

'I recognize that voice.' Kit turned his chair the better to see her. The humour left his face. 'What's up?'

Stella shook her head. 'I don't know.' It was hard to explain; a certain coalescence of mist, of flame and light and crystal that was more organic than any of these. 'I keep seeing a face, but not clearly. It comes and goes when I look at the stone.'

'The face that goes with the skull?'

'I think so. It feels like it. Is there anyone we can trust who would be able to put the face on the bones?'

'Not my field.' Kit looked up. 'Gordon?'

'There's only one that I know of.' The small Scotsman regarded Kit doubtfully. 'Did you know Davy Law went into forensic anthropology after he left here?'

There was a moment's silent pause that Stella did not understand, then, 'No,' Kit said flatly. 'Not him.'

Gordon flushed, which was almost as surprising. 'He's a Bede's man, and he knows what he's doing.'

'Oh, *please.*'

'Guys?' Stella looked from one to the other. She felt the beginnings of a warning creep under the base of her skull, sending away the face and the mists that went with it.

Kit sighed. 'David Law was a medical student who pulled out of his clinical training and ran off to do something less arduous. He's a runty little shit, with teeth like a coypu on steroids and hair like rat's tails. He coxed for the first boat the year Bede's came last.'

Stella pushed herself upright, laughing. 'That's hardly a hanging offence.'

'He assaulted the stroke of the women's team the night before the race.'

'*What?*' She swept round. 'Gordon, is this true?'

'No, it's slander and you should know better, Christian O'Connor.'

Gordon, now, was looking flushed and angry. He stared down at the floor and back up again. 'It was a rumour, there's no proof. But even the rumour wrecked Davy's career. He ducked out of his clinical training and ran off to join Médecins Sans Frontières and cut his teeth bandaging bullet wounds and sorting out infant diarrhoea in Palestinian refugee camps. When he came back, he trained as a forensic anthropologist.'

'So he spends his time cracking the bones of the dead?' Kit laughed hollowly. 'That's about right.'

Gordon glared at him. 'He's spent the past five years in Turkey pissing off the government in Ankara putting names and faces to the bones in Kurdish mass graves, which isn't something just anyone could do. He runs a forensic pathology business over by the Radcliffe Hospital at Oxford. You can cling to your prejudices if you want to, but if Stella needs someone who'll keep his mouth shut while he puts a face on the bones of her stone, Davy's the man. And he's probably one of the few who wouldn't either be afraid of it, or want to kill you for it. You're going to be hard pressed to find another like that.'

Kit raked his good hand through his hair. He looked for a moment as if he might argue, then shook his head and let all the tension drop from his body. 'This isn't my call. Stell? What do we do?'

She wanted to follow the flickering warning in her mind, but it had gone as soon as it had come. She slid the skull-stone into her backpack and closed the fastenings. The room seemed dull with it gone. When she stood, it fitted against her back as it had done in the cave.

She said, 'Tony should be back by now. It's time I cleared my conscience. Can we go and see him and take all that we've got? He wrote Owen's biography with Ursula Walker and he'll know what really happened with Davy Law. If he thinks it's a bad idea to go and see him, we'll give it a miss. If not, we'll go first thing in the morning and then go on to Ursula. Deal?'

'Deal.' Only because she knew Kit well did she see the hesitation before he spoke.

They moved slowly through the warm evening streets of Cambridge, where students not yet left for the holidays mingled with the relentless influx of tourists, where cafés spilled out into the streets and taxis ran at speed both ways along the one-way streets of the pedestrian precinct.

For ease of Kit's wheelchair they chose the less crowded route past the big colleges, King's, Trinity and John's, over the cobbles outside Heffer's bookshop, left before the Round Church and right before Magdalene Bridge to the path that led along the river's bank. The water lay blackly calm, infinitely deep and still, but for the splashes of multicoloured light spraying down from the pubs and bars at the bridge.

Kit was learning to handle the chair. Away from the town, he took more risks, pushing faster, to escape the light and noise. They slid along the edge of Jesus Green with its sporadically unquiet couples exploring each other in the grey-green grass. At Midsummer Common, they stopped under the trees.

'He's not in,' Stella said.

Bede's College lay on the far side of the river, a place of sandstone and granite, of Tudor extravagance and Georgian austerity, where the library dwarfed the chapel and was, in turn, overshadowed by the square tower that held the Master's suite.

Here and there, muted lights shone from uncurtained windows, but not from the leaded lights of Tony Bookless's study.

Kit reached up to take her hand. Shadows of starlight and moonlight combined to erase the harlequin bruises on his face. He looked younger, and untainted. He kissed the knuckle of her thumb. 'Come with me to John Dee's geometric bridge and we can wait a while. If he's walking back from the Old Schools, he'll come this way.'

The bridge was a single-span arch, built of wood, with no pins or bolts, held together by the pure mastery of geometry. It was Kit's open-air sanctuary, a place of balance where land arched over water more completely than did his rooms, where the powers of mind met the heart's needs in a form of equal function and beauty.

It was a place to mend old hurts, to re-weave the connections that were lost, or simply to sit in silence, which was what they had always done here, not needing to needle out the intricacies of the past.

The past had never before held monsters that so clearly overshadowed the present.

Stella sat, pushing her legs through the wooden spurs to dangle them over the black satin water. The skull-stone bounced gently against her back. The tingles of warning had returned; small flashes of yellow lightning that flickered through her mind like the foretaste of a storm.

'If we're going to see Davy Law,' she said, 'I need to know more about him.'

Kit kept his eyes on the window of Tony Bookless's study. 'There's nothing more to tell you. He left. He never came back.'

'But before that?'

'Before that he blew his career out of the water. End of story.'

'And he coxed a losing boat.'

'And that, yes.'

Kit shoved his wheelchair forward until he could pull himself up by the top rail of the arc and stand looking down into the water. A while later, he turned and reached for her, running his hand through her short hair. She cocked a questioning brow. 'And?'

'And this isn't worth digging up, Stell, I promise you. It's sordid and old, and it may be that Gordon's right and Davy Law's a changed man. Can we leave it at that and see what happens when we meet him tomorrow?'

'If we go at all. Tony might think we shouldn't.'

'He won't. He'll say the same as Gordon; that Davy's a Bede's man and he knows what he's doing.'

'College loyalty runs thicker than water?'

'College loyalty runs thicker than blood. If you don't know that by now, I've married the wrong woman.' He grasped her hand, grinning. 'The porters will be in, keepers of all information. They're not supposed to pass on the Master's itinerary to anyone short of the police, but I bet you a kiss to a coffee that if I show my bruises and my wheelchair, they'll tell me when he's due back.'

It was hard not to follow him in this mood, whatever the lightning flashes of the stone. She hugged him, briefly. 'If you win, do I get the kiss or the coffee?'

'Both.' He pushed himself back into his chair. 'Race you to the porter's lodge?'

'Kit— No!' She grabbed for the handles. He was already gone. It was then she found out just how fast his wheelchair could go. He won the race.

For his bruises and his wheelchair and his repu-tation in the college, the porters did, indeed, give Kit all that they knew: that the Master was expected back to his rooms thirty minutes ago, but had not appeared. In default of his being there, they had no idea where he might be.

They offered coffee or tea and the chance to sit and catch up with college gossip. Kit was relaxed in their company, open and expansive and discussing the cave as if it were a heady adventure, and all he needed was a week or two's recuperation before he went back to repeat the descent.

Stella would have sat all night listening, had the skull allowed it. She held out as long as she could. When the shards of bright yellow panic became blinding, she reached out to tap the back of his wrist.

'What's up?'

She shook her head to clear it, and failed.

'There's something wrong, but I don't know what. It's something to do with us being here when we should be . . .' A certainty took her. She pushed herself upright. 'We need to go back to the river room. Now.'

Kit could not run. Stella left him in the care of the porters and ran ahead, goaded by the skull-stone in its pack on her back.

Sprinting out past the Tudor cloisters towards the river room, she saluted in passing the bronze statue of Edward III, skipped over the never-to-be-walked-on lawn and ducked under the archway to the Lancastrian Court that led to the stairs and finally to the landing outside Kit's room, where a dragon in painted glass faced an unarmoured swordsman by the light of a high half-moon.

In daylight, she had spent hours watching the rainbow patterns of light play across the image, picking out details from the intricacies of Tudor art. In the darkness of night, a single street lamp sent uncoloured light through the dragon and the risen moon to fall on the hallway, on the place where Christopher Marlowe had carved his name on the newel post.

Once, Kit had shown her how to trace the outline of that name with her fingers, for luck. There was no luck now. The electric-yellow crisis in her head had exploded into showering stars as she ran up the stairs. The broken lock and open door were unnecessary warnings;

she already knew what she would find.

Closing her eyes, she leaned on the door frame and waited for the sick taste in her mouth and the heart-crushing outrage at the wanton destruction of beauty and age to subside.

Kit, I'm so sorry . . .

'Stell?' Kit was beside her, alone; the porters were waiting below. His hand caught hers. 'What's he done?'

She opened her mouth and tried to speak, and failed. A light-headed pressure strained behind her eyes and in the veins at her neck.

'Stell?' Kit put his hand out to touch her and let it drop again. 'What?'

The skull-stone had fallen quiet, leaving her space to think.

She had always liked Kit's river room, and felt at home in it. It was hard to feel anything but rage and horror now. She stood in a chaos of opened drawers and spilled coffee beans and scattered papers. Kit's room, his shrine to neatness and precision, had been desecrated with a venom that frightened her easily as much as the silent menace of the hunter in the cave.

'He knows you,' she said. 'Only someone who knows you would do this.'

'And hates me,' Kit said. Stella heard the whine of his chair and reached out to catch his hand. Their clasp was wordless and said everything of sympathy and horror and the sharing of both.

She squeezed his hand and let it go. Small changes registered, and added together to make something bigger. 'He wasn't just looking for the stone,' she said. 'Your computer's gone and all the files. All this afternoon's work.'

Kit was white beneath the bruises. He turned his chair in a full circle. Woodenly, he said, 'The insurance will buy a new Powerbook.'

'What's the point if we've got nothing to put in it? The ledgers have gone, the code, the shorthand. Everything.'

Kit raised his one good brow. He managed half a smile. 'Sweetheart, you're talking to a computeroid. The machine backs itself up three times a day to the server in the library and once daily offsite. There are backups of everything. And backups of the backups. I can download the latest from the .mac site in the morning and we can take them with us to Oxford.' He glanced at her sideways. 'If we're still going?'

'Definitely.' She had control of the anger now, so that it no longer paralysed her, but instead rode over the swelling ocean of her fear. 'Tonight – this minute – we're going to call the police and see if they'll take us seriously now. Then tomorrow, we're going to Oxford and we're going to find out what the skull-stone's about. And when we know that, we're a step closer to finding who did this and making him sorry.'

*   *   *

The police were quietly efficient and did take them seriously. They found no fingerprints or any other clues as to the identity of the attacker. They sealed the room and waited while Kit called the porters and arranged for somewhere else to sleep. They offered sympathy and understanding and a number to call for counselling. They promised to contact the North Yorks force and tell them of the new development. They held out little hope of a resolution.

Only late in the night, lying together for the first time since the accident, did Stella begin to shake. They were on the single bed the porters had found for them in the visiting academics' accommodation. She had thought Kit asleep and only realized otherwise when he rolled over slowly and reached his one good hand for hers. 'Stell?'

'Mmm?'

'Gordon was right.'

'About what?'

'The skull has entered a part of your soul. You're not the woman I married.'

She held on to him, shuddering uncontrollably. The blue in her mind was the only part at peace.

'Is that a bad thing?' she asked.

'I don't know.' He pressed a kiss to the soft skin of her neck. 'You are beautiful when you're murderously angry. But I'm worried for you.'

'That cuts both ways. You're not the man I married, either. I can't begin to tell you how much that worries me.'

She felt the half-grin that was becoming almost normal. 'You don't have to tell me, it's written in thirty-six point bold across your forehead. But I'm only damaged physically and if I don't mend, it won't be the end of the world. I think for you it might be different.'

'I might find the end of the world?'

'You might find the end of your world, which would also be the end of mine. Will you make me another promise? Will you swear never to go anywhere you can't come back from?'

It was not so great a request. She held him, and was held back and kissed him and was kissed back and at the end of it, when the shaking had grown less consuming, she said, 'I swear I will not go anywhere I don't think I can come back from.'

It was not exactly what he had asked, but it was close and he was already half asleep. He pulled her to his chest and wound the fingers of his good hand in her hair and they fell asleep like that and it was only as she sank into the high, blameless blue of the dream that she saw the void between what he had asked of her and what she had promised and by then it was far too late to change it.

13

Zama, New Spain, October 1556

'IN THEIR IGNORANCE, MY CHILDREN BELIEVE that we are not the first of God's creations, but the fifth and final race to inhabit the earth. They make their ornaments in testament to this, such as the one you behold now. I have preserved it exactly as it was when I first made landfall here and took this, their temple, as my home. It is a poor place, but a palace compared to the homes of my flock, and cool now, in the heat of the day. If you would care to enter? Diego will serve you with what wine we have, unless you have brought your own . . . ? Thank you. I had thought you might.'

It was becoming apparent that while Father Gonzalez Calderón, priest to the natives of Zama, had the physique of a hired thug, it was wrapped around the mind and manners of a prelate. It was equally apparent that he had invited the captain of the *Aurora* and his physician into his home as a duty, not a pleasure. A great many images of the crucified Christ adorned the walls in all their many-fold agonies, but a single look at the spartan furnishings of the place confirmed that the father was not a man given to enjoying the delights of the flesh.

Nor, evidently, did he find de Aguilar's flamboyance amusing, which was unfortunate given that the Spaniard seemed to be in a particularly expansive frame of mind. He had begun to voice his enthusiasms as he tied off the bow rope of the *Aurora* and had barely stopped, until now, when he was crouched in the centre of the priest's house, which had once been a temple, examining a coloured mosaic that took up half the floor, uttering small exclamations of wonder and delight at what he beheld.

He was doing it as a distraction, drawing all possible interest and approbation away from his physician and on to himself, and successfully so. Owen watched the priest make a physical effort to look away from the fantastic vulgarity of de Aguilar's earrings and felt a stab of remorse for his own earlier, identical prejudice.

Still, if all that had been said of the priest was correct, there was a danger in the captain's exuberance and Owen did not want his friend to come to harm on his account. Seeking harmless conversation, he said, 'This building is not

218

painted red like all the others. Did you ask for it so?'

'Of course. I required it of Diego and Domingo when first I took this place as my own. They painted it with limewash made to my own recipe and have done so annually on that same date ever since.'

'But they continue to paint the remainder of the city in the colour of blood. Is it a reminder of human sacrifice, or—'

Owen spoke in all innocence, repeating only what all of Spain knew of the natives. He regretted it at once, so suddenly and catastrophically did the thunder blacken the priest's features.

Quietly, venomously, Calderón said, 'My children do not seek, and never have sought, the death of others in appeasement of their gods. They were untutored, but they were not barbarians, unlike their enemies to the north and west, the Culhua-Mexica, known to incomers as the Aztecs, who were so successfully subjugated in God's name by his lordship Cortés and whose gold now rests with his most elegant majesty of Spain.'

Twelve years at Cambridge had taught Owen that honest ignorance served best when confronted by the anger of men who like to know most. Tipping his head a little to one side, he asked, 'Then why have they chosen such a violent colour for their decorations?'

219

The priest favoured him with a graceless stare. The great silver cross surged on the prow of his chest.

'Being more thoughtful and less savage than their neighbours, the people of Zama have come upon the idea that if they paint their buildings blood red, they will seem as do the temples of the devil-worshipping barbarians whose steps are slick with human blood. By mimicking them in this way, my children hope to deter any attackers who may— Thank you, Diego. Please do come in.'

On the order, the scar-faced native – Owen did not believe that Diego was his birth-name – slid shadow-like through the grass screen that hung to fill the doorway, bearing on a tray three clay beakers and an opened bottle of wine.

The priest treated him as any lord might treat his servant: as an obdurate child, to be seen but not heard. Cedric Owen would have been glad to do likewise, but that the piercing eyes carved holes in his mind and made deafening the background song of the blue stone.

With an effort, he lifted his wine from the tray and fixed his attention once again on the priest. 'Does it work?' he asked. 'Painting the houses red?'

'I have been here nearly ten years and the only enemy we have fought has been the pox. Therefore we can conclude that it works,' said the priest, with glorious illogic. 'And now we must deliver your captain from his knees, for otherwise there will be no part of the floor free on which to place the table. Have you found the riddle of the mosaic yet, señor?'

'I regret not.' Fernandez de Aguilar stood with evident reluctance. His eyes flashed with an excitement that was only slightly exaggerated. Stepping a little back from the design on the floor, he said, 'I think perhaps I have the beginnings of it, but it is opaque to my mind. Señor Owen, will you bend your physician's logic to the puzzle on my behalf before our host divulges its secret?'

Thus, inattentively and with his mind set all awry by the unsettling gaze of the scarred native, did Cedric Owen come to stand before the image that changed for ever the trajectory of his life.

From a distance it had looked like a child's painting done in stone; a haphazard collection of pebbles, picked for the clarity of their colour and then arrayed in stick-figure images over an area of perhaps four square yards. Here, goggle-eyed men and fantastical beasts writhed in gross, overstated struggles, eyes aflame, teeth gnashing, limbs entwined in an eternity of conflict.

On closer inspection, the shapes proved to be more complex than they had seemed. In the centre a fire was laid out in red and yellow stones, prettily lifelike, with an encircling rim made of green leaves woven thinly. About the perimeter in a deep, wide band was a map of the heavens with the constellations and planets laid out in an array that promised great understanding if studied in depth.

In the middle, between fire and sky, stood the two futures of man, held in eternal balance. To the one side, conflict, war and misery stood depicted in fierce and warring figures. To the other stood the battle's antithesis, a summer meadow carpeted with coloured flowers too beautiful to name and too many to count. A child knelt in the centre of it, peaceful in the solitude.

Separating these two was the barest thread of a dividing line, an erratic rift of black and white tiles with a thread of fat, coloured pearls strung along it, in the seven colours of the rainbow, with black and white set together at the end.

From nowhere, Owen remembered an upstairs room in a lodging house in Paris, and the smell of roasted pigeons and almonds and a delicate voice.

The colours of the world are nine in total; the seven of the rainbow, plus the black of no-light and the white of all-light. To the blue was given the heart of the beast, and the power to call together the remaining twelve parts of its spirit and flesh.

It was then, swayed by the memory, that Owen made the mistake of looking up.

Scar-faced Diego stood in a corner of the room, an invisible shadow, armed with pitiless knife-eyes that flashed and flared as much as anything in the stone-painting.

Under their gaze, it was impossible not to see the truth laid out so plainly before him.

'My God . . .'

The image was not a child's drawing. For a single heart-stopping moment, it crystallized into something quite different.

'What do you see, my friend?'

Fernandez de Aguilar asked it quietly, with the same voice he had used on the ship's deck in the morning. He was no longer clowning. If the priest saw it, if he wondered at the change in the Spaniard and his English physician, if he planned their deaths by fire and rack as a result, neither of them cared.

The question freed Owen's tongue. He said, 'I see the moment before the world's end; the held breath before the onset of Armageddon. I see a map of the heavens that gives us the date and time exactly. And I see the means by which there may be hope to avert the ultimate evil.'

He looked up at the priest. In Europe, he would have burned at the stake for even this much indiscretion. Father Calderón's black eyes were reflective, but not yet vengeful. He lifted his silver cross and kissed it. 'Pray continue.'

Owen drew breath. 'I see first the sun, greatest light of all, shining down a long, dark

223

tunnel to the place from whence all matter is born. I see Venus, the Morning Star, in wide embrace to Mercury, the Messenger, and these two dance in opposition to Jupiter, the Golden Benefactor. I see Jupiter seated at the apex of a Finger of God, with Saturn, the Great Constraint, at one arm and—'

The words snagged in his throat. 'I see the planets and constellations set in a pattern that will not happen in my lifetime, nor in many yet to come.'

The scar-faced native was watching him still, but it was Father Gonzalez Calderón who said softly, 'This shape is not made in God's heaven for four hundred and fifty-six years. What is it that the stars and planets herald?'

Owen bent back to the wonder before him. 'The image shows a frozen moment in time, as if the world has been caught on the brink of disaster and there is but this single thread of hope to save it. To the west, we see the conflict of the final Desolation. Here, men fight against all of creation, each one consumed with greed, lust, avarice, the lack of care for others, the willingness to inflict pain on them – even to take pleasure in so doing – heedless of their plight and, in the end, to trample on all that exists. This is the force that will lead to the destruction not only of all that is good in the world of men, but of the world.'

'And is there no redemption?' asked the priest.

'There may be, for set against the horror is a place of peace.' Owen laid a hand on the southern quadrant. 'Here, in the east, a girl child kneels in a summer's meadow playing knucklebones, right hand against left. She is the epitome of Innocence, of the unstained human soul that might yet be saved, and so save the future of the world.'

'It is a girl, not a boy?'

'I believe so.'

'And therefore not the young Christ. A mistake, clearly. We will change that, one day, perhaps.'

The priest held his hands clasped about the silver cross. The straight end emerged from between his steepled fingers as a pointer. He jabbed it at the image, once to each direction. 'You have spoken only of the background. What can you say about the four beasts who make the greater part of the image?'

'Ah . . .' What could he say of such things? Owen had not seen them at first, such was the wonder of the mosaic, where images hid within others. Only under the scarred native's stare had their outlines begun to shine. Now, the four beasts dazzled him, in all their might and wonder. Here was the animation, the power, the light to brighten the darkest of worlds. The words came to Owen slowly, striving to encompass the wonder he saw.

'I spoke of a thread of hope in the picture

and, in truth, the greater part of the mosaic is given over to the manifestation of that hope. Here we have four beasts, joined and yet not joined. Up here in the north-east corner is a spotted lion, a hunter to exceed all others, of sleek pelt and bright eyes. Next, in the south-east, is a serpent, long as a ship and thick as a man's waist, banded in emerald and ruby. Opposite these two an eagle sits to the north-west, its wings as wide as this house and its talons fit to lift a wolf, its eyes of sharp gold. Last, in the south-western corner sits a lizard large as a horse, with teeth that could tear a man in half. When these four join together . . .'

Even as he spoke, the beasts erupted from the mosaic; flat stone could not contain their might. They met, all four together in volcanic concatenation of flesh. Limbs entwined with wings, heads with hearts, talons and tails together.

For one luminous, heartbreaking moment, the four became one, to make a beast that was infinitely greater than all apart.

It was too bright. Owen closed his eyes against the blinding light. When he opened them again, the earth-serpent was gone, and all sign of the beasts that had made it.

The mosaic was a child's drawing again. Dizzily, Owen knelt in the band of the star map, taking care not to touch the greater picture, and ran the flat of his palm across the thread of coloured stones, half expecting shards of lightning to flash into his fingers, or a song to emerge from his blue stone.

On both counts, he was disappointed; what life there had been in the image was gone. He risked a look to the shadows beyond the priest and was not surprised to see that the scar-faced native was no longer there. Where he had been, a single bright green feather lay on the floor, pointing in, towards the fire at the heart of the mosaic.

Owen stood, feeling light-headed and a little foolish. De Aguilar was studying him in silence, his gaze sharper than Owen had ever seen it. A shadow crossed them both, breaking the intensity of the moment. Father Calderón stood in the doorway, his ox-bulk blocking both entrance and exit. His arms were folded across his chest as they had been on the pier.

'Are we to die, Father?' asked de Aguilar quietly.

'Possibly, but not at my hand. Not yet. Perhaps not ever. Father Bernardino de Saguin commends us, his children, to know the ways of the natives that we might better teach them the clear path to Christ. I have lived in Zama nearly seven years and in this house for four of those and yet I have only lately come to perceive what your ship's physician has so clearly seen at first sighting.

'With my greater knowledge, I can tell you that the spotted beast is not a lion but a jaguar, which is sacred to my children, the Maya, as are the three other beasts: the eagle, which represents the air, the serpent, which is fire, and the crocodile, which is water. The jaguar, of course, holds power over the earth. They are taught that at the End of Days, which you so clearly divined in their stone painting, these four will come together to form one beast. Can you imagine, sir, what might arise out of the union of these four?'

The presence of Nostradamus cooled the shining light in Owen's mind that he might speak calmly of what he had seen. 'Plato named it the Ouroboros,' he said. 'The many-coloured serpent which encircles the earth in endless compassion and swallows its own tail that it might never be separated. In my land, we would know it rather as a dragon or a wyvern, a beast with the body and claws of a jaguar, the head of a crocodile, the tail of a serpent and the wings and grace of an eagle. I was sent here to find how these four might join to make one, and now, having seen it, I cannot remember.'

'It would arise, perhaps, like the Phoenix, from the flames of the fire?' asked de Aguilar. A glance from Owen showed that he was not making fun of him.

'Indeed.' The priest smiled thinly. 'Or our Lord might simply call it to His hand. Such things are not for us to know, although we may praise their happening. In the lands of my children, the four-in-one is the feathered or rainbow serpent known as Kukulkan, or also Quetzalcoatl, a beast which would make a fitting mount for Christ, were He to return to save us from our own ruin.'

The priest bowed to each of them fluidly, and stepped aside from his own doorway. 'And now I have committed easily as great a heresy as yours, and we are in each other's debt. It will make for an easier evening, I believe, which is as well, for here is Domingo with our meal. The staple here is beans served with hot peppers and chillies. It will seem to you very pungent after the rude fare of the sea. Be assured that if you take to it well, all food will seem bland afterwards by comparison. In the meantime, it may help if you drink water as you eat.'

14

Zama, New Spain, October 1556

'THIS, MY FRIEND, IS THE GREEN GOLD THAT will make us the richest men in Europe, and our children and grandchildren after us.'

Fernandez de Aguilar squatted on his heels in the dust and grit of a barren landscape. A mule stood behind him, flapping its ears and flicking its tail at the insects. It had been a gift, or at least a loan, from Gonzalez Calderón, along with its saddle, bridle, and breast strap, all in local-made leather, with silver buttons at the junctions and a small image of the crucified Christ at the mid-point of the breast.

Cedric Owen leaned over and studied the plant that had taken his companion's eye. It looked no different from any of the others that grew in the arid desert around him: a fistful of long, leathery, sword-blade leaves sprouted from a thickened husk of a stem. It was small, too; this one grew no higher than a man's knee although some of those around grew to head height, so that to walk among them was to risk losing an eye on the sword-pointed leaves. The whole thing seemed designed to be inedible by man, beast or insect.

Cedric Owen took the opportunity to dismount and stood in the shade cast by his gift-mule. The flies were fewer here than in the city, but the dust more. He sat down on a flat rock with his back to the high, hot sun and skipped a pebble across the desert. He tried to imagine being rich, and failed.

'How?' he asked. Heat was teaching him an economy of language that Cambridge had never done.

De Aguilar was in expansive mood again. His arm swept the horizon. 'Do you see anything else growing here?'

Owen made a show of scanning the stretching landscape. For a long, long way in every direction, he could see rock and dust in profusion. Dotted here and there were the sword-plants of which de Aguilar was so enamoured. 'Very little,' he said drily.

'That's because you don't have great vision or great breeding. Fortunately, I have both.'

Grinning, the Spaniard stood up, sweeping the dust extravagantly from his legs with the brim of his hat.

'For most of his life, my great-uncle believed that his sojourn here in New Spain brought

231

more pain than it was worth; that the savages would never allow us to live here in peace and the earth yielded nothing more than dust, peppers, and the chillies the priest fed us last night that so offended your tongue. There is no silver to speak of and little gold; all the bullion is to the south or deep inland in the stores of the Aztecs, and Cortés has taken most of it. The art is beautiful, but it's painted on the walls or carved on the stones and, in any case, it's idolatry and the Church will destroy it all as soon as they are sure there is nothing they want to learn from it. Every member of my family has taken my great-uncle's opinion to heart and none has ever set sail away from Seville.'

'Except you,' said Owen. 'Why?'

'Because I listened to the letters and I saw the things my ancestor did not when he spoke of the sword-leaved plants that grow in the desert. There are two kinds of these plants, my friend. One can be distilled to a kind of spirit-drink more potent than the best of brandies; one beaker could leave a man insensate and two would make him wish he had never been born. The other kind is used by the natives to make a type of rope, like hemp. Cortés used this on his ships as he sailed home.'

De Aguilar went to his mule and lifted from it the coiled rope that hung across the pommel.

'This is what can be made with this plant. They call it sisal. Here, feel . . .'

It was rope. Cedric Owen was not equipped to tell one from another. He passed it between his fingers and said, 'Is it good?'

'The best. Sisal is better than hemp in every way, stronger, coarser, hardier, more fit for the needs of the ocean-going boats than anything we produce in Europe. We will grow this plant in the way the natives grow their beans and we will make ropes to fit the navies of all Christendom and beyond. We will be the richest men in Europe, trust me. Look to my birth stars and tell me I am not bound for greatness.'

Only a very confident man tempted fate with such hubris. In truth, de Aguilar's chart was, indeed, one of brilliance, marred by a single hard square from Mercury to Jupiter, on the cusp of the third house. His sun/Venus conjunction rising in Aries less than one degree above the ascendant saved that square from misery.

The natives knew something about astrology. Owen had already found that they referred to Venus in the male form and dubbed it the Morning Star, calling it a warrior. Had there been time, he would have asked their opinion of its position in Fernandez' chart. Lacking that, he had only his classical instruction, as taught by Dr Dee and Nostradamus, by whose lights it was reckoned to lead to recklessness, and possibly greatness, if impulsion could be harnessed.

None of which Owen had ever spoken aloud,

233

nor did he intend to. He lay back against his rock and pulled his hat over his eyes, shutting out the sun and the sky and the distant, disconcerting redness of the city.

'Fernandez, I trust you with my life, but perhaps not with my money. To grow these plants in quantities such as you dream of would need torrents of water and there is none here. I walked round the fields outside the town this morning while you were unloading the ship. The people have barely enough to keep their peppers from shrivelling on the stalk.'

'No, my friend, this is because they do not have my great-uncle as their adviser. He had travelled the whole land in his time as a slave to the natives and he told me things that even they have forgotten – that in the inner lands, where the cities are overgrown with jungle, or on the edges of this barren plain, the natives of old chose the sites of their cities for the great underground reservoirs that exist naturally here. The land has chalk beneath and it forms aquifers that hold the water. He never put these two facts – the water and the rope plants – together; nor did any of my family.'

The rock was warm, but not overly hot. Owen stretched his full length lazily along it, ironing out the kinks in his back.

Presently, he said, 'That sounds good. You can use the water to irrigate the plants and then if we can get Father Gonzalez who is half native by now to organize a monopoly on the rope trade for all of New Spain, you'll be able to—'

'*Cedric!* Don't move!'

It was the first time in the entirety of their acquaintance that de Aguilar had used his Christian name. Frozen, Owen lay staring up into the crown of his hat. Sweat flowed freely across his temples and soaked his shirt so suddenly that the cool of it swamped his chest.

'What?'

Evenly, Fernandez said, 'There's a snake behind the rock. One of the ones Father Gonzalez told us of last night, that is most dangerous, with the red bands on yellow with black between. It hasn't seen you yet. If you can stay still a while longer, I will kill it with my sword . . . don't breathe, my English friend, and you will be fine. It is so good that my arm is healed because I can use my sword . . . and you can lie still while I . . . bring my blade from its sheath and position it . . . so . . . and then I will— Ah! *No!*'

'Fernandez!' Owen sprang to his feet and spun round.

Red on yellow will kill a fellow. The night before, as they retired for bed, the priest had warned them of such snakes, even making a ditty in English that they might remember it better.

Owen had mocked him for it in private afterwards. He regretted that now. He regretted a great many things, most of all his choice of place to sit, and his appalling inattention. The snake was coral red banded on stripes of yellow with black at intervals between. Thrashing viciously, it hung by its teeth from the snowy white linen of the Spaniard's shirt cuff, which had been pushed lazily halfway up his once-broken arm. Small speckles of scarlet blood scattered about it, fat as rowan berries; its teeth had punctured living flesh as well as linen.

De Aguilar stood rigidly still with his eyes white all round the rims. His sword dropped from his fingers, noisily.

The snake's venom stops a man's muscles from working – first his speech slurs and then he cannot eat. In time, he can neither walk nor stand and then his chest ceases to move and his heart stops. It is inexorable. The only way to stop it is to remove the limb. Few men live through that. Ah, thank you, Diego. If you care to clear the plates, we will take port outside in the cool of the evening . . .

Owen grabbed a blade and, this once, the voice of his fencing master did not sound in his head to tell him no.

With no thought for his own safety, he swept the borrowed sword high and sliced it down again, so close to de Aguilar's arm that he removed half of the white linen sleeve.

More important, his sweep cut clean across the head of the snake, severing it. The body fell to the ground, writhing and pumping thin, dark blood. The front part of the head, with the teeth and all the venom they contained, remained fixed to de Aguilar's wrist below the light linen bandage that still covered his earlier wound.

'Fernandez? Will you sit, please? I can't take it out if you stand. I need to work with your arm low, like taking out an arrow-head. Please sit.'

Like a puppetmaster manipulating a doll made of wood and horse-sinew, he manoeuvred de Aguilar to sit on the rock. Using his eating-knife as a scalpel, and with a strip of torn linen as a tourniquet, he set about employing the battlefield skills whose descriptions he had read in Nostradamus' books and had never thought he would use.

The snake had ground its teeth deep into the flesh of the Spaniard's forearm. Owen had to disarticulate the mandible to remove it, driving the knife's point into the pinch of skin below the dead eye and wriggling it up and down to separate the upper and lower jaws. They came apart slowly and with much swearing on his part.

De Aguilar sat through it white-faced. At the end, he looked down to the four deep puncture marks in his arm.

'I am dead.' He said it without sentiment. His eyes were bright and level. His skin was a greenish white, with yellow at the corners of his mouth. 'We should go back to Zama. There is much to be arranged if I am not to captain the *Aurora* on her voyage home. If Father Gonzalez is correct in his prescription of the poison, I have half a day in which I might function as a whole man, and I would not waste it. Juan-Cruz will be a serviceable captain for daily running of the ship, but he has not the vision to make her great. You could do it, but I think your stone will not let you leave yet, and the ship should go swiftly, while the men still have heart . . . We can decide later. For now . . .' He stood up. 'Perhaps you could help me mount. I have a day's life left in me. Tomorrow . . .' He drifted to silence. His gaze rested on the sea beyond the limestone bluffs. 'I should like to see that dawn again. They say that from the lighthouse tower one can see the edge of the world on a clear day, and that all days here are clear. Will you sit through this last dawn with me, Cedric Owen?'

'No.' Owen was weeping, a thing he had not done since the blue stone became his at the age of thirteen. He kicked the limp body of the snake back to the other side of the rock and dragged de Aguilar's unwilling mule closer.

Hoarsely, he said, 'It will not be your last dawn. Father Gonzalez said amputation could save your life.'

'But he also said that this was hypothesis and that none had ever survived it.'

238

'So say the natives. They are not physicians trained in Cambridge.'

'And you, as you have often told me, are not a surgeon.' It was said gently, without rancour, as an elder brother might chide a youth for an excess of zeal.

Owen cursed again. 'You don't understand. Nostradamus made me read his books. He had me spend ten days of the princess of France's mourning sitting in his festering bloody inn reading books on surgery and answering his questions on things I had never considered and did not think I would need to know. He made me take notes, which I carry with me. He foresaw this, and did not tell me that it would break my heart. Therefore I will perform the surgery and you will not die.'

'But, Cedric, with all due respect . . .'

'Don't. Just don't . . . Just get on your mule now and come back with me. You may lose your sword arm, but I will not let you lose your life. Not when you are about to make me one of the two richest men in Europe.'

15

Law Forensic Laboratory, Oxford,
June 2007

STELLA WALKED ALONE THROUGH A CORRIDOR
of white tiles and concrete, through doors of
brushed aluminium, to a laboratory of steel
tables and glass cabinets that smelled of
chemistry and cigarette smoke and death.

Dr David Law met her at the door. He did not
look as bad as Kit had described, but the root of
it was there, enough to build the caricature. She
faced a small, wiry man with straggling, mouse-
tail hair and chisel teeth that pushed his upper lip
from his face. They were English teeth, stained
brown by years of tea and tobacco so that when
he smiled his breath preceded him into the
corridor.

'Dr Cody.' He wiped his hand on his white
coat and thrust it out. 'Professor Fraser called
to say you were on your way. Any friend of
Gordon's is welcome to my time.'

His grip was firmer than Stella had expected, with an impression of underlying strength that made five years spent exhuming Kurdish mass graves seem more plausible. Had she remained in any doubt, the photographic evidence hung on the walls; frame after frame of clean-picked bones in pits, in rows, in ordered and numbered alignments, all with fragments of hair or clothing or small bits of precious metal hooked over fleshless limbs or protruding from empty eye sockets.

Davy Law was somewhere in most of them, dressed in cut-off jeans and a dusty T-shirt with a cigarette hanging from lip or fingers. He looked more at home in the arid mountains than he did in an Oxfordshire lab.

He saw her looking. 'It isn't pretty work, but someone has to do it.' His eyes drifted past her to the corridor. 'Kit isn't with you?'

'He's asleep in the car,' she said. It was true, and sounded like an excuse.

'Right.' His too-thin lips tightened as he held open the door of his lab. His eyes glanced over hers without meeting. Walking away from her, he said, 'Gordon told me you had a skull and needed to build the face from it?'

He turned to look pointedly at her backpack. The blue skull-stone slept in it, silently. Since the warning of Kit's room, it had been quiet. She reached for it now, and felt nothing, no instinct to go or to stay. Gone, too, was the image of a face that had led her here. She stared at the floor, trapped in an unexpected uncertainty.

She followed him in, not speaking. He reached a glass-fronted cabinet on the far side of the room, a smaller version of the hyperbaric acid bath in the geology lab. She said, 'It's not a bone skull. It's carved out of stone. Gordon thought we could trust you to keep it private.'

'Did he? How touching.'

Leaning one shoulder on the wall, Davy Law rolled, and then lit, a cigarette. Blue smoke flavoured the air between them. Whatever had unsettled him earlier was gone, replaced by an acid, uncompromising stare that looked through her and past her but did not acknowledge her presence.

It was easy to imagine how this man might push against the boundaries of authority until he, or they, broke. She was beginning to understand both why Gordon had trusted him, and why Kit had loathed him.

Stella slid the backpack off her shoulders and unzipped it. Without ceremony, she lifted the blue skull-stone into the harsh lights of his lab. It no longer screamed at her, no shards of yellow lightning stabbed through her brain; they had gone as soon as she had walked into Kit's river room. It was peaceful now, watchfully alert so that all her senses were sharpened.

She held it out, letting its blue cast lighten the

clinical cold of his room. 'We found this,' she said. 'There was a cipher in Cedric Owen's ledgers that led to it.'

She was expecting a short moment of shock, of a breath taken in and let out again slowly, at first sight of the stone. She did not expect the surge of rage, or grief, or pain – she could not tell which – that warped Davy Law's gargoyle features as his eyes flicked between the stone and her face, nor the astonishing burst of feral lust that had flashed ahead of it.

'Dr Law?'

'*Keep away!*'

He flung himself away from her, to the far side of the room, and slid down the wall to sit on his heels with his knees to his chest, wrapping his arms about himself, shuddering. For a long moment, the only sound was the rasp of his breath, sawing the air.

'Should I leave?' Stella asked eventually.

'Probably.'

He stared a long time at the floor. When it was past the time for her to speak, or to leave, he dragged his stricken, bloodshot gaze up the length of her body, to rest for a blink on her face.

'But you stayed. Thank you.' He gave a small, tight smile. 'Who else has seen this?'

'Besides me and Kit? Only Gordon. Tony didn't want to look. He said it carried the blood of too many people he respected.'

'How did Gordon . . . Did he say how he felt?'

She remembered the hoarse quiet of the Scotsman's voice in that first phone call. *Your wee stone's ready. I hope you are.* And then later, *It's too beautiful. It's just asking to be picked up* . . .

'He thought I should crush it to powder with his pile driver. He offered to help.'

'Wise man.' Law's smile was broader now, full of acid irony. 'He wouldn't tell me what it was you were bringing. There's not many could keep a secret like this to himself.'

'He's a good friend.'

'Which is worth a lot, in this world of the friendless.'

Law's cigarette was gone, lost in his flight. With shaking hands, he rolled himself another and lit it, staring at the redly glowing end. 'This is Cedric Owen's blue heart-stone, yes?'

'We think so.'

For the first time, he looked at her full in the face. 'Men have killed for this, Stella. They killed Cedric Owen, and his grandmother and everyone else who held it, back up the line of his ancestors.' He pursed his lips, staring at her. 'Were you followed, coming here?'

'I don't think so. I'm not sure I'd know.'

'Stella!' He was angry with her, and did not know if he was allowed to show it. He bit on his cigarette. 'Tell me you understand the danger you're in?'

'Am I in danger from you?'

'No.' He could laugh now, and did so, coughing at the end. 'Not now. I've seen beauty and grabbed for it once in my life. I'm not going to make the same mistake twice.'

There was an edge in his voice, just as there had been in Kit's. Carefully, she said, 'Is this the reason Kit and you fell out?'

He began to answer honestly, and bit it back before the words were out. He shrugged, loosely. 'He's your husband. I can't answer for him.'

'But he was a friend of yours? A good friend?'

'Once. Not now.'

His bloodshot eyes were hard, but they did not flinch from hers. After a while, he looked round at the pictures on the wall behind her, and on both sides.

'Everywhere in the world, there are men who see something they want and think they can take it and that the cost to others doesn't matter. Always, it's the men who take and the women and children who pay.'

'That's a particularly sexist viewpoint, Dr Law.'

'Maybe, but I haven't excavated a mass grave yet where the killing was done by a woman. I promise you it'll be front-page news if I ever do.'

He was more in control of himself now, on well-trodden ground. He leaned back against the wall and blew smoke into the air between them. He looked directly at the stone for the first time since Stella had lifted it from her backpack.

'Your skull carries the heart of the world. What man would not kill to own that? Here, in one handful of blue crystal, is everything we ever wanted: splendour and nobility and passion all in one. It *aches* to be taken, to be owned, to be possessed, so that only the strongest of men, or the most broken, could turn away from it. The rabbits amongst us want to destroy it, to crush what they can't control. The wolves want to own it, to take into themselves all that it carries, not seeing that they can't ever do that. And then, perhaps, if it's what I think it is, there are the very, very few, who know what the skull can do, and want to stop that *and* take ownership. Francis Walsingham was one of these: Elizabeth's spymaster. There have been others down the centuries. There will be one or two around now, for sure.'

'What can it do? What is it they want to stop?' Her skin was raw with listening, her throat dry.

'I'm not sure yet. I may be wrong.' His cigarette was a horizontal column of ash. He tapped it into an empty coffee mug and crossed his arms across his chest. 'Does it speak to you?'

No one had asked her that, not even Kit. 'It

. . . sings. And I feel things from it: a need for care, an equal care for me.'

'Care?'

'Love, then.' She smiled weakly. 'But not only that. It has . . .' she struggled for words, 'an awareness I don't have, as if it can see the world in ways I never will, with senses I don't have. With it there, I can see more clearly, hear things beyond normal hearing, feel the scrape of my clothes. It's like being newborn and old at the same time. And the stone is like that, there's a truly ancient wisdom there, like a Buddhist statue carved into a hillside, that has life we can't see. At the same time, it's a lamb newly born that's lost its mother and I'm all it's got.' She pressed her fingers to her face. 'Why me? I haven't a clue how to take care of it.'

'But you have no choice.' Davy Law smiled sadly. 'You're the rightful keeper, just as Cedric Owen was. The rest of us, who might like to be, but are not, have to accept that.'

'I thought you said you didn't want to own it?'

Law laughed at that, softly. 'I did once, but not now. I think, of all the men on the earth, I am no longer a threat. A young woman called Jessica Warren taught me more than I can ever thank her for.'

He pushed himself upright at last. Standing, he was more professional. His eyes flickered from Stella to the skull-stone and back again, twice. 'It's modelled on a Caucasian woman,' he said. 'Did you want to know more than that?'

'If I can. I keep seeing a face – half seeing it – I think it matters to see it properly. If you can make that happen.'

'And then?' He had no trouble meeting her gaze now.

'And then I might be a step closer to understanding why this is worth killing for and who is trying to destroy our lives.'

'And?'

He understood what she had not said. For no better reason than that, she trusted him. 'And I'll have a face to put to the things that are happening in my head.'

'Fine.' Davy Law pinched his cigarette out and dropped it carefully into the breast pocket of his lab coat. 'Let's build ourselves a face and see if you like what it tells you.'

For the second time in two days, the skull-stone sat on a small plinth in a cabinet with lights shining in from different angles. Here, the background illumination was less bright than it had been in Gordon Fraser's geology lab and the work was done not by acid projected under pressure, but by pencil-thin lines of red light that streamed in from all possible angles in all possible planes.

In goggles and thin gloves, Davy Law puffed in streams of dry ice from a hand-held probe to make them visible and ensure their positioning.

To Stella, over his shoulder, he said, 'It's all done with lasers. The scan takes half an hour, though most of that's getting the settings right. It might be longer given the nature of the quartz. I've only ever worked with bone before; I'm not sure what translucency will do to the refraction indices. Kit could write us some new software in minutes to get round it. In his absence, we have to hope that the existing software will cope with the difference. We'll know soon enough.'

He screwed shut the door to the tank and took off the goggles. 'The screen's on my desk next door. I have an espresso machine. It's not quite Starbucks, but it's drinkable. Or you could go and sit in the car.'

It was neither an offer nor a request, just a statement, made without weight. Stella found she was beginning to enjoy Davy Law's quiet refusal to play the social game.

'Coffee would be fine,' she said.

He smiled, baring his appalling teeth. 'Thank you.'

He was right; the coffee wasn't Starbucks, for which she was grateful. The smell of roast beans mingled with the residues of old tobacco and came close to swamping the stench of formaldehyde.

Davy Law's office was small, with barely

room for two chairs and a desk with two over-sized computer screens and a phone. On the walls was more evidence of massacres, not all of them Turkish; Bosnia filled half of the side adjacent to the door, with the rest given to Rwanda, Darfur, and a single bulldozed site from Iraq.

Coffee in hand, Stella stood at the last, looking at the bones. 'Some of these skeletons have fractures that have begun to heal.'

'Gordon didn't say you were a medic?'

'I'm not, I'm an astronomer. If we're going to split hairs, I'm an astro-physicist. But I know enough of basic pathology to see when there's a callus forming over a break.'

From his seat behind the computer, Davy Law lit a new cigarette. The smoke was sweet and treacly and tickled the back of her throat. He picked a freckle of tobacco from his tongue and said, 'There's a lot of anger in Iraq. Some people take a long time to die.'

She held his gaze, which surprised both of them. He was the first one to look away. She said, 'Should I not have asked?'

'I don't care, as long as you can handle the answer.'

'Will it be the same when I see the face of the skull-stone?'

'Possibly.'

'But you know what it looks like?'

He tilted his chair right back and looped his

fingers behind his head and was silent so long, looking at her, that she thought he was not going to answer. Eventually, he said, 'I might be wrong.'

Before she could ask more, he tipped his chair forward and reached for his computer. 'But I don't think I am. Skulls are my obsession. And since we're both going to wait a while to find out what face we can build, there might be something to be discovered in exploring some of the more interesting skull legends from around the world. What do you know about the Mayan prophecies of 2012?'

Of all things, she had not expected that. She brought her coffee to his desk and sat down.

'I got half a million hits on Google yesterday when I searched under "Mayan" and "skull". Most of them had 2012 in the title. There wasn't one that made sense.'

Law raised his rat's-tail brow. 'Cultural imperialism has a lot to answer for.'

He blew her a thread of smoke and turned his attention to the screen in front of him, cutting her off as if she were not there.

Stella studied the remaining screen. The skull-stone revolved on it clockwise, no longer blue, but digitally converted to a solid grey set against a pale background and criss-crossed by a thousand tangential lines in shades that ranged from bright, arterial red through magenta to a range of vibrant greens and yellows.

Between these, slowly, the matt grey surface changed as flesh grew between the coloured hair lines.

Thinking aloud, she said, 'The red cross-hairs show a concave surface and the yellow ones are convex, right?'

'And the green is neutral. Right.' Law came to lean on the back of her chair, blowing smoke over her shoulder. He watched the screen a moment and said, 'It takes most people half a day to work that out. If you can guess who it's going to be, you can have a job.'

'Female? Caucasian? Around at the time of Cedric Owen?' Flattered, Stella snatched a name from history. 'Queen Elizabeth the First?'

He grinned wide, like a fox. 'Nice try.'

'I don't get the job?'

He shook his head. 'Sorry. The skulls were made at least three thousand years before Elizabeth was born. It doesn't mean it can't look like her, of course; faces come down the generations with remarkable accuracy, but Henry the Eighth's children all had high domed foreheads and almost no brows and narrow chins. It isn't her.'

'Skulls?' Stella spun her chair round. 'You said, "The *skulls* were made . . ." Plural. Are there others?'

'Allegedly.'

'How do you know?'

'I did a degree in anthropology after I

252

screwed up my medical career. It leads to strange places.'

'To an obsession with skulls?'

'That was always there.'

'What a fascinating childhood you must have had.' She looked back at the image on the screen. The face was barely human; a paste of blurred features against a blank blue background. She could no more have defined the shape of the chin than the colour of the eyes, which were not there.

Law had moved back to his seat in front of the other screen. He put his hand on the top, ready to turn it for her to see. His eyes were brown and sharp and quite serious. 'You could still walk away,' he said. 'It may be easier.'

His change of mood caught her off balance. 'David, someone tried to kill Kit in the cave where we found the stone. Someone else – or maybe the same person – trashed his room last night in a blatant act of intimidation. I can't walk away. Whatever you said about this being the most dangerous thing on the planet, I'm not ready to get out the hammer yet.'

'Davy,' he said absently. 'Not David; Davy. And don't give up on the hammer too soon. When your life's at stake, it's always good to have an exit strategy.'

He finished his coffee and his cigarette simultaneously and swung his chair round. 'Tell me what you make of this.'

The screen tilted towards her. She expected mandalas, or Mayan gods, or the other skulls. What she saw instead were Mayan glyphs, row after row of incomprehensible script, exactly as she had found in the ledger.

She leaned forward, both hands flat on his desk. 'Where did you get these?'

'From the web. There's a site where you can download them as a jpg.' Davy Law twisted his chair to see Stella and the screen equally.

'That's the Dresden Codex, one of the sacred texts of the Maya. Of the thousands they wrote, over hundreds of years, only four survived the spiritual vandalism of the Jesuits. This one ended up in the Sächsische Landesbibliothek in Dresden where it lay gathering dust until 1880 before someone finally understood what it said. Of course they could have asked the natives but by then almost everyone who could read the script was dead and so it's named after the place in which it was translated rather than anything to do with the people who wrote it.'

'Cultural imperialism again?'

'I'd say so. There are three others the same: Madrid, Paris and Grolier, although the last one may be a fake. They are the surviving remnants of a civilization that makes ours look infantile. And according to this document, the world is going to end on the twenty-first of December 2012.'

'Very funny.' There was a strange metallic

taste in her mouth. Stella spun her chair away from him.

He caught the armrest and spun her back. 'Listen to me. This isn't a joke. The Codex is the product of a civilization that could map out the planets with an accuracy that would make NASA green with envy.'

'I'm an astronomer. Don't try to blind me with science.' She hadn't mean to snap, but she did not take it back.

'Stella, I'm trying to open your eyes. Look—'

Stabbing at the keys, he opened other pages. Block upon block of glyphs flowed across the screen.

With an unexpected animation, he said, 'You're an astronomer; *listen*. The whole of the Dresden Codex is a table of Venus and Mars progressions as accurate as anything that can be done today. It's the foundations of the Mayan calendar, which makes ours look like Noddy goes to Toytown. Back in Cedric Owen's time, while we were still pissing about in the transition from Julian to Gregorian calendars, trying to find a system that didn't leave us with Christmas in midsummer, the Maya had already lived for a thousand years with a calendric system that could predict a lunar eclipse to the nearest 0.0007 of a *second* for eight millennia either way. When were we ever able to do that? Last year? Maybe eighteen months ago if we were lucky?'

'We could do it by the year 2000, easily.' Stella sat back and poured herself more coffee. 'What has this got to do with infantile Armageddon prophecies?'

Without her seeing, he had rolled and lit another cigarette. He glared at her through a haze of smoke.

'The Dresden Codex is the key to Mayan cosmology. They divided time into ages of 5,125 years each. We are living in the fifth age. According to their legends, each of the previous four ended in a cataclysm that destroyed the nascent races of men: fire, earthquake, storm, or, in the case of the last one, a flood.'

'Are you quoting scripture at me?'

'Not particularly. There are one hundred and thirty-seven culturally separate flood legends besides the one where the animals go in two by two; every civilization currently on the planet remembers that they were born out of flood water. The Maya, however, are the only ones who left us with a timetable for the next disaster. The end of the fifth age won't be like the others. It's not just the end of an age, it's the end of an era, as defined by the precession of the equinoxes. An era lasts about twenty-six thousand years and each one begins and ends when the sun lies over the Galactic Centre at twenty-eight degrees of Sagittarius, a place named by the Maya *Xibalba be*, the Road to the Underworld. When the sun walks along that path, we are finished; we'll see catastrophe on a grand scale. Nothing so small as a flood or a fire; this is complete annihilation – Armageddon, as you called it – and it will be caused by man, not by nature as were the others. This is the date that was mined out of the translations of the Dresden Codex. In the Mayan calendar it's 13 Baktun, 13.0.0.0.0.'

Davy Law wet his finger in the dregs of his coffee and drew it on the table. 'In our calendar, that's 21 December 2012.'

He stabbed out his cigarette and threw his hands behind his head and stared at her, unblinking.

Stella drank her coffee. After a while she said, 'What's it going to be? Global warming? Eco-catastrophe? Nuclear annihilation?'

'All of the above, I should think. The Maya destroyed themselves in the space of about fifty years; an entire culture wiped out by a mix of warfare and overuse of local resources. We're doing exactly the same on a planetary scale. The end result will be no different.'

'I don't see what this has got to do with the skulls.'

'Because according to the legends, the Maya – or more accurately their predecessors at the end of the fourth age, around the third millennium BC – made a group of thirteen crystal skulls which, when brought together, will help us find a path out of this catastrophe of our own making. You have one of those skulls.'

'The skulls will stop Armageddon?' She was incredulous.

'They won't stop it, they'll find us a way through. A gateway, if you like.'

'Do you actually believe this?' She stared at him, wide-eyed and disbelieving, far beyond the bounds of normal decency.

He did not smile, only shrugged and tapped again at his keyboard, to no obvious effect. 'I'm telling you what's in the old texts. The people who wrote them believed it.'

'Don't dodge the question, Davy.'

He turned his chair away from the desk and lifted one shoulder in half an apology. 'Yes, I believe it. These people knew things that we lost a long time ago when we took a wrong turning. I'm not the only one. There are a lot of other folk out there who think the same.'

'Oh, for God's sake.' She was out of the chair, pacing the length of the small room, stabbing the air for emphasis. 'There are plenty of others who believe in the second coming of Christ, the nightly perambulations of the Tooth Fairy, and that Saddam Hussein had weapons of mass destruction hidden in the Iraqi desert. They're all equally mad. What happened to realism? To evidence-based science? You're a medic, for God's sake. You deal in flesh and blood and bone, not this kind of . . . inane transcendental crap.'

She ran to a halt in front of a picture of Bosnia. Skulls lay in a neat row behind the grimly smiling figure of Davy Law. She closed her eyes and they did not go away.

From behind her, he said quietly, 'A failed medic. I didn't complete my clinical training.'

The anger left, as fast as it had come. She sat again in the chair opposite him. 'Sorry.'

'Don't be. It doesn't matter. Stella, what brought you to me?' He was not joking now. His hard eyes held her.

'I wanted to see the face of the skull.'

'You were already seeing it, that's why you came, remember? *I keep seeing a face.* Your words. And it sings to you. You *hear* a stone in your head. Tell me that's inane transcendental crap?'

She said nothing; she could think of nothing to say. He leaned forward and gripped the arms of her chair. His face was two inches away.

'What else? If the skull-stone brought you to me, is that the only thing it's done? Is there nothing else that makes it more than just a pretty lump of rock that men will fight over?'

She stared past him to the computer screen. The glyphs blurred and ran together and still made no sense.

Dully, she said, 'The skull warned me of danger in the cave; it's why Kit and I separated, why he was pushed off the ledge when I was not. Last night, it warned me of what was happening in Kit's room, I just didn't understand in time. And . . . there's a cipher in the ledgers. I think I'm the only one who can see it, but it looks exactly like this.' She jabbed her thumb towards the screen. 'It's page after page of Mayan glyphs. Another codex.'

'There's a codex hidden in Cedric Owen's ledgers?' The yearning on his face would have been comical in any other circumstance. 'Stella, *please*, you have to let me . . .'

He was close enough for her to feel the heat of his face. His hand was on her arm. The words locked in his throat, too many, or too urgent, or too desperate, to find their order and come out.

Before she could hear them, something metal cracked against the door post. A tight, acerbic voice said, 'Am I interrupting something important? Do say. I can always go away again.'

'Kit?'

He was in the doorway, leaning on his two sticks. Stella had never before seen the twisting ugliness that marred his face. He looked through her, and on to Davy Law beyond. 'Having fun?'

'Kit! He's trying to help.'

'I can see that. What kind of help this time, David?'

'Not what you think.'

Law stepped back to his own side of the lab. Stella saw him take a breath and hold it and let it out through his nose, slowly.

Looking up again, he nodded at her, stiffly. 'You were leaving, I believe? Though it might be worth looking to see if we've put a face to your skull-stone first.'

The other screen was turned away, where none of them could see it. Law walked behind both seats to turn it back, rather than reach across her. And so she was alone when she saw the face looking out at her from the screen.

'That can't be right.' She shook her head, and kept on shaking it, unable to stop, and then was just shaking, and trying not to vomit.

'What?'

Kit could not move fast enough to join her. Out of charity to them both, Davy Law turned the screen round so they could both see it equally.

Kit handled it no better. He looked from Stella to the screen and back again, twice. 'Is this some kind of joke?'

'Software,' said Davy Law, 'has no sense of humour. When you put flesh on the skull, this is what you get.'

There was no ambiguity; Stella's own face stared out at them from the screen, plastic and still, as if in sleep. She remembered the first flick of Davy Law's eyes from the stone to her face and back.

She turned on him. 'You knew it was me when I first showed you the skull.'

He smiled emptily. 'I've been in this job a long time.'

'But you've added the hair and the eyes. You've no proof they were the same.'

'Of course not. You can have black hair and blue eyes if you want, but it'll still be you.'

He tapped three keys. Her hair blinked from copper to black, her eyes from green to blue. The effect was disconcerting, but did not change the basic fact: the face that looked out at them was still hers.

Law said, 'I can get you a second opinion, or a third, but they'll come out the same. Like bone, stone doesn't lie. Whoever made this skull, they based it on someone who carried the same skeletal structure as you. Given that facial characteristics are heavily hereditary, I'd say that she was a distant ancestor. We all have them; it's not so strange. If you go back as far as the end of the last age, you have several thousand to choose from.'

Stella shook her head and held up her hand for him to be quiet. She needed time and a clear head to think and had neither. She looked to Kit, who was whitely shocked, and angry.

She said, 'Davy, what do we do?'

He shrugged, loosely, without energy. His eyes were elsewhere than her face, exploring his desk for things of greater import. She was surprised how much that hurt.

'Keep the skull hidden. Keep yourselves safe,' he said at last.

'We're going to see Ursula Walker. Is she safe?'

Sharply, he turned back round. His eyes met hers. He laughed aloud. 'As safe as anyone can be. You can show her the skull, if that's what you mean. She's one of the very few people alive today who has seen one of the others.'

He squeezed between them and held the lab door open. 'I'll help you get it out of the chamber. After that, it might be best if you left.'

Stella was turning the car in the car park, with Kit silent at her side, when Davy Law loped out of the unit. She slowed the car. His white coat flapped as he ran to catch up. He leaned in the window, blasting her with sour coffee and tobacco. In his fingers was a business card with his name and three numbers.

'Land line, mobile and international mobile. I'm in the country for the next three weeks. If you need me, call.'

She hesitated, her fingers on the card. 'Is this for my benefit or yours?'

'Just take it, Stella. It doesn't mean you have to use it.'

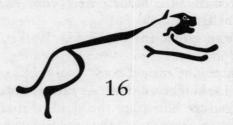

16

Zama, New Spain, October 1556

'WE DON'T HAVE ICE,' OWEN SAID. 'WE don't have mandragora or lettuce seed or hemlock, or any of the other things Ibn Sina described as necessary to keep a man at peace for the careful removal of his arm.'

'But you do have the opium poppy that Nostradamus gave you? Perhaps that will be enough.'

Fernandez de Aguilar sat in the cool of the priest's stone-built, single-roomed former temple, set about with images of the crucified Christ, which had been offered as the best place for the surgery partly because it was a house of God and therefore sanctified, but more important because it had stone floors and walls and could be scrubbed clean as the Moor El Zahrawi had said it should be before major surgery.

Finally, it was painted white inside, which

gave the best light. Two wide windows gave on to the priest's quarters, and at Owen's request they had taken away part of the roof so that clear light might fall on his operating table without great heat.

Nobody mentioned the jaguar-mosaic on the floor and Cedric Owen had forgotten it; his attention was all for his patient. De Aguilar cradled his bitten arm, which had swollen only a little so that, but for the priest's assurances, they might have believed the bite to be of no more consequence than the sting of a mosquito.

Owen reread his notes, shaking his head. 'I don't understand. Venus is in a good position – which is crucial for your chart – and the Part of Fortune is perfectly placed in Scorpio in the seventh house, which could not be better. And yet we don't have all that we need. Nostradamus had the mandragora in his stocks but sent me only with the poppy. We need both, and some ice: as the Moors described it, this surgery must be done with delicacy and tact and cannot be hurried. Your mind and soul need to be safely elsewhere for the duration. Without that, we descend to the butchery of the barber-surgeons who think it clever to take off a limb in half a minute and lose nine patients out of ten in the process. I will not do that to you.'

'And I would not ask that you live your life with my blood on your hands.' De Aguilar stood up. He was naked to the waist, with a pair of Domingo's loose cotton trousers below. The oddest thing was to see his face balanced at last, without the gold weighting his one ear.

Walking to the table, he still moved with the fluid balance of the trained fencer; the venom had not yet hampered his brain or his grace. 'We will follow my first plan to take dinner together and then sit through the night in the great square tower of the natives and watch Zama's dawn rise in all its glory. I can think of no better way to end a life.'

'Fernandez, don't give up on me so soon.'

Cedric Owen pressed the flats of his hands to his face and stared open-eyed into the blackness they made. With some effort, the black became blue, and within it the faint song of the heart-stone stirred. He was reaching for it when a scuffle in the corner of the room startled him.

In the bright, white priest's room with its icons and mosaics, only one corner held any shadows. Owen dropped his hands in time to see a figure in pale, unbleached cotton rise from the floor and step forward.

'Diego. How very . . . unsurprising.'

The scarred native held up a hand and said crisply, 'Wait,' and left.

'The tiger speaks,' said de Aguilar in some astonishment. 'I thought perhaps he could.'

'I would feel happier if he had said what he thought,' said Owen seriously. He ducked under the low lintel, peered out to the afternoon sun and ducked back in again swiftly. 'He's gone to fetch the priest. If they want to give you the last rites, will you take them?'

Fernandez de Aguilar studied the backs of his hands. 'At this juncture, I would not refuse. If you and I are wrong and the priests are right, it will serve me well. If we are right and Father Gonzalez and all the Church are wrong, I don't imagine it will do me any great harm beyond staining my soul with a little hypocrisy and I am not above that now. I do not hold my unbelief so strongly as to— Father Gonzalez!' He thrust himself to his feet. 'We were speaking of you and you are here, and in so great a hurry. Am I to die sooner than we thought that you must make such haste?'

'I trust not.'

Father Gonzalez Calderón filled the doorway of his house as an ox fills a stall, but there was a directness to his manner that had not been evident before.

'Diego understands that you are in want of something – a plant or a drench or similar – that will work together with the poppy so that the chirurgical process may go forward more smoothly, is that so?'

Owen answered. 'It is.'

'Good, then we have understanding. I was not certain.'

The priest spoke to his clerk in the fast, bird-like tongue of the natives. Diego replied in kind, fluttering his hands for emphasis. His eyes flashed back and forth between the physician, the Spaniard and the dinner table, which had been returned to the room to act as a surgical board.

Father Gonzalez held up his hand, calling a pause. 'My clerk is ashamed that so noble a visitor as Don Fernandez should be inconvenienced by the prospect of death when he has so clearly come here to help the people of Zama. He offers you a drench – perhaps "drink" is the better word – his people use to bring themselves closer to . . . God as they understand Him. This drink has never before been given to a white man, but he believes that it will combine with the poppy in the way that you need it to and that—'

A torrent of mellifluous sound interrupted him. Diego spoke urgently, staring at Owen. Partway through, Father Gonzalez, too, focused his attention on the physician.

At a pause in the word-flow, he said, 'He would have you know that this offer comes without pre-condition, but that it comes because of you, Señor Owen, in part because you read aright the mosaic that shows the End of Days, but also because of what you bring to Zama that is as yet unnamed and unshown. You should know that this . . . drink – it is not the right word, but I can find none better – is used only in the most sacred ceremonies before God. Diego believes that what you attempt is such a rite and that you will understand what it is that he offers. Do you?'

Cedric Owen took a long time to consider, during which he reached for the blue stone, and was met by it and reassured.

'Yes,' he said at length, 'I believe that I do.'

'Dear God . . . a man would have to want very badly to come closer to his eternal soul to drink this. It's foul.'

'How do you feel?'

'Sick. Horribly swimmingly sick. Like the first time aboard ship on full sea. Diego did say that I would . . . But also very . . . peaceful. I think, now, if I don't vomit all over your boots, that I could sleep even in sight of your black stone knives and that is a miracle in itself.'

De Aguilar's good hand reached out for Owen's and missed, grasping at nothing and falling back. Disappointment flickered and died in his eyes. 'Good night, my friend. Do what you can. Know that I hold . . . nothing against you and—'

'Fernandez . . .' Owen took the good, warm hand and squeezed it. 'Fernandez . . . ? God in heaven, he's asleep. I really didn't think . . .' He lowered the limp arm to the table. 'How long have I got?'

Diego shrugged. The priest, Gonzalez, said, 'Only God can know that. I would encourage

269

you to act swiftly, señor, if you would have him feel nothing as you work. Do you wish my assistance in applying the tourniquet?'

The blood made a glove that stretched from his fingertips to his elbow and dried there, stiffening.

Fernandez de Aguilar's arm was gone. Owen had dropped it in a leaf-lined basket at his side and Diego had covered it with a red, yellow and black cloth, woven in exactly the colours of the so-dangerous snake, and dragged it away.

The stumped limb remained, still pink and vital above the band of cotton that made the tourniquet. Beneath it, the tissue was grey-white and ugly. Owen fastened the last strip of flesh and skin in place with the cactus thorns he himself had picked in the frenzied planning before the surgery, when it had seemed that even to succeed in cutting the bone would be a miracle.

He had cut the bone, and the flesh before it, with a selection of knives and saws from the ship and the black stone blades of the natives, which were sharper than any razor he might have found.

Cedric Owen did not believe he had performed a miracle with these, but he dared to hope that such a thing might come from what he had done. He took hold of the tourniquet and looked again at the sand glass the priest

270

had turned as it was wound. Almost an hour had passed. It felt like a year.

Under his hand, Fernandez de Aguilar stirred and moaned for the first time since the first knife had cut him.

Owen looked up sharply. 'Diego, can you give him more to drink?'

The scarred savage was sitting in the shadows where he had been all through. He stood up now, and moved forward, bringing his gourd with him.

'No.' De Aguilar said it. His eyes were filled with shadows from the other lands his soul had visited. His voice struggled through webs of pain and the unknown alchemy of the herbs. 'Please.'

Owen said, 'The greatest pain comes when the tourniquet is released. I would have you free of that.'

'I am not . . . in pain. The poppy is still in me. And if the blood flows free from the wound, such that I die, even now after all your efforts, I would know of it, and leave this life with a mind unclouded.'

'Well then.'

Owen unwound the tourniquet and waited, counting the heartbeats in his head as colour eddied slowly at first, and then with a rush, into the finger's length of arm left below the place where the cord had been.

Quite soon, it reached the end, where Diego's

hot iron had burned the vessels, one at a time, sealing them. They were hidden beneath the skin now, and invisible. Four men held their breath. The priest, Diego, Owen and his patient all watched the neatly sutured skin grow pink and red and bulge a little as its life returned.

A spittle of blood ran from between two flaps of skin. Owen dabbed it away with the last remaining wad of folded cotton. The counting in his head reached thirty and there was nothing more. His sense of the miraculous heightened a little. He moved round the table and felt the three pulses on the remaining wrist. The one at the front was a little slippery, and the liver pulse at the back was wiry with the effort of staying awake, but in the round, the three were healthy, which was little short of astonishing.

'Fernandez? How do you feel?'

'Alive, which is more than I ever expected. My arm is . . . tingling as if it were still whole, but there is no pain. It's hard to speak but that's to be expected, is it not?'

The Spaniard's voice was badly slurred. Owen said, 'Poppy does that to a man. When it wears off, you will speak as you did before. You will need to learn to fence left-handed. I would offer to teach you, but there is chaos enough in this world without that.'

'True.' De Aguilar smiled hazily. His gaze was fixed somewhere beyond the walls. Absently, he said, 'Perhaps Diego can teach me. I think there is . . . a great deal that Diego can teach us.'

He was asleep with the last word. His good hand was cool and unfevered and the pulses rhythmic. The stump of his right arm was warm, but not hot, vital, but not engorged.

Cedric Owen looked towards the shadows in the corner and, as he had throughout the surgery, met a quiet black gaze. 'Will he live?'

From the shadows, Diego's hoarse, rusted Spanish answered. 'While the drink is in him, he will live. After that, what happens is between him and his gods. And yours.'

Owen thought he heard a question in that, and did not know how to answer it. Uncomfortably, he said, 'In that case, there is nothing to do but wait.'

The dark eyes held his. There was a measuring, but no ill judgement. 'Then we will wait.'

Twice, the sun rose at the furthest edge of the sea, spreading gold across the dazzled waves.

Twice it crossed the sky, casting shortening, lengthening shadows down the walled streets of Zama with its great tower and smaller temples and profusion of savage carvings.

Twice, the blood-copper orb sent molten ore oozing across the western horizon and out on to the cooling plains where the cicadas chirruped their way to dusk and a strange silence fell of no night beasts and not even the slap of the wind in the rigging.

Fernandez de Aguilar slept on without cease, watched by his friend and surgeon, Cedric Owen, who did not sleep at all.

At first, Owen had been relieved at his patient's ability to rest; every learned text he had ever read had recommended a good healing sleep as the best restorative following the devastation of surgery.

Thus encouraged, Owen tiptoed his way through the dressing changes in an effort not to disturb his patient to wakefulness. Sometime in the second day, when de Aguilar had neither drunk nor passed water, Owen reviewed the charts he had cast of the constellations and movements of the stars. In doing so, he found that Diego was a better source of information than his notebooks on the current position in the firmament of the three healing planets, Mercury, Venus and Mars.

Consulting the redrawn wheels, he found them all to be at least partly favourable. With that and good pulses to support his cause, he made an effort to rouse the sleeping man that he might drink.

His effort failed. Fernandez de Aguilar could not be woken. Frustrated, Owen abandoned his attempt and, with Diego's help, found a way to raise the patient and pour water into his mouth, massaging his neck to ensure that he swallowed and did not inhale.

Half the night was spent ensuring de Aguilar

drank enough to prevent the salt and sulphur in his body from becoming unbalanced. A slightly shorter span of time passed in finding a way to hold him upright so that his bladder, being pressed, might expel his urine into a gourd.

They were done with that near dusk on the second day. Three lamps burned smokily at corners of the room sending scant patches of light into the greater well of silver that flooded in through the gap in the thatch, sent by the moon.

Cedric Owen sat at one edge of that and ate the meal of beans and peppers and corn that had been brought him. The flavours were not as foreign to his tongue as they had been on the first night; he was coming to like them more.

Thus fortified, he excused himself to attend to his own needs and then, freed for the first time from his self-imposed duties, returned to his lodgings and retrieved the hessian bag in which he kept the blue heart-stone.

As ever, the first moments of meeting left him hollow and full together. Nostradamus had said, *You care for your stone, do you not?* and he had touched only the edge of the alchemy that joined human flesh and blood to a thing of cold rock, which nevertheless held so much that was perfect in humanity, and often missing.

Diego was gone from the temple when Owen returned. Relieved, he discarded the sack and set the blue stone on the table at de Aguilar's

275

head, so that its eyes faced down the length of his body. He found two candles and a small stone lamp that trailed greasy smoke as he moved it. As his grandmother had taught him, he set them to the sides and base of the skull, moving them a hair's breadth left or right until the three uncertain lights were drawn in and sent out as two certain beams along the length of de Aguilar's body.

Satisfied, Owen brought a stool from outside and set it at the Spaniard's feet, resting his chin on the table so that his eyes could look into those of the skull-stone. Sitting thus, he remained motionless a moment, listening. Outside were bats and small night creatures, but nothing of human tread.

He set his left hand on de Aguilar's left foot and said aloud, 'My friend, what we do now is outwith the realms of what you know. If you trust me, I will find you and bring you home. If you wish not to be found, that is your choice and I will honour it.'

So saying, he closed his eyes, and sought once again the place of still, high blue, within which was the single note of the heart-stone's song.

'Wait.' A hoarse word, spoken in Spanish. A quiet hand fell on his arm.

'Diego!' Owen's eyes snapped open.

It *was* Diego, not Father Gonzalez, for which he was grateful, but only barely so. He shook the hand off angrily. 'Is this necessary?'

'This is not the place.' Wide black eyes met his. They were filled with neither lust nor fear, but a solid respect that knew the stone intimately, and treated it as an equal. Diego bowed, hands on chest, before the stone and then swept his arms about, pointing to the pained bodies of the crucified Christ hung on every wall.

The rusted Spanish said, 'Once this was a place where we could talk in peace to the gods. Now it is become a place of torture, pain and loss. Your stone will be stronger elsewhere.'

Quiet in the dark night, he heard Nostradamus' whisper. *Go to the place south of here where the Mussulman once ruled ... From there, you can take ship to the New World, therein to meet those who know the heart and soul of your blue stone. They will tell you how best you may unlock its secrets ...*

Diego looked at him across the room, waiting. The skin of Owen's scalp prickled. He felt a tremor in the hands which had so steadily held the blackstone blades that cut de Aguilar's arm.

'Where must we go?' he asked. 'How far?'

'A place I know. We can take mules. Two days, maybe three.' Diego held up his fingers, to back up the numbers.

'Three days' travel? Are you quite mad? Fernandez cannot be moved two hundred yards without danger. He would die before the first morning is out.'

'He will die if you stay here. Ask your heart-stone, am I not right?'

There was no questioning the quiet certainty. Shaken, Owen closed his eyes again. The stone was there to meet him, full-voiced and ready. He had never heard such clarity. It gave no warning of danger, or loss, or grief.

He opened his eyes. Both of the candles had gone out, their flame drawn to nothing. The small smoking lamp gave muzzy light, so that the gaze of the heart-stone was dimmed to a faint blue haze. Within it, as once in Nostradamus' presence, when he had heard gulls and smelled the sea, so now he was in a place where the night beasts yarled in their hunting and a hesitant wind bent trees and grasses to the ground.

'What do you hear?' asked Diego softly.

'Bats,' Owen said. 'I hear bats flying in their thousands from a pyramid that makes your tower here seem like a child's toy house.'

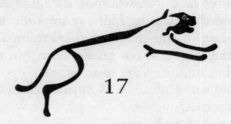

17

New Spain: southern lowlands,
October 1556

BATS. EVERYWHERE BATS. A SHRIEKING, FLITTER-ing tide that filled the clearing from treetop to treetop, blotting out the afternoon sun and bringing on such darkness as would have been unbearable, but that the soul of the heart-stone sang a paean of homecoming to drown out the noise and cast blue light, filling the false dusk with the piercing clarity of dawn.

Lost in the blinding sound, Cedric Owen swayed, and bent and lowered Fernandez de Aguilar to the ground at last, after half a day of carrying him up an ever-steepening jungle path with Diego hacking a route through the under-growth ten yards ahead.

De Aguilar did not wake as he was laid out in the long grass of the clearing, but then he had not wakened for anything, not for the shrieks of the birds through the day or the coughing

jaguar or the terrified mule whose bray had
startled the bats into flight, nor for any part of
the three-day journey that had brought him
here, to this clearing halfway up a mountain in
the heart of the jungle with nothing to show
why the trees had not grown here, but the bats
and the singing of the heart-stone.

'This is the place,' Owen said, straightening.
'I can feel it.'

'Then we make camp.'

Already, Diego was crouched on his heels,
cutting a circle of turf for a fire. Carlos and
Sanchez, his brothers, who had accompanied
them, were tying the mules and hunting for firewood. They passed Owen without a word,
although he thought that all three native men
looked at him more favourably since he had
lifted de Aguilar and carried him these last few
miles. He was not certain of it; the surprise –
and the hurt – was that he cared enough to
notice.

For something to do, Owen bent and felt the
pulse at de Aguilar's neck and at his one
remaining wrist. Of the three wrist pulses, the
liver was still thready and the heart erratic,
which told him nothing that he did not already
know. Since daybreak, he had carried the
Spaniard slung over his shoulders, and had
listened to the man's breathing worsen as fluid
gathered on his lungs and a mild pneumonia
became, over the span of hours, a dangerous

one, for which Owen could do nothing but massage water into his throat, and perhaps a little valerian and willow bark, in the knowledge that he did it for himself, to feel useful, rather than in the belief that they would be of use.

Checking for snakes, he set the satchel with his heart-stone at the side, and pulled from its depths the small bag of medicaments that he carried. Around him, the tide of bats dispersed whence they had come and life returned to the jungle, noisy and colourful as it had been the past three days. Everywhere, small jewelled birds flitted amongst the branches, sharpening the air with their calls. In the deeper depths, larger things flew and stalked and cried and killed.

Somewhere, a jaguar coughed. Owen chose to ignore it. His heart-stone remained safe in the satchel at his feet and did not augur danger. Diego walked past, carrying firewood. Owen caught at his arm. 'This is the place,' he said again. 'We must act while we may. Fernandez will not live long if we tarry.'

Diego shook his head. 'The time is not yet right. First, we light a fire. We eat a little corn and drink the last of the water. Then we wait.'

'But why? When this is the place? Do you not understand the nature of death, that you can treat it in so cavalier a fashion?'

Diego spun his blackstone axe over and over

in his hands, regarding Owen thoughtfully. He smiled a little, which was not something Owen had seen him do before.

'Cedric Owen, do you know where to go or what to do with your blue heart-stone? No? Neither do I. But one comes who does, and until then, we can do nothing. And so, we wait.'

The jaguar came in the early evening, when the shadows of the trees sawed across the clearing in sharp-edged stripes, like the bars of a cage.

Cedric Owen sat at the fireside, feeling fuddled by the smoke. The bats were returning in ones and twos with the shortening light; a few tiny shapes that flopped sporadically through the canopy.

Dusk brought everything out. The coughing grunts of the great beasts in their hunting, and the shrill deaths that followed, were all around so that the mules stamped and tugged at their tethers and even Diego did not seem at peace.

The scarred native sat with his two brothers on one side of the small fire they had built. Owen sat on the other, cradling his heart-stone in its satchel with de Aguilar's senseless body lying supine beside him.

They waited. The fire died to a red glow, and finally to ash. Owen drank water sparingly and gave some to de Aguilar and, after a while, when the waiting had stretched beyond endurance, he rose and walked a few dozen yards towards the centre of the clearing to a place where an irregular wink of yellow kept catching his eye.

It was there now, a flicker of almost-life within the grasses. He scuffed at the dead leaves and living grass with his foot and saw a smear of something hard and bright, the colour of celandines. Falling to his hands and knees, he spat on his fingers and cleaned away the gritty earth. A small, irregular rectangle of buttery stone winked up at him, catching the evening light.

Others spread out from it, of different yellows, some brighter, some deeper, and at their margins deep blood reds, and flame orange and the occasional sparkle of green. He worked harder to clear them. Soon, all the colours of sun and fire grew shining under his care to catch the dying light. He sat back on his heels. Before him was a full circle of mosaic-fire, banded by red and blue snakes.

'My God . . .'

He stood now, and swept his foot across and across, cutting arcs through the sward. Spreading out from the tiled fire were the outlines of men and animals laid out in a mosaic far larger than the one in the priest's house in Zama; this one filled the whole clearing, and very likely beyond.

If the first, smaller mosaic had seemed like a child's drawing, this was the masterpiece from which it was copied. The intricacy of detail, the dramatic use of colour and shade, the reflecting of the light from blinding shards of diamond set against dense pits of black, made this a wonder of life and teaching.

And yet it portrayed the same image: the held breath before the moment of Armageddon. Even with so little to see, Owen was certain that the wreckage of Desolation lay to the outside, but for a meadow in the south, alive with the Innocence of the girl-child and her surround of wild flowers.

He could not yet see any one of the four beasts and he wanted to. For that, he needed to cut a broom from the jungle branches, and he had no knife.

'Diego . . .?'

Even in his passion, the quality of the silence caught him. Owen turned slowly round, and realized as he did so that he had lost his awareness of the jungle and the heart-stone, and that while he had been busy, everything within and without had fallen into empty silence. The three native men stood with their backs to the fire, staring out into the velvet shadows between the trees.

His guts clenched. He ran back to the fire. 'Diego?'

'Hush.' He was a child, to be quieted with a flap of the hand. Owen bit back the retort that leaped to his lips and turned instead to look where the brothers were looking—

—and met the face of the jaguar level with his own face, and felt its fierce, sour breath burn his throat, and stared into a pair of bright eyes that were uncannily human; that knew him, and all that he had ever been, in ways that even Diego's had not done.

The jaguar snarled and its mouth gaped wide. Cedric Owen stared death in the face and tried to scream and could not; his voice had abandoned him and his legs were weak as kittens'. For one appalling moment, he thought his innards, too, were going to let him down, so that he might foul himself as he had heard men did before battle but never before so truly understood.

He managed to raise one hand, and pressed uselessly against the soft, bepatterned fur. A squeak of ultimate terror escaped his throat.

'Welcome,' said the jaguar, in Spanish.

Cedric Owen fainted.

18

*The Walker Institute, Lower Hayworth
Farmhouse, Oxfordshire, June 2007*

KIT ASKED, 'WHY ARE WE STOPPING?'
    'Because I want to know if the green
Audi that's been on our tail for the past twenty
minutes is following us.'

Stella pulled the car into a field's grassy gateway. Tall hazel hedges reared on either side,
dangling late, dried catkins. On the other side of
the gate, corn burst yellow on the stalk. A cloud
of sparrows chattered up, circled and came down
again to feed noisily on spilled grain. A hawk
passed overhead and they fell still. Somewhere
out of sight, a live band – possibly several live
bands – murdered the bucolic English calm.

A sleek green Audi slid past, almost noiseless.
It slowed at the T-junction at the foot of the
lane and turned left.

After a moment, Kit said, 'Tell me we're
turning right?'

'We're turning right,' Stella said. 'At least I am. You don't have to. I can take you to the station and put you on a train back to Cambridge if you want.' She turned to face him. 'Is that what you want?'

'Stell . . .'

'You haven't said a word since we left Davy Law's lab.'

He folded his laptop shut. 'I was working. I thought . . .'

'Working?' She laughed. An hour's glacial silence stopped her from taking it back.

Kit flushed. The colour spread blotchily over the immobile half of his face. 'I've written you a program that'll take the squiggles in Cedric Owen's ledgers and fit them together to make the Mayan glyphs. If you can get your head round using a graphics tablet, it should halve your time to translate the second cipher.'

Stella said nothing, only leaned back against the door and let him drift into silence.

He shook his head. 'I don't want to fight. Not now. Not over Davy Law.'

'He told me you were friends once.'

'We were.'

'So why won't you tell me about it? Twice now you've ducked this one. It's not good, Kit. We're supposed to be on the same side.' The anger had gone, but the void it left behind was no less.

He turned away and looked out of the window.

'If it makes any difference,' she said, 'he hates himself far more than you hate him.'

'Probably.' He caught her hand and made a clumsy attempt at weaving his fingers through hers. She let him, but did not help. 'Can we let it go for now? I'm not ducking a row, but—'

'You are.'

'OK, I am. Is there a problem with that?'

'Kit, someone is trying to kill us. I am in possession of a blue crystal skull which is modelled on my face and I can't begin to tell you how much that scares me. Davy Law knows things we don't. He's given me his number and there's a chance I might want to use it. I can't if you and I are still fighting over something that happened ten years ago that I know nothing about. I don't want the details, but I need to have an idea of what's going on between you two.'

He let go of her hand and dragged his fingers through his hair instead. Pursing his lips, he whistled out a long, tight breath.

'There's very little to tell you that Gordon hasn't already said and that little really isn't important between us, I promise you that. Mistakes happened, of omission and commission and just plain bloody stupidity, and someone I cared for was hurt. Doubtless I carried my share of the blame and I only noticed Davy's. I was young and arrogant and angry and I should have let it go then and I certainly should be big enough to let it go now, but Christ, Stell, it's hard being so bloody grown up all the time.'

He turned to her again. It was impossible to read his face when only half of it was under his control. Stella reached out and smoothed the mess of his hair from his forehead. 'Tony Bookless told me I should erase the word "should" from my vocabulary.'

'That sounds like Tony.' Kit tilted his head back on the seat rest and stared at the roof of the car. 'I'm trying not to be scared. I'm trying to pretend that all this is normal and I fell off a ledge in a caving accident. Then you pull the car over in case we're being followed and—'

'Kit, it's a sensible—'

'Hush.' He put the flat of his hand over her mouth; his fingertips pressed feather-light on her lips and stayed there, as he spoke. 'I'm scared, that's all. I just wanted to tell you that. It's as much as I can do to hold together. Being nice about Davy Law is more than I can handle at the moment.' He took his fingers from her lips. The ghost-print of them stayed behind. 'And if we're going to have another row about this, I don't want to do it on a day when either one of us might be dead by nightfall. Does the stone think we're in danger here?'

'No.' The heart-stone lay in her backpack behind her seat. It was comfortably alert, like a cat on a warm stove, watching the world with the same newborn-ancient wisdom she had first

289

felt on Ingleborough Fell. There was a comfort in it, that kept the fear manageable. She said, 'It's happier here than it was in Davy Law's lab.'

He smiled at that, properly. 'A stone with good taste. I like it better already. Are we heading for a black and white Tudor farmhouse set back from the lane on the left about a hundred yards after the turn?'

She recognized that voice. Cautiously, she said, 'We might be.'

'In that case, you might want to lean over and look down through the gap in the hedge. I think I know where the music is coming from.'

'That's not music, it's the sound of a thousand cats being strangled.' Stella leaned right over until she could see along his line of vision. There, in the fields around the only black and white farmhouse in sight, was a pop festival, complete with tents and yurts and a field full of cars and other fields full of stages and bands and marquees and the shimmering mirage that goes with mind-bending noise and uncountable numbers of people.

Experimentally, Stella opened the car door, and shut it swiftly against the hammering wall of sound. 'Kit . . . ?'

Kit laid his hands lightly over her ears. Through the gaps between his fingers, he said, 'I'd volunteer to go and investigate, but I don't think I can walk that far without help. You could go on your own, but if we've kissed and made up, then you might like company?' He leaned over and kissed the side of her cheek. 'I love you, did I mention?'

'You did. And I'm still getting over my luck on that one.' Stella caught his hand and held it. 'I'll push the wheelchair if you'll be the knight in shining armour and keep the manic music-makers at bay. Bravely and together. Don't let me down on that one.'

The farmhouse was old, all sloping black beams and layers of whitewash with a cottage garden at the front and roses in an arch over the gate. A small path led to an oak front door flanked on both sides by hanging baskets that leaked a fiery waterfall of bright orange thunbergia.

A brass plate on the wall to the left of the oak front door read:

THE WALKER INSTITUTE, OXFORD.
DIRECTOR: DR URSULA WALKER.

Beneath it was a laminated, laser-printed sign:

WELCOME TO THE 2012 CONNECTION!
PLEASE LEAVE ALL MOTORIZED TRANSPORT,
TOGETHER WITH YOUR PRECONCEPTIONS, IN THE
CAR PARK OPPOSITE.

The car park was the grass field they had passed on the lane and it was full. Ahead of them, stretching over acres of grassland, was a riot of canvas yurts, tipis and tents, surrounded by a seething, screeching mass of people, not all of them young, but all trying to seem so with their tie-dyed T-shirts and nose studs and whippets on strings dragged along behind as they swayed from tent to yurt to concert pavilion to yurt again. The air was thick with cannabis smoke and the noise was astonishing.

Stella leaned on the doorpost and stared in horror at the chaos. 'Ursula said there was a conference going on. I was expecting something more academic than this.'

'I don't think hippies do academic.' Kit swivelled his chair back to look at the sign. 'What's The 2012 Connection?'

Stella grimaced. 'Don't ask.' A yellow Post-it note lay face down in the rose bed to the side. She bent to pick it up and read aloud the neat, sharp handwriting on it.

> *Stella and Kit. The festival closes at 1:00. I'll be giving the closing speech from the podium in the centre at 12:55. If you arrive before that, feel free to wander.*

She looked at her watch. 'It's half past twelve. Shall we see if we can find the podium?'

Bright as a jewelled web, the festival caught them and reeled them in.

Ten yards down the first broad, grassy path, they stopped to buy a pineapple smoothie from a youth with lilac dreadlocks and were persuaded into tasting the wheat-grass juice – 'It gets better with practice' – and then ten yards later bought a punnet of strawberries each from a pair of enthusiastic teenagers with polished smiles and matching scarlet T-shirts who charged at least twice what the same thing would have cost on Cambridge market.

Kit was unexpectedly buoyant. As they moved away, he leaned back in the wheelchair and waved an expansive arm at the heaving, good-natured chaos around them.

'How many people here? Maybe a thousand? Four days of a festival, two punnets of straw-berries per person per day, so at a conservative estimate, they're pulling in somewhere in excess of—' He tilted his head back to look up at Stella. 'A Martian and two blue apples. You're not listening.'

'I am, honestly.' She handed him a strawberry to prove it. 'You were pointing out why we're poor and will stay that way, because we don't fleece people for fruit. But I just heard the woman with the weird blonde highlights stand-ing at that microphone say "solar wind" twice in one sentence. Why is anyone talking about astronomy in a nuthouse like this?'

She turned the wheelchair to face the small square marked out in the grass that was the blonde-streaked woman's domain. 'And now shifting magnetic poles with earthquakes in their wake. This I have to hear.'

'And I really don't.' Kit braked the chair. 'I'd fall asleep in ten seconds and the day's too good for that. There's a book tent, down there on the right.' He pointed down the pathway to where a hand-painted banner showing an open book fluttered in the breeze above a blue and white striped tent. 'We could each indulge our obsessions and meet up in twenty minutes?'

They were back, almost, to the easy company of the time before the cave. Stella stooped to kiss his brow. 'Sounds good to me.'

She stood a moment watching him manoeuvre his wheelchair through the morass of humanity towards the relative peace of the book tent, then turned the other way and pushed through a small meteoric shower of children watching a tattooed youth juggling nine raw eggs, to come at last to the square patch of grass around the blonde-streaked woman, whose own half-height banner, now Stella was close enough to read it, said, *APOCALYPSE: HOW?*'

She caught the last five minutes of the talk, and did not stop for the questions. Kit was invisible, drowned under a sea of multicoloured humanity. Stella took the easy route to reach him, meandering slowly through the gap where

294

the juggler had been towards a stall selling handmade leather belts with acrylic buckles shaped as flowers or rainbows and then on down towards the book tent.

She was fingering the belts a little wildly, not seeing particularly and still trying to make sense of what she had just heard, when a deep, classically educated voice to her left said, 'Rosita Chancellor has been talking out of her arse since the day she was born. You needn't think we all believe what she says. I'm Ursula Walker. You must be Dr Cody.'

Stella spun on her heel. Professor Ursula Walker was tall and lean with hair darker than it had seemed on the web. She wore a cream linen suit that set her instantly apart from the dreadlocks and nose studs of the festival. Her face was the deep wind-and-weather brown of a serious gardener, not the sprayed-on temporary bronze of the summer amateur. Her hands were fine and expressive, and when they pushed her hair back from her face a single gold earring winked at her right ear, the only hint of solidarity with those around her. She smiled at Stella as if they had known each other for years. Her eyes were a solid steel grey and entirely sane.

She said, 'For what it's worth, I do still think that something very, very big is going to happen around the end of 2012. What we're doing to the planet is not sustainable. I just don't give much credence to the people who are pinning everything on a blast of solar wind spinning us in the wrong direction and causing tidal waves of unimaginable proportions. It doesn't seem grounded in any recognizable physics.'

Stella said, 'My first professor would have called it pseudo-science. We were taught to run screaming from the first hint of it.'

'Very wise,' said a voice from behind them both. 'See? I did tell you she'd have a balanced intellect.'

They turned, together. In the shadows behind was an awning slung between two tents, and, beneath it, a hammock. A long, lean, silver-haired man lay there, reading a sheaf of papers. His eyes were the same dense grey as Ursula Walker's. On the hottest day of summer, he was wearing a shirt and a college tie.

Ursula sighed. 'Stella, this is my cousin Meredith Lawrence. Meri, this is Dr Stella Cody and I'd be grateful if you wouldn't make a difficult experience any more difficult for her than it already is.'

With admirable balance, Meredith swung his legs from the hammock. He was a tall man, and had learned how to fold himself smaller. From the shade at the back of the awning he produced, in order, two folding chairs, a low white table and a flask of tea and sat down.

Sitting, he seemed more compact, and less deliberately provocative. He gave a little bow.

'I'm sorry. Perhaps we should start again. Dr Cody, if I offered you tea, would you stay with me while Ursula goes to do the glad-handing that must happen before she closes this whole sorry mess?'

He had the quiet, self-deprecating humour Stella had met before in the colleges, and the sharpness of mind that she had met less frequently, but craved.

She still held a white plastic cup of wheat-grass juice in her hand. She stared at it a moment, as if considering the offer, then, with care, she set it on the ground at the side of the tent. 'For tea,' she said, 'I'd do anything.'

'Thank you. Both of you.' Ursula kissed her cousin briefly, and was gone.

They were left alone with nothing to say. 'Were you at Bede's with all the others?' Stella asked. His hair was deceptive; he was no older than Ursula, a man in his academic prime.

His grey-black brows rose a fraction as he shook his head. 'Who could compete with Tony and Ursula shining their bright lights to set everyone in the shade? No, I saw the way the wind was blowing. I'm an Oxford man; Magdalen, Classics. Which means you know as much about me as you ever need to: the college defines the youth and the subject the man. Not that there is great call for classical scholars in these days of globalization, but one finds a means to keep body and soul from parting. Milk or lemon?'

Stella said, 'Lemon, thank you.' It was a day for new experiences.

His manuscript lay on the hammock. A breeze pushed the pages around and she saw that it was not all script, and there was a coloured image she knew intimately. 'Is that the stained glass window at Bede's?'

'Outside the river rooms. Yes.' Meredith pulled a wry smile. 'For my sins, I am the external examiner for yet another post-graduate thesis examining the imagery. The little darling thinks that the complex sigil in the top right-hand corner does not depict the sun and moon together in an anchored conjunction as is generally accepted, but relics of the pre-Masonic Templar traditions denoting the two globes of the world before and after the Fall of Mankind. It's nonsense, but one mustn't say so in this era of equality and experimentation.'

'I always thought it was a set of scales, weighing the sun against the moon to show which was heavier,' Stella said. 'But then I'm not a classical scholar.'

'No, only an astronomer.' Meredith looked at her flatly for a moment, then stretched a long arm back and lifted the folded sheet from amongst the pile. Spreading it flat, he laid it across the whole of the table. The photograph had been taken well, on a day of full sun, carrying the colours beyond the density of glass to a subtler iridescence.

As always, the dragon dominated the picture, from the tip of its tail in the bottom left-hand corner to the majesty of its head in the top right. In that light, it was neither gold nor silver, but shimmered with the not-quite-rainbow of spilled mercury. The unarmoured knight raised aloft his sword, or his lance, or his staff – Stella had never known which – in a futile gesture of self-defence. The sun spread dawn across the eastern horizon. A half-moon hung at the highest point.

Stella put a thumb on each. 'The sun is rising in the east at the dragon's back. The moon is in the noon position, up here in the constellation of Virgo. Actually, it's a waxing moon reaching its zenith at dawn which is a physical impossibility but I assumed that to be poetic licence, to show us that the earth shadowed the moon and the light came from the sun. Up here, in the top right-hand corner, is this sigil you're talking about, which looks to me exactly like the scales on the Statue of Liberty, except that the sun is on the lower, heavier, side, and the moon is up there, weighing almost nothing. Relatively speaking, of course.'

Meredith Lawrence surveyed her over the top of his teacup for so long she thought he might never speak.

'If that's infantile nonsense, you can tell me,' she said.

'I would if it were.' He set the cup down. 'I could list for you the learned papers written about that window and the number of different interpretations of each of those features, none of which match the clarity, I might even say lucidity, of yours.'

'I've had help,' Stella said. 'It's on the medallion.'

Since the cave, the small bronze disc had been a part of her, taken off to shower and sleep, put back on again at waking and dressing, as necessary as her watch and as little considered. She pulled it now from under her T-shirt and laid it on the unlevel table where the sun made inroads into the dirt and oxide on the bronze.

It was oval more than round, longer from left to right than top to bottom. Here, the dragon was drawn in outline, barely recognizable as the vast, iridescent beast of the stained window. The man was a stick figure, holding aloft his sword-staff.

On the obverse was scratched the sign of Libra with the sun and the moon that she had first seen when she handed it to Kit. She said, 'There's less clutter on this, so it's more obvious. And the scales are depicted as the sign Libra, which is a bit of a giveaway.'

'May I?'

At her nod, Meredith picked the coin up and held it dangling in the slant-light coming under the awning. Distantly, he said, 'Cedric Owen designed the window, did you know? The plans were found in the cache with his ledgers and the diamonds that floated Bede's to the top of the Cambridge pile. It became the college crest only after the diamonds arrived. Before that, you had a wild boar rampant or something equally Plantagenet, but part of the conditions of Owen's bequest was that the dragon should become the crest and that the window be made and kept in place "until the ende of alle tyme". Which may or may not be five and a half years from now if we believe anything of what's going on here this weekend.'

'Do you?' Stella asked.

He grinned ruefully. 'I don't believe Rosita Chancellor and her threats of global meltdown, but it's pretty clear that we're on the downhill slope to self-destruction. We're an oil-addicted culture living on a planet that's fast running out of oil. It's pretty much a moot point now as to whether we pollute ourselves out of existence with the by-products of our overconsumption or blow ourselves to toxic fragments in the wars over the last few tankers of black gold. Either way, there won't be many folk left to pick up the pieces.'

'Someone else said as much this morning; that the Maya had destroyed themselves in the space of fifty years and we're doing the same.'

'Indeed. And they had cities of half a million people at a time when London could barely scrape together twenty thousand. And not only the Maya. Every city-based civilization has outgrown its primary resources since Gilgamesh cut down the cedars of Lebanon and turned the land to desert. Quite clearly, we have learned nothing at all from history. It's a particularly depressing thought. Whereas this . . .' Meredith rubbed his thumb over the medallion, 'is easily the most exciting thing I've seen in a long time. It is definitely Libra on here, isn't it? And the sun weighs more than the moon, which is evidently true, although how Owen knew might be a mystery for future scholars. And that dragon is really quite magnificent in its simplicity. Rather better than the stained glass, I would say; far more subtle in its subtexts.'

He handed it back, as one might hand a blown egg, or a small and fragile bird. 'Would you feel able to tell me where you got this?'

Unexpectedly, she did. 'In a cave in Yorkshire. It was round the neck of a skeleton. I asked the police. They said I could keep it.'

Ceri Jones had said she should keep it, which was close enough to be true.

'I see.' Meredith rubbed the side of his nose. Stella watched the obvious questions rise to his attention and watched him, with some control, set them aside. She looked past him, to the seething, moving crowd, and the small clot of bystanders that was growing to a larger mass in front of three young men, stripped to the waist

302

and tattooed from clavicle to navel, who began to mime the various ways by which the world might end.

At the crowd's edge was a bubble of space, and within it, a wheelchair. By a trick of the light, Kit was split momentarily in two: at once a buoyant figure sitting in his chair, laughing until the tears streaked his face; and a darker shape, standing, holding a weight of anger that could crush them both. The grim destruction that had hung around him in the doorway to Davy Law's lab clung there still.

She blinked and it was gone. She might have set it aside, but that Meredith Lawrence said, softly, 'A young man at war with himself.'

'He's lost his inner balance.' The day had fallen cold. Because it seemed to matter, Stella said, 'I'm an astronomer, I don't believe in astrology, but Kit's a Libran and he needs balance more than he needs air and water. If he goes on as he is, it'll kill him.'

'Or you?'

'Or me.' She looked away. 'I don't know how to bring him back to himself.'

'Nobody can do that, except him.' Meredith folded the image of the dragon and set it aside. 'Although you can perhaps do something for yourself? It seems to me, as an objective observer, that there is a matching imbalance within you that may need to be addressed before your Libran friend can find his own equilibrium.'

She remembered Kit's voice, dry and careful. *If I come with you, it doesn't mean I'm jealous of a stone.* And earlier, *You're in more danger. You're in love with it.* She looked over to him now. In the midst of the clowning, he had fallen fast asleep. 'Maybe.'

Somewhere in the distance, church bells chimed the hour. The sound filtered through the hubbub of the festival. Stella pushed herself to her feet. 'I should go and rescue Kit before they turn him into a prop for the pantomime. Thank you for that. It's been . . . interesting.'

Meredith stood up with her and held out his hand in a formal goodbye. His tone was lightly mocking, although of himself more than her. 'Think of it as a learning curve; it'll make the next few days easier. There is always hope in our endeavours; belief and hope together can move mountains, or at least shift the occasional molehill. Don't forget that. You can both live through this, I'm sure of it.'

19

The Walker Institute, Lower Hayworth
Farmhouse, Oxfordshire, June 2007

'THIS IS THE PLACE WHERE CEDRIC OWEN'S
ledgers were found. One of my ancestors
discovered them a century after Owen's death
bricked up in the bread oven to the right of the
fireplace, together with the diamonds that made
Bede's wealthy. Her son wrote the first thesis on
their contents in 1698. The obsession has run in
the family ever since. Take a seat. I'll get us
something to drink and we can forget the chaos
outside ever existed.'

Ursula Walker's kitchen was a haven of cool
peace; a big, high-ceilinged place of flagged
stone floors and once-white ceramic sink
and stone walls four feet thick that kept out the
heat of the day.

Stella sat at the vast oak table, big enough to
seat twelve with space to spare. Kit slept
opposite her in his wheelchair. The kitchen

windows were open, against the heat. Outside, the quality of the noise was changing as seven hundred men, women and children packed their stalls ready to leave.

Inside, Ursula made a leisurely circuit of the room, bringing together a tray of homemade elderflower lemonade and scones. She scooped clusters of ice cubes into three glasses, poured the lemonade, slid the squat tumblers across the wide oak table and came to sit at the short end, between Stella and the sleeping Kit.

Somewhere in the past five minutes, she had shed her cream linen jacket, and with it the formality of the woman who had run the festival. A streak of light crossed her face, smoothing ten years off her age. She raised her glass. 'I don't think a festival like this was necessarily the best way to meet. Shall we start again as if it didn't happen?'

'Or you could explain why it was here?' Stella said. 'You don't seem the type.'

'It wasn't all as bad as Rosita Chancellor. Bits of it were grounded in reality.' Ursula swirled the ice in her glass. 'I chaired a panel this morning that had two anthropologists and an archaeologist in the speaking team. Admittedly it was hijacked for ten minutes by the rogue element who wanted to discuss whether Cedric Owen's lost skull was in fact the Blue Skull of Albion when everybody knows – or doesn't – that the Albion skull was buried with Arthur at

Avalon and will return when he does, riding at the head of the wild hunt to save England from ruin. Apart from that it was all well within the boundaries of accepted science.'

'What were you supposed to be debating?' Stella asked.

'The interconnectedness of crystal skull legends across the globe and their relevance to the 2012 end date.'

Stella laughed. 'This is anthropology?'

'I believe so,' Ursula said. 'There are too many skull legends around the world for there not to be a kernel of truth and all of them point to 2012 as the end date, not just the Maya. All through the Americas, the indigenous tribes are gearing up for something big that will happen four to five years from now. The Hopi have been recalling their people for the past three years, exactly to meet this date. There are perfectly serious academic journals who will publish studies on that.'

She picked at a tooth with her thumbnail. 'It's harder to get them to take notice of what's happening in our own society but I've given my life to understanding the things that Cedric Owen did and the blue crystal skull drove him, therefore it drives me. If you're looking for a reason for why I am what I am, Owen's blue skull is the answer.'

'Even down to drinking reindeer urine?' Stella asked.

Ursula Walker stared into her lemonade a moment, then leaned over and reached behind Kit to where a bookcase lined the wall. She selected a slim notebook, from which she pulled, in turn, a photograph printed to full A4. She slid it on to the table, covering it with her hands.

'I went to Lapland to ask a question. The people there live with different priorities from ours and there are certain rituals that must be observed before one may even ask that kind of question, and the ceremonies I described in my paper were necessary for me to understand the answer. I'm a scientist. It is sometimes difficult for me to believe that which I have been told is impossible. The various properties, for instance, of this—'

She took her hands away from the photograph and slid it across the table to Stella.

Ursula Walker was in the picture, sitting in the background half hidden by the draped reindeer hides, with the star-specked sky over her left shoulder, but she was not the focus of the image, nor the point where Stella's eye fell.

The only thing that mattered, at first look and for a long time afterwards, was the flawless white crystal skull-stone held between the hands of a man so old that his face was cracked deep as oak bark and as brown. He wore reindeer skins and a headdress of flattened, velvet-covered antlers. His nose was a ship's prow cleaving the planes of his face. His eyes were cataract-white, exactly the same as the stone he held, and he looked straight at the lens, and through it, to Stella.

The stone shed white light from its eyes. It looked past Stella, to the pack on the floor at her feet which she had not mentioned to Ursula Walker, now or at any time previously.

Ursula said, 'This is the white spirit-stone of the Sami. I was not allowed to hold it. I was instructed, however, to bring back this one picture, and to show it to the new keeper of the blue heart-stone, that she might recognize the face of the white stone-keeper should they ever meet. His name is Ki'kaame. He is one of the most powerful people it has ever been my privilege to know. I saw him heal a child with the beams of light from the eyes of his skull-stone. Have you ever tried anything similar with yours?'

There was a long silence. Stella looked down into her glass. The lemonade smelled vaguely of cat's urine, but tasted clear and bright. White petals of elderflowers floated on the top, the same colour as the skull-stone in the picture. When she looked up, the beams of its eyes were on her. Her own stone lay mute in the bag at her feet. It was vividly alert now, sharpening her mind so that sounds became more dense and colours more saturated.

'How did you know?' she asked.

Ursula shrugged. 'A lucky guess?' She ticked the evidence off on her fingers. 'You're from Bede's. You're married to Kit O'Connor who's one of the brighter stars in the college firmament and he's been sniffing around the origins of the heart-stone since he first knew it existed. You ring out of the blue telling me you've found some Mayan glyphs in the ledgers. And when I rang Tony Bookless last night to find out who you were – he was most flattering, by the way; you have an admirer there – he asked me to do whatever I could to make sure you broke the item that had recently come into your possession. Meredith guessed first, if that makes it any easier. He has a particularly agile mind.'

She sat back and lifted her glass, eyeing Stella over the top of it. 'Were you going to tell me?'

Stella leaned back in her chair and let out the breath she had been holding. Looking up, she counted the beams in the ceiling twice over. There were nine on each side of the central ridge.

Carefully, she said, 'Someone has tried to kill Kit at least once. They – or someone else – wrecked his room yesterday and took his computer. I have no reason to believe we'd have been left alive if we'd been in there. As far as I can tell, everyone who has ever seen Cedric Owen's blue heart-stone has wanted either to possess it or to destroy it. It seems sensible, therefore, not to rush into showing it around.

And it has my face. I can't tell you how much that scares me.'

She thought Ursula might ask how she knew. Instead, she said, 'Good. Then you truly are the skull-keeper. In which case the rest of us have a duty to keep you safe long enough to do what is needed.'

'Which is what, exactly?'

Ursula clunked the ice in her glass. 'According to the Sami, you have to place your stone on the heart of the earth at the moment of sunrise on the Day of Awakening, at which point it will join with the other twelve stones which will have been set in place by their own keepers. The full array, once linked, will bring to life the dragon of the winter snows, freeing it to fight the source of all evil and thereby heal the woes of mankind and the earth.'

'The dragon of the winter snows?' Stella laughed harshly. 'Is that "within the boundaries of accepted science"?'

Ursula ran her tongue over her teeth. It was hard to tell if she was angry, offended or amused.

'You could call it the Ouroboros, or Quetzalcoatl, or the feathered serpent, or the rainbow serpent, or the Norse dragon Jörmungandr, or Arthur's dragon of Albion, or the fire-dragon of China, or the water-dragon of the Hindu that circles the elephants that hold the world on their backs. And yes, the

311

comparative cultural studies of this are written in detail in a dozen peer-reviewed journals. For the Sami, it is part of an oral legend that has remained intact for four hundred and eighty-seven generations. At the start of the ceremony, Ki'kaame invoked each of the spirit-skull's former holders by name, down the full lineage since their first making. Unless you've been there, you can't begin to understand the power of that.'

'I'm sorry.' Stella closed her eyes and hooked her two thumbs on the upper ridges of her eye sockets. A wasp whined in through the window and came to rest on the rim of the lemonade pitcher. She opened her eyes and watched it balance on a thin lip of sugared glass.

Distantly, she said, 'There was a poem in the Owen ledgers that led us to the stone. Read right, it's a set of instructions. It tells us to find "the time and place appointed", exactly the same as Ki'kaame's legend. It just doesn't tell us where to go or when.'

'Has the skull not told you?'

'I wouldn't be here if it had.' Stella turned to stare out of the window. The festival had packed itself away faster than she would have thought possible. Outside, the fields were almost quiet. She lifted her bag from the floor.

The skull was almost silent as Stella set it on the table next to the picture of the white stone. Ursula Walker was not afraid of it; nor, it seemed, did she lust for it. She folded her arms on the table and laid her chin on them and, for a long time, faced the skull on its own level. She neither spoke nor moved and the skull did not sing, but there was a communication that Stella could only guess at.

Some time later, Ursula sat back. 'There's a test that Ki'kaame showed me. Could we try it?'

'What are we testing?'

'Your connection to the stone.'

Ursula was already up and moving. She unhooked a small mirror from the wall and placed it on the ground in a patch of sunlight from one of the oak-framed windows that over-looked the back paddocks. Lifting a box of matches from near the stove, she slid it under-neath, angling the mirror so that a shaft of light speared straight upwards.

Satisfied, she stood back against the wall. 'If you can bring your heart-stone and stand here, so that it's over the mirror, and let the sun shine up through the occiput – that's the base of the skull, where the neck would join on, like that . . . thank you, yes, just a little bit left. There . . .'

Stella stood in the middle of the floor with the skull-stone held over the patch of light. Nothing happened, except that she felt desperate and foolish at once, as if she were failing an exam she had not wanted to sit.

'Ursula, I—'

'Step a little further to the left, can you?'

A hand pushed her shoulder, moving her a fraction. 'Ursula, this isn't— *Oh!*'

Stella had no words for the pulse of life that surged up between her hands and became, a moment later, two beams of soft blue light that shone from the skull's eyes.

In the blue place of her mind which had become the heart-stone's was an open doorway, or a hand extended; an invitation that she could neither read nor answer.

She hated being tested. She hated it particularly when she did not know either what was needed or how to achieve it. She closed her eyes, reaching for the open gateway, stretching for the song of the stone as she had done all day, but with more concentration.

Perversely, it grew harder to hear, lost beneath the rising whine of the wasp, which was drowning in the lemonade. Without opening her eyes, Stella could see it, caught deep in the pitcher, rocking on an ice cube, with its right wing trailing in the sticky water beneath. She might have wished it dead, simply to shut it up, but the part of her that was wedded to the stone would not allow that and so she wished it merely out of the water and silent, the better to hear the stone's song.

The wasp became silent. The stone fell silent with it. Stella opened her eyes.

'I'm sorry. I can't feel any kind of—'

'Stella, look at the wasp.'

The wasp was not caught in the pitcher as she had thought, but sat preening on the edge. The light of the blue heart-stone softened the yellow bands of its thorax to a quiet summer green.

'I thought it was drowning.'

'It was,' said Kit.

He was only just awake; she saw it in the half-dream of his eyes. The division within him had not gone; now that she had seen it, she could not un-see it. She had no idea what to do or say.

In the quiet that fell between them, Ursula Walker said, 'I saw a sick child healed with Ki'kaame's white spirit-stone.'

Ursula did not look up at Kit as she spoke. Slowly, Stella did. The heart-stone sang its almost-silent song. She turned the soft blue light towards him.

'Stella, don't. Please.'

She stopped. The blue light hovered near him, casting strange shadows on the table. Kit was white, and drawn, with new shadows beneath his cheekbones. Even in hospital, he had not looked so ill. She wanted him well again, and the stone wanted it with her; it reached for the shadows in his being as if they were strands of broken thread, to be woven whole. She closed her eyes, to keep the yearning from tearing her apart.

Again, Kit said, 'Please.'

Stella felt his resistance as a glass wall; thick and unmoving, but so easy to break. She drew breath to imagine breaking it.

From another continent, Ursula said, 'It may not help, but I don't think it can do any harm.'

'That's not the point,' Kit said thickly. 'I don't want to be able to walk again because Stell made it happen. We couldn't live the rest of our lives like that. I'd owe her too much. Stella? Are you listening? *Stop!*'

'I've stopped.' She had to say it again, to be sure he could hear it. 'I *have* stopped.'

The glass barrier was gone, and all sense of the shadows within him. She was not clear if the stone had withdrawn, or she had made it leave, or Kit had sent them both away.

Her hands burned as if she held ice in one and live coals in the other. She stepped away from the shaft of mirrored light. Cut from its source, the stone fell brutally silent. She was shaking all over. Her chest ached as an open hollow, as if she had been weeping for too long and only lately stopped.

There was a cool stone wall at her back. She slid down it until her knees were level with her chin, cradling the blue stone inside, against the soft parts of her belly, as if it were a child.

Through painful, scintillating sunlight, she looked up at Kit. 'I wouldn't have done anything if you didn't want it.'

'But you would have done it.'

316

'It's not me, it's the stone. I didn't do anything except hold it over the light. Anyone could have done that.'

'That doesn't make it better, Stell.'

'Oh, for God's sake.' She put her head in her hands, to block out the day and the light and the wounded accusation on his face. 'It's a stone. A piece of rock. If it helps you walk again, would it matter that much?' When he said nothing, she made herself look up at him again. 'Would it have been so bad to be free of this?'

He was a child, trapped in a mess of social niceties, in the company of strangers. Pointedly, he looked to Ursula and back. 'Can we drop this?'

Ursula said, 'You don't have to on my account.'

'No, but probably best if we do.' Something dense and cold had taken up residence in Stella's abdomen. 'Can we assume that I passed your test?'

'Unquestionably.'

'Right. I don't know how much Kit heard, but in essence we are no further forward than we were, except to confirm that this is Cedric Owen's stone, one of thirteen that must be taken to the place appointed, at dawn on the day appointed, and we know neither.'

The churning in her guts was less, if not her heart. She was beginning to think more clearly.

'Are the rest held by people as clueless as us, or will they know more of what they're doing?'

'I have reason to believe there's one in Hungary and one in Egypt, both held by families who still understand what they're for and what's needed. I would like to think the rest are held by people who know similarly what to do. I have no idea at all how to contact them.'

'So the Sami could tell us where to go and when?'

'I think so,' Ursula said. 'The problem is how to ask them without going there. When you first rang me yesterday, I sent an email to Lapland asking for help, but I'm not holding my breath for a reply. It's a seven-hundred-mile trek from the herding grounds to the internet café in Rovaniemi in Finland and only one of Ki'kaame's great-grandsons has ever learned how to use a PC.'

Kit said, 'How long would it take you to get to Finland?' His voice was brittle, as if he was asking the question simply to be heard.

'Too long. The stone wouldn't risk coming out of hiding unless we were very close indeed to the Day of Awakening.'

'And I thought we'd been so clever finding the code.' The irony in his smile, at least, was real.

Ursula liked him. There was a different warmth in her eyes. 'You were,' she said. 'If there had been no one left with a strength of heart and mind to match it, it would have stayed hidden for the rest of eternity and the arc of the nine would never be lit at all. Our problem now is how to begin to find the answers when we don't even know how long we've got.'

'We have the codex we found in Cedric Owen's ledgers,' said Stella. 'It's why we came here in the first place. It must have the answers, surely.'

It was worth a lot of the past half-hour simply to see the world crash to a stop in Ursula's face. She said, 'I don't understand.'

'Here.' Kit lifted his bag from his chair and gave it to Stella. She opened it and spread everything neatly across the floor: the original copies of the ledgers, the prose poem they had found from the shorthand in the final volume, and her attempts at recreating the Mayan glyphs in the other volumes.

She said, 'I told you on the phone that we'd found some glyphs. They're part of a code – you build them up from marks in the ledgers. They come out in a twelve by twelve array.' Stella spun the opened file across the floor. 'Can you read them?'

Ursula was already on her hands and knees, pulling the pages into a line across the flagstones, reading as she went.

'*I, friend of the . . . jaguar-woman . . . I write this . . . account of my life, my knowledge, my learning*— That one isn't clear, I'll need to look

319

it up, it goes deeper than that. *I begin in . . . the city with the great river* – that would be Paris. He was never in London – *and my meeting with the . . . star-gazer and teller of . . . true futures*. That has to be Nostradamus; we know they shared a lodging in Paris . . . My God—'

Ursula was shaking; the page fluttered in her hand. Her eyes were alight with a startling fervour. 'Stella, this is a gold mine, the mother lode of all gold mines. Cedric Owen spent thirty-two years among the Maya of the New World. If he wrote down what they taught him, it will be more than enough. Somewhere in here will be the detail of where we have to take the stone and when. How fast can you transcribe this?'

'Faster than I could have done now we've got Kit's software.'

'What are you waiting for?' Ursula flushed like a schoolgirl. 'You write, I'll translate. If we do nothing else, we could conceivably have all thirty-two volumes done within the week.'

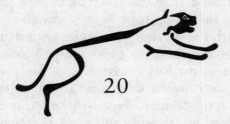

20

Southern Mayalands, New Spain,
October 1556

CEDRIC OWEN WOKE TO RAIN THAT WAS NOT
rain, but Diego standing over him flicking
water hard and fast at his face. His heart-stone,
safe in its satchel, dug into the small of his back
where he had fallen on it. He rolled over to find
that the jaguar was squatting at his side, gazing
at him curiously.

From this new angle, he could see that the
gape of its jaw was the pelt of a beast, with
the still-boned head set atop wiry native hair;
that the lines flaring back from the bared teeth
were not whiskers, but scars gouged deep into
the cheeks of a dark native face; that the great
white jaguar teeth below were not set in the
jaws of a beast, but only threaded on to a
necklace, hung there for decoration like the
two paws of the jaguar skin cape that dangled
below, and beneath them, pushing them

out in two gently swollen curves, were . . .

Very much too late, Cedric Owen came to understand that the beast that now stood up beside his prone form was a woman, and that beneath the spotted beast-skin, with its head set on her head and its claws draped loose about her neck, she was naked.

He had been a long time at sea, in the company only of men. His eyes had travelled the length of her from head to toe and back to the swell of her chest again before he had a grip on himself and remembered that he was a physician, and the human body held no mysteries for him, nor allure.

From the place he no longer cared to look, a rusted voice of vast amusement and great depth said, 'Cedric Owen, keeper of the blue heart-stone, are you afraid to set your eyes on me?'

He was afraid, but not as he had been when he believed he faced a living jaguar. Now, he was afraid for his pride and his deportment rather than for his body and soul. He was not so much a child as to give in to that.

He stood, and made himself look. The jaguar-woman was a head shorter than Diego, who was not tall to begin with, but she bore herself with an assurance that Owen had never seen in any woman, not even the Medici Queen of France.

Viewed in greater detail, she was as well muscled as any fighting man, only fuller of the hips and with the soft swell to her belly that men never carried, and her breasts ... In his professional opinion, she had borne at least three children.

He tried to drag more light from the falling sun that he might better estimate her age. In the shock of first seeing, he had thought her of his own age, not far into her third decade. She stepped closer to him now, to let him look better, and he saw beyond the startling dis-figurement of the jaguar-scars on her face to the fine-branched lines in the brown skin at her eyes and the thicker skin at her throat and the silvering hair at her temples under the jaguar's head cap. At the end, he believed her closer to forty than twenty. The thought made her no less terrifying, or beautiful.

He was staring at her, dumbly, which was not decent. He closed his mouth and averted his gaze. She took hold of his jaw and turned him forcibly back to face her. 'Do you not know me?'

'I regret not, madam.' Discomfort made him formal. He bowed stiffly against the pressure of her hand and flushed when she laughed aloud. 'I came in search of help for my friend who is dying.'

'Only that?'

... *therein to meet those who know the heart and soul of your blue stone. They will tell you how best you may unlock its secrets and pre-serve them for all eternity.*

'No, madam. I came also to find how I may recover what was lost: the knowledge of how best to use my blue heart-stone. I am led to believe I may find these two together; the healing of my friend and the secrets of my stone that once were known and have long since been lost to my family.'

Raising a brow, the jaguar-woman took a step back the better to view him as he had her. The starkness of her scrutiny was as discomfiting as anything else she had done. Owen's heart twisted in his chest. Very badly, he did not want this woman to be disappointed in him.

He said, 'I have not yet the honour of your acquaintance, while you know me in all ways. May we redress the balance?'

'Cedric Owen, ninth of that name.' She ran her tongue across her teeth in a gesture that spiked terror and desire in him equally. He felt an unfortunate movement in his groin and prayed she might not notice.

She did him the service of not looking down. 'I have known you since before you were born,' she said. 'I have known you since before you last died, when you were not Cedric Owen, and before that, and before that. I know who you will be when next you walk upon the earth.'

There was nothing he could say. Something in his silence drew her to a decision. She bowed her head as he had done, but with more grace.

'I am Najakmul. You may call me Dolores, if you find it easier – that name was given me by the Spanish priest when he still believed that by dipping me in cold water he could bring me closer to his man-god.'

She was no more Dolores than the man who had summoned her was Diego. Owen said, 'I would prefer to call you Najakmul.'

She nodded. Her scrutiny seemed less scathing. 'We have little time. Are you prepared?'

'I don't know.'

'My sons have not told you what is required?'

'Your *sons*?' Owen spun with all the force of an aggrieved and injured pride. 'Diego!'

The scarred native shrugged sheepishly. 'What could I say that you would have believed? Among your people, the women have no power. They cannot talk to the god of the black-robed priests, they cannot talk to the kings and generals of the armies. Even among my people who live in Zama and Mérida, the women were already accounted less than the men long before Spain came. Only those of us who still live in the jungle, by the ways of the jungle, know that the she-jaguar is the more powerful, the she-eagle the bigger, the she-snake the more deadly.'

'And your mother?'

'Is all of these.' White teeth flashed him a many-layered smile. The complexities of love and respect and a deeper awe weathered into Diego's face spoke more depth than his voice ever could. 'When she talks, we listen. What she needs of us, we give her.'

'Of course.' He turned to Najakmul, swept off an imaginary hat and bowed. Fernandez de Aguilar could have done it with no greater panache. The Spaniard breathed painfully at their feet. Owen knelt, and lifted the sleeping man's hand, that they might all remember why he had come.

'Perhaps then, you can tell me what is required to achieve the healing of my friend?'

Catlike, the jaguar-woman stalked thrice around him and came to kneel on de Aguilar's other side, bringing her face close to his. Her eyes shone with the light of the moon, dazzling him. 'Can you light a fire, Cedric Owen, keeper of the blue heart-stone?'

This at least he could answer. 'I have been lighting fires since I was six years old.'

'Then do so now.'

'Diego has already—'

She shook her head, grinning savagely. He turned round in time to see Diego kick the remains of his fire to smouldering cinders.

'You are the keeper of the heart-stone. It must be your fire.' Najakmul saw him reach for his flint and tinder and shook her head again, handing him instead the loose-strung bow and charred rod that the natives used with such

326

ease and Cedric Owen had never used at all.

'Not here, there,' said Najakmul, pointing. 'On the fire circle of the mosaic. There must you raise your heart-fire.'

Under the critical gaze of Najakmul and her three sons, he crouched in the sweating heat and bent his back to slide the blackened tip of the stick into its socket and did his best to draw the bow back and forth as deftly as Diego had done.

None of them laughed, for which he was grateful. He sweated and swore and snagged his fingers in the bow-string and cursed and slowly, as the late sun honed its light across the sharp edge of the pyramid, he brought forth a spidery thread of smoke and saw a reddening glow come alive in the tinder and fed it the hairs from his head and small fragments of dried moss and grasses and knew a satisfaction that surprised him; he had long since forgotten the child's unfettered joy in a new task mastered.

The smoke was rich with the scents of the jungle. Owen's eyes began to water. Diego and his brothers gathered at his back, whence the light breeze was coming. In the forgiving shelter of their bodies, his flame became two flames, and then many. The buttery yellow mosaic tiles took the flames to their hearts and glowed as if from within, so that his fire burned down into the earth as much as it did up to the evening sky.

At a certain point, when the flames were bright to match the fading sun, Diego leaned over his shoulder and pressed a fresh knot of grasses and leaves into his hand. 'Burn this. Drink the smoke.'

The bundle burned with a high, blue flame, the colour of his skull-stone. The smoke was fine and peppery and slid down his throat to fill his heart and spread through his chest, warming him, lightening him, lifting him to heaven. He drank, and grieved when it was done.

'Stand. Look. Listen.'

He stood. He looked. He listened to a world in which every breath of every beast of the jungle was made suddenly clear to him, as if his ears had been stopped all his life with cotton and were only now laid open.

All around, the cries of the small jewelled birds spilled out as individual notes, clear as chimed crystal; to his left, high overhead, the wings of a passing butterfly rasped through the air thick as crows' feathers; he heard the scales on a snake slide past the loose bark on a tree.

His eyes were similarly deafened. Before, he had thought the jungle blindingly iridescent. Now, he saw the colours within the colours and was dazzled. He could have lost himself in the single mote of light of a quetzal bird's eye, or the veins on a hanging leaf, or the scattering of tiles on the mosaic, which were not separate any more, but flowed together to make a living image of the held breath before the world's end.

Light-headed, he began to kneel, the better to see the shape of a single blue flower picked out in turquoise pebbles in the meadow of Innocence.

His balance was bad. Careful hands caught him, and wrapped his head, tilting it backwards. Diego's voice, light and brisk, said, 'Do not look down yet, Cedric Owen, lest we lose you for ever in the other times.'

Afraid, he let his gaze be directed west, to the setting sun and the open blue sky whereon were painted the colours of the coming night.

He might have launched himself into the sweep of saffron yellow and deep plum reds flaring out from the sun's globe, letting go the fragile boundaries of his body, but that Fernandez de Aguilar coughed – a chaotic sound, cracked across by shearing scarlets, whites and blacks.

Owen followed the bubbling in-breath that came after and knew the depth of it, and the pockets of water in the lungs where it sought to rest, and the pressure of blood in the great pulmonary vessels that even now was beginning to fade.

He reached forward for his friend's wrist, and found it, and read the truth in the three pulses. 'He is dying. We must act now!'

His voice swayed out to the trees and

rebounded. From the far side of the fire, Najakmul answered, 'Then look at me, Cedric Owen, keeper of the blue heart-stone. The time is right.'

She sat in shadow. Two beams of light came from between her hands, as if she had reached to the sky and pulled the sun twice from its mooring and brought it here to shine on him.

Against the brightness, Owen squinted at the space between her bony fingers. Slowly, a shape grew: the silvering outline of a jaguar skull crafted from perfectly clear, colourless stone that drew in the wavering firelight and the haze of distant, jungle-screened moonlight and wove from them two beams of silver light that sang with a tone so pure it came near to breaking his mind apart.

So it was, in the throbbing night, with all his senses sharpened beyond bearing, that Owen saw for the first time in his life another skull wrought of stone and shaped by hands that knew the secrets of the stars. Almost, it came near to the perfection of his own stone. Almost.

Softly, Najakmul said, 'It is strange, is it not, to see another?'

'It breaks my heart.'

Owen felt his soul rise to his eyes; a kind of nakedness he had never known before. 'What have you done to me?'

'Opened the eyes and ears of your heart. You can see now as we see, hear as we hear, feel as we feel. Thus equipped, you are fit to walk the rift between the worlds, to bind the four beast-stones, and join together the nine stones of the races of men.'

A half-remembered shadow rose to him from the mosaic, and a chance remark by the priest.

At the End of Days . . . these four will come together to form one beast. Can you imagine, sir, what might arise out of the union of these four?

The hairs rose on his scalp, prickling and cold in the warm night. Afraid, he said, 'You want me to raise the dragon Kukulkan, the rainbow serpent? The end times are not yet upon us, surely?'

Najakmul shook her head. 'Not yet. But in a time yet to come, the whole must be made from the sum of its parts. The nine stones of men must be joined in the hoop that will girdle the earth. If we were asked to do this now, we would fail; a piece is missing from our knowledge. Only you can find it. When it is found, then may the four beasts come together as one.'

Najakmul leaned forward over the fire. Thick smoke furled about her head. She did not cough. 'Will you believe me, Cedric Owen, if I tell you that time is a path along which you may walk if we open the gates and send you?'

Something in her dark eyes warned him, and a simple question from Nostradamus. 'Does death attend the trying?' he asked.

331

'Death attends all things.'

'And yet, if I succeed, will the death that presently attends Fernandez de Aguilar depart so that he might live?'

She nodded, and it was almost a bow. 'If you can do this, it is possible your friend may be healed. If you fail, more than you and he will die, for the last rift will be joined and Desolation will spread over all the earth without hope of redemption. Are you prepared for this? Are you willing to risk all for the life of the one you care for?'

'I am.'

He spoke with a certainty that surprised them both. Through the swirling smoke, he heard Najakmul's soft laugh. 'Then look down now, Cedric Owen, and see at last the world at your feet.'

21

SOME TIME BEFORE NIGHT FELL, DE AGUILAR had been brought to lie on the very centre of the mosaic that mapped the end time. At his right hand was devastation, grief, destruction and death, made so real Owen could taste the fear, could see the colours of the tears, could hear the soul-death of those who struggled simply to survive.

At his left, place of the rising moon, a girl-child played knucklebones in a summer's meadow with wild flowers scattered around.

Caught in the rift between these two was the string of many-coloured pearls; a thin thread of hope for Fernandez de Aguilar and for the world.

From the far side of the fire, Najakmul said, 'They must be joined by the song-line of your stone.'

His blue stone languished in the satchel bumping at his hip. With the care of a father to his firstborn, Owen delivered it into the firelight.

He felt shy of it, in the presence of another, and then proud, for Najakmul showed her soul in her eyes as she gazed on it.

Tilting his hands, he played with the light until the stone gathered enough of fire and moon to weave them together and send them out to meet and match the clear, uncoloured crystal of her snarling jaguar.

In their meeting was an alchemy of tone and light he had not witnessed before. Seeing how each wove into the other, to make a third thing that was greater than either apart, Cedric Owen understood how the thread of the song-line might perhaps be made to join the nine skulls together and then to unite the four beasts as one. The question was whether he could do it.

'So.' He lifted the skull and moved it, that the shine from its eyes and the thread of its song might be directed downwards, on to the tiled rift in the mosaic.

He began in the south, with the red stone, colour of the fire's heart. The rift widened as he sent the blue song of the heart-stone on to it, so that what had been a red-stained pearl became a skull-stone of deepest carnelian, and what had seemed a single line of plain black obsidian pebbles set into the earth became instead a widening place of night-time shadows and soft breath, waiting.

Drawn by his own stone, sent by Najakmul's beast-stone, he moved on and in.

The rift was a valley, now, that led on to a broad, sandy desert. Owen walked on warm, coarse sand, which sifted up between his toes. He smelled a bittersweet smoke, quite different from that which he had left. He looked up to a crisp night sky with stars he had never imagined, and could not name.

The red fire-stone was held by a woman his own age, with skin black as pitch. She sat naked before him. Firelight cascaded gold and red down the satin valley of her breasts. She nodded to a log on which a visitor might sit. As Owen bent to take his seat, he heard a slither on the sand behind.

The blue skull-stone sang a bright note of warning and command. Time warped and slowed in the place where he stood. In leisurely fashion, he spun on one foot and hooked the toe of the other under the red-bellied black snake that struck for him, sending it sailing far into the night.

He felt no fear, only a strange, dry exhilaration. In a separate place of his mind, he apologized to Fernandez de Aguilar, his friend, that he had not moved with such swiftness when the last snake came upon him.

Turning back, he found the black-skinned

woman standing. Her skull-stone was the colour of blood, of birth, of raging, red-fanged death, the colour of the snake's belly. It took in the light of the fire and spilled it out again in a scarlet song-line that stained the earth to make a path that did not depart when she turned away. Owen turned his blue stone the same way, and the paths wove together, to make something greater than either apart.

'Come,' said Cedric Owen. 'Ours is the time, the joy and the duty.' The words were not his; they came from the night and the earth and the place beyond the scuffing shadows of the fire whence they must walk.

In silence they followed the red-blue path into the darkness, and presently came upon a rock that reared out of the desert, vast and smooth as the hump of a whale. High on its side, punched clear out of the stone, was a rounded cleft, of a size to take a man's head, with or without the flesh.

Owen said, 'We must make the whole from the sum of its parts. Your stone must join with the soul of the earth.' The woman was already reaching up.

Her stone slid home to its place in the root of the earth with a sound like the birth of a star, a blinding, deafening implosion that rocked Owen back on his heels and robbed him momentarily of his senses so that he did not see the second snake, that came for the black-skinned woman.

She was dying when next he opened his eyes, but gladly so. Her smile lit the night. She waved and he fell backwards on to earth that opened to let him through into darkness.

'That was the first,' said Najakmul. 'You faced the serpent and lived.'

He was already in a new place by the time he realized she was speaking to him.

Eight times in all did Cedric Owen cast his song-line along the rift that held back the Desolation. Eight times he met a skull-holder, each with a stone of a different colour, who gave it to the earth, that its song might join with the song of the blue stone, which was also the song of all that had gone before, and greater.

Eight times did he face death in its many guises, from a scorpion at the foot of a pyramid to a charging boar in the forests of a wet, windy plain, to a rockfall in a wooded river valley so beautiful that he wept to leave it. Eight times did he see the skull-holder greet the same death he had just avoided after the stone had been given to its place in the earth.

Thus did he fulfil the prophecy of Nostradamus, who had cast the seven colours of light in the shape of a fan across a table in a lodging house in Paris, and shown him that after them came the black of no-light and the white of all-light to make the full nine.

He came last to the all-light. An old, old man

with a hooked nose and an antlered headdress held the white skull-stone in a place of snow and ice with harsh-coated deer in the background and a young woman weaving the song-line in her throat. Death came for Owen as an avalanche, which he ran from, returning later through thigh-deep snow. The cleft that joined the skull to the earth was dug deep into the living ice and bedrock and the old man had to be lowered in on a rope and lifted out afterwards, when the white stone was set.

The old man and the young woman left him, swept away in an avalanche they made no effort to escape.

Alone, and untouched, Owen stood in the black night on a landscape so vast and white that the reflected starlight hurt his eyes.

He stood on the boundary between white snow and black night and his own blue stone sang to him, spinning and holding at once the complex thread of eight colours that encircled the earth.

Only eight.

The shadow of Nostradamus whispered in his ear. *Nine are shaped for the races of men. Remember this. You will need knowledge of it later.*

Owen looked down at the blue stone. Thinking back, it came to him that he had passed without stopping from a green forested place with high foaming cataracts on to indigo mountains where a monk with a shaved head and prayer wheels had set a deep blue stone into a carved place in an altar so old the rock was almost gone. There had been no chance between these two to go to England, whence the blue stone had come and must return.

Over the thousand leagues of snow and ice Najakmul's voice came to him in tatters, torn by the razor wind. 'You must set your will to go there.'

Aloud, he said, 'But where? I know not the place.'

'The place will call you. Send out your care for your friend, and follow the song of your heart.'

To his shame, Owen had all but forgotten Fernandez de Aguilar. He remembered him now, lying flat on the mosaic with one arm gone and the fluid rattles in his lungs that were killing him. He smelled the smoke of the fire, suddenly more pungent, with the same peppery sweetness of earlier.

He sneezed. Najakmul said, 'Drink, and remember. Your friend cares for you. You have staked your life on his. *Think* and remember.'

Owen sneezed again, fluidly, and watched the stars in the high firmament shudder in their tracks.

Think.

He said it himself this time, without Najakmul's help. With a grinding effort, he trawled his mind and found at last something he could hold to: the image of de Aguilar sitting with his back to the mast of his ship, looking out at the dawn before Zama, offering friendship without attachment or condition.

Perhaps you would not wish so to burden a friend?

The light, acerbic voice reached Owen across the wastes, and the burn of the sun and the sea wind, and the flap of the sails, and the salt-sour taste of the sea on his lips and the sway of the ship underfoot.

Even as he matched it, the ship swayed less. The wind grew warmer and did not cut him so. The mewling cries of a distant gull came closer, and were instead the tremulous call of a tawny owlet, that was from neither the tundra of the reindeer-people nor the humid jungle of Najakmul's jaguar night.

Owen opened his eyes, only then aware that he had closed them. He was in England; he knew it by the smell of damp turf, and the hushing breeze and the creak and sway of the beech trees in the moonlight. Most, he knew it by the heartfelt silence of the blue stone, which had come home at last.

He did not know the place to which he had been brought. Standing stones ringed him, of harsh grey rock, the height of a man and half as much again. Their shadows made thin black streaks that fell across the earth.

They made the forefront to a low mound of barrowed earth, grown over with grass, as wide as de Aguilar's ship. At its end, facing Owen, was a stone-lintelled entrance, into which a tunnel bored, guarded by the four sentinel stones and a few others, shorter and squatter with carnivorous points, set about with carved runes that caught and held the moonlight. Unreadable syllables whispered softly in the night.

The land was the same; from all directions came faint, ghosted pathways, tracking in like the spokes of a wheel to centre on the mound within the ring of standing stones. They chimed softly, dissonantly, so that Owen was caught in a web of the moon's weaving and all of it tugged him, whether he willed it or not, to the square-edged black mouth of the mound.

It was a grave; he could hear the sighs of the once-living that still gathered close.

The owl called again, more harshly. Owen felt the skin on his back shrink from an unknown threat. His blue stone gave no warning as it had done before the storm, but sat in the silence of a held breath, waiting.

Does it require your death, this stone?

The owl called for the third time. Owen lifted his blue stone that it might better catch the moonlight at his back and send it forth to light his way.

For the first time, the colours it sent forward were all nine of the races of men, woven together to make the shimmer on the surface of water, or of the ice on a high mountain, split and re-formed, a colour that had no name, but was precious beyond imagining.

It arced forward, as an inverted rainbow, with the red to the inner edge and a line of diamond white to the outside. Along the ghost-light of this path, Cedric Owen walked into the mouth of the grave mound, which opened to receive him, and down the length of the tunnel beyond.

The light was swallowed by the dark. Owen stood at the blind end of the grave mound. It was larger than it had seemed from the outside. He could feel stone all about; the tunnel walls brushed the top of his head and his two shoulders. If he stretched out both arms, he could touch the lateral margins.

There were bones on the floor. Kneeling, he felt the length of them, and the curved ends, and knew them for parts of human and horse; more than one of each. His fingers brushed against something metallic: a brooch or a coin. He rubbed his thumb across it to clear the dust of the tomb, but could not see clearly what was printed thereon. He dropped it into his satchel and felt on for the socket into which the heart-stone must be seated. He felt no danger, although death was all around.

A noise made him turn; the sound of voices,

arguing. Swaying back against the tomb wall, he found an alcove and pressed himself into it. With his two hands, he covered the eyes of his heart-stone so that it might not shed light and give him away.

In the black, his eyes made shapes that could not be there. A young woman passed him, out-landishly dressed, speaking words in a language Owen did not recognize. She reached the end of the grave mound and looked about and, in the light of her presence, he saw the socket that would take the blue skull-stone.

Without wishing it, Owen gave a small and breathless gasp.

She turned, and Owen gasped aloud, for between her two hands, with the care of a mother cradling her infant, she held a blue stone, exactly like his own. In the curved mirror surface of its cranium, he saw himself reflected exactly as now, but that his hair was silver. The shock of both these two things – the stone and his hair – rendered him mute.

The girl peered at him, and frowned. He saw his grandmother in her face and was likewise recognized. He might have spoken, but that she turned and looked back behind her in alarm, and ran on to the end of the mound, and knelt, and lifted her stone towards its resting place.

Urged by his own fears, Owen said, aloud, 'Do not delay.'

She turned to him, shocked. He reached out

to help her as he had helped the others. Before his hands could find flesh, there fell a fog of such density that it swallowed both girl and stone. From outside, whence had come the roiling fog, came a shout, and a crack, like thunder. In the darkness was a stifled scream and the sound of a body, falling.

Owen did not believe the girl had set her stone as was needed. Fog-blind, he felt his way forward to where she had been. By touch, he found the socket, and would have set his own blue stone into it as he had seen done eight times already, but that his skin pricked a warning.

He turned. A draught brushed up his left side. There, in the dark where there had been a blank wall, was a wide space. In the centre, Fernandez de Aguilar lay on a mosaic, lit by a dying fire. The signature stench of lungs in putrefaction rose from him. His breath rattled. Bloody foam leaked from his nose.

'Fernandez?'

Owen knelt to take a pulse that fluttered and leaped under his fingers in a way he knew well, and had always hated.

'Fernandez, no!' He leaned in, ready to do what he could with his breath, but too late. With the closeness of a lover, he saw the moment when the soul of his friend lifted away from the body that had so lately held it.

He rocked back on his heels. The shade of de

Aguilar bowed before him. 'Do not grieve for me, my friend. Death is not so bad a thing when it has been preceded by joy, and I have known great joy in your company.'

'No! You cannot die!' Owen was wretched, swaying and grieving as he had seen so many others do and never yet done himself, even for his grandmother.

He still held the blue stone, and it sang for him. Scattered bones scraped at his knuckles. He swept them away and shifted round to fit his back to the wall, where the sharp stones of the mound dug into his flesh, giving him another kind of anchor.

The boundary between life and death was a tangible thing, a fine membrane of shimmering black, that shaped the air in front of him. Holding to the blue stone, with the grinding sharpness of the rocks as a second anchor behind, Owen thrust his free hand through the barrier to the place where de Aguilar's body lay in the worlds of death.

There came flesh-scorching heat, as if he had just plunged his hand into a furnace. Paired with it was a bitter, aching cold that turned his ruined fingers to stubs of iron that would not bend.

Cursing, and then screaming, Owen strained one outstretched hand forward to touch his own life to the dark place of de Aguilar's death.

Death came for him, faster than the serpent

or the scorpion, more crushing than the rocks or the avalanche. His smoke-given gift of speed was no longer sufficient to evade it. As a fist of dark ice, it sprang up the full length of his arm, clutching for his heart—

—and met the steadfast song of the blue heart-stone, in the core of his own soul.

The world exploded into shards of blue and black and scarlet.

Cedric Owen fell backward, striking his head on stone. Fire scorched him on one side, cold on the other. A small, terrified part of his mind told him that he had entered hell, and that the priests had been right and he had all eternity to regret his hubris.

The rest of him only knew that the blue heart-stone was lying heavily on his abdomen, and that he needed urgently to be sick.

He rolled to his knees and puked violently, retching afterwards on nothing until he thought the lining of his stomach would fall to shreds and pour out of his throat. A beaker was pressed into his hand, made of a leaf coiled into a cone and stitched with fine tree shoots. He drank the thick, bitter liquid without comment or complaint.

Three times, he was sick. Three times, he was held and given comfort and the foul liquid to drink. At last, heaving, he sat up and opened his eyes to find which god or devil, or some monster between, was now his keeper.

He turned his eyes towards the half-seen figure in the white shirt who sat near the fire with one arm draped across its knees. He blinked, and again, and the shape would not go away.

'Welcome back,' said Fernandez de Aguilar peacefully. 'It would seem that, once again, I am in debt to you for my life.'

For the second time in too few days, Cedric Owen fainted.

22

Southern Mayalands, New Spain,
October 1556

H E WOKE IN DAYLIGHT, IN THAT COOL PART OF
the morning when the fire was still
welcome.

He lay on grass, not on the mosaic, and there
were trees overhead, full of coloured birds and
soft-furred mammals that hung from the
branches and gazed at him with fat, black eyes.

He could no longer hear their breathing, nor
lose himself in the spark of light from a feather.
He mourned that loss as he would have
mourned his hearing or his sight.

He sat up and was sick again; a thing so rou-
tine that his body no longer fought it. This time,
Najakmul held him, and gave him the black
drink; he felt the press of her breasts on his
back. A shiver of fear made him pull away.

'Cedric Owen?' Her hands held him loosely.
He did not look at her; could not do so without

348

remembering how she had sat through the night on the mosaic, exactly at the boundary line between Desolation and Innocence.

Owen said, 'I failed you.'

She was exhausted; the deepening lines on her face told him so. She smiled stiffly, as if her muscles had forgotten how to work. 'You did not fail.'

'But I am alive, when the others all died.

'You think that failure?' She smiled her disbelief.

He was not in the mood to be taunted. 'I thought only of Fernandez. I did not marry the blue heart-stone to the earth; I have it here with me still.' It was not only in his hand, it was in his heart. Something had changed, so that he no longer reached for the stone as a thing outside himself. It had *become* him, or he it; its song was his heartbeat, his heartbeat its song.

'It was not up to you to set it, only to find where it should be. And your friend lives, therefore you did not fail. This is yours, as proof of it.'

Najakmul pressed a coin into his hand. On closer inspection, squinting through blurry eyes, he saw rather a bronze medallion, with a dragon worked into its front face. The wings were an eagle's, the body lithe as a jaguar; the gaping jaws were of the crocodile and the tail curled up after the manner of a serpent. The whole thing stood with the rising sun at its back and a half-moon high above. A man stood before it, in the west; a small, insignificant thing before the might of the beast.

A leather thong of a hide he did not recognize made the coin something to be worn. Najakmul took it from him and hooked it over his head. Owen looked up, holding it to the sun.

'Is this Kukulkan?'

'It is indeed; that which will arise from the four beasts when the arc of the nine comes together. Only the keeper of the blue stone may wear such a thing, and must do so at the end times. You should keep it now, and ensure that it stays with the stone.'

He felt his brow furrow along its length. 'How can I—'

'You think too much. Drink now, and sleep. We will talk of it later.'

She held the leaf cone to his lips again. The loathsome black drink crept into his head and stole his mind. He slept and when he woke it was night time, and then daytime again with the sun slanting in from the west, to light a different clearing; he lay under a shelter this time, made of branches standing on end, with their leaves trailing his face. From the opening, he could see the peak of a mountain; he was on the slopes near its height.

Najakmul was bending over him, pressing her fingers to his lips, forcing them open. He bit down on something bitter and choked. The cone she handed him had water in it. Never had he been so glad to drink.

He sat up and was not sick.

'I'm sorry.'

He remembered saying it before, but could not remember her answer. Saying nothing, she gave him cooked meat. The smell assaulted his stomach, kindly. He ate, and felt the heat spread to his fingertips. The world ceased to move, although the true colours did not come back, nor the songs that went with them.

He fingered the medallion at his neck. 'Will Desolation rule the land?'

Najakmul sat on her heels at his side. She swept the hair from his brow and let her hand dally on his forehead, skin to skin. Her eyes were warm and dark and still tired, but less so than they had been.

She said, 'The time of Desolation will not come upon us until the sun treads the path to the Underworld four hundred years from now.'

'Then why did we set the stones into the earth? All but this?' He fumbled at his side for the satchel. Someone had slipped his blue stone inside and fastened the buckles. 'I did not set this one. The arc of the nine is not made. Kukulkan will not arise.'

'The stone is not for you to place. Now is not the time.'

'You make no sense.'

Knees splayed, she crouched before him. He

was becoming more comfortable with her nakedness.

'You moved across more than miles in your journeys, Cedric Owen; you moved also across centuries. What you saw did not take place here or now. You have travelled the song-line of your stone, which is not only distance, but also time. This is why you did not place the heart-stone. In that distant time – many years from now – another will be asked to place it, and may do so, if you can leave true word of where it must go and when.'

'Then why . . . ?'

Her hand clasped either side of his face. Her scarred cheeks were so close he went cross-eyed trying to see them properly. Her eyes held his and made them still.

She said, 'Listen to me, and try to understand. Your task was to find where the heart-stone must go. Only that. I can tell you the day and the time at which Kukulkan may be summoned, but the location itself can come only from you. Having found it, you must leave word of both the time and place of Awakening for your successor in a way that cannot be lost a second time, but also cannot be found by those who would misuse it. You must do this; it is what you were born for.'

'Then I have truly failed because I don't know where the place was.'

He read the shock in her eyes. She shook her

head in wordless horror. At length, frowning, she said, 'Would you recognize it again if you saw it?'

'Of course. The sight is burned on my soul. But I could search the length and breadth of Britain and never find it again.'

'You will find it.' She nodded to make them both believe it. 'It is the second of your three life's tasks. You have completed the first: to find the secret of the heart-stone. The second is to find where the stone must be placed at the end times, and the third is to hide the stone safely, leaving word of where it must go at the time when Kukulkan arises. The fate of the world rests on you, Cedric Owen. Therefore you will find it. It must be so.'

'And I will die when all is done?'

'The keeper always dies. It is the way of things. If you have lived for the stone, you will die at its passing.' She squinted at him. 'Better to die in the joy of a task fulfilled than simply at the end of a life. The stone grants life's meaning. There can be no greater gift.'

Owen looked down at the blue stone in his hand. The feeling of it as part of him was new and to be cherished. He saw himself reflected in the shine of its cranium, and remembered having done so before.

He said, 'I had silver hair in the grave mound.'

Najakmul leaned in to touch her brow to his. 'Show me.'

'I don't . . .'

'Make a picture in your head and show it to me in the stone.'

He was not thinking clearly, which was as well. He brought forward the memory of his own reflection in the blue stone; a scar lay across one cheek that he did not presently have, and his hair was as thick as it had always been, but silver almost to white. Because the stone was part of him, it shared the memory. He saw the mirrored image of himself change, and struggled to hold it.

'Enough.'

Najakmul sat back. She reached up for him, and grasped both hands to his face and drew him forward and kissed his brow. The touch of it shuddered to his core. He felt himself flush with a child's joy and a man's pleasure.

'Hush. You should sleep. Where you have been and what you have done is not easy.'

He was already half sleeping. Memories came to him, ethereal as dreams.

Thickly, he said, 'In the time-yet-to-come I saw a young woman in the grave mound. She carried a blue stone, but I did not see if she placed it in its seating. A fog came and my sight was taken from me. I saw nothing of her after.'

Najakmul chewed her lip, nodding slowly. 'Then it is not certain that she will succeed. We can only do our best to make it so. Kukulkan's arising depends on it.'

She picked a stick and stabbed it into the fire to good effect; sparks flew high into the cool blue sky. 'You excelled yourself, and we are proud of you, we who brought you to this. As we measure time, you laboured for four days and four nights without cease and you brought back the soul of your friend. Not one of us could have done better.'

'Four days?'

'And four nights. It is why you are so far gone and we must feed you to bring you home.' She handed him another strip of meat. Through the chewing, he asked, 'You sat with me through it all?'

She grinned, showing him white teeth. 'It is what I was born for. This and to send you home when the time is right. Sleep and enjoy the marriage of your heart to your stone. It has been a long time waiting and it requires that you give thought to it.'

The pressure of his bladder woke him next time. The sun had moved backwards, from which he concluded that he had slept through at least one night and on into the following day.

He was alone, lying on a bed of grasses. A gourd of water was propped nearby. He drank and then rose and went out to relieve himself.

Najakmul no longer watched over him. Instead, Diego and his brothers fussed with the mules a short distance away. De Aguilar was nearby, dressed in the white linen shirt that Owen had brought for him, with the empty sleeve pinned up neatly. He had cut a long stick and was practising fencing moves, left-handed. He saw Owen and threw his stick away and came to sit by the fire at the mouth of the shelter.

'Welcome. I had thought perhaps you would sleep until the snows come. Would you like food? I can cook corn pancakes now.'

'Thank you, yes. Do the snows come here?'

'They might do, eventually. There is some on the mountain peak.' One-handed, de Aguilar cooked them both a pancake. The moves had the fluent look of sustained practice.

Owen said, 'How long did I sleep?'

'Perhaps best that you do not ask. It is a great thing you have done, even so little as I understand of it.'

'It did not seem so at the time.'

'Then it will not lead to arrogance, which is a good thing. I could not bear to be so indebted to an arrogant man.' There was a new calm in de Aguilar's eyes as he rolled the pancake and passed it across.

Owen said, 'You are different.'

'I have seen death and stepped past it. There is little to be afraid of now.'

'What will you do?'

'Whatever you ask of me. I am your swordsman. No—' He held up his hand. 'You cannot

356

gainsay it. I will go where you say and do as you ask of me, but I will not leave, even if you plead, so spare us both the embarrassment of that.'

De Aguilar was relaxed and at the same time vibrantly alive, as he once had been after an attack on a dark night. It was a magnificent thing to see.

Owen felt the warm press of the bronze dragon on his chest. He lifted it and rubbed it lightly with his thumb. 'I suppose we should return to England and seek out the place of the stone circle.' He rubbed his face with his hands. He loved England, but he had no real wish to abandon all that he had found in the jungles of the jaguars.

Circumspectly, de Aguilar said, 'Would you care to go back to your homeland a rich man or a poor one?'

'Do I have a choice?'

'I believe so. Najakmul has been called into the jungle to tend a woman in childbirth but she gave me to understand . . . that you had grey hair in your journeys?'

'I did. Bright silver, like pewter. It was a strange thing to see.'

'She said as much. It would seem that while the stone demands great things of you, it grants you also a great gift. We are given some grace to rest and enjoy each other's company, this place and its people before we must return to England to fulfil your destiny.'

'Some grace? How long? A week? A month? A season?'

'Until you have silver hair, my friend.' De Aguilar leaned forward and lifted a lock of Owen's hair. With exaggerated interest, he studied the roots. 'Unless you have a bad shock, I would say perhaps thirty years . . . ?'

'Thirty . . . ?' Owen stared at him, and laughed, and went on laughing, knowing himself a fool but enjoying the feel of it, as he enjoyed the shiver of the leaves and the smell of the jungle and the murmured voices of Diego and his brothers as they quieted the mules against the sudden outburst from the crazy Englishman.

'Half a lifetime and then you will come with me to England? Really?'

De Aguilar held a straight face a moment, then let a long, slow smile stretch to his eyes and beyond. 'To England, where the unsullied grace of my king has married the damp and dusty shrew of your queen. Yes, I insist upon it. But not yet. First, we will live out the best parts of our lives in paradise, and make our fortunes in doing so.'

23

Lower Hayworth Farm, Oxfordshire,
June 2007

O N THE LAPTOP IN FRONT OF STELLA WERE
two more lines of text to finish the page.

3 Julye 1586, From Jan de Groot, trader, For:
three shyps' hold of Strong Sisal unmade into
rope and one shyp of rope readie-made:
diamonds to the value of £100 (one hundred
pounds).

3 Julye 1586, Also from Meinheer de Groot,
ane sword for a left-handed manne, craftit with
grate skylle by the Brothers Gallucci in Turino,
Italy, to the worth of £5, a gift.

The transcription of the ledgers had become
her obsession, and she was glad of it. She picked
out a line and drew it, and another, then pressed
the keys to form the glyphs and sat back, rolling
her shoulders as the techno-magic happened.

She was in Ursula Walker's study, a place of
high oak beams and limewashed plaster. Two

French windows at the back opened on to an orchard and herb garden, unchanged since medieval times.

Ursula worked under the apple trees outside. Her legs were visible, poking out across a stretch of shaded grass. The paddocks beyond were silent; the brown patches where the tents had been had returned nearly to green.

A dragging footstep sounded from the doorway to the kitchen. Stella bent her head back to the laptop.

'Coffee?' Kit asked.

'Thank you.' She did not lift her head. 'What time is it?'

'Half past five. You've been at it for eleven hours. You should take a break.'

'Soon. I'm nearly done.'

'Gordon rang,' said Kit. 'He's finished the analysis of the limestone section. He thinks the skull was immersed in the cave in the spring of 1589 – *after* Cedric Owen died.'

'So we still don't know who the skeleton was,' Stella said. And then, 'How's the translation going?'

'Slowly.' Kit swayed on his two sticks. He had done everything he could to give up the wheelchair; he was walking better than he had been, but still badly. He still needed Stella's help to dress and undress, and each time was less gracious about it.

Now, he leaned back against a wall for

stability. 'Cedric Owen is in the Mayalands, drinking smoke in the jungle with a woman who is also a jaguar. I think we forget how impenetrable Elizabethan writing can be even when it hasn't been warped through the prism of ancient Mayan glyphs. Ursula's asked Meredith Lawrence to come and help.'

'I know. He came to say hello when he arrived. You were there.'

'Of course. I'd forgotten.

They spoke as strangers and could not change it. In the four days since she had tried to heal him with the skull-stone, the hairline crack between them had become an unbridged, unbridgeable divide. They talked to each other only when they must and then in dislocated sentences, going through the motions of friendship and kindness.

What shocked Stella most was how easily and how fast they had fallen apart. She could remember that she had loved him, but she could not remember how or why. The cold in Kit's eyes had become a steel wall and he no longer tried to pretend he was letting her in.

Nor did he make any effort to hide his loathing of the blue skull-stone. She had brought it out when Meredith had first come in and Kit had walked away rather than stay in its presence. He would not have come into the room now if she had not kept the backpack hidden under the desk.

There was nothing left to say. Stella pressed a key to open a new page and began to draw the lines that only she could see. When she heard him leave, she was more relieved than sorry.

Meredith Lawrence came to find her later, when she was halfway through the next volume. He leaned on the edge of the French windows, relaxed with his tie gone and his shirt sleeves rolled up. 'Can you take a break?'

'If you can give me a good enough reason.'

'Not the one you want.' He smiled an apology. 'No date and time appointed. But possibly some pointers in the right direction. If you'd care to join us for some iced tea, we could show you what we've got?'

The garden was small and wild, with a roughly mown lawn and borders filled with kitchen herbs and straggling tomato plants tied loosely to the trunks of crab apple trees. Ursula worked on a tartan blanket under a cluster of late-flowering apples. Papers lay in an arc around her, weighted by small stones against the breeze.

She sat up and cleared a space as Stella approached. 'Sorry, it's a bit rustic. I lost the habit of working at a desk in Ki'kaame's reindeer lands and never got it back. Would you like a chair?'

'The blanket's fine. I'm becoming chair-shaped as it is.' Stella stretched out in the sun on the red and black tartan, resting her forearm across her eyes for shade. Kit was nowhere to be seen, for which she was grateful.

Some while later, she felt the shadow of Meredith pass across her, bringing the tea. She was warm and mellow by then, and not inclined to get up. Still with one arm over her eyes, she asked, 'What have you got?' Her voice had a tinge of Irish; a part of Kit she had not yet shed.

'A dog and a bat,' said Ursula. 'To be more accurate, we have a pair of recurring glyphs that have no obvious bearing on the narrative. One depicts the head of a dog facing left, and one has a bat flying towards us. In isolation, they could mean all kinds of things from loyalty to hunting to dreaming to a specific member of a classical Mayan dynasty headed by Two Jaguar. Put together, they are almost certainly Oc and Zotz, part of a date in the Long Count of years.'

Stella lifted her arm from her eyes. 'And in English, that would be . . . ?'

Meredith was in her field of view. He spread his hands. 'If we knew that, I'd have come to you a little more cheerfully.'

'Without numbers, the glyphs are meaningless.' Ursula's voice floated on the late afternoon sun. 'It's like saying today is a Tuesday in June. If I don't say it's Tuesday the nineteenth of June 2007, you're not actually any the wiser.'

'Is that it?'

'So far. We're working on it.'

'Great.' Stella rolled over on to her stomach. 'Four days' work for a Tuesday in June. Why did Owen not just give us the date in plain text?'

'He didn't know which calendar to use,' Meredith said, and when Stella looked him a question, 'Owen had just lived through the administrative chaos that was the transition from the Julian to the Gregorian in which some – but not all – of the Catholic countries in Europe had cut nine days from their calendars while the Protestant ones, including England, chose to ignore the deviations of a Catholic pope. Half of Europe didn't know what the date was and nobody could have predicted which version we'd be using five centuries later, if either. He had no choice but to use a system that he knew was accurate.'

'And Mayan calendrics is accurate to 0.0007 of a second for sixteen thousand years, so he'd be safe with that,' Stella said. Davy Law had told her so. It did not stop both Ursula and Meredith from being impressed. Briefly, she basked in that.

'Where do we go from here?' she asked, when the silence had stretched long enough.

'We make an effort to think as Owen thought.'

Ursula reached for a pile of papers and

fanned them out on the grass. The paired glyphs recurred on each page, outlined in yellow highlighter.

'Looking at it logically, if we assume that Owen knew the date, the time and the place to which the heart-stone needs to be taken, he was left with the almost impossible task of passing that information to you uncorrupted, while at the same time ensuring that it didn't fall into the hands of Walsingham, or anyone else who might want to destroy the skull, or use it for their own ends. He will have done whatever he thought was best.'

Meredith said, 'One obvious route would be to break up the information into fragments and hide each part in a different place. It's what I would do, in Owen's place. Which leads us directly to the medallion you found in the cave of the skull-stone, the one with the mark of Libra on the back.'

'This?'

Stella reached into her shirt, pulled the thong over her head and held it out to him. There was a slide of cotton on linen as Ursula bent over Meredith to look, and a sigh of disappointment.

'No numbers,' Meredith said. 'Not in English, not in Arabic or Roman numerals, not in the Mayan counting system, not even notches on the rim. I thought there must be something I'd missed the other day, but not a thing.' He threw himself back against the tree. 'Damn and blast.'

Ursula took the medallion, turning it over and over in her hand. 'And nothing to link us to Libra, either, unless we can find a date in October that fits with Oc and Zotz. But that's five months away, which is too long. Ki'kaame said the stone would only dare to show itself in the last weeks before the date.' She held the medallion up, angling it into the light where the sun made honey of the bronze. There was a pause, and a sudden catch of breath.

Stella sat up.

Quietly, Ursula said, 'Meri, when was the last time you saw a dragon facing right instead of left?'

'Apart from every other vertical surface at Bede's?' He cocked his head. 'Hardly ever. Pretty much every other dragon ever painted in the canon of European art points left, facing a knight in the left foreground.'

'Not on a hillside, less than half an hour's drive from here?'

'Ah.' A broad smile dawned on his face. 'The horse that might not be a horse. I never really thought it was. And if you took the wings from Stella's dragon here, it would be very much like it. Well done, cousin mine. I knew there would be something.'

The flush of understanding made him boyish. He raked both hands through his hair. 'Stella, have you ever seen the White Horse of Uffington?'

'Not that I know of.'

'You'd know.' He grinned cheerfully. 'It's a Neolithic monument, at least five thousand years old, probably older. Our ancestors carved the shape of a horse into the hillside, taking away the turf to show the white chalk beneath. It's best seen from the air, but even close up it's a breathtaking sight and the best place from which to sit and look at it is called Dragon Hill. At this time of day, you can park right at the side and walk straight up. Take your medallion and your skull and see if they think it's a good place to be. And take Kit while you're at it.'

'I can't . . .'

'You can. You're four volumes ahead of us in your transcriptions. You deserve an hour or two off.'

The misunderstanding was deliberate. Stella might have argued, but Kit was there, standing at the French windows, blocking her route back into the study. For a moment, she believed it an accident, then remembered the length of time Meredith had taken to bring the iced tea. She had not thought to look back at the house since.

Feeling hotly cold, light-headed and leaden, she stood up. She could think of nothing to say.

Woodenly, Kit said, 'I've been there once, a long time ago. I know the way, but you'll have to drive.'

'Do you want to go?'

He shrugged. 'Do you?'

'Oh, for God's sake,' said Ursula Walker from behind her. 'Just go. Go together. Walk up the hill together, sit at the top together, and for heaven's sake talk about something other than the weather when you get there. It'll be worth it, trust me.'

'There are steps,' Stella said. 'You don't have to crawl up the side of the hill.'

'I don't want to use the steps. They're an affront to the wildness of the place. Just go ahead and stop looking at me. It doesn't help.'

Already, the sun was a lavender bruise on the western horizon with washed veils of tangerine above. A waxing half-moon hung high overhead, the light more amber than mercury.

The car was parked illegally at the roadside. The small, flat-topped hill grew out of the road, with the steps newly cut and faced in wood. On the far side, where Kit climbed, the slope was tussocked and steep. Stella used her hands to pull herself up and did her best to study the grasses and white-starred meadow flowers against the surprising urge to look back at Kit and help him.

He was more agile on all fours than trying to walk, and going up was easier than going down. He put on a burst of speed at the end and reached the top before her. In silence, he offered his hand to haul her up the last strides. His hands were soft again; three weeks in a bed had worn off the calluses of the cave. His fingers were long and fine.

Uncertainly, she hooked her own through them, and drew herself up. The top was a place of sun-dried turf worn away at one point to make a patch of white chalk in the shape of a sickle moon. There was room there for two people to sit. Perforce, they sat together, staring down at the grass. The silence stretched.

Kit said, 'Have you looked at the horse yet?'

'Not yet.' She did not think he had, either. A shared perversity kept them both from it.

Kit lay back on the turf. The late sun cast long spears of gold across his face. The green harlequin bruises were a faded remnant, merging with the grey mosses. 'Is this the place appointed?' he asked.

'No. I'm sorry.'

'The skull-stone says so?'

'Yes. It feels safe here, as it does at Ursula's farmhouse, but no more than that.' The back-pack that held the stone lay openly at her side. For the drive and all the way up the hill, Kit had ignored it. Stella was surprised that he mentioned it now. She did not say more, that the stone was awake, and sharply aware, and that there was a sense of threat for which she had no name and no direction, save that it was not for now.

After a while, when she could think of nothing to say and the silence was too thick to break, she lay back on the grass and let her eyes rest on the sky. A plane grew out of the burning sun and moved across from west to east, slow as an ant. Long after it had gone, the white vapour trail stayed behind, a single linear flaw cutting across a domed sky that was the same perfect blue as her skull-stone.

Kit was warm at her side. She could feel him breathing in the push of his arm against hers. She remembered other summer days, on other grass, when a blue sky was simply blue and did not hurt like this.

She said, 'I should have thrown the stone away when Tony Bookless asked me to.'

'I don't think so. Unless Ursula and Meredith are both mad and—'

'They're pretty strange.'

She felt him smile. 'Granted, but I don't think they're delusional. In which case you are the skull's rightful keeper with all that entails. I don't want to be responsible for the end of time just because I can't handle how you feel for a stone.'

'Is it about the stone? Or is it the stone and me together? I am no longer the woman you married. You said that the night you got back from hospital and I'm sure it hasn't changed. It's probably grounds for divorce. If that's what you want, I won't contest it.'

'Stell?' He tried to push himself up on one elbow, but she was on his bad side, and his arm would not hold him. Trout-like, he flopped on his belly with one arm across her. She lay very still while he sorted himself out and came to rest on his elbow, with his weight carefully kept from her torso. His eyes were above hers, looking into her. 'Why do you think I want a divorce?'

'You haven't spoken a complete sentence to me since we first got to Ursula's. Actually, not since we left Davy Law's. And if you're jealous of him too, we really are finished.'

This close, he could not hide the flicker of panic in his eyes. 'Do I have reason to be?'

'Kit? Tell him that's a joke . . . ?'

He braced himself and rocked away from her. 'You wouldn't be the first woman I've loved who's fallen for him. I really don't want to go there again.'

'Davy Law?' She laughed aloud. 'Give me a break. He's not quite as bad as you made out, but he's probably the least attractive man I've ever seen. He has the peculiar integrity that only the truly ugly ever really have and for that I respect him enormously. I'd like him as a friend, but I don't love him. I'm not sure I could love anyone else just yet. You'll be a very hard act to follow.'

She had not meant to say that. She blinked,

harshly. 'Was it Jessica Warren you lost to him before?'

He did not answer. She thought he could not. Understanding dawned on her, bright and sure and not, after all, so complicated. She could have laughed at the ease of it. Lightly, she said, 'Is that what this is all about? Hurt pride over a lost lover you've never told me about?'

He was shy, which she had never seen. 'She wasn't a lover. But I wanted her to be. I never even asked her out for a drink.'

'Kit, you daft—'

'Davy doesn't bother about things like that. He doesn't do diffident, or humble, or socially inept. He simply asked her out, and she said yes and that was it, they were joined at the hip. She thought the same as you, that he shone from the inside.' He gave a wry smile. 'I was very grown up about it.'

'And then he tried to rape her? Or did he actually do it?'

'That's what everyone said – but then so many people hated him for being brighter than they were; they were all too happy to kick him when he was down.'

'What did Davy say?'

'He didn't. Jess was out of it – she'd screwed up spectacularly in the race, then left and went home to her mother's without telling anyone anything. And Davy went missing. I spent the next few days defending him to everyone who was ready to think the worst, all the while waiting for him to come back and explain that it had all been a ghastly mistake – that maybe he'd been overenthusiastic, wanting to celebrate the boat race before it had ever happened; that Jess had told him to sod off and they'd had a screaming match and he was sorry; something like that. He wouldn't have raped her; he really wouldn't. He hated the "all men are rapists" argument; it was one of the few things guaranteed to make him see red.'

'What happened next?' Stella asked.

'Nothing. He never came back. He was halfway through his surgical houseman's year, all set to be a world class neuro-surgeon or a paediatric cardio-thoracic specialist – whatever he wanted, really – and he threw it away. He just disappeared from the face of the earth. The college hierarchy clearly knew something because they weren't dredging the Cam for his body or checking to see if he'd gassed himself with a car exhaust, but they said nothing to the rest of us. I didn't know where he'd gone until the other day when Gordon told us about the refugee camps. I hadn't seen or spoken to him in over ten years.'

'Until last Friday.'

'When he was practically crawling into your lap, looking like he wanted to eat you, and he'd planted your face on the skull on his computer.

I could have killed him. I'm not quite sure why I didn't.'

'Because he was your best friend once and you know better.' Stella sat up, hugging her knees. 'If it makes any difference, Davy told me he'd tried to take something beautiful once and he was never going to make the same mistake again. I'd say he's had a hard lesson and taken it to heart.' She stared up at the evening sky. 'Why didn't you tell me this before?'

'Jealousy isn't pretty, Stell. Am I not allowed some pride?'

'Of course. Just not stupid, idiot, dumb' – she reached for his hand and pulled him close – 'heartbreaking pride. Not the kind where I can't reach you through the walls you build from it.'

'You nearly did.' He was near enough to kiss, and she did not dare. His eyes were gateways through which she could pass, but not yet.

'With the stone? I'm so sorry, Kit. I fucked up so very badly.'

'You didn't fuck up. You just—'

'I just didn't think. I had the skull in my hands and I knew what to do and I didn't question whether it was right until you told me to stop. It was fantastically stupid.'

'But you did know what to do? You could have made me better?'

'It seemed like it.' She touched her lips to his cheek. 'I'm sorry. It shouldn't be like this.'

'But it is, that's the point.' He was silent a

while. The sunlight deepened to amber. The high moon brightened with it. 'I'm trying to imagine what might happen to end the world, and how a scary lump of blue crystal might change it. I get stuck until I remember a wasp that didn't drown. Then anything seems possible, even the solar flares and global meltdown and dragons arising to battle the ultimate evil. Unless the dragon *is* the ultimate evil, and we're letting it out of its lair, which would be unfortunate.' He pressed his own lips to hers, chastely. 'The sun's nearly gone. Shall we look at the horse while it's still there to be seen?'

'Go on then.'

She rolled away, letting Kit sit up. Later than him, she looked up.

'My God . . .'

It was only a horse, a white horse, carved in simple, flowing lines from a green hillside to show the white chalk beneath. It was only chance that the sun and the moon spilled even light across it, so that the white glowed as liquid fire. It was only a buzzard that spiralled down to lift a kill from the heart of the horse, and looked at her a moment, eye to living eye, before it rose again, flapping, to the high, vaulting sky.

It was not chance at all that the horse on the hillside was exactly the dragon on Cedric Owen's medallion, alive in all its wild beauty. All it lacked was wings.

'Kit, do you see . . . ?'

He dragged her hand to his lips and crushed them with it. 'Don't speak. We're here at the balance between day and night and no one can take it from us. It's perfect. Please don't speak.'

For full thirty seconds, she held herself silent against the breaking ocean within. Then, 'Kit, say that again?'

He huffed amused frustration. 'It's perfect. Please don't—'

'No, before that, about balance.'

He frowned, caught by her tone. 'I don't remember.'

' "We're here at the balance between day and night." Balance. It isn't Libra on the medallion. It *is* the scales. And it isn't weighing the sun against the moon in Bede's window. We were all wrong!' With one hand, she was scrabbling in her shirt, pulling out the medallion; with the other, fighting to get into her pockets for her mobile phone. 'Why did we not see this before? Meredith was right, Owen *did* leave us what we needed in more than one place.'

'Stell, you're not making sense.'

'Hush.' She flapped one hand. With the thumb of the other, she speed-dialled Ursula's number. The phone rang once and was answered.

'Ursula, it's the summer solstice! The day after tomorrow!' The words tumbled over themselves. Kit made a sign to slow down and be calm.

Stella took a breath and tried again, spacing the words. 'The scales on the stained glass window and the sign of Libra scratched on the back of the medallion show the same thing. They're weighing day against night, not sun against moon. On the longest day, the light weighs most against the dark. Does that fit with the dogs and the bats?'

'Wait, I'll check.' There was a tight, cluttered moment, filled with the rattle of keyboard and the muted chimes of a PC in action, and Ursula shouting for Meredith, then a pause.

Hoarsely, Ursula said, '9 Oc, 18 Zotz is the 21st of June 2007. That's the day after to-morrow. I can't think why we didn't look before.'

'It doesn't matter, we have it now. And we've got the time of day to go with it. The stained glass window shows the dragon arising at dawn on a day when there's a waxing half-moon in Virgo. So the time appointed is thirty-six hours from now, give or take twenty minutes. All we need now is the place.'

'Is it not the white horse?'

'The skull-stone doesn't think so.'

'Then we're stuck because it's nowhere in the manuscript and we've translated all you've transcribed.' For the first time, Stella heard panic in Ursula's voice. 'Meredith's gone into town to check some of the glyphs against the dictionaries in the Bodleian, but I don't hold out much hope. In the last bit we've translated, Owen has just come back from the New World to England. He's fought his way across half of Europe – or de Aguilar has on his behalf. But he doesn't know the location of the place he's looking for in England. He says so clearly in the text.'

'Well he must have found it before he died. There are four volumes to go. We'll come home now and I'll finish the transcription. It has to be in there.'

It was ten o'clock on the night before the solstice and Stella had one more page left to transcribe.

She was alone in the study; Kit had gone to bed and Ursula was working upstairs in her bedroom; too much proximity had not helped either her or Stella work.

Outside, it was night. The half-moon was setting. It lay on the far horizon, bright against a backwash of stars.

The last page wavered on the screen.

12 March 1589, From Francis Walker, who was once another man, my thanks for all you have done . . .

She could not focus. The skull-stone sat on the desk in plain view; Kit had asked her to put it there. The blue eyes observed her, uncannily sharp, too much like life for comfort. Aloud, she said, 'You look like my grandfather.'

It was not entirely true, only that, of all her family, her mother's father had looked most like Stella. For sixty years, he had raised sheep on Ingleborough Fell, through summer heat and winter snow and at the end, when she was small and he was old, she had thought the weather had taken all the flesh from him and laid his skin in brown wrinkles on the planes of his skull.

From the hazy hollows of her memory, her grandfather said, *You should wake, child. It is not a time for sleeping.*

'I'm not sleeping. I'm working. It just feels like sleep.'

No. The voice was different. Stella blinked again. Where had been her grandfather was a younger woman, like her and yet unlike, with darker hair braided to her elbows, and skin more brown than white. *You dream, and should wake, else it was all for nothing. Wake now!*

She clapped her hands. The noise was like a falling plank. Stella woke.

In the study was smoke, sliding at floor height, coiling up the legs of the chair. The skull-stone sat in darkness, and had no points of light in its eyes. The flat screen of the computer was blank, the machine itself quiet in sleep.

Stella rubbed her eyes and inhaled, deeply. In

the blue place of her mind, the skull-stone awoke as if from a deeper dreaming.

The scything yellow of its panic met the force of her own terror. She grabbed the laptop and ran for the door and filled her lungs and shouted.

'*Fire!*'

24

Trinity Street, Cambridge,
Christmas Eve 1588

DR BARNABAS TYTHE, READER OF PHYSIC AND philosophy and Vice Master of Bede's College, Cambridge, was enjoying the blaze and crackle of his own fire, alone in the blessed privacy of his own lodgings, when the rap came at the door.

He ignored it, being lost in contemplation of a letter. Solitude had slowly become him. His wife's death was an old thing, to be dusted off and remembered awhiles on the nights when the city was quiet and sleep would not part its curtains to allow him entry.

The pain of loss was present still; Eloise had been a friend and confidante as much as a bed-mate, but the early knife-ache of her absence was a dull prodding now, so familiar as to be part of his fabric, knit deep into his flesh and bones.

Early, he had mourned the absence of children, and considered the taking of another wife, but none of those who had been offered had matched Ella's intellect or sharpness of wit and those who he thought might be bearable had invariably chosen greater men, or at least those possessed of greater incomes than anything to which a mere don might aspire. In any case, he had come to realize that he loved his college, which was immortal, more than he might ever love another too-mortal woman. He had set his mind and his soul to serving the stones and structure, the students and staff, and was happier then than he could ever rightly remember.

There had been whisperings on his elevation to Vice Master to the effect that a man is only half made without a wife to keep home for him, but by now, three years into the post, those who carped had turned their attentions elsewhere and, in the absence of a well-favoured woman of childbearing age to manage the servants and see to the menus, Tythe had reverted to the old practice of taking in students to share his rooms and had found the youthful company more to his liking as his middle years gave grudging way to white-haired old age.

Even so, he enjoyed the peace of the holidays and his house was hardly difficult to manage. Thus it was that this year, he had given leave to those of his serving staff who wished it to visit relatives for Christ's Mass, that they might be in the company of their loved ones when they gave thanks to God that the English forces under my Lord Howard and the more famous Drake had this summer so roundly defeated King Philip of Spain's Armada and thus delivered England from the Duke of Parma's invading army.

Tythe had not been called up to arms in defence of the realm. His position as one of the country's foremost academic physicians, added to his age and the old injury to his left knee, ensured he was not required to strap on the sword he could barely use and stand shoulder to shoulder with others equally unsuited to warfare. His friends, colleagues and students had gone in his stead, to stand in the sweltering heat of the south coast, under-armed and entirely untrained, awaiting the eviscerating energy that was Parma and the brilliantly trained, fully provisioned army with which he had so efficiently laid waste to the Netherlands.

Archibald Harling had gone, the medical student who had slept for two years in the antechamber to Tythe's room, and he had taken with him his friend and room-mate, the unfortunate Jethro Missul, whose misformed shoulder had made him the butt of so much talk in his childhood days that he had developed a permanent stutter. His grasp of law, though, was exceptional, and, as his tutor, Tythe had argued hotly against his throwing all that learning away on the smashing blades of Parma's army.

That he himself was not a swordsman had not aided the force of his rhetoric and he had been forced to concede, in the end, that law such as they knew and loved it would have no place in a Catholic England ruled from Spain, and young Jethro had limped off, intent on hurling himself before the Spanish wave, if only to delay them for the time it took them to step over his corpse.

Miraculously, the army had not come, and the pair had returned to Cambridge whole in body, if not entirely of mind, with stories of food poisoning and cholera amongst the ranks, of no food and water for the waiting men and of previously chaste women offering themselves openly in broad daylight, to keep the men from absconding and leaving the coast to the murdering Spaniards, which, reports from the Netherlands suggested, would have been immeasurably worse than mere dysentery.

They spoke in their sleep of their dread at seeing the vast glittering hulks of the Spanish fleet, sailing together with a majesty never seen in English waters.

They had seen the size of the Spanish guns and had thought themselves facing certain death, but then the pirate Drake had come, setting his small, weasel-fast boats to harry the lumbering oxen of Medina-Sidonia, and God had sent a blessed wind to aid the English and it seemed as if the new Puritan religion was better served than the mother church of the Catholics because Parma had turned his army round and gone back to murdering the Flemish peasants and the tag-ends of the burned and defeated Armada had sailed all the way up to Scotland, which was said to be all clothed in ice from one year's end to the next, and had come back down the other side and even when Archie and his friends had ridden to the west coast to repel them, they had not had the grace to land and give him a battle, but had let God's wind drive them on to the Irish rocks, losing more ships than before.

Of the one hundred and thirty ships that had left Spain, less than seventy limped back to face the wrath of a monarch whose pride and mother church had been crushed in full view of all Europe.

Archie and Jethro and their friends had ridden home to celebrate and none spoke too loudly of the English sailors who had not been paid or the men who had died needlessly for lack of provisions.

Thus had summer given way to a good, rich autumn, full of relief and relaxation, ripe with the air of a term's end even before the Michaelmas term had fully begun. Little of real worth had been taught or learned but there was no great harm in that, and the holidays had come and the snow had followed soon after and Cambridge had passed quietly into Christ's Mass, pleased to remember that God loved the Puritans more than the Catholics and, by way of evidence, had left their Queen Elizabeth to blaze in all her glory on the throne.

Nobody, in all of this, thought greatly of Sir Francis Walsingham, secretary and spymaster to the Queen and very likely, in Barnabas Tythe's opinion, the true architect of the Spanish defeat.

Nobody, that is, except Walsingham himself, and his extensive network of spies who worked tirelessly to feed the avaricious spider who wove his intrigue from the centre of their web.

Nobody knew the full count of those in Walsingham's pay, and it was well known that his agents were frequently set to spy on one another, which was, in part, what kept them all honest and diligent. The other, greater part of their diligence grew from the fact that they had all seen at least once what happened to men with whom the Queen's secretary was displeased; no man in his right mind would choose to risk ending his life in the Tower of London, answering unanswerable questions on the rack.

Which made it unsettling, therefore, to have received a letter in Walsingham's own hand, demanding action that was, in Tythe's opinion, impossible to take. It was, in fact, bordering on the insane even to ask it. Three feet of snow combined with the onset of Christmas gave him grace to consider his reply. Tythe had been doing just that for two days, since the letter arrived and the snow first started to fall. He was no closer to finding an answer.

He leaned forward and threw another log on the fire and read the letter for the fifth, or maybe sixth, time that evening, and drank a sip of good Greek malmsey and shook his head.

The second knock rattled the door on its hinges. A voice he had not heard for years hissed, 'Barnabas? Barnabas Tythe. If you would not have us perish on your doorstep of cold and hunger, would you open up and let us in?'

The malmsey spilled all over the hearth, sending aromatic vapours into the air. The goblet received a dent that would take the town's silversmith some skill to repair. Tythe paid attention to neither, but stared in shock at the letter lying across his hand and tried to understand how that which had been impossible was rendered otherwise, and how, in God's name, Sir Francis Walsingham could have known it aforehand.

He did not like any of the answers that presented themselves, nor his prognostications for the immediate future. The dark shadow of the Tower loomed suddenly darker and stretched the hundred miles north to fall on Cambridge and Bede's College in particular.

Some time after the third knock, the Vice

Master of the college stood up and hobbled forward to open the door.

'*Written this 20th day of December in the year of our Lord et cetera, et cetera ... to Sir Barnabas Tythe, from Sir Francis Walsingham, greetings.*

'*The most momentous year in our history draws to a close. We have fought off the Spanish evil and kept whole the sovereign borders of our land and the rights and sufferance of our most Beloved Queen.* He despises her, does he not know we all know it? *But the Papists never rest and nor must we. I have it on good authority* – whose? Who could possibly have known you were coming here? – *that one Cedric Owen, formerly of your acquaintance, is travelling in the company of a Spaniard and for this alone is to be considered an Enemy of the Realm. Moreover, he is carrying with him certain items of witchcraft which must be taken and held for further examination.*

'*I believe, due to your former friendship with him – a friendship in which you are blameless –* Walsingham holds nobody blameless. He would cut up his own daughter if he thought it would serve his own ends – *that he will endeavour to reach you within the closing days of the year. You are to apprehend him with all necessary force and deliver him alive to London with all speed. Should you require assistance in this matter, raise your own banner above your house and those who are our friends in this matter will come to you.*

'Deliver him alive to London.' Barnabas Tythe lowered the letter he had been reading and stared across the top of it to his friend. 'I would rather die penniless in a leper colony than be delivered alive to Francis Walsingham in London. Whatever you have done to make an enemy of this man, Cedric Owen, you should undo it if such is in your power, or flee England – nay, flee *Europe* – to escape him.'

'Certainly that's one option. I would like to think there might be others, though, before we take ourselves back to New Spain to no benefit.'

The night, which had been strange, was descending rapidly into unreality. The first of the two men standing warming themselves in a steam of damp riding habits by the fire was sixty years old, almost to the day. Barnabas Tythe knew this because he had attended Cedric Owen's twenty-first birthday celebrations thirty-nine years before. It was a matter of some concern, therefore, that Owen should look so exuberantly, youthfully healthy, when all accounts had laid him dead in a French dock-side tavern thirty years before.

And he had brought an accomplice, who spoke now, in a soulful not-quite-English. 'Have I not said already that Walsingham is the agent of the Enemy? You should listen to your swordsman, my friend, for your life is mine to protect, and I scented danger before ever we left Sluis.'

Manifestly more disconcerting than the presence of a once-friend whose death he still mourned every Twelfth Night was the growing understanding that the light-footed, one-armed man with the astonishingly inappropriate nugget of gold at his left earlobe, and the ostentatious crushed velvet doublet, was both a Spaniard, and Cedric Owen's friend.

A Spaniard, which is to say a Papist and a subject of the hell-born Philip of Spain, was thus drinking Tythe's best mulled wine on the eve of a Christmas in which every one of her Britannic majesty's subjects was celebrating wholeheartedly the comprehensive defeat of Spain and all it stood for.

Gangs of youths had burned effigies of Philip at the start of Advent. Later into the month, older men who should have known better had skinned cats alive and crucified them, to send the message back to the Pope that his false religion was doomed. No man in his right mind would contemplate playing host now to a Spaniard, however exuberant his tailoring, however good his command of the English language, however close his association with a man recently returned from the grave.

And then there was Walsingham's letter, the

implications of which were beginning to set Tythe's bowels to water. And the one-armed popinjay had just spoken of Sluis. Which was in the Netherlands. Which was, in fact, one of the last of the key strategic trading towns to fall to the besieging army of Alessandro Farnese, Duke of Parma, loyal servant to King Philip II of Spain and the greatest enemy England had ever known.

And the Spaniard had just defined Sir Francis Walsingham as the Enemy.

Tythe was neither a weak man nor a coward. Nevertheless, he felt sick in every part of his body and soul. His left knee ached. His chest refused to answer the bellows-call of his diaphragm, and his breathing whistled tightly.

He had been in the Tower once, and had caught a whiff of the stench of utter despair, which was worse than the charnel house and the abattoir put together. It had made him vomit then, much to his own disgrace, and had haunted him ever since. He smelled it again now, in the comfortable warm-damp of his own room, with the ruined spice of the malmsey still trickling into the fire. Sir Francis Walsingham had been present when he was sick. The man had smiled at the sight of it. It was that smile, and the penetrating eyes above it, that left that solid citizen, Barnabas Tythe, shaking like an agued woman now.

He said, 'Cedric, I have loved you like a son,

but I ask you now to leave. Please. I beg of you. Go now while the streets are empty and the falling snow will cover your tracks. I will tell no one you were here, I swear to it.'

He was croaking like a jackdaw. He heard it and bit his lip and swore inwardly.

'Barnabas.' Cedric Owen folded himself neatly on knees that showed no sign of rheumatics and sat cross-legged on the hearth. He smiled, and Tythe remembered the effervescent student, only five years his junior, who had so enchanted him in the summer-days of his youth. A faint haze of steam arose from the back of Owen's doublet and a greater one from the bulk of his riding cloak, on which the snow was not quite melted. The room began to take on a launder-house atmosphere.

'Barnabas, it's Christmas Eve and the snow is falling. We would not be here if there were any danger to you. We can stay safely for two days, I think, before anyone considers it necessary to call on you, and even then, surely you can trust the men of Bede's?'

'No. That's just it. You don't understand. Robert Maplethorpe is Master these past two years. He is Walsingham's man as much as I. More so, if the truth be told.'

That was it. In less than five minutes of a dead man's company, he had said more than he had ever dared to any living soul.

'Barnabas?' Cedric Owen blinked artlessly at

him, as he had used to do when they drank together in the Old Bull on Trinity Street. Tythe thought of Eloise and prayed for fortitude. 'Can we safely assume that Sir Francis, archest of all arch-Puritans, does *not* know that you are still a Catholic at heart?'

There was a choking noise in the quiet that was Barnabas Tythe's answer. The bejewelled Spaniard said softly, 'That was not friendly, my friend. Now you have made your other friend sick with fear. He believes himself undone and in the company of witches, or at least of black-mailers.' He spread his one arm wide with a theatrical flourish. 'I am a Catholic, señor, if not a very good one; we who are alike know one another. You will find no witchcraft in that. Nor will you find threat. We will not hurt one who has once befriended us.'

Barnabas Tythe considered pointing out that he had not befriended any man of Spain, but the bejewelled one carried at his hip a plain sword whose very lack of adornment spoke volumes on a man otherwise given to grotesque bad taste. Owen had never been a fighter and yet he had come through the Low Countries alive. His self-appointed swordsman, therefore, was a man to be respected, not offended, and, in any case, Owen had just opened his riding pack, and was unwrapping the spare cloak which, Tythe greatly feared, hid the evidence of all-too-real witchcraft and was therefore of far greater concern.

He was right. A corner of the cloak fell away and the placid amber light of his fire was warped to a cold ice blue. It was thirty years since he had seen its like and it still haunted his dreams, inspiring yearning and revulsion equally.

Tythe groaned aloud and thrust himself up from his chair.

'Not the blue heart-stone. Please God, Cedric, in thirty years, have you not had the sense to rid yourself of that? Queen Mary and that idiot Pole may have wanted to burn you for it, but Walsingham will do far, far worse; he will want to use it for his own ends. He may be an avowed Puritan, but he will take a short spoon to sup with the devil if it gets him where he wants to be.'

'Ha!' The Spaniard had startling grey-blue eyes and hair long and glossy as a girl's. When he threw his head back and laughed, his teeth were white as the winter's snow. 'My friend, your other friend is right; we should be gone from here. If Walsingham knows where we are, so simple a thing as the birth of Christ will not keep him from us.'

'No, but the snow will. And it gives us time to plan. In any case, I have more wealth than he has.'

Sir Francis Walsingham was one of the richest men in England. Tythe assumed that Owen was speaking in allegory and was about to recount how the sparkle of a dawn's sunshine filled his soul with greater riches than anything England's spymaster could draw to his coffers.

It was with some surprise, therefore, that he saw the other corner of Cedric Owen's riding cloak fall back to reveal the spark of a diamond button that did not look in the least allegorical. In fact, when Tythe thrust himself up from his chair to study it more closely, he found himself holding a life-sized mask of a woman's face cast of gold with a crusting of diamonds at both ears that made the Spaniard look positively restrained in his attire. The item was as thick as his thumb's first knuckle and was well in excess of five pounds in weight. He attempted to estimate its worth, compared to, say, his annual salary, and abandoned the task; the two were not comparable.

'Cedric?' Barnabas Tythe found his mouth gone dry. 'Where did you get this? Does it carry men's blood?'

'It carries a woman's blood, certainly. It was cast from the face of a woman for whom I had the highest respect. Her son made it on the occasion of her death, as our leaving gift. I will be sad to see it go, but if anyone can gaze upon Walsingham and cause him ill, it is Najakmul.'

'But why? This would buy you freedom if you used it wisely.'

Owen tilted a smile. 'If I sought freedom, and if it were all that I had, I might consider your suggestion. But I seek more than freedom, which makes it fortunate that this is not all that I have.'

Tythe gaped. 'There is more?'

'Indeed. Clearly I do not choose to carry it all with me. The rest is largely in gemstones, which are more easily hidden. They are in the false bottoms of barrels of sack, housed in a cellar near the port in Harwich which is owned by a Dutch smuggler who owes me his life. I believe he will not touch that which is mine while he believes that I live. Given that I must die soon, then we must find a way for you to reach it, and then for you to hide it until such time as Walsingham and all like him are gone.'

The wine sat unexpectedly sour in Tythe's mouth. 'I don't understand. Why must you die?'

'How else will Walsingham leave me? He has issued a warrant for my arrest. I am a traitor, to be held on sight and taken alive to the Tower. Only if I am dead will he desist.'

'But if you are a traitor and die, your entire estate becomes forfeit to the Crown. If you have such gold as you say, Elizabeth will use it to fund her navy to retake Calais. She will steal the New World from the Spanish and the Portuguese; she will—'

'Which is why I must die a pauper and the wealth be hidden for your lifetime and beyond.' Owen smiled and cocked his grey-tinged head. 'What is your greatest love, Barnabas?'

That answer was easy. 'Bede's,' said the Vice Master. 'My college is my life.'

'So then will you help me to give my diamonds to the college in such a way that Walsingham cannot get his hands on them?'

'God, yes!'

'Even if it means my death?'

Tythe felt a pang of sorrow. 'Would you fall on your sword for this man?'

'Well, I would fall on *somebody's* sword. My own might not be public enough for Walsingham's tastes and we must not disappoint him.'

Owen grinned at that, but the humour fell away all too suddenly, leaving him thoughtful. His face took on the keen sharpness of a falcon, not dissimilar to Walsingham's own. It came to Tythe that he did not want to make an enemy of this man who had been his friend.

'Who else is in Walsingham's pay?' Owen asked it sharply, with a new hardness to his voice.

Tythe said, 'Besides Maplethorpe, I cannot say for certain. I doubt there's a Master of any college in Cambridge, or Oxford for that matter, who isn't taking money from him in some form. After the Lutheran heresies here in the twenties, to refuse aid to the Queen would be as good as confessing treason. There will be others, but I know not their names; the spymaster does not keep his servants privy to his secrets.'

'Then we must be doubly cautious.'

The blue stone was fully clear of the cloak now, held balanced on one hand so that, from Tythe's seat an arm's length away, it appeared that the fire came from the centre point of its cranium.

Owen stared into it a moment and then turned to the one-armed Spaniard who purported to be his bodyguard. There passed a wordless conversation at the end of which Cedric Owen cast his cloak once again over his blue skull-stone to hide it, turned to Tythe and said, 'Barnabas, it is Christmas Eve. If I were to offer you the Mastership of Bede's as my Christmas gift, what would you say?'

Tythe laughed, with little humour. 'That you should sleep and perhaps take laudanum and we should begin again with the clean slate of forgetfulness on the morrow.'

'You don't want to be Master?'

'Of course I do! I have given my life to my college and am vain enough to want her to grant me her ultimate accolade in return. I would prefer it to being the next King of England, but it is every bit as unlikely and not a safe thing to consider. Maplethorpe is not a man to cross lightly. He has three manservants any one of whom could beat the best in London. He calls them his human mastiffs and they are well known for killing men on dark nights with no questions asked or answered. He hides behind a veil of abstinent piety and murders those who stand against him. It's one of the reasons he was elected Master; none of us dared do anything else.'

The Spaniard flashed a ferocious smile. 'A challenge! At last! England is a good place, Señor Tythe.'

Cedric Owen ignored him and thus, blessedly, Tythe could do likewise. He was about to turn the conversation to less dangerous ground when Owen rose and drained his goblet.

He said, 'Now would be a good time, then, for you to go to Robert Maplethorpe and tell him that you have unexpected visitors. Show him the letter and ask his advice as the Master of Bede's, not as Walsingham's spy. Tell him we are exhausted and came to prevail upon your Christian charity. It is Christmas and the roads are blocked. We cannot therefore be dispatched to London and so you seek his advice on what best to do.'

'He'll kill you,' said Tythe flatly.

Owen bowed. 'Then you will have done your duty and will fly high in Walsingham's favour. If I cannot give you the Mastership, what better gift than this, that we have not endangered your life or your standing?'

25

Bede's College, Cambridge,
Christmas Eve 1588

BUT FOR THE FALLING ECHOES OF THE NIGHT
bell, the streets of Cambridge were softly
quiet, and absolutely dark.

Snow fell lightly, with less wind behind it
than before. The young moon had fallen below
the earth's edge, leaving only a scattering of
stars by which to see.

This once, Cedric Owen did not need sight to
find his way. Guided by instinct and memory,
and with his hands held out in front of him for
when these two failed, he followed Barnabas
Tythe down the path from Magdalene Street
and along the river towards Midsummer
Common.

His knuckles brushed against wood and he
turned left on to the arch of John Dee's geometric
bridge. By the changed timbre of his snow-
muffled footsteps, and the sudden warming of

his heart-strings, did he know that he had come home.

He squeezed his old mentor's arm. Tythe was not a fearless man by instinct; he had a different kind of courage, that acted in spite of gut-emptying terror. 'We'll wait here,' Owen said. 'You are safe this far. Keep out of the fighting and you will remain so.'

'What if your subterfuge with the torches fails?' Tythe asked. His voice was not firm.

'It worked in Sluis and twice before that,' Owen said, 'it will work again. Men fight more poorly if they do not know the true numbers they face. Dark is our ally and their enemy.'

'He has three men to guard him and he can fight as well as any of them. Probably better.'

'And there were six in Rheims. All are dead. If you can trust anything in this world, it is the speed of Fernandez' blade.'

'You will not fight?'

'I won't have to.'

Owen made his own voice certain. He watched Tythe screw up his courage and step out into the cushioned night. The flame of the old man's torch made oblique progress to the gates of the college and was presently drawn inside.

They were two men alone in the dark of a Christmas night. Putting out his hand, Owen felt the familiar press of de Aguilar's tawny velvet against his palm. He heard the scrape of iron against tallowed leather and saw the faintest smirr of a polished blade sweep across the starlight.

'Thirty years of preparation and all for this,' de Aguilar said softly. 'It does not seem so long.' He, too, was breathing more deeply, without the overstrung tension of Barnabas Tythe's house.

'It was long enough,' Owen said. 'The heart-stone gave us three decades' gift. All that remains is to find if we can fulfil the tasks it requires of us, for if we fail it has all been for nothing.'

'It is far from certain, my friend.' He felt the Spaniard's eyes on him. 'There were only five men in Rheims and two of them too drunk to move. Maplethorpe forbids drink to his men. We will be harder pushed here than there.'

'I know. But Tythe needed courage. You and I have sufficient to succeed.'

They waited a while, who were well versed in patience and could bear a little cold.

The blue stone sang quietly. Just before the darkness parted, it changed the tenor of its tune.

There was no sound from the porter's lodge of Bede's College, but the small side door opened and this time three torches appeared where there had been one.

'Only three. Maplethorpe has not come,' de Aguilar hissed.

'He will. I knew him as a student. Even then, he baited bears for pleasure. He will not miss a chance to kill men now for the sport of it. Wait and he will be here.'

They waited. The torches came forward in a line abreast. At a certain moment, a line of light blazed briefly wide as the porter's door opened and shut on the candles within. Two shapes stepped out into snow and were lost in the cloaking dark.

'Now,' said Owen.

He struck flint against tinder to light a single torch, and then two others from it. Handing one to de Aguilar, he emerged from the line of trees at the edge of the river walking crabwise, bearing a torch in each hand, with his arms spread wide apart. De Aguilar followed in like manner, his torch held behind him so that it might seem as if three or four men walking line astern had crossed the small arched bridge and entered the college grounds.

Approaching the porter's door, Owen let out an oath in Fenland brogue, and doused his torches. In more of an academic voice, he said, 'God's bones! Did you not bring a better light on such a night as this?'

'Hush now. Silence about the Master's work.' In thirty years, de Aguilar had learned English as if born to it. On board the smuggler's skiff from the Netherlands, he had perfected both the scholar's drawl and the sliding, nasal east

Anglian vowels. In these latter, gruffly, he said, 'We'd best douse the torches. There's no need for more than one when all we're hunting is a one-armed man and a fop.'

'No need even for one, when we have three.' The authority in the voice that came from the porter's lodge exceeded that of any porter, however far above his station he might set himself.

Robert Maplethorpe stepped out into the crescent of churned snow that marked the gateway to Bede's College. The blade of his sword flickered naked in the grey snowlight so that Owen's eye was drawn to it first, and the unshaven darkness of his visage second.

His three men came behind him, each bearing aloft a lit torch of a quality that did not spit pitch on their master. In their other hands, with the carelessness of men for whom the breaking of limbs is a daily delight, they bore ironwood cudgels bound about with wool and cloth that they might more silently maim those against whom they were set.

Barnabas Tythe stood framed in the doorway, leaning a little to the left, to support his lame leg. He pitched his voice out over the heads of Maplethorpe's three thugs. 'Joseph, is that you?'

Cedric Owen said, 'Aye,' and hawked and spat into the snow. 'At your service, Master Tythe. We are come as you asked, bringing all we could muster. Your enemies remain in your

404

rooms still, making free of your hospitality.'

He thrust his own torch into the snow, creating a flash of darkness that engulfed him; by chance, or good luck, or skill, he and de Aguilar stood beyond the semicircle of light cast by Maplethorpe's men.

De Aguilar cursed, and appeared to trip, and stumbled out to the side.

'You're drunk!' Maplethorpe hissed it with a venom that made his men seem mild as milkmaids.

'N-nay, Master.' De Aguilar cowered at the margins of the light. He threw his hand up and staggered further backward in evident terror. As far as anyone could see, he was not armed.

The three men behind Maplethorpe leered knowingly as their Master brought his blade up to fighting height. He was a fit man. In two strides, he was beyond the arc of the blazing torches, and in two more he had passed beyond the grey-silver of the snow's reflection so that he, like the man he pursued, became a dark, uncertain shape.

'Hold! I will have no man of mine drunk at any time, and least so on the day of Our Lord's birth.'

Maplethorpe spoke with no sense of irony. The three armed men rolled their eyes. From the dark, coarsely, Cedric Owen said, 'Master, is it not the Spaniard that we seek, not the death of your loyal servants?'

'I will not kill him, only . . . teach him a . . . lesson.'

The sentence was twice punctuated by the scuffling of feet and the sleek whistle of a sword blade slashing air.

On that last, higher, note, a man gave that sound, partway between a grunt and a squeal, that is the earnest signature of death. All of those listening heard a body fold to the ground. None of them was so innocent as to believe that the man had learned any lesson other than that which his Maker might choose to offer at his final reckoning.

Maplethorpe's voice said, 'A pity, but a lesson learned.' The bulk of his shape loomed in the darkness, hand on hip, cloak a-flying. 'Why are we still lit like a festive bonfire? Can you not find your way to Tythe's lodgings by starlight?'

His three thugs doused their lights. The man they believed to be Maplethorpe strode to the nearest – who had just time to see that his assailant was thrusting left-handed before the sword thus deployed cut through the leather of his vest, sliding in up a line from the sternum to pierce his heart.

He fell back, choking blood. Of his two companions, only one had the speed of reflex to leap forward, swearing. Barnabas Tythe, with a surprising courage, knifed the other in the back and kicked his legs out from under him so that he fell forward on to the snow.

Which left only the third of Maplethorpe's three mastiffs still dangerously alive.

That man had no care that he was outnumbered. Already he had deduced the source of greatest threat and was advancing on de Aguilar. Breathing hard, he made a feint with his unarmed hand and then swung in ruinously hard with the other.

Cudgel met blade – and broke it. There was a moment's shattered silence before de Aguilar threw himself sideways, rolling, and rose with the stolen cloak already off his shoulders and spinning round his only arm. He danced light-footed on the snow, dodging and ducking the swinging cudgel. His assailant aimed half a dozen fruitless times at the Spaniard's wraith-like shape, then cursed and drew his eating dagger and held it out, fish-silver in the starlight.

He was harder to avoid then. For all his bulk, he, too, was light on his feet and he had the full-shadowed dark at his back, with the greyer light in front of the college to his fore. The starlight was not great, but it was enough for eyes that knew night as a friend. He had more practice of fighting in snow than de Aguilar, and he had two weapons, against a one-armed, disarmed man who had only a rolled cloak for protection.

He moved fast and hard and in three breathless moves had jabbed his dagger into de Aguilar's thigh and swung the cudgel at his head. Owen watched the Spaniard crumple to the snow.

The cudgel-man stepped in to finish his work. 'No!'

A long time ago, Cedric Owen had promised Fernandez de Aguilar that he was never going to wield his own sword in anger.

In the Jesuit bloodbath at Zama that had seen Najakmul dead, in Rheims, in Sluis, in the harbour at Harwich, where they had nearly been taken by Walsingham's agents, he had used his knife, or a club, or – in Zama – a Dutch musket, and let the Spaniard set his serpent-fastness against other men's flesh and blood. He had seen it strike from the dark against greater numbers so often now that he had begun to believe his friend invulnerable.

And yet there was that one night in Seville, where he had used his own blade in de Aguilar's defence. He had no sword now, and his knife had not the reach he needed, but a dead man's cudgel lay at his feet. He swept it up and waded forward through the snow and let the cold, heavy wood carry him past his own incompetence.

He was not too late. That thought filled him as he measured the distance to his adversary; he was not too late and he had once used his sword to good effect in de Aguilar's name.

He was thinking of that when the cudgel-man struck. The first blow took him in the ribs and he felt three of them crack. The reverse swing struck his head, with the full, skull-cracking force of the big man's arm, and felled him.

In the long, long moment of falling, Cedric Owen heard Barnabas Tythe shout his name and fancied he saw his old tutor hobble up to stab a dagger into the back of his assailant – his murderer, in fact, because he had no doubt that he was dying.

His one thought, as the snow received him into its embrace, was that he was about to meet Najakmul and that she would know that he had failed.

26

Oxfordshire, June 2007

IN A SMALL SIDE ROOM OFF THE ICU IN THE
Radcliffe Infirmary in Oxford, a consultant
physician in a white coat spoke to the senior
nurse, ignoring Stella and Kit who sat at the
bedside.

They smelled of smoke and hurt and fear but
were not in need of medical aid. Ursula Walker,
by contrast, lay bandaged and unconscious. Her
strong, expressive face was slack with sleep and
drugs. Her veins stood out blue against grey-
white skin, streaked with angry red lines along
her arms and across her forehead.

A ventilator breathed for her, through the
endotracheal tube that poked out of the side of
her mouth. Plasma expanders dripped into the
veins in her arms. Other bags delivered their
drips more slowly into the veins of her neck.

A drain sucked fluid from the side of her
chest. A urine bag tied to the end of the bed

filled slowly. An array of green traces on the monitor recorded her pulse pressures and expired gases. A twelve-lead ECG bleeped as it threw up patterns that Stella could not read.

The consultant signed a note and left. The nurse drew the curtains round the bed.

Left alone with Kit in the clinical white, Stella pressed her fingers to her eyes. The skull was quiet now, its warning given. In its place, where had been blue peace, a wash of flame filled her mind, and the sting of smoke, and the stench of burning flesh. When she opened her eyes, the flames were less, but not gone. The smell of smoke and burned hair remained.

'Why did I let her go back in?'

'You couldn't have stopped her,' Kit said. His breath still smelled of smoke. His words came out wreathed in it.

'But I didn't try. She said she knew what she was doing, that she had found something vital in the diaries. I believed her. I *wanted* to believe her.'

'I didn't stop her either, Stell. If we're going to fall into recrimination, we should at least split it equally.'

'You were barely conscious. I don't think—'

The nurse was there, swiftly kind. She held open the curtain. 'Mrs O'Connor? Your brother's here.'

'My bro— *Davy?*'

He embraced her briefly, drily. He shook

411

hands with a shocked and silent Kit. He said, 'You shouldn't beat yourself up about it. Nobody could stop Mother when she set her mind to something, you know that as well as I do.' He nodded to the nurse. 'Thank you. Can we be alone with her for a while?'

She stepped back, neatly. 'I'll let you know the blood results when we get them.' He was wearing a white coat. The smile she gave him had a different quality from the one she gave Kit and Stella as she left.

Davy stood at the foot of the bed and studied the monitors and winced at what they told him.

Tonelessly, he said, 'She's damaged the endothel— the lining of her lungs. There was chlorine in the smoke. This wasn't just arson, it was designed to kill whoever was in the farmhouse. Ursula – that is, my mother – seems to have realized the danger in time. I don't think the firemen fully understood it when they brought her out to you, but apparently she had a linen tea towel over her face and she'd poured lemonade on it, to act as an acid barrier. It's probably the only reason she's still alive.'

He was speaking automatically, in the clinical rhythms of the medics. His eyes fixed on the monitor screen and never left it. Stella took his shoulders and guided him to a seat and pressed gently, until he sat. 'Will she get better?' she asked.

'If she lives through tonight, she'll probably

survive. She may end up as a respiratory cripple dragging an oxygen bottle strapped to a Zimmer frame everywhere she goes, but she'll be alive. I'm not sure she'd thank us for inflicting that kind of life on her.'

Kit said, 'It's not as bad as you think. Hope's worth a lot.'

There was a moment's hard, bright silence. Davy Law dragged his gaze from the monitors and looked across the bed for the first time. His eyes were rimmed red. His skin was yellow beneath the brown of the Kurdish summer. His hands shook, from nicotine famine, or grief for his mother, or the presence of Kit, or all three. He said, 'I heard what happened in the cave. I'm sorry.'

Kit said, 'So am I. But I'd rather be here, the object of everyone's pity, than not be here at all.'

There was a gap when either of the other two could have contradicted him, protested the absence of pity, and did not.

Stella felt Kit's knee against her own; for that reason alone, she held silent. She watched Davy Law take a breath and hold it and let it out slowly, shaking his head.

After a moment, he said, 'I think I would rather be hated than pitied. But it goes hardest when there's both together.'

'I never pitied you, Davy.'

'But you did hate?'

'What else was left?'

That was when they faced each other fully, eye to eye, so that the past was laid bare between them.

The curtains contained them, soft veils that kept the world at bay while something broken was mended, or not; she could not tell. On the bed, Ursula Walker's chest lifted and fell with the sigh of the ventilator.

Stella felt a change in the knee that pressed against hers. Kit said, 'Why did we not know Ursula was your mother?'

Davy Law smiled crookedly, showing his bad teeth. 'We don't talk about it much. And you didn't see the family resemblance.'

'There isn't any.'

'There is.' He leaned over the bed, turning so that his head was next to hers on the pillow with his bloodshot grey eyes fixed wide. With great care, he lifted his mother's eyelid, so they could see the steely grey-blue beneath. It was possible to imagine his without the bloodshot and yellowing and to see them the same. He said, 'The eyes have it.'

Stella said, 'We should have seen.'

Davy shrugged. 'Nobody else ever does. But if you want to beat yourself up about this on top of everything else, don't let me stop you.' He let go and sat up. 'Beyond that, you're right, I am the nightmare of my mother's days. She wanted a beautiful, striking, intelligent child to carry on the line unbroken since before the Romans landed and what did she get but a runt of a son with teeth like a coypu on steroids and hair like rats' tails.'

Stella stared at him. He grimaced. 'I made that up. If Kit said it to you, he was plagiarizing.'

From her side, Kit said, 'Guilty.'

Davy shrugged it off. 'But she let me come back home to the farmhouse when I screwed up so badly at Cambridge that I couldn't go on with medicine, and she opened doors for me in anthropology, so in the end I followed in her footsteps after all.'

He reached out and smoothed a single finger down her cheek. 'She took me with her to Lapland. It's the one place left on earth where they don't judge a book by its cover. My mother and I found a degree of mutual respect out there in the ice and the snow and the reindeer piss, which is more than we've ever had before. I would like for it not to be taken from us just yet.'

Shorn of all irony, wrapped in grief, the profile of his face was quite different. Through a tight throat, Stella said, 'I have the heart-stone. If there's anything we can do with it . . .'

He shook his head. 'All you can do is find the heart of the world and take the stone there at the right time. Her whole life has been pushing towards this.'

Kit said, 'The time appointed is dawn tomorrow, but we still don't know the place. Unless someone else can translate the last two volumes, we're finished. Can you read Mayan script?'

There was a window beyond the head of the bed. Davy looked out of it into the dark night. 'I can, but not without my mother's dictionaries and they were all in the farmhouse. There are copies in the Bodleian Library. It won't be open before dawn.'

The urine bag was nearly full. Davy reached for an empty measuring cylinder and filled it. Briefly, the curtained space smelled sharp.

He read the volume, wrote it on a chart and held up the cylinder. 'I'll go and empty this and then we can work out a game plan for the next few—' It was the second set of ring tones that stopped him. His eyes flashed wide. 'Please tell me one of you hasn't left your mobile on? You've never seen vengeance till you've met an ICU nurse who thinks her monitors are in danger of electronic interference. She'll slaughter us and we'll deserve every bit of— Stella!'

'It's not mine,' she said, 'it's yours. It's a text.' His phone was in his coat, which he had taken off and hung on the back of her chair. She lifted it out and handed it to him, and saw the moment when the blood fled from his face.

'Davy?' She reached for his arm.

He sat down heavily. 'It's from my mother. I didn't know she had my number.'

'Is someone else using her phone?'

'Doesn't look like it.' He thumbed down the screen. 'It's timed at 10:27 this evening. You called the fire brigade at 10:23 and they pulled her out at 10:51. She must have sent this when she was still in the house.' He was speaking woodenly, not truly thinking, staring at his mother with the green lights of the monitors casting ugly shades across his skin.

Gently, Kit said, 'What does it say, Davy?'

'*Now is the time to open that which was closed in the fire's heart. Please.*' He was weeping and had not noticed. 'I have to go back to the farmhouse.'

'You can't. It's an inferno. The whole sky was orange when we left. And it was crawling with firemen.'

'They've gone. I listened to the short wave on the way here.' He was already reaching for his coat. 'I still have to go.'

'Then we're coming with you,' Stella said.

There were no firemen, no flames, no orange sky at Ursula Walker's farmhouse, only a dark night, lit by half a moon and sharp stars and the smell, everywhere, of smoke and ash. Stella parked the car where she had on the first afternoon. She and Davy helped Kit out. They walked together down the hill, through air that became thicker and hotter the closer they came to the house.

White limewash showed grey through a smear of soot and ash, but the frame was intact. At the gate, they stopped; a single band of yellow and black tape blocked the way. Where there had once been posters announcing The 2012 Connection was a new notice: SAFETY HAZARD, DO NOT ENTER.

Stella said, 'Do we need to go inside?'

'I do,' said Davy. 'You can stay out here if you want, it might be safer.' He was more on edge than she had ever seen him. Looking past her into the night, he said, 'Does either of you think we were followed?'

Kit stood between them, where he could lean easily on either shoulder. 'No, and I was watching,' he said. 'Ursula was in the kitchen when the firemen found her.'

'Best try the back door, then.' Davy forced a grin. 'Less of the house to fall on our heads as we go through.'

They went slowly down the path, past the debris of the garden fence. From the dark, Davy said, 'I don't suppose you happened to bring a torch?'

'Use your phone,' Stella said and took her own out and switched it on.

Along two faint beams of light, between scorched and sodden roses, over fallen slates from the roof, they picked their way round the side of the house. The back door was gone. The door frame was warped and scorched.

Davy Law ran one hand down the ruined wood. 'Whoever did this knew what they were doing.' He dusted his hands on his jeans. His face was still and hard as stone. 'Breathe shallowly. If you feel anything bad, get out fast.'

Stella followed him in over the threshold. She swept the poor light of her phone in an arc across the remains of the oak table, the bentwood chairs, the charred and pocked walls and floors, the broken fireplace.

Kit came after them, taking his time, watching where he placed his feet among the debris. He stopped in a smear of moonlight. 'Davy, you don't need to see this. Why don't you tell us what you're after and you can stay in the car while we get it.'

'Hardly. You forget, I've spent the past five years in war zones.'

'They weren't burning the house you grew up in.'

'Even so . . . There are things only I can do.' He stepped in and stood by the table. More faintly, he said, 'I didn't do much of my growing up here. We fell out too soon for that.' He turned on his heel, looking for something. Absently, he said, 'Can you wait here a moment?'

Wraithlike, he was gone. They waited in the

dark with the noise of settling timbers going off like firecrackers about them.

'Scared?' asked Kit.

'Terrified,' Stella said. 'Do you trust Davy?'

'Yes. You?'

'I always have. From the moment I met him.' A sound came from the broken doorway. She looked up. 'Davy? What's that?'

'A lump hammer. There's been one in the garden shed for as long as there's been a garden shed, which takes us back to 1588, or thereabouts. Martha Walker had the first one built, the woman who married Francis Walker to found the dynasty. She's my great-great-great-several other greats grandmother and she left a rather strange instruction in her will that the hammer was never to be beyond reach of the kitchen. I had an idea why this might be when I was a teenager and tried to use it. My mother was . . . not impressed. That was the day I moved out to live with cousin Meredith.'

'Meredith Lawrence?' Stella asked, surprised. 'He's been helping decode the ledgers.'

'Of course. The obsession runs in the family. You must have noticed.' Davy turned the hammer over in his hand. In the light of their phones, the mass of metal that was the head gave off a dull blue sheen. He said, 'He was a good man to grow up with and we all learned to speak to each other after a while. I took half of his name, though. I thought Mother had never forgiven me for that. Maybe I was wrong. She's never said please to me before in the whole of my life.'

'What are you going to do?' Kit asked.

'What she told me to do, open that which was closed in the heart of the fire. It does make sense, but you have to know the family history fully to understand, which was why it was safe to put it in a text. If I didn't get it, nobody else would figure it out.' He lifted his head and smiled quite beautifully. 'Could you do the thing with the mobile phones, and shine the light here, on the hearthstones at the back of the inglenook?'

He swung the hammer even as he spoke, not hard, but with focused precision, aiming it at the solid stone floor at the place where it met the wall in the heart of the inglenook fireplace.

Three times, the hammer rebounded off solid stone. On the fourth, the sound was different; stone ground against stone. Davy turned the hammer over and used the handle to crack the mortar, then spun it again and rained softer, more precise blows against the opening gap. Between each one, he said, 'This is the . . . second secret of the fire. Cedric Owen's ledgers were . . . found in the bread oven a century after his death but . . . nobody has ever opened this . . . for the obvious reason that my family's history required that it not be until the time of

. . . final reckoning, which my mother . . . clearly considers to have— Damn. Could you make more light?'

'Can't,' Stella said. 'The mobiles are running low. Kit, kill yours. We need to keep the batteries for later.' He did and they stood in darkness lit by stars. She said, 'Davy, are there candles?'

'Under the sink. On the left, with the dusters. There's a box of matches on the shelf above. If we're lucky, the stone of the sink will have protected them from the fire. If not, we're stuffed.'

Stella felt her way there and found a pack of six misshapen candles and the matches, not yet burned in the heat. 'We're lucky,' she said. She took three, set them in a triangle on the floor and lit them. 'Did you ever see this done in Lapland?'

'I don't think so.' For the first time, she heard Davy Law sound cautious.

The skull-stone tingled in her hands, more than it had done when she held it over the sunlight. She held it over the triple flame and caught the centre point, where the firelight became blue heart-light, shining softly from the skull's eyes.

'God,' said Davy Law reverently.

Stella took care not to shine it at him, or at Kit, but at the chipped place on the floor where the hammer had hit. 'Go on,' she said. 'Finish it.'

He did, swiftly, chipping into the gap.

'Done.'

He smelled of brick dust now, as much as smoke. He was shaking all over. Where he had worked, in the deepest shadow at the back of the fireplace, was a rectangular gap. Carefully, he pushed against the stone at its edge. 'I should be a gentleman and let ladies go first, but in this particular instance . . . Could we have more light inside, please?' There was a sound of stone falling on stone. Davy stepped forward uncertainly, and angled the light of his phone into the hole.

'Oh, yes. Oh, very, very yes.'

From the denser dark, from amidst the dust and the ash and the broken flagstone, he drew a roll of parchment tied about with a scrap of linen, and a small notebook.

Stella said, 'Tell me that's a map?' She laid the stone down. The yellow candle flames changed the colour of the night.

'I think so. I hope so.' Davy knelt, and began to push back the ash and debris from the floor. 'Can we clear a space? And perhaps look in whatever's left of the pantry? There were plastic bags on the floor under the stone shelf. If there's one left intact, we could open it up and spread it out. I think this' – he held up the parchment – 'was old when Cedric Owen was alive, and if it's not a map, or, at least, proof of where to go, I'll eat the kitchen table. While this' – he held up the book – 'was hidden for a very good reason and I badly want to know what it was.'

Stella found a roll of bin liners in a corner where the fire had not reached. She swept a place on the floor and unrolled them to make a clean bed.

She reached for the bundle. Kit said, 'You need to be wearing gloves. If it's that old, we can't get finger grease on it.'

'But—'

'Marigolds,' said Davy. 'Also under the sink.' They were all shaking now.

She found them and came back and fumbled with the knots in the linen that bound the scroll together. It came undone suddenly, in a snap and flurry of old threads. With unsteady hands, she eased it open. 'I'll break it.'

From somewhere in the dark to her left, Davy Law said, 'Stella, we have less than six hours until dawn. If we can see where it shows, breaking it doesn't matter.'

She did break it, but only in one place. Laid out together, the two pieces made a whole – a charcoal-drawn sketch of a landscape, dyed here and there with patches of old, worn pigment. The lines were nearly gone, just enough to show a landscape, a circle of stones with a grassy mound inside and a shaped stone gateway. Trees swayed behind, and a quarter-moon stood overhead, with the sun sketched as a curved arc on the horizon. Stella squinted and stared and looked up at Davy Law, who was pale as glass and plastic-faced, as if all the feeling had drained into his fingertips.

'Do you know where it is?' she asked.

He barely heard her. He made a small, desperate noise in the back of his throat.

Quietly, Kit said, 'It's Weyland's Smithy. It's been there since before the Romans came. The Saxons believed that if you left a horse there overnight with a silver piece, the god-smith Weyland would have shod it again by the morning.'

'And it's a grave mound,' said Davy Law hoarsely. 'Where else would you take the stone that mirrors the head of your ancestors?'

'Is it near?'

'Ten minutes away.' His eyes were shining. 'We'll make it before dawn, no problem at all. And we still have time to look at the book.'

He laid the notebook alongside the curled edges of the parchment. As Cedric Owen's ledgers had been, it was bound in dull red leather. Unlike them, it bore the letters *BT, YULE, 1588* on the front cover in spidery capitals. Davy opened it with a finger's end, touching only the corner. Inside, the writing angled steeply across the page, barely more legible than the Mayan glyphs. He said, 'They never found Barnabas Tythe's first diary.' And then, 'Read it for us, Stella. You're the one with the practice reading Elizabethan script.'

And so she did, slowly, by the light of the

three candles, kneeling in the ash and smoke of his mother's ruined farmhouse, starting at the first entry.

'*Twenty-sixth of December, in the year of Our Lord one thousand five hundred and eighty-eight, thirtieth in the reign of our most Soveriegne Lady, Queen Elizabeth, Monarch of England, France and Ireland.*

I, Barnabas Tythe, have this day become Master of Bede's Colledge, Cambridge, most honoured position of owr lande. To my grate shame, my first act in this post was a lie.

May God and my colledge forgive me, for I have performed a funeral for a living man. Cedric Owen is not dead.'

27

Lodgings, Trinity Street, Cambridge,
27 December 1588

WRITTEN THIS 26TH DAY OF DECEMBER, IN
the year of our Lord, 1588. To Sir Francis
Walsingham, from Sir Barnabas Tythe, Master
of Bede's College, Cambridge, greetings.

It is with great regret that I inform you of
the deaths, not only of your loyal servant Sir
Robert Maplethorpe, but also of the traitor
Cedric Owen.

He did indeed come to my lodgings for
succour as you had suggested. I went forthwith
with all haste to the Master of my college to ask
his assistance in taking him prisoner. Professor
Maplethorpe came with armed men, intent on
taking him alive, but in such we failed; he
fought with a ferocity unknown to us, and had
clearly been most succinctly tutored. The man
who killed him has been punished for his
recklessness, but not by our hand – he died of

his wounds even as Owen lay bleeding his last.

The Spaniard of whom you wrote was wounded. His body has since been dredged from the Cam and burned. On the order of the college authorities, of whom I am now Master, Owen's corpse has been consigned to the paupers' graves beyond the crossroads at Madingley. I searched it myself and found not one whit about it to tell us of his purpose, or even to confirm his identity, but I found in his saddle bags an item – herewith enclosed for your perusal – of quite exceptional workmanship in what I believe to be gold.

Owen was a traitor and died fighting her majesty's loyal servants, and thus all of his property belongs now to the Crown. I send you this now, in earnest understanding that you will know how best to deal with it.

I would ask, however, that for the sake of the college, Cedric Owen be known to the future as a good man. It would sit ill with us to have nurtured a traitor, however unwittingly. I would not give our enemies ammunition to use against us in future centuries.

I await your further instructions on all matters.

I remain, sir, your most humble and loyal servant before God,

Professor Barnabas Tythe, Master-elect of Bede's College, Cambridge.

* * *

'Are you sure you want to give it to him?'

The solid gold funeral mask lay on the folds of Cedric Owen's good riding cloak. Barnabas Tythe's fingers strayed across the clustered diamonds. He said, 'Walsingham does not expect it, surely, nor does he need it. I could write the letter again and say that your saddle bags were empty save for a few gold coins from New Spain.'

From his chair by the fire, Cedric Owen shook his head. 'It is a gamble, admittedly. But if he thinks there is more, he may chase down the means of our arrival from Sluis, which would go ill with a certain Dutch smuggler flying under the flag of Portugal. I owe Jan de Groot enough already without drawing down Walsingham's pursuivants on his head.'

Owen spoke thinly; the bandage circling his brow successfully kept his brains from curdling, but in the two days since his injury he had found that if he gave rein to the full texture of his voice the pain in his head became unbearable.

He said, 'The mask will buy Walsingham a great deal of information. My hope is that he puts his remaining energies into spending the revenues it generates, not into hunting for more. How goes his health? I had heard it was not good.'

Tythe shrugged expansively. 'He is dying, but then so are we all. The only consolation for those who continue to suffer under his ministration is that Sir Francis is living in constant pain from stones in his kidneys and his faith will not permit him to seek a swift and painless ending by his own hand. Those of us who wish to can see it as God's punishment on him for his evil.'

Tythe was thinly fragile, still nursing a terror that the truth of the Christmas Day massacre might yet be exposed.

In the chaotic aftermath of the fight outside the college, Tythe had certainly believed Owen to be dead. Fernandez de Aguilar, whose own wounds were fortunately superficial, had been alone in believing otherwise, but had not let his care for his friend overtake the necessities of the moment. He it had been who had pulped the face of Maplethorpe's second henchman with his own cudgel, and then handed the weapon to Barnabas Tythe, ordering him to make the last three strokes that there might be some blood on his hands and hose, 'for verisimilitude' as the Spaniard had said.

De Aguilar, further, had so arranged the bodies that anyone else with an eye for a fight might see how Owen, the master-swordsman, had slain Maplethorpe and one of his henchmen before losing his own sword to a cudgel. How, immediately thereafter, the traitor had taken a like weapon from the ground, allowing him to defeat the last of Maplethorpe's men, before

Barnabas Tythe, hero of the hour, had taken his knife and finally killed him.

The good fortune of it was that the third man did bear some passing resemblance to Owen, and a few cracks with a cudgel made any close inspection unlikely. They moved swiftly to clothe him in Owen's cloak and boots, and for the rest, the ever-stronger flurries of snow had covered the battle site, concealing any inconsistencies that might have given the lie to their tale.

De Aguilar, then, had carried Owen to safety, sending Barnabas Tythe to convey the two parts of good news to his fellow scholars: that they were free of Maplethorpe at last, and that Cedric Owen, enemy of Walsingham, and so of the state, had been slain.

For the greater part of Christmas Day, while Barnabas Tythe had cemented his authority on the college that he loved, Fernandez de Aguilar had set aside his popinjay's clothes and the gold at his ear and wrapped a bandage about his own leg before tending to the unconscious Owen.

For a man with only one arm and no medical training to speak of, he had bound the broken ribs and skull with a dexterity that Tythe envied when finally the old man returned, stamping the snow from his boots, to tell of his unopposed election as Master and the successful passing off of Maplethorpe's thug as Cedric Owen.

In this they had been lucky; the seasonal festivities were well under way, the choir was making ready in Bede's College chapel and the men of the college council had better things to do than to stand in the mortuary examining bodies on the day of Christ's Mass.

Maplethorpe they looked at, covering their faces against the charnel-house stench. It was a duty to the dead man, and, more, a need that they could each relay afterwards the precision of the sword thrust to his chest that had killed him, and the same also to the manservant who had died immediately after. More than that they did not deign to do; the other bodies lay deeper in the oozing dark where the bracketed torches on both sides of the door barely reached.

It was possible to see the battered face of the swordsman Cedric Owen, and to wonder at the rich stuff of his cloak, but not a man among them wished to soil his boots to study the traitor or the man he had beaten to death in closer detail. When Tythe himself, the only physician present, had hinted that there was a risk of infection from the ill humours of the dead, they were all too grateful for his offer to arrange for their appropriate burials.

That had left the issue of Maplethorpe's remaining henchman, who appeared to be missing, there being only two other bodies besides Cedric Owen and Maplethorpe himself. A rumour arose that shortly before his death

Maplethorpe had confided to his Vice Master that the wretch was a suspect in the matter of some missing silver, and it was quickly accepted that he had seized the opportunity to flee with his ill-gotten treasure. For the preservation of the college's good name, no hue and cry was raised. As for Owen's accomplice, Tythe had taken it upon himself to have his personal servants dredge the Cam, and when they returned with a body – a not unlikely outcome, and one that Tythe had banked on – had identified it himself as the Spaniard who had accompanied Owen. The Master's sword could not be found but that was of no great moment.

The twelve men of the council had given vent to a collective sigh of relief at an ugly matter neatly closed, agreed a memorial to the memory of a 'much beloved and sadly missed' Master and unanimously voted the bloodstained hero, Barnabas Tythe, as their new Master.

That he kept neither henchmen nor a ferociously sober college was not their first consideration in his appointment, but both factors acted greatly in his favour. They raised their glasses in a toast to his new position, granted him the professorship he should have had long before and waded home through the still-falling snow in time to take their families to the Christmas morning Service of Thanks Giving in Bede's College chapel. The priest, roused early from bed, was able to pen a few moving lines about the dearly departed that would serve also for the funeral.

'What do we do now?' asked the new Master of Bede's of his guests.

'We wait,' said Owen. 'We eat, we keep silent when men pass in the street below your windows and we hope most fervently that we are both fit to mount a horse and ride by the time the snow stops falling. How much of the goose is left?'

Tythe grimaced. 'Enough for three good meals and a broth for your friend. Her majesty may command that we eat goose in honour of the Armada's defeat, but she is not the one who must continue to eat it for a four-night after the first meal until she wishes death and dissolution on every goose and gander in Christendom.'

'Maybe she does, maybe that's why she commanded we eat them at Christmas; so that the land might be devoid of goose and she will never be forced to eat it again. Did you know they were importing them from the Netherlands, that her majesty's loyal subjects might not go hungry for lack of goose?'

'Nothing would surprise me,' Tythe said sourly.

It occurred to him that his question had not been answered and, further, that this happened a lot when he spoke to Owen. 'And if we were not using time in the discussion of poultry, how better might we use it? I, for instance, must begin the daily diary that is required of me as the new Master of Bede's which will see me hang if I write the truth and it is discovered. What are you going to do when the snow stops falling?'

'I don't know.'

It came as a hard admission from Cedric Owen. He leaned back, looping his fingers over the curve of his knee, and directed his attention to the wavering ice-shadows on the hearth where sat his blue heart-stone.

Presently, he said, 'I have certain tasks to perform in this life, the first of which was to go to the New World, find the secrets of the stone and record them in such a way that only one truly wedded to the stone might find them. By the magics of the jaguar-people, Fernandez and I have together done just that; we have left in hiding in Harwich a set of volumes which will marry past to future and sometime soon we must find a safe place to hide them.'

'I think—' Tythe began.

'Not here, my friend; we would not so presume on your hospitality.' Owen made a fist, closing the possibility. 'We will concern ourselves therewith in due course, but first, and more onerously, we must remain alive long enough to find a certain very old place, somewhere that was sacred to our forebears long before the time of Christ. To my shame, and very great distress, I know not where to look. I had hoped that the stone might direct me, but it has not done so. Without its further aid, we are rudderless ships in a storm.'

'How will you recognize that which you seek?'

'I have dreamed it. The first time was thirty years ago, but the dream has remained with me since.' A flop of hair fell over Owen's eyes, the stifled end of a move to rise. 'It is a wild place, in a flat wooded plain with a circle of standing stones and the wind howling around. In the dreams, I see the black silhouettes of leafless trees bent against a storm and lightning in the sky, but that could be a hundred places from the southernmost coast of Cornwall to the far north of Northumberland. We cannot search them all.'

Tythe pressed his fingers to his lips. A memory danced somewhere just out of reach, insubstantial as fog, elusive as summer trout. He was trying to see its form and substance when he became aware of the blue stone that sat so crisply on his hearth and shed its light into the room. In the space of two breaths, there was a change in the texture of the flowing blues – their boundaries had spread out to reach him.

Barnabas Tythe watched this alchemy and felt the hairs rise along his forearms. He saw Cedric Owen's head turn uncertainly, as might a hound's that hears a distant echo of its master's whistle, and then saw the whole man jerk back a little in the chair as if the whistle had come again, so close as to be deafening.

Tythe fancied he heard something; a faint tune that played at the borders of his imaginings and was not of any instrument or voice that he had ever heard.

Owen said, 'Barnabas? What is it that you have forgotten?'

'I don't know,' Tythe said. 'There's something . . . somebody . . . but I can't remember who or—'

It seemed to him that the blue stone turned so that its fire-lit eyes were focused directly on his. Held by that unworldly gaze, his thoughts scattered as clouds before a storm, leaving a clear blue sky where before had always been cobwebs and clutter. The stone-song became a summoning. A gateway opened and the elusive memory stepped up to meet him, sharp and clear and bright.

Into the song-filled silence, he said, 'I have a cousin, recently bereaved, who lives in a farmhouse near Oxford. We have not met in person since the death of Queen Mary, but we correspond twice a year on family matters. The relationship is through my mother's side, but before the late king destroyed the monasteries my cousin's father was retained at the rate of one gold piece per year by the late Richard Whiting, the Abbot of Glastonbury, may God rest his burned and broken soul, to maintain the ancient byways and sacred paths of the ancestors that pass through the abbey and assorted other churches and monasteries. The Catholic Church was not as ignorant of these things as the Puritans prefer to be, and my cousin's father was the one amongst them who understood the old ways best.'

Owen's eyes were large as an owl's. They fed on Tythe's face. 'Would your cousin's father help us?'

'If he is yet alive. He will be ninety-three in June, so it may be that he has died. If he still lives, there is no other man who knows more of the standing stone circles and the dragon-ways of England than he.'

Tythe stood up briskly, relieved at one stroke both of the stone's song and the burden of his guests.

Cheerily, he said, 'If you would travel thither, I will give you a letter of introduction to my cousin that should smooth your way. You can leave as soon as the snow stops, preferably tonight. If you and de Aguilar can ride well enough to allow you good speed, you will reach Oxford before ever my letter to Walsingham reaches London.'

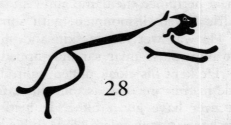

28

Lower Hayworth Farm, Oxfordshire, 30 December 1588

Eᴺɢʟᴀɴᴅ ʟᴀʏ ɪɴ ᴀ ᴡᴀsʜ ᴏꜰ ᴍᴇʟᴛɪɴɢ sɴᴏᴡ. Trees dripped steadily on to grey, slush-ridden pathways. Horses stumbled and slipped on patches of hidden ice. Even at noon, it was dark as dusk; travelling at night had proved impossibly dangerous and Owen relied for secrecy on the fact that no one ventured abroad without exceptional reason.

They came to the farmhouse in the early evening, as true night was falling. It was a newly built, prosperous-looking place, of good timber, stone and thatch in the latest design. Behind them, the countryside lay mired in grey fog. In a kennel nearby, a pair of bloodhounds belled musically. A mastiff snarled and snapped, but not yet at them.

Ahead, a pathway of level stone led to a gate and through it to an oak door that looked built to repel an army. Smoke rose in dark ribbons from the chimney stacks and the smell of roasting meat perfumed the damp air.

Cedric Owen dismounted, with some difficulty. He was wet to the skin and shivering. Beside him, de Aguilar sat blue-lipped on his horse. He kept his cloak pulled tight, as much to hide his missing arm as for what warmth it might ever have given him. He held Robert Maplethorpe's stout, plain blade in his hand.

'Knock,' he said. 'We have nothing to lose. If Tythe's cousin turns us down and we sleep out of doors another night, we will both die.' He essayed a feeble grin. 'The warmth of hell would be a blessing after this. Do you suppose there is a cold hell reserved for those who died in wintertime?'

'We haven't come this far to die,' Owen said, and tried to believe it. He raised the handle of his dagger and rapped it against the new wood of Barnabas Tythe's cousin's farmhouse door.

He was too cold to move fast, and too blinded by the wet hair that streaked across his face to see the club that angled down at his head in time to avoid it. He heard de Aguilar shout hoarsely in Spanish and heard the scrabble of a wrenched horse on the slushy path and was trying to frame an appropriate reaction when his brains fell to water and his knees ceased to hold him up.

He was not awake enough to be aware of

the slight hands that caught him as he fell, or the shocked, delicately moulded face that stared into his own.

The warmth in his feet was Owen's first sense on waking, the unutterable luxury of dryness and tingling heat when he had ridden the last three days believing he would never again feel anything but cold and wet.

He lay a while, restricting his attention to his nether regions in an effort to avoid the bruising pain in his cranium or the waxing and waning of his consciousness.

In one of his more lucid moments, he thought he heard mellifluous Spanish spoken in two voices, which was, of course, impossible. But it was there again when next he surfaced. With an effort, he organized his thoughts and made connection with all four of his limbs and finally, regretfully, with his ribs and then his head. Raising himself half to sitting, he opened his eyes.

'Ah. Señor Owen awakens. And not before time.'

It was not Fernandez de Aguilar who spoke; thirty years of close company had woven that voice to his soul so that he knew it better than his own. Against the protestations of his body, Owen opened his eyes and made his head turn towards the source of speech.

He was in a large, comfortable farmhouse

441

kitchen, with flagstones upon the floor and a vast stone-built inglenook fireplace currently burning what appeared to be an entire oak tree in sizeable logs. The room was radiantly warm. Seated at a long oak table of aching newness was Fernandez de Aguilar in manifestly less pain than he had been since the injury to his leg. Beside him sat a figure robed appropriately in black. *I have a cousin, recently bereaved . . .*

That one rose now, and came over to where Owen lay on a truckle bed before the fire.

'I'm sorry, sir. I live alone but for my widowed father and England in this weather is not a place where honest men choose to travel. I took you for brigands, come for what little silver we have saved. Had not your friend shouted in Spanish, I might have done you more damage. You have his exhaustion to thank for the wholeness of your limbs; had he not been tired and fevered almost to insanity, he would have manufactured a shout in English and I fear it would have been the end of you.'

Owen stared, dizzily, trying to make sense of an upturned world. The face on which he made such an effort to focus was sage and well weathered, broad at brow and cheek, narrowing to an oval chin of commendable firmness above a slender neck. The eyes were a dense steel grey and catlike, teasing and savage together. The lips were perfect, and framed about by deeply etched lines of laughter that put their maker on the wrong side of forty, but cheerfully so.

The overall effect was of a fierce, intelligent face, framed about by hair the same colour and curl and sprinkling of not-quite-grey as Barnabas Tythe's. It was this, then, that identified the speaker incontrovertibly as Tythe's cousin, child of his mother's sister, whose father had been geomancer to the abbots of Glastonbury before the reformation.

Which begged the sizeable question of why Tythe had omitted to mention that his cousin was a woman, or that she was quite astonishingly handsome, or that Fernandez de Aguilar, who had spent his entire adult life happily disregarding the comforts of the fairer sex, might suddenly – if with perfect reason – become infatuated with her.

Or perhaps not quite so suddenly. Owen said, 'How long have I been asleep?'

De Aguilar said, 'Not long. It is evening of the day we arrived. Martha has spoken to her father. He knows that we are fugitives from Walsingham's pursuivants and that there is a risk in our being here. He has insisted that we must stay and, moreover, has asked to see the blue stone. We waited until you were awake to show him.'

Martha . . . We . . . The greatest change was not in de Aguilar's language, although that was great enough, but in the texture of his voice, which had become soft and rich and rolling, like malmsey drunk at the sea's edge of a summer's evening.

It should not have hurt so. There had, after all, been thirty years of Najakmul, and not once had her importance to Owen come between himself and the Spaniard whose life he had saved.

Even so . . .

'May I know to whom I am speaking?' Owen sat up too fast, and closed his eyes against the pain in his head.

There was a perceptible pause from his right. He fancied that the woman had asked a silent question of de Aguilar with her steel-grey eyes, and the man had answered with a nod.

The voice which had spun such silken Spanish said, 'My apologies, sir. I am Martha Huntley, daughter to Edward Wainwright who sits yet by the fire and wife to Sir William Huntley, who died aboard ship this summer defending England from the enemy.'

Owen opened his eyes. The woman stood just out of arm's reach, watching him. He wished himself less vulnerable. He said, 'And you speak Spanish like a native. Did that set you apart from your neighbours when the Armada threatened?'

She was very like Najakmul; her eyes flared with a new fire. 'My neighbours know that I am not a traitor, but fully loyal to Queen and country. My family fled to Spain in my youth when Queen Elizabeth first came to the throne. I was young, my mother was not of robust health and they feared that the burnings would start again except that they would be of Catholics this time, not Protestants.'

'You came back because you were wrong?'

She turned her hands outwards in a way that she could have learned from de Aguilar, but had most likely known since childhood. 'We were English in Spain, which was not a safe thing. There, we *would* have been traitors, at least in our hearts. The Queen had shown by her actions that she was serious in her intent not to carve windows into men's souls. My father missed the land he had grown with and my mother wished to die here. She was granted that wish.'

'I'm sorry,' Owen said. 'With your mother and husband both dead, you are doubly bereaved.'

The frankness of her gaze acknowledged his courtesy and yet denied the need for it. 'My mother died many years ago. I am more concerned now that my father is also fast approaching his final communion with his Maker. He remains tied to this life because he will not leave me as a woman alone, forced to marry to keep my good name and my home.'

Owen switched his gaze from her to de

445

Aguilar and back again. Artlessly, he asked, 'Do you fear his imminent death?'

She flushed, but did not lower her gaze. 'I do, but for other grounds than those you think. He holds to life for a second reason: he has had dreams of a certain stone which he must see before he dies, of blue crystal sapphire, fashioned in the shape of an unfleshed man's head.'

Owen did not answer at once, but waited for the stone to speak to him – and waited in vain, for it was unaccountably silent. From the moment they had left Cambridge – actually, from the moment they left New Spain – it had been leading Owen and de Aguilar to this place. At each point on their journey, its song had been a constant presence, stronger when they took the propitious turn at any given cross-roads, weaker when they did not. At the killing of Maplethorpe, it had fairly hollered its appreciation, and in its connection to Barnabas Tythe, to prompt him to send them here, it had excelled itself. To find it silent now left the world a poorer place.

Risking the knifing pain in his head, Owen turned to search the room.

From his left, de Aguilar said, 'Cedric, your bags are here.'

For thirty years, Fernandez de Aguilar had divined whatever Owen wanted before any need to ask. Yet again, he was there at his side, holding the saddle packs, a sober flounce of oak-brown velvet and gold. His long, lean face was no longer blue with cold and pain, but warily alive; the creases etched by the sun of New Spain were lit with laughter and a new hope even as his eyes spoke complex silent messages of apology and insecurity and reassurance. He wanted Owen to know that nothing had changed, that the widow Martha Huntley was not going to come between them, but that the sun had risen in his life in a new way and he craved the freedom to enjoy it.

Patiently, as to a child, Owen said, 'Fernandez, you are a Spaniard. England is at war with Spain. The first time you open your mouth as your true self, you're a dead man.'

The Spaniard grinned. 'But I am already a dead man; my body has been found and burned. If you and I are to be safe from Walsingham's pursuivants then it must be that Fernandez de Aguilar no longer exists. If I can be made to have light hair, not dark, and a new, more patriotic reason for having lost my arm, I could be another man and nobody could prove I was not.'

'You would leave behind all that you were?'

'I would – no – I must. But not yet. I am still the man whose life you saved. I am bound to you yet, and will fulfil my duty.'

Something unkind grabbed at Owen's gut. 'I had thought it more than a duty.'

'It is.' De Aguilar's one hand held his shoulder. Black Spanish eyes sought his and held them. 'Truly, it is. I love you as much as I have loved any man. But I would have sons to live after me. And not only that . . .'

In thirty years, de Aguilar had never been lost for words. The novelty of it eased the moment even while the rest of him proclaimed a peace newly found that was beyond language.

More gently than before, Owen said, 'Then let us bring the blue heart-stone into the light of the fire and perhaps we can find why it has fallen silent.'

The stone was asleep, or it seemed so to Owen. It felt heavy and limp in his hand as he drew it out of the saddle bags, like a fireside cat that has fallen drowsy in the heat and wakes with reluctance.

Presently, when it did not, in fact, wake, he came to believe it was exhausted. He had thought it immortal, immune to the aches and ills of men, but as he held it by the vast oak-log fire in Martha Huntley's farmhouse and spoke to it in his head as he had done these past few decades, he felt the numbness of true fatigue, the sluggish glue-eyed return to the world of men. Its song then was a slender thread of sound, spun out from the aeons of space wherein it had found shelter.

He had never considered himself the stone's master, capable of summoning it against its will.

It lay passive between his hands, so that the firelight barely leaked through it and the colour that came out was more amber than blue.

'I'm sorry,' Owen said to the thread that wove in his head, 'there is one who would meet you. I must interfere with your repose.'

'Thank you.' The voice came aloud, in response to a thought he had spoken only inwardly. Owen turned, too swiftly, and slowed, for the pain in his head.

The fire had hidden Edward Wainwright. He sat so close that it seemed the flames must consume him ere ever they were done with the oak. He sat in his armchair, swaddled in fine-woven blankets, an animated skeleton, barely clinging on to life. His veins showed blue and knotted through the paper thinness of his skin. His tendons stood out like pulleys so that Barnabas Tythe could have held an anatomy master class on his just-breathing body and never had need of dissection. His eyes were filled with cataracts and swollen conjunctiva with crusting pus at the inferior canthus where his daughter had not seen fit to wipe it away, or had chosen not to so invade him, for it did no harm, Owen thought, and its leaving gave him some dignity.

He was stronger than he appeared. He reached out to grasp Owen's wrist and the clawed fingers were strong as a snake that wraps its prey to crush it. 'Have I your permission to look at your jewel?'

'Of course.' The stone said nothing different, gave no warning. Owen set it down, nestling it on the bony knees deep in the wrap of the yellow blanket. 'You may hold it if you wish.'

There was a moment's hiatus when the old man simply looked. His face was a study in awe, as a child who is given the gift of his heart after long years of disappointment.

The skull was facing him, the empty eye sockets turned up to face the deep pits of his own gaze. It was contained still, sleepily inhaling the light from the fire and even more sleepily sending it out. Slowly, in wonder, Edward Wainwright's hands closed around its smoothly perfect temples.

At the moment of their meeting, the stone wept, or so it seemed to Owen; in the quiet of the firelight, he felt such a melting as he had never known from it.

Certainly, the old man was weeping. Sparse tears made tracks of living gold down his cheeks, as if all the fluids of his life were saved for this.

None the less, his eyes were dry when eventually he raised them to Owen again. 'There is a place in this land that was fashioned to hold this stone, and must do so in the end times. Do you know where it is?'

Owen felt his heart stop, and then start again,

erratically. 'I have dreamed of this place every night for the past thirty years, but I have never been there, and do not know where it is. I have been sent to England to find it.'

'Then my last year has not been wasted.' A warmth lit Wainwright's face, easing the weight of age. 'For my daughter's joy and for your arrival have I waited, and today both are fulfilled. And yet our quest is not so simple, for we who walk the old, straight tracks were never told which of the five places we guard was the one that mattered most. Could you draw for me the place of your dream?'

Like a flood tide, racing, the blood flowed too fast in Owen's veins. 'If you furnish pen and paper, I can try.'

At her father's direction, Martha took a candle upstairs and presently returned with a goose quill and black ink and a sheet of good, flat paper, which held the ink perfectly.

'I use it for casting maps of the stars,' Edward Wainwright said. 'If I live to morning, I will take the time and place of your birth and create your own.'

Out of politeness, Owen thanked him, and did not say that he could cast his own chart, and had done so too many times to count.

He sat by the fire with a wooden tray inverted as a resting-board on his knee. By the dancing orange light, with his eyes half closed, he sketched out the place he had first seen in the smoke dreams of the jungle over three decades previously.

He talked as he drew. 'The place is shrouded by mist; when I first come to it, all I can see are the half-shapes of beech trees all along one side. And yet the moon gazes upon it, a week before full, so that the shadows of the standing stones are crisp.'

'There are stones, then? Will you describe them to me?'

'I cannot be certain.' In the process of drawing, Owen found the gaps where the dream was not clear. On the paper already were vague outlines of the beech trees, and the beginnings of a circle of stones that carried its own magic without his having to make it happen, but not the detail Edward Wainwright required.

Owen tilted the board to gain better light. 'As I approach, I come to a row of four upright stones, each one taller than a man, and, at the base, twice as broad, pointed at their upper ends. They surround a long, low mound, bowl-like in its shaping, and there are lower, rounder stones before it. The mound itself is made of stone covered with earth and turf that hides a tunnel at its heart. It has lintel stones, squared at the edges and ends so that they fit together as a joiner fits timber to make a door frame.' He scratched his chin with the feathered end of the quill. 'Shamingly, I cannot count the stones in the circle. I try, but each time the number is different.'

From the far side of the inglenook, Edward Wainwright said, 'There is no shame in that. No one can ever count the stones in the old circles; they are not made for eyes such as ours. In your dream, do you enter the grave mound?'

Owen lifted his head. 'It is a grave? I had thought it might be; there were bones of men and horses in its heart. In each dream, I do indeed go into the tunnel. It is completely dark, and yet I can see as if it were day; thus have sleep and the blue stone changed my sight.'

He began another sketch, this time of the interior of the mound. 'The grave is long and narrow, except for two blind arms to either side just within the entrance, so that if one were to look on it from above, it would be shaped a little like a short-armed cross. The niche made for the heart-stone is at the far end, within the wall. I have never seen it clearly, but believe it to be exactly of a size and depth to bring the heart-stone to bear on the earth's surface, while encased in the hewn rock of the mound.'

He finished his sketch, both of the mound from the outside, and of the inside, and labelled the niche with an arrow and a short phrase. Turning the board, he showed his sketch to Edward Wainwright. 'I would not hasten your death by any measure, but if this helps you to fulfil your life, it will be well done.'

'It is well done.' Wainwright's eyes were alight with a new life. He looked beyond Owen to where Martha Huntley sat. 'For this we have lived, you and I. Now is the time of revealing.'

Wordless, Martha left the Spaniard and took her candle to the great fireplace within which oak logs each as thick as a man's thigh gave off a fierce heat.

To dismantle such a fire took some skill, such as might come of practice. Presently, when the logs were pushed aside, Martha swept her skirts tight around her ankles and, kneeling near the back of the fire, performed a minor miracle, pushing her hand through the thick stone hearth to a cavity beneath. Owen took his own candle closer, and by its light found that it was not so much a miracle as a sleight of hand; a single stone in the midst of the hearth was balanced about a mid-pin, so that, when pushed, one side slotted inwards while the other rolled outwards, leaving a gap such as a man's arm might fit through.

From the hollow space thus hidden, Martha brought out a bundle of vellum scrolls, rolled and tied with braided horsehair. She carried them as if they were the leg bones of a long-dead saint, like to crumble to dust at any moment. Kneeling, she laid them with reverence on her father's knee.

He sorted through them with the feathered end of the quill pen, lifted one, and held it out to Owen.

'Would you do me the honour of opening this?'

'May I do so safely? It looks too old to be handled by such as I.'

'It was made for such as you. If it crumbles as you touch it, still it will have served its use. But best if you treat it kindly and can leave it for those who come after.'

Owen held his breath, and did not know until afterwards that he had done so. With unsteady fingers, he untied the binding and unrolled the parchment. It was softer than he had imagined, and did not split along the cracks, but eased out into a single sheet the length of his forearm and the height of his hand upon which was sketched, in thin, faded charcoal, a landscape.

It was Fernandez de Aguilar, leaning over his shoulder, who understood first.

'It is the same place . . . Cedric, this is your dream!'

And so it was, drawn with charcoal and coloured by ochre and lime and copper oxide, held fast by water, or egg white, or somesuch that had caused the tints to fade greatly with age.

The place was the one he had seen. Still the number of the stones was impossible to count, as if the firelight made them sway whenever Owen looked directly. In any case, it was the mound that drew his eye and held it, for it was not empty and silent as he had met it first, but the centre of a gathered crowd, with a man holding a raised staff near its mouth. He leaned in to the fire and brought the vellum close, then lowered it again.

'How old is this?' His voice was dry as dust.

'It has been in my family for a little over one hundred generations,' said Edward Wainwright. 'I could name them for you, but fear my life would end ere I was finished. Someday, if you have the time and the interest, Martha will do so for you.'

Owen said, 'In my family also, we can name the generations of those who have held the blue stone. It is the first thing I learned from my grandmother. The reciting of names takes over half a day.'

'Of course, for you are the keeper and your line is as unbroken as ours. We are the walkers of the trackways. To us has fallen the task of keeping the life in the old places. Why, then, do you ask the age of the picture?'

By a small miracle, Owen found sufficient spit to speak. 'I thought I recognized myself. Now I look more closely, I see that it is but a man with silvered hair, and could be anyone of like height and colouring. My apologies.'

He held the two pictures side by side, his and the older one. 'These are unquestionably the same place, but even now I don't know where in England it is.'

Wainwright looked at him, shocked. 'Of

course not! For if you knew, you might speak it aloud. Only by keeping stone and knowledge separate are we safe in this world where fire and torment are used to pull the truth from unwilling minds.'

He took back the older picture and began carefully to fold it. 'And still, there is no need for you to know, for it is many years before your stone must be set there, to form the heart of the beast that will arise from the land. As we have done since before the birth of Christ, we who walk the trackways will hold this knowledge safe until such time as man's evil requires that it be drawn forth in the earth's defence. Your task is to hide the skull in a place of great secrecy that will thwart all those who seek its destruction, while yet leaving it to be found by the one who must bring it here.'

Edward Wainwright's eyes were the same dense steel grey as his daughter's. He used them as a fencer uses his foil, to catch Owen and hold him. 'You did know that the heart-stone must be hidden somewhere distant from here?'

'In a place of white water, yes. My grandmother described to me the place and a wise Frenchman spoke of it again, long ago, in the summer of my youth, so that I understood why she had done so.'

'Is it within reach of here? Can you go there now?'

'If need be, although the route will not be

easy if it must be travelled in secrecy. The place is in Yorkshire, where I grew up, a good ten days' ride from here.'

'Then we can each fulfil our tasks. I will hide again the map that my family may keep the secret of it, and you must set forth to York that you may keep the final part of your bargain with the stone. Martha? Will you return the scroll to its resting place?'

His daughter did as she was bid, closing over the hidden place and returning the fire to its bed. The heat it gave off was not as great, afterwards, but quite sufficient.

'Thank you.' In a creak of old limbs, Edward Wainwright lifted himself to standing. With no small regret, he handed back the heart-stone to Owen, bowing deeply to him and then to Fernandez de Aguilar.

'Sirs, it has given me untold pleasure to see the stone and yourselves in the last days of my life and I cannot thank you enough. By all rights, I should send you swiftly to complete your final task, but tonight is not a night for travel and I cannot doubt but that the morning will suffice. In the meantime, we can set the beds to warming and we have food enough for four, if you have not yet tired of the taste of roast goose?'

29

Lower Hayworth Farm, Oxfordshire,
31 December 1588

NOT FAR AWAY, A CHURCH BELL TOLLED midnight.

Cedric Owen lay awake, staring up at the dark ceiling. The sheets of his bed were cold and damp and starched so that they did not fold around him. The room smelled of unuse and cobwebs draped thickly across the corners of the roof beams. The mattress was of uneven horse hair with ends that poked out to stab through his shirt to his skin. With all of this, it was luxury compared to where he had slept in the journey from Cambridge, and he was glad of it. Pushing his feet down to the last heat of the warming brick, wrapped in its own woollen sock, he listened to the slow heartbeat of a new house, settling, and to the breathing of the man on the bed next to his own.

He knew the signatures of that breath as well

as he knew his own; he had slept in its company, although not in the same bed, for the past thirty years. Presently, into the dark, he said, 'Fernandez, if you cannot sleep, why do you not go to her? Likely she is as awake as you.'

There was a silence, in which the breathing changed and changed again. Eventually, Fernandez de Aguilar said, 'She is a lady. I would not sully her good name.'

'And if Walsingham's men come tomorrow and we are slain? Would you not rather at least have let her choose what she does with her good name? You can be married in days if you and she wish it.'

'And if she does not?'

'Then you will have your answer. Go to her, man. You have nothing to lose.'

A bed creaked in the dark. He heard the slide of starched sheets and a blanket thrown back and the subtle noises of de Aguilar's dressing, broken by the briefest pause.

Amused, Owen said, 'You need not change your doublet. If she does not love you in the tawny velvet, she will not love you better in the blue. You will wear neither for long if she feels as you do.'

'I had thought to find something with less mud on it, but you are right, there is nothing to be gained by dissembling.' For a man who had never been uncertain, there was a shadow of doubt in de Aguilar's voice now. 'If she does not want me, we may have to leave before morning.'

'Then we will be spared more goose. Go, and do not expect to be back before cockcrow.'

Soft-footed, de Aguilar left. Owen lay awake in the dark and heard, presently, the murmur of voices and the scrape and rattle of the hearth as the fire was roused. He smelled its smoke, and the cinnamon sweetness of wine newly mulled and let himself drift into a doze, that he might not offend his friend, whom he dearly loved, by listening to his courtship.

He woke some time later to the baying of bloodhounds; a sound to rouse the moon and make it flee from its course. The heart-stone sang with them, a song of alarm that had penetrated the clouds of his dreams, spreading streaks of yellow lightning in a warning he had neither heard nor seen in the whole forty years of their time together.

Owen sat bolt upright in the dark, reaching with one hand for his knife and with the other for de Aguilar, and only when he had found neither did he remember where he was and to what purpose.

He was rolling out of bed even as the evening's events were sorting themselves in his head. Last came the knowledge of where he might find de Aguilar, and in what frame of mind.

Barnabas Tythe had given him a sword. He buckled it on, for the show, and ran along the corridor to the room at the east end, where slept his host's daughter. 'Fernandez? Fernandez, are you there? We are assaulted!'

'Wait for me downstairs.' The voice was only a little disgruntled.

They met downstairs in front of the red-ashed fire. Fernandez was sharply awake, his eyes alight with the life of newly consummated love. He buckled on his sword belt one-handed.

'Walsingham?' he asked.

'I believe so. The heart-stone sounds a warning to match the hounds.'

'And who else would be abroad in the dark morning hours of the year's last day?' De Aguilar swung round as he spoke, studying the room. 'The house is well built. We can fortify the doors and shutter the windows but we cannot withstand a long siege. It might be better if you and I were to go outside and meet the enemy in the open, which will leave our host and his daughter safely inside to—'

'No.'

Edward Wainwright and his daughter spoke with one voice. The old man was surprisingly sprightly, for his age and the time of night. He leaned on the doorway to the kitchen. 'I do not impugn your courage or your abilities, but we are too close to the end to risk failure now. The blue heart-stone must not fall into the hands of the enemy, nor must the secret of its final destination in the heart of the earth. If these two are lost together, then far more than we are lost with them.'

'What do you advise?' De Aguilar was politely attentive, even as he found wood to brace the shutters and sought vessels in which to gather water against fire.

'I will stay here. You and the skull-keeper must leave. My daughter may do as she will; go with you or stay here. Either way is fraught with danger and I would not impose on her a mean death against her own choosing.'

'Father . . .' She was torn; any man could see it.

The blue heart-stone was still sounding its warning. Finding courage in that, Owen said, 'Go with Fernandez. He will keep you safe. I will leave first and ride north from here and thus lead them away. When they have followed me, you can both return in safety to your father.'

'No.' De Aguilar spoke alone this time. Moving closer to Martha, he said, 'Cedric, you have the blue heart-stone and I still have my sworn duty, which is, as you said last night, far more than that. Your life is in my care, and that of the blue stone, and thus the hope of the world for all eternity. Therefore, I will trust you to guard Martha and her father, or perhaps trust her to guard both of you, for I suspect her skill with a blade may exceed yours. I will be the one to act as decoy. Martha and her father will tell me now which trackways I may follow that will most confuse those who hunt us and I will do whatever I must to draw them away while all three of you travel north. Please – there is no time to be lost and this is our only hope.'

He held up his hand against the chorus that came against him. In the space of moments, he became again the man Owen remembered, who had captained the *Aurora* through a storm to a strange land: confident, organized to the point of arrogance and brooking no argument. He stalked the length of the kitchen, firing instructions. As he had so many years ago, Cedric found himself doing as he was bid, too busy to think of other avenues that might be taken.

'Pack what little you must carry and leave the rest. Take sufficient diamonds to keep you in good heart for half a year and hide the rest. Leave a little of the gold where it might appear to have been hidden in haste; if it is found, it may be enough to buy us freedom. If we live, we can come back for the rest later. Cedric, you take my horse; I will take yours. If we were recognized on our journey, that will help the deception, for you rode a grey and it will be seen in the light of the coming morning. I will take whatever spare horses Edward can lend us and use them to make diversion.' They were running to his command. As he stopped, Owen and Martha were both close. De Aguilar caught them each, one after the other, with his one arm. 'I am not seeking my death, only to buy life for us all. You must trust me to do this, both of you.'

Martha was the braver of the two. She had a square of linen and was already gathering into it bread and hard cheese and – miraculously – a small squared honeycomb from the pantry in the corner of the kitchen. She moulded herself to de Aguilar's embrace and received a brief, chaste kiss. Stepping back, she said to Owen, 'Name a place where he may meet us when he has lost them,' and thus was the decision sealed.

They moved swiftly, goaded by the worsening noise of the hounds and the frantic urgings of the heart-stone. The candle had burned down less than a quarter of an inch by the time they embraced their last goodbyes. Their diamonds and as much of the gold as they dared were hidden in the resting place at the back of the fire; the rest of the gold was left in a place where searching men might find it without undue difficulty, and think they had come across a hoard. Owen was packed and ready with Edward Wainwright and his daughter. De Aguilar had committed to memory, but not written anywhere about his person, the name of the place where they might meet.

He was mounted on the grey gelding that had been Owen's since they left Cambridge. Owen reached up a hand to the bridle. In the dark, his friend was a bare outline, seen against the crisp cold of a frosted night. 'We will wait for you ten days from now, and every alternate day for a month. After that, we will return monthly, in case you have been there. If you come and we are not there, tie a square of linen to the hawthorn tree near the ford and we will come every day at dawn. If you are taken, and made to talk, tell them to tie white wool and we will know we must flee.'

De Aguilar leaned down from his horse. His breath made pale mist in the greying air of morning. 'I will not be taken. Wait for me there. I shall join you as soon as I may.'

His parting from Martha was brief and heart-felt. Owen turned away from it, that he might not interfere. They stood together, he and Martha, in the sharp cold of the stables, and listened to de Aguilar make noise enough for three, if those three were doing their best not to be heard.

The bloodhounds bayed, and the heart-stone sang a quiet song of farewell that caused Owen more heartbreak than had even Najakmul's timely death in the jungles beyond Zama. Martha Huntley could not hear it and he did her the service of not explaining why he wept. By the flickering light of the single candle, he saw that her fingers, which had been bare, now wore a gold ring of great quality on the marriage finger of her left hand.

Too soon, he heard a shout, and the sound of many horsemen, and the whistle that was de Aguilar's signal that he had been spotted. The patter of bound hooves became a thunder with the iron-on-stone of shod hooves behind. Very quickly, the sound of a hunt grew loud and fell away into the night.

'We should go now,' said Owen gruffly, to Martha and her father. 'For it is a ten-day ride north to York and we must travel circumspectly, and not arouse attention.'

30

Oxfordshire, England, 4:00 a.m.
21 June 2007

'WE'RE BEING FOLLOWED.' STELLA TURNED to look out of the back window. Somewhere behind in the black night were twin points of light. For a moment, she smelled damp rock, tasted earth on her tongue, felt the acid wrench of fear from the cave. Anger washed it away, made blue by the stone. 'The pearl-hunter,' she said softly, viciously. 'We're being hunted.'

Kit was in the car's back seat. He leaned forward. 'Davy, can you drive without the lights?'

'Not unless you want to die before dawn.' Davy knew the way to the grave mound and so Davy was driving. Already they were going too fast.

'How far to go?' Kit asked.

'Another two or three miles.'

'Then stop the car and go without me. I'll catch you up.'

'Kit?' Stella turned to catch his hand. 'You can't walk.'

'I can walk, I just can't run. You can, and it's you two who need to be there. Davy knows where you need to be, you have the stone. So leave me behind.' In a gesture as intimate as any Stella had seen, he reached forward to touch Davy's wrist. 'You know I'm right. Don't piss about. Just do it.'

Davy kept his eyes on the road. After a moment, he said, 'Junction coming up. There's a field just past the turning where we can park the car behind the hedge. Stella, there's a torch in the glove compartment. We'll need it to see where we're going. Kit, if you're walking, stick to the road. Go up the hill to the white horse car park and turn right on to the Ridgeway. Head for the line of beech trees; it's quarter of a mile after those. You truly can't miss it.'

'I won't miss anything tonight,' Kit said. 'After everything else, I'm expecting fireworks at the very least. Or a dragon arising.'

'I hope not,' Davy said grimly. 'Ki'kaame, skull-holder of the Sami, said if we ever saw the dragon, we would know we were already dead. Hold tight. Here's the turn.'

He flicked off the headlights and pulled hard left on the wheel. In the blinding darkness, only hope and luck kept them safe. Stella found the torch and shone it out through the windscreen. Davy cut the engine. In silence, they bounced over rutted ground into the field.

'Out,' Davy said. 'Fast.'

He had been in war zones; it showed in the ways he moved, keeping close to the hedge line, away from the grey starlight.

Standing knee deep in uncut barley, Stella gave Kit the torch and her phone. They stood in the dark, with stars above showing outlines of faces and hands and eyes. Somewhere, not too far back, a car paused and came on.

Kit said, 'It's like the cave, but this time you're running ahead.'

'I have nowhere to fall.' She felt him falter, and sit. 'Kit—'

'I'm fine. I'll sit here a bit and catch you up. Go on. Tonight is about you and the stone. Afterwards, we can find the balance.'

She found his shoulders in the dark, and then his face, and his lips, and kissed him. 'I love you, did I mention?'

'Not today.' His eyes were wet. He made himself smile. 'Thank you.'

'I'm not choosing between you and the stone.'

'I never really thought you were. Please go.' His voice was steadier. He drew back and she could not see his face. He turned her round and gave a small shove between her shoulders. 'I'll catch you up, I promise.'

Davy caught her arm. 'Run, or we'll lose the advantage. How fit are you?'

'I ran the Paris marathon last year.'

'Good. So pace yourself. You've had no - warm-up and there's a big hill coming.'

Pacing herself, she ran. In the dark, under sharp stars, with cold night air on her face and the first hint of dawn dew, with the breath rasping hot in her throat and the taste of blood on the back of her tongue and a stitch knifing her side and sweat rolling in a steady stream down her back, with the heart-stone bouncing in her backpack, urging her faster onward, she followed Davy up the never ending hill which did end eventually when they turned right on to the track that led to the Ridgeway. No car lights followed.

'Davy—' She had to stop. She leaned forward, with her hands on her knees, spitting bloody mucus on to the tussocked turf. He came back to her and stood the same, breathing in a whistle.

'How much further?' she asked.

Wordless, he pointed. Ahead, in a corn field, a circle of trees blotted out the stars. He said, 'Nearly there. No need to run now. Dawn's not for an hour.'

They walked the last quarter of a mile down the track and along the narrow turf path that led out through a desert of planted barley to an oasis of trees and green grass. Stella was blind with exhaustion, seeing black against red in the backs of her eyes and feeling the ground with her feet. Gradually, the night settled to black and shadows of black and the pinprick stars above. The corn field was undulant as a grey sea. The circle of beeches whispered in the night. An owl crossed them. Somewhere, a dog fox barked. Down in the valley, a cock crowed, early. She heard no cars.

'We're there.' They were among the trees, looking in to the centre, to the place of the ancient charcoal drawing Cedric Owen had hidden in the heart of the fire so long ago. The sketch had made her spine tingle. The real thing left her in a strained, light-headed place, where the world seemed suddenly far older, and the soft voices of the stones were as real as morning birdsong.

Ahead, a circle of ground rose in a squat, flat mound, circular and covered in turf. Its circumference was bounded by stone and at the front, facing her, four tall, sharp-topped stones reared into the black night. Between these, a low, stone-sided channel led to the squared stone entrance. Inside that, only black.

It was not a spectacular place; it had neither the majesty of Stonehenge nor the artistry of the running horse at Dragon Hill, but in its very simplicity was a power each of these lacked.

Davy came to stand beside her, his shoulder warm on hers. Presently, Stella said, 'There were more standing stones in the picture.'

'I think it was drawn a long time ago, when

this was first built. Stone's too valuable for building to leave it standing around doing nothing, and the Church wasn't going to protect a place consecrated to the devil.'

Davy had caught his breath. The familiar sharp edge was back in his voice. He stepped up to the channel that led to the low doorway; a perfect alignment of two upright stones and a capstone, set back from the surrounding circle, fitted for thousands of years and proof against wind, rain and storm.

On either side, the four upright sentinels marked the front of the grave mound; tall as a man and as wide, but here, this close, it was the smaller, carved stone in the entrance that held Stella. Under the starlight, lines and shadows moved on it, undulant as the corn-sea in the field beyond. It spoke to her in the same tongue as the heart-stone sang, but she could not understand the words.

She said, 'I had thought there would be more of a tunnel. It seems very short.'

'It'll open when you need it to.' Davy stepped in front of her, blocking the route to the door-way. 'It's too early to place the stone in its setting,' he said. 'If I understood anything in Lapland, it was that timing is crucial. If you set the stone before dawn, or too late, you might as well not have bothered. And we can't go in early – the entrance is blocked by solid stone. I tried it once when I was a kid; there's a

473

cruciform shape at the entrance with two small side arms, but then it's just rock.'

'Then we can't go in,' Stella said. 'We're finished.'

'No. It'll open. You have to believe that. It's hollow inside. The archaeologists have been the full length. It will open.'

'Once we're in, how do we get out?' Stella asked.

'The same way we went in. There's only the one entrance.'

'Then it's a death trap.' Something was tugging at Stella's mind, fainter than it had been in the car, but enough; that sense of a hound following a scent. The skull-stone was a hunting cat, crouched and waiting. She felt no fear from it now, only a sharpened awareness of the passing time. She said, 'We're still being followed. If we go into the mound and can't get out, we're dead. Don't ask me how I know that.'

With no edge to his voice at all, Davy Law said, 'What do you want to do?'

'Find somewhere among the trees where we can see but not be seen while we wait for dawn.'

They stepped back under the whispering beeches. Davy brushed old leaves from a stone and lay down with his head on it, cushioned on his arm. Stella hunched her shoulders against a tree, hugging her knees to her chest for warmth. She lifted the heart-stone from its bag and pulled it into the foetal circle of her abdomen, keeping the backpack to sit on.

The stone crouched in her mind, watching and waiting. From the mound came the same sense of old life, newly awakened. If she allowed it, she could see more sharply, hear more clearly, taste the growth of the trees in the air, name the small creatures feeding in the foot of the corn, stitch together the constellations to make words that she might try to read.

She blinked and the sharpening was gone, except that the stone and the mound were still there and still spoke one to the other, if not to her. She tipped her head back and stared up at the unshifting patterns of the stars.

'Why are we here, Davy? You and I are scientists. We don't believe Rosita Chancellor's hysterical nonsense that the sun will walk down the path to the Underworld in five and a half years' time and the earth will vaporize in a puff of superheated steam. It doesn't happen like that.'

His voice came from the dark, scathing in its humour. 'We might not think it happens like that. The Sami would tell you differently. They wouldn't talk about superheated steam, but Ki'kaame can speak for nights on end about how the infantile white man is destroying the planet with his need to own everything.'

'So what's going to happen?'

'I have absolutely no idea, but I'll bet you the pension I don't have that something big is coming soon that we're too blind to see.'

'Cultural imperialism?'

'Cultural arrogance, certainly.' He was angry now, quietly so, forgetting the approaching threat. 'The Sami have it that we have fallen foul of the Enemy. They say that the gods made us self-reflective so we might venerate their wisdom and the beauty of their creation and instead we have used the powers of introspection to create hell on earth. As far as they're concerned, when the nine skulls of the races of men join with the four beasts to raise the dragon, it's more than likely that the end result will be a nuclear winter and the end of all human life. They're quite resigned to the extinction of all their people if it will cleanse the earth of what we have become. The question is whether it's likely, and frankly, every time I turn on the radio and listen to the news, I think we'll be lucky if we get as far as 2012.'

Stella chewed the edge of a nail. 'You can't write off the whole human race just like that. Most of us are decent, peaceful, honest folk going about our lives without threatening anyone.'

He shrugged. 'You're missing the point. Compared to other cultures, we stink. We don't care for our elderly, we don't venerate the earth, we worship a cult of youth and pretend that death doesn't happen when it's the only certainty we've got, we destroy the old places that might have saved us – actually, if you listen to some of my mother's wilder friends, we go out of our way to build motorway service stations on the nodes of the ley lines specifically in order to obliterate them. Ki'kaame will tell you that we are the fallen, while his people are still in Eden. If Lapland wasn't so bloody cold, I'd agree with him.'

'You'd rather live in a reindeer skin tent than in your mother's farmhouse?'

'I'd rather live amongst people who didn't think mass graves were an unfortunate but necessary side effect of equally necessary violence. Or even that killing my mother is a sad but essential step on the road to sainthood.'

His voice was different; the edge of grief was not new, but underscored with a loathing Stella had not heard from him before. Slowly, she said, 'Davy, do you know who's hunting us?'

It was growing lighter, not yet dawn but with a greyness that lit his eyes and smoothed the strange angles of his face until he looked very like his mother. His eyes met hers now, unwavering. He said, 'I might be wrong.'

She felt sick. The stone was fully awake now, sharpening her senses beyond bearing. Her skin was raw. She could hear too much of the night. 'Who, Davy?'

He shrugged. 'Is it important to find a name? Every mass grave I've ever exhumed has been dug by someone who's crossed the line to a place where the ends justify the means; where one person's life, or ten, or a thousand, is a fair price for what they believe is right. Look at the people who rule over us if you want to understand what happens to men who listen to the whispering evil. Whatever they've sold their souls to doesn't have the best interests of humanity at heart, but by God, they're convinced they're in the right.'

Stella said, 'I read your mother's translation of the ledgers. If she's got it right, Nostradamus said the same to Cedric Owen when they met in Paris: that there's a force that feeds on death and destruction, fear and pain, and needs these things to continue into the nadir of Armageddon.' She closed her eyes, remembering. '*It bends men to its will; intelligent, thoughtful men who believe that they can take the power they are offered and wield it only for good. But the nature of power is otherwise; it breaks them, always, and its greatest desire is that the thirteen stones might never again conjoin to deliver our world from misery.*'

'You learned it by heart?' Stella could not see his face well enough to read the irony, or lack of it.

'It made an impression,' she said. 'But it doesn't bring us any closer to who's doing it.'

'Oh, come *on*.' He turned his head. His gaze scoured her face. 'Who knew where you were going to look for the skull? Who knew you were coming to see me? Who knows my mother so well he won't even countenance the possibility that he's spent his *entire life* working to keep the blue heart-stone hidden?' He sat up on one elbow, close enough now for her to smell the cigarettes on his breath. 'Who's the big fish in a tiny pond who has never really pushed himself into the limelight? Who served with the King's Troop in Northern Ireland and has advised on the carnage in Iraq and knows how to make the kind of chlorine bombs that destroyed my mother's farm and put her in hospital? Who—'

'*Who is walking down the Ridgeway, now, towards us?*' Stella said. She did not need the stone's piercing warning to tell her that the hunter had found her; the mound itself was screaming in silent agony. With a sudden lucidity, she saw past, present and future come together. 'Davy, would you take a risk for Cedric Owen's heart-stone?'

'I would give my life for it,' he said, and she believed him.

'Then take it into the mouth of the mound and wait until the tunnel opens. I'll stay outside and keep them occupied. Dawn can't be more than half an hour away. You know what needs to be done as well as I do.'

'No.' He was smiling in a way that froze her blood. For a heart-stopping moment, she thought she had made the ultimate mistake, and that he was the hunter. She raised the backpack, her only weapon.

'Stella, don't.' He held up a hand. 'I said I would die for it. I meant it. You have to place the stone, only you. It has your face and you are the one it speaks to. Ki'kaame told me eight, maybe nine times, *Only the keeper can place the stone in the heart of the earth at the end of time*. You go into the mound. I'll do whatever it takes to keep him away. Go on. There isn't time to argue.'

'But I'm the one they're looking for. They'll go straight through you and I'll be trapped. It's half an hour till dawn.'

'They?'

'There are two of them, and they have a gun. If you won't take the skull, go to the woods at the back of the mound and stay there. I'll tell them you've already left. Go! You're the only wild card we've got.'

'OK.' In one more astonishing moment in an astonishing night, Davy Law hugged her, and was gone, running more quietly than she had expected of him. She walked forward, along the circle of beech trees to the narrow green avenue that passed through the barley and the figure that limped slowly along it.

'Kit!' She reached for him, smiling.

'Hey.' He leaned on her shoulder and ruffled her hair. She could see the two parts of him as clearly as if he were two people. 'Where's Davy?'

The lie was the easiest she had ever told. 'He's gone back to the hospital. He's worried about Ursula and I didn't need him once I knew where to go. The mound's here, in the clearing. It's amazing. Come and see.' She turned, tugging him by the wrist. He came slowly, using both sticks. The heart-stone had not ceased its warning. 'You're not walking well. Did you hurt yourself coming up the hill?'

'No. I'd never have made it like this. I got a lift.' He stopped and leaned against the first of the upright stones to catch his breath. 'Tony brought me. I know what you think, but you have to trust him. He's come to help. He's just parking the car. He'll be here any moment.'

She said, 'He's here now.'

A thin torch beam bobbed up the grassy track. The figure behind it emerged slowly from the pre-dawn mist that hugged the field, distorted and shrunken and not at all like Sir Anthony Bookless. With the blue heart-stone tensely silent, she stepped forward. 'Tony?'

'Not Tony,' said Gordon Fraser grimly. He stopped at the edge of the clearing, a small, stumpy dwarf of a man; her friend, the best caver in Britain. He was unshaven and tired. His red hair made an unruly hedge about his head.

Stella lifted the blue heart-stone in greeting. He stood suddenly still. In his eyes was the same terror that had been there in his lab when the stone was first cleaned of its limestone coat.

Stella had forgotten that. Smiling, she said, 'It's all right. It's a friend. It'll help us.'

'Aye?' The small man shook his head sourly. Crab-wise, he shuffled towards her and found a seat on a stone. 'Like Tony Bookless is a friend and he'll help us and all. He's a yard or two behind. It's going to be one big grand reunion when the sun comes up, and then won't the fireworks be spectacular?'

31

*Skirwith village, near Ingleborough Fell,
Yorkshire, April 1589*

E ASTER WAS PAST, AND THE PRIVATIONS OF LENT;
the lambs were white in the fields and the
primroses grew yellow at the field edges.

A late frost rimed the scar of turned earth;
where the sun fell was dew. Cedric Owen, now
named Francis Walker, trader and would-be
farmer, bent and laid a wreath of catkins on the
grave of his wife's father. The cracked bell of
Skirwith's church echoed a single note across
the Yorkshire moor.

At his side, Martha Huntley, now Martha
Walker, four months pregnant and just
beginning to show it, bent also, and laid a lace
of freshly picked daisies on the raw earth,
which was what the old man had asked of her
when he knew his final hours had come.

They stood together a while, listening to the
start of the day, a man and the wife with whom

he had not lain, and had no intention ever so to do. At length, Martha said, 'He is dead a week. We gave our word that the heart-stone would be delivered to its place of safe keeping within a ten-day of his death. There is nothing to be gained by waiting.'

'Except that Fernandez might come.'

'He will not.' She said it sharply, a poor disguise for the grief that still caused her nightly to weep in her sleep. 'We should not wait for it.'

'But still, the route to the cave's mouth leads past the hawthorn. We can look on the way.'

He held their one chestnut gelding for her to mount. Of the three good horses they had brought north with them, one had died of colic soon after they arrived, and the bay mare, gift of Barnabas Tythe, had surprised them all by giving birth to a weedy, undernourished colt foal on the last day of the spring's snow fall, a week to the day before Edward Wainwright's death.

Martha settled her skirts and clucked for the horse to move on. Cedric walked at its shoulder in easy silence. They had not chosen each other, but their shared grief over the loss of Fernandez, and Owen's obvious care for Edward Wainwright in his dying days, had brought them together much as a man might be with his sister, or she with her brother, so that each knew what the other thought without need to ask.

Their route took them out of the tiny church-yard with its squat church, past the grey hard-stone manor house, past the huddle of farmworkers' cottages, of rough cobble and thatch, past the well and the small single-roomed inn that marked the ending of the village and out to the grey-green moorland, where only sheep could thrive.

Owen was still coming to grips with the land-scape around him. By force of habit, he marked in his mind the places where willow grew along the beck, and the new holes that marked an active coney warren. A trio of young, fat rabbits skittered away from their approach. He noted them for later, and allowed himself to feel the small skip of joy at the thought of a hunt. He had not lain in wait for a coney since his child-hood and had not realized how much he missed it until the chance was there again before him.

From above his shoulder, Martha said, 'We could begin to sell the diamonds slowly now, I think, saying they were my legacy from my father. That would not arouse comment.'

'As long as it does not arouse Walsingham's interest, we will be safe. I would not relish having to flee again as we did that night.'

'No.' Martha shuddered and pulled her shoulder cloak more tightly about her. 'With only one horse, that would go hard on us.'

The journey had killed her father. Edward Wainwright had never truly recovered from the cold and misery of ten days spent on the roads in the January snows. Neither of them said it; they had never indulged in recriminations, but it was there between them as yet another thing to keep them separate.

Whatever happened to Fernandez, Owen did not rate highly the chances that this marriage might ever become anything but a convenience for either of those enmeshed in it. He kept his thoughts for the growing child, whom he must rear as his own, in the hope that one day he would be able safely to tell it the history of its true father.

Steepening, the path rose up Ingleborough Fell. They picked up a new river and followed its bank to the sharp turn and the ford Owen had remembered from his childhood. The hawthorn tree that was their marker grew gnarled and bent and there was neither linen nor a square of white wool tied to it, to show any hint of the fate of Fernandez de Aguilar.

Owen watched the shadow of hope pass from Martha's face, saw her set her jaw and shrug on the weight of another day's disappointment. He feared that the weight one day would crack her, and mourned in his own right that he was powerless to make it different.

He smiled for her, thinly, and wondered if she saw the same in him; he thought it likely.

She turned the horse away from the thorn

bush. 'We should go to the cave,' she said. 'I brought candles and a skein of wool and a pitch torch. Do you need aught else?'

'Only courage,' Owen said. 'I was never enamoured of the dark.'

He spoke to her retreating back; she was urging the horse to a fast walk, so that he had to run to catch up. She slowed for him, out of pity, and they walked along together in the growing clamour of the morning.

Presently, over the high trilling of the larks, she said, 'When today is over, we need never return here again. We could go west towards the coast. Since Spain, I have had a liking for the sea air.'

'Due west of here is Ulverston. We could do far worse than buy some land there and farm it. The sea air makes it harsh, but it is beautiful in the early morning.'

They were talking for the sound of their own voices and soon stopped. The mare was sure-footed and Owen let her pick her own way up the hill. A buzzard made wide lazy sweeps over-head. Half a mile to their right, a handful of crows erupted from behind a gorse thicket and sprang upwards, flung rags, tumbling high into the air.

'A dead lamb,' Owen said, not thinking. 'Or a ewe—' He stopped.

'Died at birthing,' Martha finished for him. 'I had thought of that. But is it not strange that the carrion birds have left their feast when we are so far away?'

'It would seem we are not alone on this hill-side, even now, when the morning is so newly broken.' Owen slowed the horse to a stop. The blue heart-stone lay warm and heavy against his side. He heard from it the faintest warning, not a certain thing, but a caution to be wary.

He said, 'It might be a shepherd, but we should take no chances. You should go back. If we are betrayed, it will do no good for both of us to be caught in the open.'

'If we are betrayed, I would rather be caught in the open than die in my bed at night. Or in the Tower, at Walsingham's pleasure.' Martha shuddered, and he thought she might be sick again, as she had been on first waking. 'Promise me that if we are assaulted and you think we may die, you will give me a swift end before it is too late?' She sensed his hesitation. 'Fernandez would have done such a thing for me; he said so on the night we . . .'

She was an honourable woman; Owen had never known her to lie. Against his every instinct, he said, 'I give you my word that if we are assaulted, I will do whatever I may to see you on the road to freedom. If that is impossible, I will not let you be taken to London. In return, will you wait here and let me go ahead?'

She set her jaw obstinately. 'You carry the heart-stone. Yours is the greater risk.'

'And it has never yet let me walk into danger. Please – you carry Fernandez' child, which must be protected. The horse cannot come much further anyway. We must go on foot beyond here.'

'Then we go together. Fernandez left you in my care as much as me in yours.'

He had tried to argue with her once or twice before in their four months together and had found her almost uniquely intransigent. He gave way with what grace he could muster and helped her down from the gelding, setting hobbles about its forelegs that it might not wander too far should they need it.

'Let us go then. The opening to the cave is upwards and to our right. If you see a flare of yellow gorse with sharp grey rock behind it, it is to the right of that. Climb with your head low. We cannot avoid being seen, but perhaps they can be confused as to how many of us there are.'

The heart-stone did not want to go into the cave, that much was obvious. Owen felt from it the same fierce, wordless grief he had sensed from women dying in childbed; knowing that something worthwhile must come of their ending, but grieving that they cannot live to see it.

It was disconcertingly different from the two most recent deaths he had attended in friendship. Edward Wainwright and Najakmul had both reached the end of a good life fully lived and had stepped up to meet death's embrace with something close to enthusiasm.

Both, with their dying breaths, had urged on him the absolute necessity to bring the blue heart-stone home to this place and leave it there. Both had warned him that it would not want to come.

Only now, as he stepped into the cave's mouth, did he realize the strength of its resistance. He had pushed up the last half-mile of hillside against a force as strong as gravity that held him back, listening all the while to the keening in his mind that was either a warning of mortal danger or a desperate grief and he could not tell which.

'We'll wait here a while,' he said. 'If someone is following, we shall see them before they see us.'

The opening was a slantwise crack in the wall of rock ahead of them, half hidden by a stand of thorns. Owen caught Martha's elbow and drew her in and sideways, to a dry, flat place where they could see out while being hidden from without by the trees. They stood in the half-darkness, breathing heavily from the climb.

At their back, solid, chalky rock reached up to a high-pitched ceiling. To their left, the sun moved on to the moor, drawing brighter shades from the heather and bracken. To their right, a tunnel sloped into darkness, wide enough at its start for them both to pass together, although in Owen's memory it narrowed a good deal towards its end.

He waited, letting his eyes adjust to the grey light. Old swallows' nests tucked into the nook of the roof's peak came slowly into focus. A wren flitted in and out again swiftly, a splash of colour in the gloom. Presently, when nobody came and there was no further excuse for delay, Owen did what he had done as a youth exploring these caves; he brought to mind his grandmother, and her care of the blue heart-stone.

There was a particular memory from his early teens when she had begun to show him the ways of the stone. On a mellow evening in autumn, with piles of russet leaves burning in the orchards and gooseberries cooking for an evening tart, she had taken him to the quiet room to the north of their house and shown him what might be done with candles to make the light come from the skull's eyes.

He had practised under her tuition until he got it right, feeling the growing bond to the stone as he might feel it with a newly leashed hound, or – better – a hawk that came willing to the fist. Slowly, concentration gave way to elation until his world sparked brightly alive.

At the end, he had almost turned the soft beams of blue on to his grandmother, but she had put up her hand to stop him, saying that she liked her hair white and did not want it to go dark again. He had taken it as a joke and had lowered the skull and lifted instead the candles, one in either hand, and framed her face in their light. She had been beautiful then, and at peace.

Later that evening, she had described to him the caves she knew of, and the way to find the cathedral of the earth. She had not asked him to go, only mentioned where it was, believing that, however great his fear of small, cramped places, he would have to see it.

His fear was greater than she had known. He had not gone that autumn, but waited until spring, which was too late to tell her of the beauty he had found for she was dead by then.

As his gift to her, he had gone into the labyrinth of tunnels, carrying as his bastion against the dark the memory of that one moment when the light of two candles had lit her face to wise gold.

Robbed of the heart-stone's solace, he did the same again now, although it was hard to know if the face that lit his mind was hers or Najakmul's; these two had begun to blur in his memory. Whichever it was, either or both, he used her to anchor his courage much as he anchored the loose end of the woollen thread, that he might find his way out to daylight again safely.

Martha was at his side, watching him knot

the wool and fix the end in a crack where it would not pull out. As with all gravid women, her hand lay over the small swell of her belly.

Owen said, 'If you wish to remain here, I will come back to you as fast as the tunnel permits.'

'I would gladly accept, but I promised my father I would see the place where the heart-stone lay,' she said grimly. 'We who walk the trackways have our own fates to fulfil.'

She had his grandmother's courage. As they turned towards the dark, he saw the last colour leak from her cheeks and the fine lines about her eyes grow sharper.

He gave her a chaste hug, swiftly gone. 'It's worth seeing, when we get there,' he said, 'and the first part is easy. Just imagine you are walking the corridor in your house at night with no candles.'

The route in was not as bad as his childhood memories had told him, but it was not something he wished ever to repeat again.

At length, they stood side by side on flat ground, with the roof too high above their heads to feel, and no walls pressing in on either side. The sound of a waterfall surrounded them, so that it seemed as if they must stand within it.

'Here, we can light the candle, and the lantern,' Owen said, and then, with a child's love of mystery, 'Would you close your eyes?'

He carried flint and tinder, and a spill of woven grass. Even for one who had seen it before, the wonder of the place struck the heart, so that he had to remind himself to light the lantern and hold it up and say, with unexpected shyness, 'If it please you, would you look now?'

'Oh, Cedric . . .'

It was worth the dark and the cold and the fear. Almost, it was worth there being only two of them there, not the three it should have been, for the moment when his wife, Martha Walker, turned to him with her soul in her eyes and could not find the words to say what she felt.

He moved close and hugged her again, one-armed, as Fernandez had done. 'There is no need to speak. Only look and remember, so that the generations after may know that the cathedral of the earth is worth the route they must take to find it.' He gave her the lantern, and took forward only the candle. 'If you will stay here, I will place the heart-stone in its resting place.'

'I should come—'

'No.' A swift pain grabbed at his heart. 'I must do this alone.'

He lit four more candles and set them on ledges about the arched entrance, that she might sit in ample light, then left her and retraced the steps he had taken once before, east for twenty paces, and then across the river on stones that rolled unsteadily underfoot. Turning west again, he followed the line of the river's edge to the astonishing, soul-lifting beauty of the waterfall.

Caught in the sooty light of the lantern, it cascaded as living gold into the wide stone crucible at its foot, where the white rock caught it and made it quicksilver.

His grandmother had described the place as the well of the living water and he could think of no better words.

Balancing the lantern on his knee, Owen sat on the edge, ignoring the wet, and drew the heart-stone at last from the leather satchel in which it had travelled half a world and back again.

It rested quietly between his hands, silent now that the end had come. He felt its mourning as a heaviness about his heart, that dragged him down and down until he sank to kneeling on the cold chalk of the cavern's floor.

All elation drained from him, all sense of beauty, all joy in his own success. In the heart of the cavern, his world emptied of light and colour, scent and touch, song and love. In this new deadness, he understood for the first time how his life must be with the heart-stone gone. He could not bear it.

'Why must it be so?'

He cried aloud and the sound sank into the well of white water and was gone. He did not speak again, only sat in the dark space of his soul and looked back at his life with a bitter wonder that he had not thought to ask the question until it sprang now to his lips.

In his childhood, his grandmother had told him of the stone's resting place, and he had accepted it without question, as he had done everything else from her. In the springtime of his life, Nostradamus had spoken this destiny and Owen had wondered only that another man could know it. Najakmul had said it again, more clearly, had trained him for it through thirty years in paradise and he had thanked her daily for it and had come to England driven only by the need to reach this place and leave his record for the ones who must come after.

Most bleakly, Fernandez de Aguilar, a man with everything to live for, had given his life that the skull might be brought here to its place of safe keeping, that future generations might find it when the world had greatest need.

Cedric Owen did not care about the world's need. He wept for his own pain, and for Fernandez, and for Martha, and for the stone.

You would undo all that we have done?

The voice was one he knew most intimately, else he would not have looked up. Najakmul was there, standing in the power of the waterfall. She reached a hand for him. *If I tell you that the stone will be here, where I am, would that ease for you the pain of parting? You will not be long without it.*

A spray of water reached him, lighter than

rain. Najakmul said, *Have you asked the stone what it wants of you?*

He had not. He had thought its will was his, its heart was his. A quiet blue reached him, from the still place of his soul. It grieved. It did not challenge its destiny, or his. And it attested Najakmul's truth.

Through the cascading water, she spoke again. *Give it to the living water, son of my heart. Your life's work is near to done.*

Son of my heart. So she had called him in her last days alive. It was that that gave him the courage to rise, to lift the heart-stone so that it might hold for one last moment the light of the candles and the cascading silver of the waterfall.

The well of white water boiled beneath, and opened, as a heart opens, to show the still black of its core.

'*Cedric!*'

Bright searing yellow sliced across his mind, with Martha's voice twined through it, from the far side of the chamber. Across the river, in the flaming light of four candles, he saw her struggling with one, maybe two, assailants.

His need balanced on a knife edge, his two duties opposed. With a courage unmatched, Cedric Owen launched the stone that carried his soul into the bowl beneath the cataract. White water rose around it as a crown. The flash of its last blue lay stitched across his vision for an age after it was gone.

* * *

He was already running, lantern in one hand, eating knife – uselessly – in the other, back across the river to where Martha Walker battled with the men who would take her life and that of her unborn child.

32

Weyland's Smithy, Oxfordshire, 5:00 a.m.
21 June 2007

DAWN CAME SLOWLY TO THE OXFORDSHIRE countryside. The stones about the grave mound were the first thing to show colour; splashes of grey lichen became, as Stella watched them, more subtly green. In the valley, the cock gained confidence. Overhead, a crow barked from the highest beech. Lately, a wren had begun to reply.

Branches cracked near the road. Tony Bookless was a formless shape, striding up the avenue of trees towards Weyland's Smithy, sending his voice ahead as a beacon in the poor light.

'Stella, you're there!' He fairly ran the last few yards, crashing in through the trees to come, breathless, to the open space before the mound. 'And Kit. And Gordon. And the skull-stone. That's good.' He named them off like a roll call, but his eyes never left Stella and the blue stone that lit the air around her. His right hand was jammed awkwardly in his pocket. She could count the flat ridges of his knuckles. 'Where's Davy?'

Somewhere to her right, a moving branch became suddenly still. 'He went back into Oxford,' Stella said. 'I didn't need him here once he'd shown me the mound and he's worried about his mother.' She could lie to him now with a clear conscience. It gave weight to the words.

'Of course.' He nodded, solemnly, the Master dealing with unfortunate news. 'Kit told me there had been an accident.'

An accident? Stella stared at Kit. His eyes flashed a frantic, silent warning. *Trust me. Danger! Please, trust me?*

Flatly, she said, 'An accident, yes.'

She no longer knew whom to trust. Gordon was nearest, almost within reach. His fear of the stone was a palpable thing but even so, he had stood up when Tony Bookless arrived and taken one more protective step towards her.

Kit was not angry; he was miserable and caught up in something beyond his control. He was out of reach, stuck in the open away from the mound, swaying on his feet.

Whatever his silent pleas, he and Tony Bookless had a common understanding. They were both moving now, edging round, slowly, absently, with no obvious place to go, except that Bookless came closer each time to Stella and the skull-stone and Kit further away.

The stone gave no help. Here, so close to the end, it offered nothing but a desperate need to enter the tunnel of Weyland's Smithy. The grave mound ached equally for her, as a lover might ache on the wrong side of a prison wall, seeing, but unable to embrace.

The spiralling marks on the entrance stone were more solid now; were she close enough, Stella could have traced her fingers along their grooves. Their magic seemed less, but the draw was as strong. As lodestone to lodestone, she knew exactly where to go and what to do and when to do it; without ever looking at her watch, she could count the falling minutes: six, perhaps five, until dawn.

Tony Bookless was less than ten paces away. She could not tell if the hand that remained in his pocket held a gun, but she could see his face clearly in the growing light. His flat, hard eyes held hers, grey as the pale sky. There was no friendship there, only warnings of violence.

Davy's voice rolled through her head. *Whatever they've sold their souls to doesn't have the best interests of humanity at heart, but by God, they're convinced they're right.* And long before, when she knew him less well, *Your skull carries the heart of the world. What man would not kill to own that?*

Stella made herself stare back, and not into the beeches to her left wherein branch rasped upon branch in the dawn wind. Under it, she could believe Davy Law was crawling.

Stella lifted the skull level with her own head. Grey light became blue around it. Gordon made a small, hurt noise in his throat. Abruptly, Tony Bookless stopped moving. As if merely curious, Stella said, 'Tony, what are you doing?'

'Trying to keep you alive.' He gave a smile she knew well. It did not soften his eyes. 'I told you before, the skull-keeper always dies. For all of my life I've believed Ursula was going to be the keeper and I could protect her. Clearly I was wrong, so I'm here to see what I can do to rectify matters.'

He took another idle step towards her, waving a hand towards the grave mound. 'I know you think the fate of the world hangs on its going in there, but I remain of the belief that no stone is worth dying for. I promised Kit I'd keep you alive. I am doing my best to achieve that.'

He was so plausible. The fragile safety of the morning hung on the fiction that she believed him. Too late, Stella took breath to answer, to keep the fiction going. To her right, Gordon Fraser had already lost the last threads of control.

'You did your best to murder Ursula Walker, you hypocritical bastard. Don't pretend you're here to help.'

'I'm sorry?' There was ice in Bookless's voice, of a weight to crush the heat of Gordon's rage. He was so tall, so cool, so composed. Beside him the small Scotsman was a burr of unkempt fury, catastrophically lacking in self-control.

Tony Bookless ignored him. With perfect diction, he said, 'Stella, what *exactly* happened to Ursula?'

'Don't pretend you don't know, Anthony sir fucking Bookless. I worked you out days ago. You're a cold-blooded killer, hiding behind your sham charm. You—'

'Gordon, stop.'

Once started, the small Scotsman was all but unstoppable. He spat on the ground. Propelled by his own rage, he took the final bound towards Stella, making of himself a wall between her and Tony Bookless. He was her friend, her mentor, the man who had courage in the dark places. In the silence of her heart, she thanked him even as she reached out to catch his arm and hold him silent.

She said, 'It's kind, but I don't need you to fight my battles for me. I'll do this for myself.'

She directed her coolest smile at Tony Bookless. 'Ursula's on a ventilator in the Radcliffe ICU suffering from smoke inhalation. She stayed in the farmhouse too long after Kit and I got out. The fire caught her in the kitchen. There was chlorine in the smoke. The police *will* be investigating this one as attempted murder.'

503

'*Chlorine?!*'

Bookless was an exceptional actor. Stella saw the blacks of his eyes flare out to the rims, squeezing away the colour. More slowly, she saw the colour leach from his face. He raised his head to look past her. 'Kit, why did you not tell me this in the car?'

They had all his attention. If ever there was a time to act, it was that moment. Stella gave a silent call, and was answered the same by the shifting leaf patterns in the woods behind. The murmur of birdsong broke off suddenly.

'Stella, go to Kit, *now.*'

Tony Bookless snapped in a way she had never heard from him. Gone was the urbane, cultured humour. Left behind was the man who had served in Northern Ireland and advised in Iraq, the man who gave orders and was heard and obeyed. There was a relief in the honesty of that.

The time for pretending was past. Stella did not move. 'Why?' she asked. 'So you can kill us both as you tried to kill Ursula?'

'Quite the reverse, so that I can do my utmost to keep you safe while— *Davy Law, don't do it! You've got the wrong man!*'

He took his hand from his pocket. He did not hold a gun, but a bunch of keys. He threw them, hard, straight at Stella, who ducked sideways with a speed she did not know she had, and rolled, holding the stone.

Tony Bookless filled her spinning world, and

Gordon, closing in on him, and at last Davy Law, running low and hard from the encircling trees from quite another place than she – or anyone else – had expected.

The morning was lost in a brutal collision of flesh and the crack of a shattered bone – and after it, a gunshot. Someone grabbed for the skull-stone. Stella clutched it, kicking, and was pulled clear by her elbow.

Davy Law stood over her, in a breath of nicotine and wrath. One arm hung useless at his side. With the other, he shoved the small of her back.

'It's dawn. The mound's waiting. *Go!*'

In broadest Aberdonian, Gordon Fraser shouted, 'Stay where you are!'

'*No, Stell, go for it!*'

She trusted Gordon with her life, but she would not have stopped for him, whatever he had shouted. It was the unrooted terror in Kit's voice, even as he urged her forward, that cut through the pull of the stone. She tripped to a halt, with the mound's mouth an arm's length away, and turned.

Kit was standing rigid. A gun held at his temple kept him still; it kept everybody still. Gordon Fraser, her friend in this world of the friendless, was the person holding it.

'Step back from the tunnel,' he said, when he saw her looking. 'Put down the stone, and nobody else gets hurt.'

'Gordon?' Stella stared at him, not believing. His red hair was everywhere. His face was a pale and sallow green. His eyes fed on the skull and it was not fear that fired them, but a depth of yearning she had never seen before, in him or any man.

Floundering, she said, 'Is this a joke?'

A grunt from the ground made her look down. Tony Bookless lay there, holding his arm across his body. Blood spread in a narrow band, staining the dawn turf. His eyes burned. He shrugged something that might have been an apology. 'First rule of warfare,' he said, drily. 'Always do what the man with the gun tells you.'

'Right.' Gordon gestured with his free arm. 'So put it down and step away.'

She could not; the stone would not have let her even if her mind had encompassed the need. Numbly, she said, 'I thought you were here to help.'

'Some things are beyond helping.' He sneered, unprettily. 'You won't save the world like this, whatever Davy Law's told you. The time for that's long past. It's every man for himself now, just like it's always been.'

Stella said, 'What do you want?'

'The stone, what else?'

She gaped. 'But you're scared of it. You could hardly go near it the day you washed the chalk off. You wanted me to crush it under the pile driver.'

'There was no danger you'd do it, though, was there? And you'd not think of me wanting to take it if I'd told you to grind it to dust.'

'Come off it, Gordon, that wasn't a bluff; you were terrified of it.'

He flushed a sore, angry red. 'We just need time to get to know each other, it and me.' His hand was steady if his voice was not. 'It'll be different when this dawn's past and it's lost its hope. It'll not be so savage, then. You just keep clear of that doorway until the sun's well up and we'll all be happy.'

Dawn was already upon them. The birds had fallen silent at the gunshot, but the sun was a razor line of light melting the horizon.

Flatly, Davy Law said, 'What makes you think the stone will be anything but a piece of flashy sapphire when the dawn's past? If you stop it from going into the mound now, you'll break its soul, then what will you have?'

Gordon's grin was fast and full of loathing. 'I'll have the biggest gemstone in the western world at no risk to myself. But I don't think it'll be like that; it's not going to let go of its power that easily. And don't even try to say you wouldn't do this in my place, David Law. You've done your taking of beautiful things and you know the power of this one. You'd do the same if you had the guts.'

'I would never have pushed someone off a cliff for it.' Even as he spoke, Davy was moving, sliding his nearest foot slowly towards Stella.

Gordon laughed. He sounded perfectly sane. 'I've been looking for Cedric Owen's blue heart-stone since I came up to the college thirty years ago. I've looked in every cave in England and a few beyond. I've risked my life more times than you've had women; a lot more times. Kit O'Connor had barely been in a real cave in his life. What right had he to find the stone for half a day's looking? The Rescue are a bunch of wet pansies. They'd never have found the thing if it had gone over the edge with him. I'd have got it later, no problem at all, and there's not a caver in Europe could have done that alone but me. I'll have it now and there'll be justice done for once.'

As if to commend him, the band of sun to the east broke through a thin strap of cloud. Gordon looked at it and back. He gave a short nod and squared his shoulders, as Stella had seen him do in countless caves before the big descents.

With military sharpness, he said, 'David, if you move another muscle, Kit dies and you after him. If you don't believe me, you only have to try. Stella, put the stone down by the count of three or he's a dead man anyway. *One.*'

'Don't do it, Stell.' Kit had more colour, suddenly. Heedless of the gun, he turned his head. 'He can't kill both of us in time to stop you.'

'You're welcome to try me. *Two*.'

'Stella, you have a choice: me or the stone. We've been coming to this all along. You *know* which matters more.'

Suddenly, unexpectedly, she did.

'*Thr*—'

Against the scything panic in her head, she bent and set Cedric Owen's blue skull-stone on the earth before the mound. The noise did not become less as she straightened, but was lost in the sudden cacophony of small birds that rose to announce the moment of dawn.

The lust in Gordon Fraser's eyes was a hard thing to contemplate. The cry of the stone broke open her mind. She set her heart against it.

'Have it then.' She stepped back. 'It won't give you what you think— Kit! *No!*'

He was unsteady and half-maimed and he made the choice she had just turned down. She saw him wrench to his left, heard the gunshot, louder than thunder, saw blood, and did not know if it was his or Gordon's before they fell together to the ground.

From the hard earth, Kit shouted, 'Stella, run!

He was alive; it was all she needed. She was already snatching up the stone, running like a hare from its form, over the sworl-scripted stone that blocked the entrance to the mound, down the short tunnel into the embracing darkness. As Davy Law had said, the solid rock did, indeed, open to let her through.

She heard the gun fire again, and the crack of an impact, and a man's scream, but she was in the dark by then with the dawn blazing behind and the stone and the mound sang to her, equally, so that it was impossible not to go on, and on and in to meet the light waiting at the tunnel's end.

33

*Ingleborough Fell, Yorkshire Dales,
April 1589*

OWEN HAD NOT KNOWN MARTHA CARRIED A knife, but in the time it took him to cross the water, he saw her use it once to good effect.

That her attackers were Walsingham's men was not in doubt; all that remained to be learned was how many of them were there and whether they had seen the blue stone fall into the pool.

Before that, he had a promise to keep: that Martha Walker would not be captured and taken alive to London to face the agonies of the Tower at Walsingham's pleasure.

It was this promise that spurred him to leap the river, a feat he would have believed impossible. He met the ground running and flung himself forward, screaming the same high note as the blue stone, so that the sound seemed to lance out of his head and shatter from the walls.

511

Even so, he thought he was too late. There were at least two of them fighting Martha, and only one wounded by her knife. He had hold of her hair with his one good arm and was pulling her head back and round, towards the tunnel. The other seemed intent on grabbing her feet, but that her kicking was stopping him. By the half-light of the candles, Owen saw him abandon that endeavour and reach to his hip for his sword.

'Martha!'

The sound of her name, or the closeness of the shout, caused her to cease her struggling and temporarily spared her life. The sword-bearer spun snarling to face the new danger. At the sight of Owen and his three-inch knife, he barked a laugh.

'They said you were no swordsman. I had not hoped to find they spoke so true.'

The man was black-haired and bearded and spoke with a Devonshire accent. He held a blade easily the equal of the one owned for so many years by Fernandez de Aguilar; that much Owen could tell as he skidded to a halt on the wet limestone floor of the cave.

'Drop your knife, *doctor*.' Blackbeard used it as an insult. 'Be sensible and we'll let you live.'

'In the Tower? I would rather be dead.'

The man grinned, showing white teeth in the fuzz of his beard. He had the same build, the same easy way with a weapon as had

512

Maplethorpe's mastiffs. He said, 'Join your friend, then, the one-armed Spaniard. Though he died slowly enough. We only need one of you and we'll have the wife if we can't have the husband.'

At the mention of Fernandez, the fight went out of Martha. Owen heard it, even although he could not see it. Before Blackbeard could turn, he dropped his knife. The clatter was lost in the rush of the waterfall. He held out both hands, palms up. 'Let her go and I'll come with you.'

The man advanced, raising his black brows high. 'Or we'll take you both, now that you've so kindly offered, and then you can both tell us what we need to know and we'll compare your answers.'

The knife was useless anyway. Owen kicked it sideways. It skittered across the floor and splashed into the river, taking Blackbeard's attention with it for the moment Owen needed to scoop and pick up a stone the size of his hand from the cave's floor.

He was no swordsman, but he had spent thirty years in New Spain playing 'catch-and-throw' with generations of children. In England, it would have been a pretty game, to keep them amused. In Zama, it was the beginnings of the hunt and Owen had found a flair for it.

The piece he held now was light, if satisfyingly jagged. He balanced its weight in his palm. Behind Blackbeard was a flurry of action. He thought Martha was fighting again, but could not see to be sure.

'What of Fernandez?' Owen asked. 'Did he tell you to come here?'

Blackbeard sneered. 'He told us everything we asked of him.'

Owen wanted to disbelieve him, but Barnabas Tythe had told them of Walsingham and he could believe any man would reveal his soul if asked aright.

'When did he die?' he asked. His heart was a hollow void. He dared not look at Martha.

Blackbeard made a show of counting back on his fingers. 'February,' he said, 'near the end of the month.' He was wary of the stone, and began to circle, pushing Owen away from the candle's light to the darker, less even places in the back of the cavern. His sword moved always ahead of him, a streak of dull light that marked him even as they stepped further away from the tunnel's mouth.

Owen stepped sideways, and ducked under an outcrop of rock. He felt pressure on his right sleeve and knew that the wall was there. He slid left and found that way, too, blocked.

'Come out, doctor. Why make me hamstring you when you could ride to London in comfort?'

There were loose pebbles underfoot. Owen stooped and dragged up a handful and threw them into the man's eyes. The point of the sword lowered enough. He flung his rock, as well as he had ever done.

Not well enough.

It was a difficult throw; Blackbeard was twisting away, thinking more pebbles were coming, and the candles played tricks with their light, shoving it sideways and then pulling it back. Thus did Owen hit the shape of where Blackbeard had been, and not the man himself. The stone sank into his shoulder, biting deep into flesh and sinew and bone, but it did not hit his head and make a kill.

Some men retreat when injured, others rouse themselves to fury. Blackbeard was of the latter mould. He raised his sword before him like a lance and ran at Owen, roaring fit to drown the river.

Slow as a dream, Cedric Owen saw his death approach. Somewhere far away, at the tunnel's mouth, he heard Martha scream his name and then a man's shout and then Blackbeard was on him and he heard the iron pierce his shirt, his skin, his flesh, his lungs, and felt the wet gush of blood long before he felt the fierce, hot pain.

Owen's body crashed against the limestone wall. His left elbow shattered; in his new place of distant objectivity, he could count the pieces and knew it would never mend. His knees buckled and he felt his back slide down the wall, and was surprised to see Blackbeard topple also, but in the other direction.

And then he knew he was truly dying, for Fernandez de Aguilar was standing in front of him, with Robert Maplethorpe's dark-wet sword in his hand and anguish on his face.

A memory came, sharply. With grim humour, Owen said, 'Do not grieve for me, my friend. Death is not so bad a thing when it has been preceded by joy.' He tried to lift his hand and failed. 'Your presence gives me great joy. I had not thought that death would be so forgiving as to bring us both together.'

'Cedric . . .' De Aguilar was weeping openly, a thing Owen had never seen from him in life. He lifted Owen's hand and the touch of his skin was surprisingly warm for a dead man. He said, 'I was as fast as I could. I have been following Jack Dempsey and his brother for four months, and they following me – we played cat and mouse across the length and breadth of England. I could not leave the linen square because it would have led them to you. I lost them just before they entered the cave. I heard the blue stone cry out once, loudly. Only that brought me to you. I am so, so sorry.'

The world was beginning to sway. Straight lines became curves and the air dense as water. Owen frowned. The meaning of the words strayed into his mind and out again. He grasped at them, as at passing fish. One of them stayed. 'Fernandez? You're . . . alive?'

'Alive and unhurt, against all my vows to protect you.'

'I had to see if . . . I could . . . fight just once.' He managed to grin but stopped at what it did to Fernandez. He caught another passing fish. 'Martha?'

'Hurt, but not badly so. I can tend her. I cannot tend you, my friend. I am so, so sorry. You should not have died now when you have achieved your life's tasks.'

A bigger fish passed, and lingered. 'Not . . . finished. Need to . . . finish ledgers. Must leave record for . . . those who come.'

'I will finish the ledgers, I swear it. Martha will help. We will bring to pass all that you and I and Barnabas have planned. The college shall have its legacy and the world shall see the ledgers and understand them, but not while Walsingham lives. It will all be done.'

'Thank you.' The feeling in Owen's fingers was leaving. His head fell back and struck the limestone, but he felt no pain. He could sense the blue heart-stone waiting for him, as if it straddled the line between life and death, and could ferry him across. His soul leaped for it, salmon-wise.

A moment's lucency struck him. He grasped again for Fernandez' hand. There were two of him now. Owen frowned, to bring them both into focus, and saw one of them was Martha.

Dark bruises marked the smoothness of her face and she was bleeding on to her shift. He wanted to say how to heal her and could not. Instead, he said, 'Sell the diamonds . . . for you. Make your . . . daughter . . . a wealthy woman.'

'She shall be. In your name shall the Walkers keep open the trackways. I swear it. Goodbye, my friend. Do not forget me where you travel; I would meet with you again if we may.'

Owen could not speak. He felt a warm hand on his brow and fingers on his eyelids that made the world black and gave him peace, so that he could turn now and see a chalk-riven hillside, on which waited an arc of colour, and four beasts becoming one.

Najakmul was there, glorious in her majesty, as she had promised she would be. She swept open her arms and there came a rush of welcome and choice and one final request.

34

Weyland's Smithy, Oxfordshire, 5:12 a.m.
21 June 2007

THE TUNNEL INTO THE GRAVE MOUND WAS NOT long. It did not muffle the noises from the clearing outside; the sounds of men in conflict flowed in on a liquid bed of birdsong.

Another shot rang out, and another. The part of Stella that could still think clearly knew that Gordon Fraser was free now to follow her. That same part grieved for Kit, even while the rest held the blue stone and knew that he had made the right choice where she had not; that it mattered more than her life or his for the stone to be in the heart of the earth at the sun's rise.

There was no time properly to grieve. The sun spread gold across the eastern line of the earth. From inside the true black dark of the mound, she could feel it. The song of the stone was the song of the birds and they reached for the same rising point. She could count the time in heartbeats.

At the tunnel's end was a fire, with shadowy figures about it. One was clearer than the rest: a lean man with a quirked smile and gold in his ear. Bowing, he said, 'My lady, we who care for you are here as guardians, but we cannot guard for long. The place is known to you. Will you set the stone into it?' He bore a sword that she recognized in his one hand. She looked for a medallion about his neck but did not see it.

Words burned across her mind, written long ago, to bring her to this place. She spoke them aloud: '*Follow the path that is herein shewn and be with me at the time and place appointed. Do then as the guardians of night foretell. Thereafter, follow your heart and mine, for these are one and the same. Do not fail me, for in doing so, you fail yourself, and all the worlds of waiting.*'

'Indeed.' His smile was that of a god, free of all worldly care. His earring was a pearl of sunlight, sent to guide and guard her.

A recess in the back wall glowed with a blue light all its own. With too-slow fingers, Stella fumbled the heart-stone to the lip of stone and the recess that had been made for it at the dawn of time. There was no warning from it now, no push, no flashes of colour in her mind, only a need that went beyond words. It was a lover and the mound the beloved, waiting, yearning. She was the one who held back a moment, simply for the ecstasy of it.

Behind her, a figure of flesh and leaking blood blocked the entrance to the tunnel.

A voice she had never heard before spoke from the earth, saying, *Do not delay.*

Stella Cody stepped over the fire and lowered the stone that bore her own face down to the place that had waited for over five thousand years.

The gunshot came afterwards, or before, she could not tell which, only that her world exploded in damaged flesh and blue light and a bluer, harder pain.

She was blinded a moment by the fire and the glow of a man's earring, and Gordon Fraser was there, looking dazed, and an old man with the skin of an oak tree and a nose like a ship's prow who stood with his staff raised in summoning, and so they were all dead together, which explained why she saw the dragon of the winter snows rise up from the side of Uffington hill and unfurl its wings and tip back its head and roar out its yearning to turn back the tide of all evil and save the world from ruin.

And yet, it could not fly; only eight colours made its form. The sky blue of the heart-stone was missing.

Stella looked down. In the lands of the dead, she carried the stone, as she had in life. Here, the stone was more alive than she, vibrant

521

in ways she had felt before, but never seen.

On the hillside, twelve people stood in an arc about the dragon. At their head, the old man crowned by reindeer horns, whose face she knew. Ki'kaame said, 'Will you join us, last of the keepers, and return the heart of the earth?'

'Of course.' She was already walking.

From the other half of her heart, faintly, Kit said, 'Stell? Please don't go.'

Stella stopped. Ki'kaame stopped.

The air parted and came together again. To her left, where there had been only the dragon, was also a man of medium height with silvered hair. The medallion about his neck was the image of hers. His smile was old as time, and as wise. He looked exactly like her grandfather.

He said, 'You are the latest and the youngest. Your life has not been shaped for this. If you wish, I will take the stone to the heart of the dragon. You have that choice.'

The dragon called to her once, with all the yearning of the stone. From another, less bright, place, Kit's voice whispered, 'Stella?'

'*Kit.*' The word came from the depths of her soul, an answer and a choosing.

Already the cold was inside her, welling upwards.

'Thank you. We have followed our hearts, you and I. There must always be love, as well as duty.' Cedric Owen reached for her and for the skull together. His hand was a clear sky blue.

In the core of Stella's heart, a fist of ice met the song of the blue stone. Her world exploded into shards of blue and black and scarlet.

'Stell?'

She was in sunlight, lying on grass with bird-song quiet around. Her shoulder was on fire.

Kit was leaning over her. His face was a kaleidoscope of grief and wonder.

'Stell. God, Stell . . .'

With both arms, he lifted her. The pain in her shoulder was blinding, so that she was slow to understand.

'You're whole!' she said presently, in wonder. 'You can walk.' He was walking, carrying her to a place where the sun fell on the short grass.

He said, 'And you're alive.'

His smile was a lopsided thing, not fit for such a dawn. He tried again and it was even, both sides the same. He said, 'You've been shot, but the bleeding's stopped, and the hole's not a hole any more. And your medallion has changed.'

He lifted it up. On the flat surface was a dragon alone, with no man to raise it. On the other side, the scales that balanced sun and moon had gone.

Unsteadily, he said, 'As a scientist, I'd rather not ask how this happened.' And then, because she needed to know and could not make the words, 'Gordon Fraser's dead; Tony got the gun and shot him. Davy's cracked his arm, but otherwise he's OK.'

'Ursula?'

'We don't know yet. Davy's calling the hospital.'

She let Kit help her to sitting. The mound was the same as it had always been, but that the stones were not singing.

She said, '*Thereafter, follow your heart and mine, for these are one and the same.* Cedric Owen was there. He gave me the choice. I followed my heart. I came back to you.'

'I felt you do it. I can't tell you how glad I am.'

In a daze of pain and sunshine, she held his hand. '*Do not fail me, for in doing so, you fail yourself, and all the worlds of waiting.* I don't know what the worlds are waiting for, but we didn't fail, either of us.'

Kit smiled again, and the world lit bright and was perfect. 'I know.'

EPILOGUE

To Professor Sir Barnabas Tythe, Master of Bede's College, Cambridge, greetings.

Sir – My thanks for your kind letter and the gift of pearls sent to our daughter Frances Elizabeth on the occasion of her Christening. She thrives but is peaceful, as she has been since her birth. Martha, too, is thriving and once again managing the farm. We have completed the writing project that was our joint concern and the results are sealed as we have agreed to be opened at a time long hence. I have deposited a letter with your lawyer in Oxford as you suggested.

There remains nothing outstanding, except only our deceased friend requested that you be given the enclosed, which I trust finds you in good health. If sold, it should, I believe, generate approximately £100 for it is unflawed and of good cut. If you wish to have it divided, I know of a man in Sluis whom you may wish to contact in that regard. He has regular contact with Harwich and was known to milord Walsingham before his untimely death last month, for which we all, of course, have offered our sympathies to the family and to the Queen.

I trust this finds you in good health and that you and your college continue to prosper.

Yours, etc.

Francis Walker esq. Written this tenth day of May, in the year of Our Lord, Fifteen Hundred and Ninety, at the farm of Lower Hayworth, Oxford-Shire.

Translated from the Elizabethan by Anthony Bookless and Ursula Walker, in their *New Comprehensive Biography of Cedric Owen*, Cambridge University Press, 1972. Excerpts available on line at www.bedescambridge.ac.uk

POSTSCRIPT

It is with great regret that the Master and Fellows of St Bede's College, Cambridge, announce the death of Professor Gordon Fraser after a short illness. At his own request, his body was cremated and the ashes were scattered into the Gaping Ghyll pothole on Ingleborough Hill in the Yorkshire Dales.

A service of remembrance, open to all current and former members of the college, will be held in Bede's chapel on Friday 3 August 2007, to which you are cordially invited. Donations should be sent to the Bursar.

Signed, Sir Anthony Bookless MA PhD OBE, Master, Bede's College, Cambridge.

Davy, Ursula, can you come? Stella will be out of hospital. Tony will be able to take time off after the ceremonies. It would be good to see you. And Jess is here. She wants to meet. Let me know, Kit.

THE END

AUTHOR'S NOTE

I am writing and you are reading in the 'end times', the period in which a man-made catastrophe assails the world.

The translations of the Dresden Codex are disputed in their detail, but the broad picture is widely accepted: that the ancient Maya, a race of quite astonishingly accomplished astronomer/mathematicians, whose culture flourished from AD 200 to 900, nevertheless set their calendar with a 'zero date' of 11 August 3114 BC, in order that it might reach its end date of 13 Baktun (roughly 5,125 of our years) on 21 December 2012.

This is the date when the winter solstice sun returns to its full conjunction with the galactic centre, the dark rift in the centre of the Milky Way. We name this place 28 degrees of Sagittarius. For the Maya, it was *Xibalba be*, the Road to the

Underworld, considered to be the womb of the galaxy.

Thus they set their calendar to mark the moment when the sun dies and is reborn from the galactic womb – an event which happens only once every 26,000 years. For the Maya, it represented the end of the fifth and final cycle of human existence.

A whole body of myths, prophecies and legends surrounds this time, not only of Mayan origin. If Geoff Stray is right (see *Beyond 2012* in the bibliography), the I Ching can be read as a lunar calendar which also indicates an ending – or a transformation in consciousness so vast that it might seem like an ending – in 2012. Others have found similar references in Vedic and Egyptian traditions and yet others link the associated Venus/Pleiades alignments with Christian or Judaic theology and the promise of Armageddon.

Among all of the plethora of myths and legends surrounding the 2012 end-date, those relating to the crystal skulls are the most colourful – and they are pale artifice compared to the real thing.

This book grew from the astonishing, beautiful, compelling, and inspiring life-sized crystal skull that is on display in the British Museum. It sits in a quiet corner of the main gallery opposite a particularly moving statue of a boy on a horse (whose story I will write one day).

Whatever you wish to believe of the skull's origins and purpose, it is impossible not to be struck silent in its presence.

Of the many accounts of its creation, the ones I have chosen to nurture are those which say it was birthed in the pyramids of the Maya, and that it is one of a series of thirteen which, when brought together, will either avert the end of the world, or provide us with the means to transcend it.

Whoever made it and when, the skull is a piece of extraordinary craftsmanship. To carve a fully life-sized skull with such a degree of anatomical accuracy from a single piece of crystal is, even by modern standards, a gargantuan task. If it was genuinely made in Mayan times, by polishing raw crystal with ever-decreasing grades of sand, knowing that any mistake would destroy generations of work, it is exceptional.

The Museum skull is not alone. The best known of the others is the Mitchell-Hedges skull which is kept in Canada. Like Cedric Owen's blue heart-stone, this skull was carved from a single piece of solid crystal, with a hinged mandible and the ability to take light up through the occiput and focus it out through the eyes.

Facial reconstructions have been made of this and other skulls, showing faces from a range of readily recognizable racial types. All of these skulls are said to have a solid, calm, quiet presence and to change the lives of those they touch. (For a more detailed description see *The Mystery of the Crystal Skulls* by Chris Morton and Ceri Louise Thomas.)

Those, then, are the two foundations of this novel: the 2012 end-date and the legends of the thirteen skulls. For the novel's history, I have woven my fiction around pillars of known fact: the reign of Bloody Mary Tudor did reach its nadir in the spring of 1556, when Thomas Cranmer, former Archbishop of Canterbury, was burned at the stake.

In June of that same year, Catherine de' Medici, the much-traduced Queen of France, gave birth to twins, one of which died within days while the other survived to mid-August. Michel de Nostradame, better known as Nostradamus, and renowned for his skills as a physician, was summoned to court in the summer and was present around the time of the death of the second twin.

History does not record the reason for the summoning but it doesn't seem to me to be too much of a stretch of the imagination to link him to the Queen's need for a new and better physician to save the life of her child.

This was a time of massive developments in medicine, although in the western nations surgeons – as opposed to the university-educated physicians – were considered little better than butchers.

By contrast, the Arabic and Moorish worlds had textbooks going back centuries that detailed intricate surgical techniques, together with an understanding of anaesthetics that permitted them to take place. As a former anaesthetist, I could easily become lost in the descriptions of amputations, mastectomies and enucleations and wonder at the skills of those who went before, while lamenting that our insane cultural blindness led them to be ignored for centuries as unclean and unworthy. As a writer, I have endeavoured to bring life to the texts without becoming overly technical.

The remaining characters are largely fictional, although Fernandez de Aguilar's putative ancestor Geronimo de Aguilar was taken captive by the natives, along with Gonzalo de Guerrero, in 1511. The latter did defect to the Maya and led a longstanding resistance on behalf of his new people against the Spanish invaders until his death in battle in 1535. De Aguilar never gave his heart to his captors. He escaped in 1519 and joined Cortés' expeditionary forces as an interpreter. In later life, he settled and married a native woman. He did not make his fortune selling sisal rope to Europe, but a great many of his successors did exactly that from their estancias in what are now Mexican lands.

* * *

In terms of location, Zama is now named Tulum, but the temples and the walls remain. The view of the dawn from the top of the temple/lighthouse is exceptional.

In England, the White Horse of Uffington and Weyland's Smithy (also spelled Wayland's) are both uniquely powerful places to visit and are linked by the Ridgeway, which is currently classified as a long-distance path but has been part of the backbone of Britain for far longer than the bureaucrats of the current age. It is not actually possible to see the one from the other, but they seem to me to be linked in just about every other way and for the flow of the text I have made it so in the final scenes of the novel. There is also no tunnel apparent into the depths of the grave mound at the Smithy, although the local archaeological details record that one was found on excavation of the site. Both of these places are well worth a visit, with due respect to the ancestors who made them.

Bede's College is fictional. It sits on the banks of the Cam at a place currently occupied by modern and costly flats that would be much improved if there were an ancient sandstone college there instead. The kernels of its history grew up from the early fourteenth-century colleges; Clare, for instance, was founded in 1326 by a granddaughter of Edward I, while Trinity Hall was founded in 1350 by the Bishop of Norwich for 'the promotion of divine worship and of canon and civil science and direction of the commonwealth'. That said, I would emphasize that not one of the Cambridge colleges could ever be described as a 'second-rate Plantagenet project', nor has any been rescued from poverty by a massive bequest from a man arraigned for treachery. Academia being what it is, I have culled the concepts of Master's Lodges, Courts, and the internal political structure – particularly the loyalty of graduates for their alma mater – as nearly as I can from life.

The remainder of Cambridge, its colleges, students and details of the city, are drawn from the memory of several happy decades spent living within easy reach.

For those of you interested in astrology, I have tried, in so far as possible, to keep the planetary aspects and transits accurate within the text. I have drawn up charts for all of the major players and the various end-dates and worked within the limits of those.

In the end, whether the ancients were right or not is a moot point, and if we're all still here and untouched on Hogmanay 2012 then we can perhaps laugh off the predictions much as we did the hysteria of the Y2K bug and all that led up to it – except that I suspect the end-date is an approximation and was set to indicate a general time rather then a specific twenty-four hours, and there can be little doubt that we are living through a period in which man-made catastrophes assail the world.

You may believe that you wake up each day to news that exemplifies the heights of human achievement. I am inclined to think that if this is the best we can do, we're in deep, deep trouble, and to hope that those people who believe that the next evolutionary step is spiritual are right. If they are, we need to get on with that evolution soon.

If the thirteen skulls come together to kick us forward into a transformation in consciousness that leads to a better, more sustainable way of living, I'll be first in the queue for the paradigm shift.

Summer Solstice, 2007
Shropshire
UK

BIBLIOGRAPHY

The research for this book was enormous and a true bibliography would be unwieldy and unnecessary. I have appended those books that were of most interest or of most use, plus some of the more useful websites that give details of the various theories of past and present concerning the legends of 2012.

A proportion of the detail came from conversations with chance-met people with a specific interest but for whom I have no secondary back-up. I have been told, for instance, that the Hopi are recalling their people in time for 2012, but have no firm evidence. If anyone with any credibility has any better information, on this or any other part of the book, please contact me through the website www.thecrystalskull.co.uk

Calleman, Carl Johann: *The Mayan Calendar*, Garve Publishing International, 2001, ISBN 0-9707558-0-5

Calleman, Carl Johann: *The Mayan Calendar and the Transformation of Consciousness*, Bear & Co., 2004, ISBN 1-59143-028-3

Coe, Michael D. and van Stone, Mark: *Reading the Maya Glyphs*, Thames & Hudson, 2001, ISBN 0-500-05110-0

Drew, David: *The Lost Chronicles of the Maya Kings*, Phoenix, 1999, ISBN 978-0-7538-0989-1

Geryl, Patrick: *The World Cataclysm in 2012*, Adventures Unlimited Press, 2005, ISBN 1-931882-46-0

Geryl, Patrick and Ratinckx, Gino: *The Orion Prophecy: Will the worlds be destroyed in 2012?*, Adventures Unlimited Press, 2001, ISBN 0-932813-91-7

Hartmann, Thom: *The Last Hours of Ancient Sunlight*, Hodder Mobius, 2001, ISBN 0-340-822430

Jenkins, John Major: *Galactic Alignment*, Bear & Co., 2002, ISBN 1-879181-84-3

Jenkins, John Major and Matz, Martin: *Pyramid of Fire: The Lost Aztec Codex*, Bear & Co., 2004, ISBN 1-59143-032-1

Mercier, Alloa Patricia: *The Maya Shamans*, Vega, 2002, ISBN 1-84333-596-4

Morton, Chris and Thomas, Ceri Louise: *The Mystery of the Crystal Skulls*, Thorsons,

1977, ISBN 0-7225-3486-8

Pinchbeck, Daniel: *2012: The Return of Quetzalcoatl*, Penguin, 2006, ISBN 1-58542-483-8

Rees, Martin: *Our Final Century*, Random House, 2004, ISBN 0-099-43686-8

Stray, Geoff: *Beyond 2012: Catastrophe or Ecstasy. A complete guide to end of time predictions*, Vital Signs Publishing, 2005, ISBN 0-9550608-0-X.

See also www.diagnosis2012.co.uk This is the website from which the book *Beyond 2012* was culled. At the time of writing, this is probably the best of the websites devoted to the 2012 phenomenon, although, given that Google currently registers 60,000 hits to the search phrase '2012 mayan', there may well be a few others I haven't found that are almost as good.

DREAMING THE EAGLE

*The first novel in the
acclaimed* Boudica *series.*

**Boudica: at twelve, she killed
her first warrior. At twenty-
one, she defended her land
against an invasion by the
most powerful empire the
world had ever seen. At
forty, she led her people in a
bloody revolt - and became
a legend.**

Set in a Britain before the
Romans came, Manda Scott's thrillingly imagined
novel brings the brutal world of warriors and their gods to vivid
life – the opening chapter in a story of passion, courage and
spectacular heroism pitched against overwhelming odds…

*'A powerful novel, alive with the love, deceit, wisdom and the
heroics of humanity'*   JEAN M. AUEL

*'Manda Scott has created a fictional universe all her own, but
close enough to our reality for it both to warm and break our
hearts. Breathtakingly good, it reveals the best and worst in
all of us'*   VAL McDERMID

9780553814064

BANTAM BOOKS

DREAMING THE BULL

The second novel in the
acclaimed Boudica series.

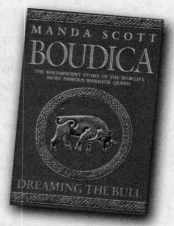

Hailed by her people as the
Bringer of Victory, Boudica
now leads the resistance
against the occupying legions
of Rome.

Opposing her is Julius Valerius,
an auxiliary cavalry officer
whose increasing brutality in
the service of his god and
emperor cannot shield him
from the ghosts of his past.
Caught in the middle are two children, pawns in a game of
unthinkable savagery.

Continuing her unforgettable retelling of the story of Britain's
great warrior queen, Manda Scott has written a novel that
captivates the heart as Boudica and the man who calls himself
Julius Valerius confront each other – and their own inescapable
destinies…

'*Richly textured, robustly plotted … it's strong,*
sophisticated stuff' *Independent*

'*A cry for freedom cloaked in lyrical and sensitive prose*'
Oxford Times

9780553814071

DREAMING THE HOUND

The third novel in the
acclaimed Boudica series.

**AD 57: Much of Britannia lies
under Roman occupation.**

Only in the far West, where
Boudica leads a guerrilla war
against the hated invader, does
the flame of independence burn.

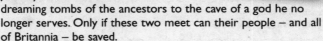

Across the sea, Boudica's half-
brother seeks peace on a
journey that takes him from the
dreaming tombs of the ancestors to the cave of a god he no
longer serves. Only if these two meet can their people – and all
of Britannia – be saved.

But the new Governor has been ordered to subdue the tribes,
and he has twenty thousand legionaries ready to stop anyone
from bringing Britain to the edge of revolt …

'One of the boldest recent adventures in historical fiction'
INDEPENDENT

'Of the recent historical novels set in Roman times, this is the best
one I've read' MAIL ON SUNDAY

9780553816365

BANTAM BOOKS

DREAMING THE SERPENT SPEAR

The final novel in the acclaimed Boudica series.

Britannia, AD 60: The tribes of Britannia are ready to seek bloody vengeance. Twenty thousand warriors ache to reclaim their land from their captors.

Now is their chance: the Roman governor has marched his legions west, leaving his capital and a vital port undefended.

There is no going back.

Colchester is burning. London has been destroyed. Amidst fire and bloody revolution, the Boudica and those around her must fight to keep what matters most – now and for all time.

'Fast moving action, spine-tingling battles ... a deep understanding of the relationship between the world of the sword and the world of the spirit. Wonderful'
KATE MOSSE, AUTHOR OF LABYRINTH

'Boudica is brilliantly realised. Her battles against Rome – the super power of its day – are both heart rending and magnificent' DAVID GEMMELL

9780555381|4088

BANTAM BOOKS